LIFE AS A SANDWICH

a novel

To Boris,
A great dad and a great
friend!

Best always,
— [signature]

September 2015

LIFE AS A SANDWICH

a novel

by

Eric Peterson

Huckleberry House

Escondido, California • Lake Tahoe, Nevada

Life as a Sandwich
Huckleberry House
P.O. Box 460928, Escondido, California 92046-0928

Cover and book design by Armadillo Creative
Edited by Leah Cooper
Printed in the United States of America

This novel is a work of fiction. The characters, settings, events, and
corporate entities described are fictitious. Any similarity to real persons,
living or dead, is coincidental. Wherever certain established government
agencies and institutions appear in this story, the characters associated
with them are fictitious and are products of the author's imagination.

Special discounts may be available for bulk purchases. Please direct
inquiries to info@huckleberryhousebooks.com

Library of Congress Control Number: 2009931963

ISBN 978-0-9824860-5-4 (hardcover)
ISBN 978-0-9824860-4-7 (paperback)

For Teresa
And in case my pen falters,
for Katie and Caroline
You are the loves of my life.

ACKNOWLEDGMENTS

For his colorful account of the next generation of venture capitalists, I am indebted to Randall Stross and his book *eBoys*. I also wish to thank Herant Katchadourian, whose Vienna lectures on Gustav Klimt's *Beethoven Frieze* provided a much-needed framework for this story. For added character resonance, I drew certain details from Dr. Katchadourian's *Cream of the Crop*, co-written by John Boli. For technical guidance, I owe a debt of gratitude to the editorial staff at *Model Railroader* magazine.

This novel would not have been possible without the help of John Cornfield, who generously gave his heart—and criticism—to the manuscript. For their time, encouragement, and contributions to this story I also thank Chris Peterson, Phil Winters, Pat McGovern, Marty Schmidt, Steven Winther, John Jennings, Patrick Flynn, Fred Farr, Julynn Suhs, Michelle Tremblay Schulze, Jill Treadwell Svendsen, and G. Bruce Dunn. My friend Nikki Niciphor introduced me to a superb editor, Leah Cooper, and for both relationships I am truly grateful. Finally, for their unwavering support for this project, I thank my parents: George F. Russell, Jr., Dion Peterson Russell, and Gregor G. Peterson, himself a pioneering venture capitalist and the founder, in 1989, of Huckleberry Press, Lake Tahoe, Nevada.

"Squeezed between raising children and caring for elderly parents, consumed by demanding careers, it's little wonder the men and women of the Sandwich Generation feel pressed like cold cuts in a heavy Dagwood. The pressure takes its toll. As these baby boomers hit middle age, proclivities for destructive or wanton behavior can be rife."

Dr. William L. Ricketts
Capicola, Couples, and Cuckoldry: A Treatise on Middle-Aged Marriage in a New Century

PROLOGUE

The Mexican soldiers had the U.S. troops pinned down on the boulder-strewn hill. It was December 1846. A cold rain fell. Hunger set in. The troops, a detachment of First U.S. Dragoons, resorted to eating their mules.

Western scout Kit Carson, presumably neither a fan of dining on mule meat nor of becoming a human piñata at the hands of Mexican *Californios* wielding eight-foot lances, voted with his feet. He and two others snuck away in the dark of night and walked some thirty miles over jagged rocks and cactus to the U.S. outpost in San Diego—walked it shoeless, according to historians.

A relief party was quickly dispatched from Fort San Diego, and the cornered U.S. troops were saved. They had just survived the Battle of San Pasqual, the bloodiest California conflict of the Mexican-American War. The hill on which they'd made their stand would thereafter be known as Mule Hill.

By November 1998 Mule Hill was a stone's throw from a super-regional shopping mall. The trail that Kit Carson traveled on his way to San Diego was a major interstate highway, eight lanes and growing. And the Battle of San Pasqual was virtually unknown to most Americans—all but the few who took the time to stop by the tiny visitor's center at the San Pasqual Battlefield State Park, usually on their way to the much larger, and infinitely more popular, San Diego Wild Animal Park.

Wallace Noe was a regular commuter on car-clogged Interstate 15 to San Diego—roughly the same route that Kit Carson traveled shoeless. The father of two young daughters, Wallace had pushed his share of baby strollers over the meandering trails at the Wild Animal Park, which gave the illusion of being a zoo without fences. He purchased the lion's share of his clothes at Nordstrom, an anchor tenant in the mall that was a stone's throw from Mule Hill. He liked their men's department for its reliable selection of conservative gray and blue business suits. On his shopping sprees, which occurred about every two years, the Nordstrom sales associates—invariably attractive women about Wallace's same age—were astonished at the speed with which he could do his shopping, choosing suits, selecting shirts (all-cotton, always white) and picking out ties.

The decisiveness that so impressed people on the outside, however, was viewed as a serious character flaw by Wallace's wife, Hannah, who knew that most of his decisions were driven by irrational fears: the fear of loss or appearing incompetent; an attempt to quiet a denigrating, inner voice. ("You dress just like your father," she'd say, seeing all those white shirts, rolling her eyes.) Though Wallace's father was no longer living—he was killed along with Wallace's mother in the freak crash of a sightseeing helicopter in Skagway, Alaska—Wallace would invariably take this as a compliment; over the years, fashions hadn't changed much in the American boardroom.

The signing of the Treaty of Guadalupe Hidalgo, in 1848, may have formally ended the territorial fight that was the Mexican-American War, but 150 years later, on the California border, undercurrents of tension remained. Trapped in gridlock traffic and listening to talk radio, Wallace heard almost daily reports of the latest skirmishes in the still-unresolved turf fight between Mexico and America. Illegal aliens crossed nearly unchecked into the United States, committing crimes, clogging hospital emergency rooms, and overcrowding public schools. There was little doubt the faces in the public schoolrooms were becoming increasingly Hispanic. The situation was forcing middle-class, white Americans like Wallace to come to terms with their own fears and prejudices about the "browning" of California.

For a family that had exhausted its savings on a start-up company and was living virtually week-to-week on paychecks and credit card float, the decision to enroll two young girls in a private Christian school was a thorny one. True, it was a recurring expense they could ill afford. But, in the end, both Wallace and Hannah decided they were willing to make the sacrifice, though for different reasons: Hannah wanted to instill in her daughters a healthy dose of Protestant-Christian ethics, whereas Wallace was afraid if he sent them to public school, the hoodlums would jump them for their lunch money.

CHAPTER ONE

"What now?" Julie asked. "You pick today of all days to have a brawl with a meatball sandwich?"

Wallace had stepped out for a late bite of lunch, and the moment he returned she was on him like a bird, flapping her wings, fussing. His white shirt had the telltale stains of tomato sauce. He knew he was cutting it close for the meeting with the venture capitalists, but he needed the walk even more than the sandwich.

"Maybe we should put some club soda on that," she said, following him.

Julie was the secretary Wallace shared in the executive suite, a fresh-faced East County farm girl who embraced her budding corporate career with the zeal of a college intern. She had traded in her Lee jeans for Anne Klein, her riding boots for heels, her Ford pickup for a Volkswagen Jetta. She was efficient in the way Wallace imagined a much older woman would be. She anticipated things.

"Your stapler was almost out of staples," she said, giving Wallace a brief tour of his own office. "And I refilled your tape dispenser. Here. Take this." She pressed a new copy of the business plan into his hands.

This one was bound in leather and had an embossed cover. "The new number is $8.75 million. Remember that. Oh, and I moved your printer. It's over there now."

The printer lurked on the credenza like an iguana. The books that normally occupied the space were missing. Wallace carried a small reference library with him wherever he worked: Drucker's *Management*; Strunk and White's *The Elements of Style*; Ayn Rand's *Atlas Shrugged*; Schmidlap's *Trains of the Feather River Canyon*. These were books he liked having close at hand; they helped him get things right.

"What have you done with my books?"

"They're on the bookshelf, where they belong."

Often Wallace would go to meetings and return to find his files purged, pictures changed, or a different leather chair behind his desk. He was tempted to ditch the printer and move his reference library back to the credenza, but there wasn't time. He was late for the meeting in the conference room.

"You need a boyfriend," Wallace said. "Go home to your dogs."

Julie blocked Wallace from getting out the door. To his relief it wasn't to douse him with club soda.

"Wait. Let's fix your tie." She had brawny hands, no rings on her fingers, no reservations about helping herself to the knot on Wallace's tie. "Is this a Robert Talbott? From Nordstrom?"

"I think so."

"I approve." She caressed the silk necktie once with her open palm, then gave him a push out the door. "Get going. You have a company to save."

It was a meeting that couldn't seem to get started.

Trek Reese kept stepping out to take calls.

The Trek Reese. Of venture capital fame. Trek was a general partner at Jacaranda Associates—the renegade, freewheeling firm that flew in the face of convention, that took companies public before they made a dime of profit, that, as punishment, shut out corporate pension funds, university endowments, and investment banking firms for dragging their feet on a deal, for a perceived slight in the press, for failing to return a phone call. Jacaranda was housed in a stone, glass, and hewn-timber architectural wonder tucked away under craggy oaks in the rolling hills above Palo Alto. It was situated quite literally at the heart of Silicon Valley's de facto financial capital, dead-center at the junction of Sand Hill Road and Highway 280, at the confluence of three raging, uniquely Northern California rivers: unlimited money, inexhaustible entrepreneurship, and the infinite brainpower flowing out of the engineering programs at Stanford University and UC Berkeley.

Whenever Trek stepped out to the hallway, a reverential silence fell over the conference room—as if to speak in his absence would be the height of disrespect.

Trek's junior associate, introduced simply as Jeter, knew the drill. He stayed behind organizing his notes, checking his cell phone for incoming calls, fidgeting. He wore the same black slacks, black blazer, and deeply expensive wool turtleneck as his boss, but Jeter was fresh out of business school. He looked like a kid waiting to move scenery at a high school play.

Something about Trek Reese—beyond his haughty arrogance—bothered Wallace. Studying the logo on the venture capitalist's business card, he suddenly realized what it was: the jacaranda tree. There had been a jacaranda next to the swimming pool at the home of Wallace's parents. Early in the summer it would come alive with throngs of neon blue, trumpet-shaped blossoms—a promise of glory. But the blossoms would soon fall like raindrops, making a colossal mess of the patio, lawn, and pool. Wallace spent weeks, even months, of his childhood cleaning up after that tree with a pool skimmer, push broom, and garden hose. The jacaranda was a shallow-rooted, ostentatious menace.

"Damn this thing."

Wallace looked up. Michael Merksamer was flummoxed by the narrow buttons of the computer projector. He was Wallace's boss: president of the company, also chairman and CEO. Middle-aged, slightly paunchy, with reddish-gray hair—he was already breaking a sweat. The sagging skin around his eyes and jowls gave him the downtrodden look of a basset hound. He did the talking when it came to dealing with the venture guys.

"Where's Julie?" Michael demanded of Wallace. "Get her in here." He jabbed nervously at the controls with stumblebum fingers, but the lamp wouldn't come on. The projector fan cycled on and off, hissing at him like a cornered opossum.

Some high-tech company, Wallace thought.

Wallace grew up in the 1960s in Sunnyvale, California, an unassuming town located midway along the tail of the sophisticated, urbane comet that was San Francisco. Sunnyvale was a sprawling bedroom community comprised of endless tracts of compact, ranch-style homes that encroached upon equally endless orchards of apricots, prunes, and apples. It was a place where stay-at-home moms drove their kids to swim lessons in Mercury station wagons; where every house had a basketball hoop over the garage. On weekend nights, teenagers blackened their faces and marauded the streets while their parents—IBM executives, dentists, and airline pilots—got blasted on whiskey sours, Cold Duck, and Harvey Wallbangers.

At Sunnyvale's Robert F. Stockton High School, Wallace made decent grades but refused to join the honor society. (Even in his earliest days, Wallace was never a joiner.) The memorable accomplishment of his senior year was being voted "Most Congenial" for the school yearbook, heavy-handedly entitled *The Anvil*. Wallace was not a class clown, but he used his humor to help pass the time. Two girls, flirtations but not serious romances, wrote in Wallace's *Anvil* that they never would have made it through the year without his sense of humor to carry them through. Both girls prayed he'd find God over the summer. Another girl who *was* a girlfriend wrote that she considered him to be an insignificant speck of crud and hoped that someday he'd get serious and make something of his life. In addition to being somewhat prescient, she was his high school sweetheart—the first girl he ever kissed. She did not take their breakup (just before senior prom) well at all.

For college, Wallace enrolled at the University of California at San Diego, in La Jolla. It was the only school he applied to. The allure of San Diego included blue waters, pristine beaches, majestic palms, and a climate that supported year-round golf. Best of all was its far reach from Sunnyvale—about five hundred miles. In Wallace's mind there was also something appealing, even romantic, about UC San Diego's affiliation with the Scripps Institution of Oceanography. In the mid-'70s Jacques Cousteau was a folk hero, John Denver was singing "Calypso," and Wallace could picture himself as one of those rugged, full-bearded men posing cross-armed in the Scripps catalog. He imagined himself on the cover, skin sunburned and sandy hair tousled, with a fog-shrouded pier, a gray sea, and the world beckoning in the background beyond.

In studying oceanography, Wallace imagined a world of excitement, exploration, and possibilities. It was a world of travel to exotic destinations, backbreaking physical work in the harsh elements, and deepwater dives where the only sound was your own breathing. Success meant merely to survive.

It was neither physical toil nor numbing cold that derailed Wallace's oceanographic career. The certification dive was what did him in—the stinky little boat and its incessant bobbing. Wallace vomited in his face mask. He would never again smell the pungent odor of kelp beds at low tide, hear the squawk of seagulls, or taste dry salt on his lips without feeling a corresponding twinge in his stomach. He wanted nothing to do with the open ocean ever again.

College, however, was not all misery.

In his days at UC San Diego, Wallace excelled at finding the easiest classes in the school's most unchallenging major (communication). He was also head and shoulders above his classmates at formulating a sluggard's schedule. For four straight years, he slept until almost ten every morning. He took Tuesdays and Thursdays off.

"The path of least resistance to a college degree," he told his roommates, who proved to be more intellectually serious than he. (One went on to teach history at Yale, another earned a law degree and was a practicing attorney in San Diego, and a third was an anesthesiologist in Houston.)

Considering that Wallace was armed with a bachelor's degree from one of the nation's top public universities and that his father, who was well connected in business circles, was willing to make any number of introductory telephone calls on his son's behalf, the decade of Wallace's twenties was a testament to his immaturity and lack of ambition.

In contrast to his father and grandfather, who both had strived for a good education, and then doggedly pursued their chosen careers—one in insurance and one in finance—Wallace's postcollege days were marred by indecision and complacency. His strengths were also his weakness. He was personable and friendly, but his career aspirations blew with the wind. His lifestyle fit the pattern of the classic underachiever: Wallace sought ease over challenge, pleasure over self-sacrifice. His early career results were inconsequential.

The jobs Wallace took were suggestive of a ship without a rudder: engineer at a Christian radio station (The Almighty 96.3); gofer for an egomaniacal real estate developer who ran his company like a religious cult; staff copywriter for a vainglorious witch who ran her ad agency like a private serfdom.

It was in his twenties that Wallace truly merited the title "Most Congenial," though "Most Unfulfilled Potential" would have been more accurate. He spent the majority of his evenings at neighborhood bars in the company of workplace companions, drinking scotch, ridiculing his bosses, filching food, and casting an eye out for the right pretty face that somehow never came walking through the door. Wallace played golf incessantly; he threw wild drinking parties in his rented apartment. He never connected with the right girl. The fast, floozy ones were offensive and tacky; the attractive, intelligent ones were invariably taken—usually by someone wealthier and much older. The plain-Jane, meat-and-potatoes girls who practically threw themselves at Wallace's feet were, well, *dull*.

Wallace's parents—especially his father, Wendell Noe III—were beginning to wonder what might be wrong with their son. Underachievers, as a rule, did not run in the Noe family. Wallace's only sister, Jennifer, had a good job with a bank. She lived in Mount Vernon, Washington, with her husband, an epidemiologist for the state. (He had a name for what ailed Wallace—"lazyitis!")

One day, Wendell III flew in to San Diego for the afternoon. Wallace took his father to a popular harbor restaurant for lunch. The view included jaunty sailboats riding wind-chopped water with the naval aircraft carriers of NAS North Island standing sentinel in the background. Wallace's father had thinned noticeably, the result of a strict, post-heart attack diet. He walked stiffly and sat inflexibly upright. With his silver hair, square head, and chiseled nose it was like having lunch with a canoe paddle.

"You disappoint me," Wallace's father said. "Drinking beer in the middle of the day." He was picking over a plate of steamed opah and stewed tomatoes. For some reason he had ordered plain hot water.

"Fine," Wallace said, "then I'll drink Bloody Marys like you and Mom." He drank his beer straight from the bottle. He had consumed the better part of a bacon cheeseburger and was picking at fries.

"What time are you due back at this third-rate agency of yours?"

"I'm taking the day off. I called in sick."

Wendell III tensed. "That isn't how you were raised. Work is a privilege."

"It's not exactly the Great Depression." Wallace gazed out the window at the bay. "I'm thinking about taking a job with Amtrak. Or the police academy."

Wendell III went crimson. "What's the matter with you, boy? Are you mentally ill?"

People at the next table stopped eating and stared.

"No, Dad," Wallace said. "I'm nothing like you. I intend to be happy when I'm old."

Wallace called for another Budweiser.

Wendell III—not one for scenes in restaurants—stiffened in his chair, as if prodded by an electrical device.

"I want you to see a doctor," he said in a bare whisper.

"I'm perfectly healthy."

"Not a medical doctor. An industrial psychologist. He has tests. He can help you find your way."

"What makes you think I'm lost?"

Wendell III made a wan fist and stared out the window. His bushy eyebrows were absurdly pronounced—balls of cotton pasted on by a mirthful child.

"Son, listen to me. See those aircraft carriers? They're safe in the harbor, but that's not the purpose of a battleship. Life is short. You're watching from the sidelines. You need to show the world who you really are."

A number of months passed and Wallace spoke little to his father. He became increasingly unhappy with his low-level job at the ad agency. He resented having to churn out, day after day, the forced press releases, phony product brochures, and inane service-club speeches. Bottom line: it wasn't what he had in mind for the rest of his life. He had to agree with his father. Career-wise, he was lost.

On the eve of his twenty-sixth birthday, Wallace called the industrial psychologist. He scheduled an appointment for the following week.

At the doctor's office, Wallace was given a battery of aptitude and preference tests; he answered long lists of open-ended questions. According to the psychologist, the results were revealing: Wallace's favorite work experiences were teaching golf at a summer camp, driving the camp bus, and working at the Christian radio station, in that order.

From these pleasurable events, the doctor explained, certain inferences could be drawn. Wallace was adept at imparting technical information (explaining the rules of golf, announcing to his campers the daily bus schedule); he was good at demonstrating concepts (the golf swing takeaway, the follow-through); and he was patient and empathetic with his students. He was fascinated (some would say obsessed) with making painstaking adjustments to intricate dials and gauges (this from driving the old Ford bus and working at the radio station). He was a good communicator (both written and verbal), an effective organizer of diverse sources of information, and he had a penchant for coalescing divergent opinions.

To the psychologist the conclusion was clear: Wallace was a people pleaser. He should become a consultant.

"But what kind of a consultant?" Wallace asked.

"That's for you to decide," the psychologist said, leaning back in his chair and giving his breath a shot of Binaca. "You can be your own first client."

Wallace did research. He chose a field of interest: human resources. Eventually he scored a technical writing position with a well-known employee benefits consulting firm. The psychologist was right—corporate consulting suited Wallace well and he advanced rapidly. Hannah's father was an actuary working in the same firm. That was how Wallace and Hannah met—at a summer actuaries' picnic amidst a sea of white shorts, black socks, and pallid faces under the protective shade of wide-brimmed Panama hats. At the picnic Wallace and Hannah became coconspirators. They spiked the party punch and ran off before the sack race.

Hannah Taylor embodied the most appealing traits of Wallace's past girlfriends—she was well educated and had traveled the world. A lithe, stunning brunette, she worked for a major airline. To Wallace the contradictions in her personality were seductive: she was a hellish partier and an avid churchgoer, a daddy's girl with a fierce independent streak, a lover of gardening who resented getting her hands dirty. She was also conveniently between boyfriends.

Within a year Wallace and Hannah were married. Two years later Addison was born. Three years after that, they christened their second daughter, Tiffany. (Like brand managers bringing new products to market, Wallace and Hannah chose names for their daughters that brought to mind upscale, aristocratic themes—names suitable for patterns of fine china or floor plans in a tony La Jolla condominium complex.)

Tiffany was still in diapers when Wallace was revisited by the vague feeling of listlessness at the office. The consulting business was taking its toll: the out-of-town travel, the interminable meetings, the infighting among members of the same team.

"There's nothing wrong with consulting per se," Wallace's father said to him one night on the telephone. "It's just that by definition a consultant is always working for someone else, and I'm not sure that's your charge in life. By the way, how are Hannah and the girls?"

"They're fine," Wallace replied. "Addison's the CEO. She treats Tiffany like her own employee. At least that's what Hannah tells me. With the work and travel I hardly ever see them."

"Mind you, this is really about making your way in the world," Wallace's father continued. "Somewhere along the way, most people make wrong choices. They never live up to their potential. Most lawyers never become Supreme Court justices, most senators never become president. You see what I mean. Most consultants never become—" Wallace's father was at a loss for the term.

"CIC," Wallace said.

"What?"

"Consultant-in-charge."

"Well then, most consultants never become the consultant-in-charge. And you know what they say: if you ain't the lead dog, the scenery never changes. That's all I'm saying."

Few people experience a death as categorically violent as a helicopter crash. The tail rotor fails and the engine torque forces the aircraft into a savage spin. The helicopter pitches sharply and drops like a stone. For those trapped inside, the blare of the alarm horns, the howl of the failing engine, the sound of the blades clawing heavily through the air, must add a certain hopeless surrealism to the experience. Imagine the thoughts that must pass through your mind in the final five seconds of your life.

"I fly in fixed-wing aircraft," Hannah would remind Wallace every time they argued over her career with the airline, whenever Wallace brought up the danger factor. "Your parents died in a rotary-wing aircraft. There's a big difference. Commercial airliners do not fall out of the sky with the frequency of sightseeing helicopters."

There were many things Wallace liked about Hannah—indeed, some that he loved—but it disturbed him to be married to a woman who used a term like *fixed-wing aircraft*. Wallace wanted Hannah to quit her job as a flight attendant. He wanted the girls to have a stay-at-home mom. He wanted *Sunnyvale*.

"Understand, I have nothing against the path you've chosen if it's really what you want to do," Wallace's father said in one of their last telephone conversations. "We Noes have always been a can-do kind of people—*Noe can do, I like to say!*" Wallace closed his eyes and grimaced. This again. "Success is not something that just happens to you, like catching a flu bug. You have to lay your own groundwork. No one's going to do it for you. Understand what I'm trying to say?"

Wallace understood perfectly what his father was trying to say. He had been saying it all of Wallace's life.

"Why don't you and Hannah move back to Northern California? People are more serious up here."

"Listen, Dad, we'd like to do something for you and Mom."

Wendell III chuckled dismissively. "What could you possibly do for us? We have everything we need."

"I mean for your Alaska cruise. We'd like to treat you to an excursion."

"Nonsense. Save your money. You may need it one day to start a business."

Wallace was insistent. "There's a helicopter tour when you get to Skagway. It looks like something you and Mom might enjoy, something you two wouldn't normally do."

Wallace arranged for the helicopter tour directly with the cruise line. His sister, whose name was on the ship's emergency contact form, got the call. The helicopter had gone down, there was a fire, her parents never reboarded the ship. They asked her to send dental records.

Wallace was executor of the estate. The plan put in place by his father was meticulous and thorough. The house in Sunnyvale was owned free and clear. There were stocks, bonds, and life insurance policies to be divided equally between Wallace and his sister. The personal property was similarly apportioned—Wallace inherited his father's Cadillac, Jennifer her mother's Louis XVI bedroom set and knock-off collection of Fabergé eggs.

The difficulties in settling the estate came in trying to sort out backdated medical bills for procedures undergone in the prior year: the heart bypass for Wallace's father, a hip replacement for his mother.

"Your billing paperwork is a nightmare," Wallace complained once to a supervisor's supervisor in the insurance company's claims department. "I have no idea what I'm looking at, and I'm in the business."

One day the billing nightmare led to a casual conversation with a systems analyst at the consulting firm.

"I hate these big insurance companies," Wallace said. "If only you could log onto your personal computer and track all these medical expenses. You know, like co-payments and what's covered and what's not, what's already been paid. Think of the hours of paperwork and agony you could avoid. Solve this and you'd be a billionaire."

The systems analyst agreed. "But first you'd have to capture the enrollment record to know what coverage was in place."

One week later, Wallace walked into the office of the consultant-in-charge and resigned.

"I'm going to start a software company," Wallace said. "Call it a gift from my late father."

The consultant-in-charge, a pension actuary, knew the risks of a start-up company. "Are you sure you want to do this?"

Wallace smiled, knowing that his father would be pleased.

"If you ain't the lead dog, the scenery never changes."

Hannah felt slighted, and she let Wallace know. What kind of a husband quits his job and starts a new company without first discussing it with his wife?

Hannah's genetic makeup included her mother's frugality and her actuary-father's aversion to risk. As a result she misunderstood the nature of entrepreneurship. She mistook Wallace's tenacity for folly, the company's lack of revenue for failure. She couldn't see that in a start-up, success often hinges on pressing ahead when others would have long since let go, that Thomas Edison first had to learn a thousand ways *not* to make a light bulb.

As their savings vanished, Hannah grew moody and dissociated from Wallace. She wore her financial worries like a yoke. She spent time in the evenings combing through newspapers and junk mail, cutting out coupons. She called off landscaping the back yard, which would indefinitely consist of a small concrete patio and a wooden hot tub on a pad of hard, flat dirt. In the fall she sent the girls to school in last year's uniforms, which were too small. In the winter she insisted on keeping the thermostat at sixty degrees—there were times that Addison and Tiffany ate their dinner in front of a roaring fire, dressed in ski parkas and scarves.

There were tearful nights when Hannah would beg Wallace to return to his consulting job.

"You can't steal second while keeping one foot on first," Wallace would answer, holding her and wiping away her tears. "Please. I need to do this."

Wallace was determined to make the new company work, whatever the price. It wasn't about a burning desire to automate enrollment; it was more personal than that. It was about strength of character, perseverance in the face of adversity, redemption.

It felt like somebody up there was watching.

By March of the second year, the situation was grim. There was a painful string of layoffs—for Wallace, employees were like family—and now, in addition to Wallace, only three people remained in the company: an older salesman named Charlie Dye, and two young programmers from Provo, Utah. It was a tight-knit group with a clear-cut division of labor. Wallace and Charlie made cold calls while the programmers tried to rein in the company's prototype software program, nicknamed, out of frustration, the Beast.

Often in the course of a live demonstration, the Beast would suddenly take over Wallace's computer, making the program crash in a humiliating sequence of events: first the surprise strum of a guitar chord, then the appearance of a cryptic message in the center of the screen. The software would freeze up. Then, with a carnival-like series of bongs, chimes, and doorbell tones, the computer would shut itself down and reboot—the Beast's signature work, one invisible hand on the keyboard, the other on the calliope. In the crowded conference room at a Blue Cross plan halfway across the country, a computer crash was a mortifying experience. It made Wallace want to climb into a hole.

By Wallace's estimate, the company was within a few weeks of folding when he attended a Nexus Enterprise Forum. Nexus was a San Diego-based, nonprofit support group whose purpose was to link entrepreneurs with community resources—all the local legal, accounting, and financial service firms that didn't want to miss out on the next hot IPO, the next *Qualcomm*. The setting for the breakfast meeting was The Lodge at Torrey Pines. In his college days Wallace had tromped both the North and South courses of Torrey Pines more times than he could count—the thirty-six holes, just up the road from UC San Diego, were cut like giant fingers through the maritime chaparral and scrub oaks atop a sandstone cliff high above the beach—but he had never been there for a business meeting dressed in a suit.

On that morning in March, the view from the veranda of The Lodge was spectacular: a cloudless sky; green fairways pointing to the ocean; windswept Torrey pines perched precariously on the rims of deep ravines; the waves of the Pacific glistening on the horizon. Beyond the cliff's edge, sunlit hang gliders soared. (Wallace thought hang gliding was a stupid, risky avocation—fools jumping off cliffs, banking on serendipity and chance to keep them aloft—but now, going into the Nexus meeting, it was he who was on the verge of hitting the rocks, in desperate need of an updraft.)

The speaker that morning was Michael Merksamer. According to his biography he was a seasoned executive and a practiced master of start-ups. He was the driving force behind Merksamer Digital, a local software company that developed custom applications across multiple platforms. At first glance Michael Merksamer was Wallace's type of businessman—he wore a blue suit, white shirt, and red tie. "Growing a Software Business" was the title of his talk.

The food was better than the talk, but the audience was receptive—posturing suits, mostly, representing a myriad of costly financial and professional services, grateful to be out of the office, equally relieved not to have their own money on the line. Michael Merksamer seemed to have a good grasp of the basic pitfalls inherent in a start-up technology company. Coming off the high of his speech, he was approachable. He gave Wallace his card. That same afternoon, Wallace made the drive south on Interstate 15 and hand-delivered a copy of his business plan to the receptionist at Merksamer Digital.

Two days later, the telephone rang. It was Michael.

He had read the plan, liked it, and proposed meeting over lunch at his country club in Rancho Santa Fe, a haven for millionaires and Thoroughbred horses about twenty-five miles north of San Diego. He was dressed in the familiar blue suit and waiting for Wallace under the porte cochere of the Tudor-style clubhouse. The entrance resembled the turret of a castle. A uniformed valet held open the heavy door.

"We'll eat in the men's grill," Michael said. "The main dining room is full of blue-hairs who like to eavesdrop and gossip."

Wallace followed Michael through the lavishly carpeted, wood-paneled corridors of the clubhouse. The place was as silent as a museum. They passed two white-haired members in garish golf attire who nodded tersely, as if greetings were currency.

The men's grill was empty. Michael and Wallace took a table overlooking the first tee. Across the lake was a grandiose Tuscan mansion with vine-covered chimneys, clipped hedges, and a stone pool house. The community was gated and heavily patrolled.

"Look at that place," Wallace said. "Talk about a monstrosity."

"That's my house," Michael said. "That thing would cost a fortune if I had to build it today."

One-on-one, Michael Merksamer was surprisingly awkward. He fidgeted with his knife and fork and spoke rapidly and distractedly, first about the fees at the club (quite stiff), then the feedback he'd received from the Nexus event (overwhelmingly positive), then the overall business climate for start-ups (not easy). He seemed relieved for the interruption when the white-jacketed waiter came over and poured water.

"I won't beat around the bush," Michael said, clearing his throat and folding his hands on the table, looking at Wallace without blinking. "I thought we could explore combining our two companies. You'd be stepping into a ready-made organization."

The waiter brought bowls of black bean and chorizo soup. Michael pushed his aside. With his Montblanc pen, he sketched on the white linen tablecloth the organization he had in mind.

"We'll do a reverse merger, into my shell, for tax purposes," he said. "Recapitalize it with new money. Equal partners. I'll be CEO, you can run sales and marketing. I've got a young guy out of India, very bright, he can build anything. And my chief financial officer is top-notch, a former tax partner at Cooper's. He can help you flesh out the metrics in your plan."

"I think this can really work," Wallace said to Hannah that night, electrified, pouring champagne. Time, experience, capital—it was everything he needed to keep the business alive.

"So when do we get our money back?" Hannah asked.

"Not so fast," Wallace said. "Be patient."

Wallace would have a seat on the board. Within a few years, Michael claimed, the investment bankers would be champing at the bit to take the company public.

"Equal partners, yes," Michael said to Wallace, backpedaling in his lawyer's office as they worked out the details of the acquisition. "But that's in theory only. We need to discount the value of your investment, since you bring so little to the table."

"No, Michael. I'm bringing everything."

"You know what I mean," Michael said. "No customers, no revenue. The code is crap. I'm putting in all the new money. We have to value this thing like a rank start-up."

It was a rude awakening. The experienced industry statesman who Wallace thought was going to save his company was, in fact, a self-serving bully, a corporate shakedown artist with the charm of a buzz saw.

In the end, Wallace came away owning twenty percent of Merksamer Digital.

"Believe me, Hannah," Wallace said hotly, when she accused him of being a pushover, of allowing Michael to steal the company. "Twenty percent of something is a lot better than a hundred percent of nothing."

On move-in day, Charlie Dye promptly had a heart attack. He survived, but only because the paramedics brought him back to life on the way to the hospital.

It wasn't all tragedy. In May, Wallace signed their first customer. Cal Max was the third-largest insurance company doing business in the state of California. It controlled the state's second-largest HMO. There was a directive from higher-ups to embrace future technologies, and the health plan's management wanted to use Merksamer Digital's software system for open enrollment in the fall.

For Wallace and Michael, it wasn't simply a matter of filling the order; they still had to build the system. They needed personnel and equipment to pull it off, cash to keep it going. Michael insisted they should raise venture capital.

"Go up to Palo Alto," he directed Otto Foreman, his chief financial officer. "Call on every venture firm you can find—I don't care who it is. Tell them we're going to the moon, and we need the money to do it."

Otto was beginning to regret his decision to leave public accounting. Like Wallace, he increasingly found himself playing shepherd to Michael's mercurial personality. He was often confounded by the illogical things Michael asked him to do.

"Michael, there are a lot of venture firms between here and Palo Alto. What's wrong with Orange County or Los Angeles?"

"Small potatoes or they wouldn't be down here," Michael said, dismissively. "Don't get mealymouthed on me, Otto. We're swinging for the fences here."

Wallace thought they were raising too much money, too soon. They had yet to see how Cal Max would proforma out. The most recent version of the Merksamer Digital business plan said the company was seeking $8.75 million.

"*Eight point seven five?*" Wallace questioned.

"An odd number makes the venture guys think we've put a lot of thought into it," Michael explained. "When they see that level of detail they're more likely to fund the plan."

It took Otto almost a week of manipulating spreadsheets to back into a set of numbers that showed the company needing exactly $8.75 million.

"And call the insurance broker," Michael said. "Tell him to move our health insurance over to Cal Max."

Otto was incredulous. "Change plans now? In the middle of the year? But that's crazy. It's a lot of work. It's disruptive to people's lives."

"Do it," Michael said. "If they're going to be our customer then we need to be theirs, too. That's how the game is played." He shook his head disgustedly at Wallace, who happened to be in the room.

Otto couldn't stop grousing about Michael. "Jesus, this guys needs a padded cell," he complained one night to Wallace, when they were both working late. "He'd bawl out a rut in the road for running the wrong way."

Charlie Dye returned to work a few months after his heart attack, the recipient of a double bypass. He was short-tempered and easily fatigued. It infuriated him to learn that Otto had switched health plans; he was afraid Cal Max wouldn't pay his medical bills, which were substantial and continuing to mount. He left the office that day in a blind rage. A few blocks away, he swerved to miss a squirrel, ran his Bonneville into a Taco Bell, and was readmitted to the hospital.

Wallace was working on overload—he had his marketing job to do, the Cal Max implementation to oversee, Charlie's sales work to juggle, and budgets and sales forecasts to track—but it wasn't in his nature to complain. It was the first time he'd ever applied himself fully, without reservation, and he pitched in wherever the need arose, taking on new tasks.

Still, there were days when he felt caught in the path of an oncoming storm: dilution, capital calls, Michael's manic mood swings, Hannah's dispirited reticence.

For Wallace the signs were unmistakable—his dream was rapidly turning into a nightmare.

Trek Reese returned to the conference room, passing Julie in the doorway. She had managed to get the projector working, even with Michael moaning and pacing behind her.

"Okay, gents, where were we?" Trek asked. He was tall and had the exaggerated chin of a college athlete.

"We were talking about my vision for the company," Michael said. "I've taken the liberty of preparing a few slides."

"Save your slides," Trek said. "You've got fifteen seconds. Why the hell should I give you money?"

"Fifteen seconds?" Michael was stunned. He froze, caught in a half-crouch behind the projector. Wallace enjoyed the look of utter humiliation on Michael's face—the ruler with the iron fist, caught under the contemptuous thumb of the venture capitalist, this raffish jackass with money.

Jeter stepped in. "Trek, the market's at a critical inflection point. Paper enrollment is analog. These guys are digital."

"First mover?" Trek asked. "Across the category?"

"Pure Trojan horse," Jeter said. "With a component of McDonald's. You start with enrolling for health benefits. Then it's like, 'You want fries with that order? Life insurance? Dental? 401(k)?' With a first-mover like this, you'll crater your competition."

Trek stewed on this a moment. "They've signed Cal Max?"

"The dogs are eating the dog food," Jeter said.

"Future rounds?" Trek asked. "Or we talking big bang?"

"Big bang," Jeter said. "You don't bunt here."

Trek looked at Michael. "What's the cap table look like?"

"What?" Michael asked.

"Who owns what?"

"I make all the decisions around here," Michael said.

Trek turned to Wallace. "You just a worker bee?"

"When he brought me the company it was on wobbly wheels," Michael said. "The code was spaghetti, they weren't making sales. I gave an infusion of capital, straightened out the code, built out our management team to where it is today." He paused to let this all sink in—how he had single-handedly saved the company.

"Holes?"

"I'd prefer to talk about that off-line," Michael said.

There was a knock at the door.

"This better be important," Michael said to the closed door.

Julie stepped in. "I have an urgent message for Wallace."

Wallace knew that look on Julie's face. The news was bad.

She walked purposefully around the perimeter of the conference room, away from Trek and Jeter, who lolled insolently in their swivel chairs, tyrannizing the near side of the table. The floor around them was littered with empty coffee cups, strewn newspapers, and cleaved computer bags.

Julie handed Wallace a note. She spoke in a whisper. "Hannah called. She needs you to pick up the girls."

Wallace stared foolishly at the piece of paper. Was this Julie's idea of a joke?

"Wallace, she's stuck in a snowstorm," Julie said. "A ground-hold in Denver. She said I should remind you of the school's new late policy."

Wallace didn't need reminding. While the public schools had recently embarked on campaigns of zero tolerance for guns, drugs, and knives, the Edelweiss Christian School had recently instituted a similar policy for parents who were late picking up their kids from daycare. Wallace was a frequent offender. To date his punishment had been simply to endure the irked, self-righteous stares of the Christian women in smocks—the teachers and teacher's aides who had no choice but to await his arrival. But with the ratification of the new late policy, the shoe had passed to the other foot. The penalty was harsh—detention for the parents, the time to be served stuffing envelopes at the theological seminary. The formula for calculating the term of detention was sadistically Gordian: one hour per child for every minute past six o'clock, and for every quarter hour past six fifteen, another hour licking envelopes.

"Okay. I'll deal with it." Wallace folded the note and stuffed it in his shirt pocket. He could feel the eyes of the others in the room. The displeasure was palpable.

Jeter's mouth gaped open: *no one ever walks out on a meeting with Trek Reese!*

"Don't tell me you have to leave," Michael said.

"Sorry," Wallace said. "Duty calls."

His outward nonchalance masked the growing resentment he felt for Hannah's longstanding career. He had fires to put out on an almost daily basis: settling turf wars, usually between the temperamental engineering staff and the rest of the company; making payroll; beating down doors of decision makers at health plans across the country. There was also the full-time job of keeping Michael from making irrational, knee-jerk decisions that increasingly whipped the company into a dysfunctional, reeking stew. Delays in Hannah's schedule wreaked havoc on Wallace's. He was constantly leaving this or canceling that to fend for himself and his girls. It didn't help that Hannah's airline was run by idiots who couldn't quantify manpower requirements and as a result were calling at all hours of the day and night, asking her to fill in on short-staffed flights.

"Isn't there someone else you can call?" Michael asked. Pursed lips, imploring eyes—his face looked like a human exclamation point.

Yes there is, and no there's not, Wallace thought. There is, for example, my eighty-year-old mother-in-law. But Trek Reese is probably not interested in hearing about her driving challenges: how she blows through red lights in her Buick, how she doesn't hear sirens, how the accelerator on her car sticks for reasons no one at the car dealership can explain. No, Wallace knew, there was no one else to pick up his girls. That is, nobody he'd let them ride with. He looked at his watch. Assuming traffic was light, the Edelweiss Christian School was exactly sixteen minutes from the office. That meant he could leave at 5:43 and still make it to school by six o'clock.

"I don't have to go just yet," Wallace said brightly, looking at his watch. "I've still got half an hour."

CHAPTER TWO

W allace rushed from the low-profile suburban office building into the moonless night. He passed beneath the neon glow of the sign that bore Michael Merksamer's name—a reminder of something he once owned wholly that was now slipping through his fingers. With new money, Wallace's ownership interest in the company would diminish even further.

Wallace slid behind the wheel of his father's Cadillac SLS. It felt good to be out of the stuffy conference room, to have his freedom again. He made a left out of the parking lot and accelerated toward the freeway. It wasn't exactly a new car, but it beat all the unproven junk hitting the streets these days: clean, bright instrumentation; a solid sound system; turn indicators that were clear, frank, and certain. It handled well and was a reliable performer, extraordinary for a big American car.

Wallace turned the corner leading to the on-ramp and braked suddenly. The meter lights were on. Four lanes of freeway traffic were at a standstill. He picked up his cell phone to call the office.

Julie answered.

"I hate this," Wallace said. "Traffic is horrible."

"You want me to call the school and tell them you're running late?"

"Please."

"I'm sorry, Wallace. Is everything all right?"

"Sure. Fine."

"Hang on. I'll put you through to Michael."

Wallace drove this way for the next hour—one hand on the steering wheel, the other holding the cell phone to his ear. It was the same ridiculous position he'd been in hundreds of times before, counting out money at the drive-up window, passing greasy bags of hamburgers and fries over his shoulder to his girls in the back seat, participating fully in a business conversation on the phone. Julie liked to say she could tell whenever Wallace's coworkers rode in his car—there'd be people walking through the hallways with pieces of crayon and stale french fries stuck to their butts.

The meeting droned on, with Michael pitching and Trek and Jeter countering in their speak-speak. Wallace inched up the freeway, claiming territory one-tenth of a mile at a time.

There were times Wallace swore he could walk it faster.

He allowed his mind to wander.

First to Lenore: blond hair, cut just above the shoulder. She was thorough, engaging, smart—a rising star in the organization. Earlier that day he was standing in her office when she told him about the e-mail from Cal Max. It was her account, everything was all screwed up. "Here. Come see for yourself." Moving behind her chair, he had to squint to make out the tiny type of the e-mail message on her screen. He was so close he could smell the air around her, scented like the perfume counter at Neiman Marcus. He discerned the way her graceful neck rose from the open collar of her silk blouse, the way a renegade strand of hair rested on her shoulder. He let himself imagine for a moment what it might be like to nuzzle the back of her neck, to kiss her softly behind the ear.

But Wallace knew no good would come of an affair with a married colleague. So he turned his mind instead to something less perilous: Hannah walking across the yard in black Nike running shorts, tending the herbs and roses in her garden. That was her thing—stuff growing out of the dirt. You're either big on that or you're not. Wallace definitely was not. He preferred to be holed up in his garage, working on his model railroad—no, make that *buying* stuff for his model railroad, since he didn't know jack about electricity, which made it really difficult trying to get an electric train to run. Plus the trains would fly off the track all the time. Sometimes, watching his favorite engine hit the cement floor, he'd cuss a blue streak and the girls would come running into the garage, gleefully charging him a dollar for each cuss word they heard. *A dollar!* If only he could fix that spot where the engines flew off the track, then he could start on the tunnels. The girls would like that project, sinking their arms in plaster of paris, shaping the mountains while a football game played on the old TV in the background.

"Guys, I'm going to have to sign off now," Wallace said into the cell phone when he finally arrived at the school.

The parking lot was empty. Behind the church, in the last school building, the lights were burning in a single classroom. The nuns would not be happy with him. Or whatever they were called—those heinous daycare ladies in orthopedic shoes.

Mrs. Hogan, the bossy one, unlocked the door and let Wallace in.

He knew what she was thinking: *what kind of an asshole would be more than an hour late to pick up his own kids?*

"Sorry I'm late," Wallace said. "I'll just take my treasures and go."

Mrs. Hogan used a key to bolt the door behind him. "Thanks to you I've missed Bible study." Her skin, usually pale and Irish-looking, was blotchy and sheeny with salve. She wore a powder blue smock that was intricately embroidered—Noah's ark overflowing with cartoonish animals. "Please don't look at my face. I spent the morning picketing Planned Parenthood and got a sunburn. All that honking—people today have no grace."

"Daddy!" Addison cried. She was pushing a janitor's broom over the linoleum floor. Addison was a lanky nine-year-old, a willowy bundle of twigs who wielded the tall broomstick like a pole-vaulter. Whenever she worked at a task, she sang Disney songs to herself: "Zip a Dee Doo Dah," "Whistle While You Work."

Across the room Tiffany, her six-year-old sister, sat at a small desk. She was sniffling and had her head down.

"No talking to that one," Mrs. Hogan said. "She's in time-out."

Wallace caught Tiffany sneaking peeks through her crossed arms. "Don't tell me. What did she do?"

"She was being inappropriately silly," Mrs. Hogan said. "She said Galatians wore galoshes and Deuteronomy was for doo-doo heads. When I asked her to empty the wastebaskets she refused. She's been crying ever since."

"She gets that stubbornness from her mother," Wallace said. "Hannah won't take out the garbage, either."

Whenever Wallace went out of town, Hannah would bag the kitchen trash and leave it in a pile at the garage door. It was her airline training; she was used to the ramp monkeys coming to the aft door, restocking the ice and soda pop, and taking away the refuse. She could adeptly step around a mound of tied-off, clear-plastic bags, stacked in a small area, for extended periods of time—days, if necessary. Often, coming home after a long trip, Wallace would be unable to enter the house through the garage for the great mountain of garbage blocking the door. It was lost on Hannah that airplane doors opened out but house doors opened *in.*

"We're trying to teach an important life lesson," Mrs. Hogan added. "The way to the top is by getting off your bottom. Refusing to work begs the lesson."

"I can see that it would."

"Headstrong is what she is."

"It's genetic. You ought to meet her grandmother."

"I know her grandmother very well. She's a lovely lady. Tell me, does she know her granddaughter sees space aliens?"

"You mean Beatrice? She was here?"

"Asleep in the trash can. That's why it couldn't be emptied."

Tiffany was sneaking another look at Wallace. She was as timorous as her older sister was self-assured. Beatrice was Tiffany's extraterrestrial friend. She often visited for tea and stayed to debunk the daily Bible lesson: Moses never walked a parted Red Sea; there were no apples at the Garden of Eden. It was exasperating for the teachers, but Tiffany was adamant that Beatrice was a real Martian. Wallace had to admit he rather enjoyed Beatrice's pluck.

"I hope my secretary caught you," Wallace said. "To tell you I was running late."

"That one who called, she was very nice. I was surprised to hear you had an office."

Wallace stared back blankly. Surprised?

"One of the mothers speculated that you played football, with your size and all. But then I don't suppose a football player would have an office and a secretary, or be as thoughtless as you, seeing as how they're in the public eye.

"'Thinking Like a Leper,'" Mrs. Hogan added. "That was tonight's Bible study. Now I may never know how a leper thinks."

"You could always ask one of your friends," Wallace said.

Mrs. Hogan regarded Wallace with scorn, probably out of the mistaken impression that he was antireligious. Church was the one wedge in Wallace's marriage. Hannah found comfort in attending Sunday services, whereas Wallace felt he was always on the outside looking in. It was the implausible cocktail, the man-made concoction of organized religion, that pushed him away: the rigid belief systems, the inflexible doctrine, the forced march of worship, the corruption and scandal of people in power, and the utter determination to grow the congregation—its coffers—through Sunday morning media broadcasts. Wallace knew a business when he saw one.

"Let's go, girls," he called. "Addison, put down that broom."

Tiffany raised her head. She was looking for permission to leave time-out.

"Yes, Tiff, now."

The spectacle of Wallace usurping her authority in the classroom caused Mrs. Hogan to shake her head and cluck like a hen. She made no move to unlock the door. Instead she went to her desk and began leafing through a thick binder.

"Bear with me," she said, massaging her temples. "If I don't enforce the new late policy there will be heck to pay tomorrow."

Wallace said, "How about I make a donation to the teacher's fund and we'll call it even?"

"I swear, you parents are more flighty than your offspring—"

Wallace reached for his checkbook. "I'll make it an even hundred."

"We don't want your money, Mr. Noe. We want your toil. The seminary is behind the church. Report at eight sharp."

The girls ambushed Wallace with things from their cubbies: back-packs, lunch boxes, artwork, graded papers, school sweaters.

"Daddy, we thought you forgot us," Addison said.

Wallace crouched down to eye level with his daughters. He took each one by the hand. "Sorry, girls. I had an important meeting—a man with lots of money."

"You know what the Bible says about rich men and heaven," Mrs. Hogan said. "You'd easier pass a camel through the eye of a needle."

Addison and Tiffany looked confused.

"The eye of a needle," Mrs. Hogan said, showing the fraction of an inch between her thumb and forefinger. "And a great big camel." She revealed her full wingspan. She looked like a fat blue goose that could never fly.

Mrs. Hogan was a Biblical literalist, a hard-core fundamentalist. The Edelweiss Christian School was full of them. Wallace was incensed on principle. Wealth had built this country; most of the rich people Wallace knew were generous to a fault. It was the pious ones, the ones who wore religion on their sleeve, that you had to watch for: the fly-by-night pool contractors, the appliance repairmen, anyone who plastered that stupid fish symbol all over his signs and business cards. Given the chance they'd beat their own mother out of an extra dime.

"Don't pay any attention, girls," Wallace said. "Heaven is like community college. Everyone gets in."

Mrs. Hogan glowered. "Everyone but heathens and sinners."

Wallace wasn't about to cede any more of his daughters' mind-share to the daycare ladies of Edelweiss Christian. Still fresh in his memory was the night Addison and Tiffany had gone to bed in tears, convinced their father would spend eternity burning in hell—something a teacher's aide asserted, since Wallace rarely attended Sunday service.

"If it's all true then explain about the boat," Wallace said.

Mrs. Hogan looked up. "Excuse me?"

With a nod of his head, Wallace indicated the Noah's ark embroi-dery on her smock. "Two of every kind of animal in the world? How is that possible?"

"It was a big boat."

"The Wild Animal Park is two thousand acres," Wallace said. "How big was the boat?"

Mrs. Hogan put on her reading glasses menacingly, a warrior girding her loins.

"I think I see where we got Deuteronomy for doo-doo heads," she said, reaching for a pencil and powering up the calculator. The school was technologically backward. The adding machine was ancient—as big as a typewriter, with keys the size of garden stepping stones.

"We may not be able to put dads in time-out," she said. "But they can lick stamps at the seminary."

She punched angrily at the calculator keys, clearly yearning to slap Wallace with a hefty detention. She glanced between the written late policy and the adding machine, tallying hours on a yellow legal pad, unwilling to give an inch.

Wallace looked on, somewhat amused. "How about I just volunteer my mother-in-law for the school board?"

Mrs. Hogan finished totaling. She took off her reading glasses.

"Congratulations," she said, a sanctimonious smile forming across the oil slick of her face. "You've got the record. Thirty-six hours of detention, starting tomorrow."

"Sorry," Wallace lied. "I'm playing golf."

"I will remind you," Mrs. Hogan said, "the girls are on automatic suspension until you serve your time. They can't set foot on school grounds. They'll get failing grades for the quarter."

"Fine. We'll pull them out and homeschool."

Addison and Tiffany traded astonished stares.

"You don't mean it," Mrs. Hogan said, sizing up Wallace skeptically. "Your mother-in-law is a prominent member of this church. She'd be humiliated."

"Try me."

"You expect me to believe this—you'd drop your own flesh and blood out of Edelweiss Christian, just to avoid detention?"

"In a heartbeat," Wallace said. "Your field trips suck."

Mrs. Hogan made a show of unlocking the door. "It's your funeral. There was talk of purging the heathens, anyway. Enrollment's up and there's a waiting list."

"Good. Bend *their* minds."

Wallace felt a tug on his sleeve. Addison was quietly crying.

"What's the matter with you?" Wallace asked.

"I can't leave school," Addison said. "My California Mission project is due."

"Not anymore, it isn't."

"But Mom already bought the stuff. She said it cost a lot of money."

"We'll build a fort for your Barbies."

"Dad, please," Addison begged. "Why can't you just do detention?"

Wallace didn't take time to explain. He pushed his girls out the door.

On the way to the parking lot they passed a janitor working in a brightly lit classroom, emptying the trash. Tiffany suddenly insisted they had to go back to the daycare room. It seemed they had forgotten Beatrice in the garbage can.

CHAPTER 3 THREE

The sprawling Spanish Colonial Revival campus that housed the Edelweiss Christian School, the Four Gospels Theological Seminary, and the Hidden Valley Presbyterian Church was situated at the top of a hill—a perfect landing spot for an alien spacecraft. A thick marine layer cloaked the night in fog. At the edge of the parking lot, near the grove of eucalyptus trees, Tiffany bade Beatrice good-bye.

Wallace's plan was to make a quick pass by the bank for cash, circle back for hamburger meals, and go home. Addison and Tiffany always enjoyed the short ride into town—the plummeting drop down Idaho Avenue followed by the roller-coaster hill that was Ninth Avenue.

Ninth Avenue bisected Old Escondido, a neighborhood of architectural curiosities, some dating back to the 1800s: painted Craftsman bungalows alongside renovated Victorians; disintegrating California ranch houses next to restored Cape Cods; storybook cottages abutting hunkered-down adobes; overcrowded cinderblock apartments and white stucco duplexes, doors open, Radio Latina blaring. The trees—peppers, oaks, and eucalyptus, mostly—were old and overgrown; there were whole blocks where thick canopies enveloped the street. Security bars and cyclone-fenced front yards suggested not all was well in Old Escondido.

Wallace dialed his cell phone.

"Daddy, who are you calling?" Addison asked.

"I promised Michael."

"I'm really hungry."

"I know, Tiff. Hang on."

The phones were on night ring. Julie had gone home.

What was the extension to the conference room? Wallace tried *202 pound.*

Encouraging. It was ringing.

Yellow streetlights shone over the once-thriving business district where broken sidewalks ushered in a modern-day, cultural mishmash—Sasha Liquor, *!Qué Bueno!* Used Cars, third-world markets *La Fiesta, El Gato,* and Abdul's Four Star. Royal's Corner, an all-night donut shop, was ablaze in light, its sterile stainless steel counters looking like an operating room through the big windows. *El Cantinero,* a Mexican tavern, and Body Fresco, a tattoo parlor, occupied two storefronts on an otherwise abandoned block.

Michael picked up.

"Wallace, where've you been? We've got a lot of questions."

Michael was a circus performer who didn't like working without a net.

"Sorry. I got held up."

"Trek has a question," Michael said. "How many insured lives at Cal Max?"

"About six million, total."

"About six million total!" And Michael was off and running, a tap dancer with a top hat and cane, pitching, wheedling, cajoling.

At the drive-up ATM Wallace kept the cell phone to his ear and used his free hand to lower the window. Then he noticed the sign. An out-of-order sign was taped across the screen, and it was a shitty-looking sign at that. Now he'd have to use the walk-up ATM at the front of the bank, which meant backing the car around, getting out, and locking the girls inside—more time wasted. He cursed his bankers. *Is it that tough to keep your mission-critical systems up and running? In this day and age?*

He threw the car in reverse.

"You said a swear word!" the girls cried from the back seat.

"No, *Christ* is not a swear word."

"Yes, Mrs. Hogan said it was."

"Wallace, what are you saying?" Michael asked. "You're on speaker."

"Owe us a dollar!" the girls said. "Daddy, you owe us a dollar!"

"Okay, I owe you a dollar—"

"Listen, Wallace, Trek has another question," Michael was saying. "What would a typical employer group pay to a benefits consultant—"

Trek interrupted. "—if they did a big enrollment project for that group?"

"How much would your user stand to save?" Jeter asked, pushing in.

"Hard to say," Wallace answered. "Benefits consultants typically charge a fee plus production costs based on the number of employees."

"Like how much would they charge?" Trek sounded testy.

"I don't know. Anywhere from ten to fifty dollars a head. It all depends." Wallace put the car in park and turned off the ignition. If Trek and Jeter still had questions, it could be a while.

"That's a big spread," Trek said. "So you're saying production costs plus some sort of fee?"

"Well, hold on," Wallace said. "We may be talking apples and oranges. Most groups we deal with have less than a thousand employees, and big consulting firms aren't much interested in that market. If anything your per-employee cost would go up on a smaller group because you wouldn't be spreading production costs over so many people—"

Something was not right.

Girls, what are you doing now?

A toy knife?

Wallace tried to make sense of what he was seeing.

Where did you kids come up with a toy knife? And how did you get out of the car?

Surprised, Wallace pulled the cell phone away from his ear. A man held a large, serrated knife at the open window. The blade was polished steel, with a tip that curved up like a scimitar. Wallace took in the details of his would-be assailant: the sideways Raiders cap; the frantic eyes; the narrow, blighted face; the baggy Lakers jersey over the white T-shirt. The young robber was muttering in a voice too soft to understand.

"C'mon," the robber said, stepping closer. "Gimme your bank card."

Wallace would never fully understand how—or why—he then did what he did. He would be compelled to recount his every thought, his every move, lord knows how many times over the coming year. He would be asked by friends and family members to defend his actions, which no reasonable man could do given that his children were in the car. He just did what he did. The only time it seemed like a good idea was as he was doing it.

That would be his explanation. Forever.

Wallace used his free hand to quietly unlatch the door. Then he pivoted in the driver's seat and kicked explosively with both feet at a spot just above the armrest. Like a battering ram the steel door swung unfettered and struck the robber in the legs. He buckled from sight.

In an instant Wallace was out of the car.

The robber quavered on injured legs.

Wallace knew he had two things going for him: his daunting physical size and a dexterous ability to posture, honed from years in the consulting business. He decided his best bet was to bluff, to try a sort of streetwise tromp l'oeil.

No one would dare fight a cop, Wallace reasoned. Cops carry guns. They have radios. They're backed up quickly by other cops.

Wallace wielded his cell phone like a .38 snub-nosed revolver. He drew down with both hands, taking aim, using the antenna to paint a bull's-eye on the robber's forehead.

"Police officer!" Wallace shouted. "Get on the ground!"

The robber went face down on the ground.

"Drop the weapon!"

The knife went free.

Good, Wallace thought. It's working.

Wallace took a step and gave the knife a kick. It skidded across the parking lot and came to a rest at the base of a planter box.

"Hands where I can see 'em!"

The robber lay spread-eagle on the ground.

Wallace's heart raced. What next? He saw that he easily out-weighed the boy by at least a hundred pounds. He thought his best chance of holding him was to sit on him, literally.

Wallace sprang onto the robber's back and rode him like a pool mattress.

"Hey—" the robber said.

"Shut your mouth, prisoner." With a forearm Wallace cuffed the robber at the base of his skull. The blow sent the baseball cap flying.

"I'm sorry, officer—"

Wallace grabbed a handful of hair.

"My kids are in that car," Wallace hissed through clenched teeth. "Nobody screws with me in front of my kids!" With each word Wallace slammed the robber's face into the asphalt, for emphasis. The boy came up with bloody nostrils and pebbles embedded in his forehead.

Wallace became increasingly aware of people gathering at the scene—bank customers and passersby—eager to lend a hand. He also became conscious of the rising stench of urine; his young prisoner had apparently wet himself.

"Would somebody please call the police?" Wallace said to the onlookers. "I'm holding a robber here."

Within seconds the air was filled with the sound of sirens descending on the bank. The lead cruiser, its *eyeaaaah-woop-woop* wailing and lights flashing, came to a heavy stop behind the Cadillac. Wallace and his prisoner were instantly illuminated by a wall of bright light. Soon the parking lot was filled with squad cars. They were angled every which way, their lights flashing, doors open, and brakes smelling hot. The robber was quickly handcuffed, dragged to his feet, and marched to a waiting patrol car.

Long after it was over, most of the cops were still in the parking lot loitering, talking, and joking. They took turns congratulating Wallace and making small talk with Addison and Tiffany. An officer in blue fatigues walked a police dog through the crowd. He brought the dog over for the girls to see.

Wallace's ordeal had come to an end. And fortunately for him, his prisoner never moved a muscle.

CHAPTER FOUR

The next day Wallace went into the office on less than five hours of sleep. It was early morning, and the fog was still thick. His first stop was the outdoor coffee cart in the center courtyard. Lenore was there, right on time, her blond hair spilling over the collar of her black wool jacket. Their morning rendezvous was getting to be a regular thing.

"Congratulations," she said, her face flushed pink from cold. She grasped a paper coffee cup in two hands, tying to keep warm. "Is there anything you don't do?"

Already the story was around: Wallace the hero, taking down an armed robber, Michael and Trek Reese listening on the line.

"What kind of a question is that?" Wallace asked.

"Indecent, for all you know." Lenore often surprised him with impertinent remarks—alluring tidbits that caught him off guard. As far as he could tell, she only did this with him; around others she was the model of propriety. It left him with the bewildering suspicion that he was the butt of her joke. She followed with a wry smile, eyes gleaming, her crow's feet crinkling—she could turn it on at will, like her Corpus Christi drawl.

"Come on," she said. "Hurry and order. Then we can go sit."

Wallace ordered his usual—a tall coffee, black. When Lenore reached for the cream, the neck of her blouse widened faintly.

"I'll pay for hers," Wallace said to the coffee vendor.

"No," Lenore said.

"I insist." Wallace slid his credit card across the narrow counter. He had no cash.

The coffee vendor accepted the card with a forced smile. He recognized Wallace as a man of distinction—a company owner.

"But Wallace, weren't you terrified?" Lenore asked.

"I missed my calling. I should have been a cop."

"What about Hannah? Was she suitably impressed?"

"If you hear anything let me know."

"You haven't told her?"

"She doesn't need to know everything." Wallace hadn't spoken to Hannah in two days. The surprise snowstorm in Denver had jumbled up everyone's flight schedule. As a favor to a friend, she took an extra trip to Chicago, according to the message on the answering machine.

"You men and your secrets," Lenore said. "Knocking out a bank robber with your bare hands and not even telling your wife."

"I like your version better."

They carried their coffee cups around the corner to an out-of-the-way café table—a recent progression to their early morning routine. A lattice of honeysuckle vines gave them a shred of privacy. Near the table, a staked twig that was supposed to pass for a mulberry tree stuck out from a planter box like a bone.

Lenore gazed at the scrawny tree. "Think it'll ever make it?"

"Maybe," Wallace said. "If they don't kill it first." He turned toward her and caught a forlorn look. "You all right?"

"Hardly slept a wink."

"Ricky?"

"Ten thousand dollars. He wants me to wire it to a Guamanian bank."

"What this time?"

"A bent shaft. The usual nonsense, you know the drill. Don't give up the ship."

Lenore's husband, Ricky, captained a tuna boat out of American Samoa. His trips home were increasingly rare. Once, in an aside to

Wallace, he claimed working the waters of the Western Tropical Pacific was the Triple Crown of fishing: wages were low, his purse seine nets were beyond the reach of United States law, and his personal life was beyond the clutches of an overly ambitious, increasingly discontented wife. Wallace wanted to tell Lenore to cut her losses and file for divorce, but he held his tongue in deference to their employer-employee relationship. It was a line he didn't dare cross.

"Are you going to send it?" he asked.

"Like hell."

They sipped their coffee in silence. Wallace pictured Ricky Terry holed up in a cheap hotel room in American Samoa, stoned on vodka, in the clutches of some tropical cutie, waiting for a bank wire that would never come.

"I think I hate him," Lenore said.

"Thank God no children."

Lenore managed a smile. "Distance has its advantages. Shall we?"

There was a legitimate business reason for these early morning meetings: Lenore gave Wallace the rundown on Cal Max. Wallace listened, less intently than usual, preoccupied by the events of the night before. As a businessman and entrepreneur, he strived to achieve a modicum of control over the people and events around him. Then it happened suddenly, unexpectedly, like a camera strobe in the dark. It was a euphoric feeling turning the tables on an armed robber, holding him for the police, being treated as one of their own at the station. The patrol sergeant was a congenial ex-marine with salt-and-pepper hair. When he learned that Addison and Tiffany were hungry, he sent two retired senior volunteers out for food. The volunteers, who wore starched white shirts and looked older than fossil dirt, got into their white police sedan and drove away with a great sense of purpose. They returned a half hour later with two hamburger meals for the girls and a third for the prisoner.

"I'd rather have fed him liver and sour owl shit," the sergeant said.

While in the station, Wallace picked up a reserve officer recruiting brochure. To him, community service was uncharted territory. He had never given any thought to setting aside a certain number of hours each month to pitch in, to make the world a safer place. The time commitment alone, he realized, made it virtually impossible to join the police reserves. He already worked a sixty- or seventy-hour week, and his travel schedule would only intensify in the coming months. Still, police work intrigued him. He couldn't get the idea out of his head. He could guess what the women in his life would say: Hannah would kill him, Julie would laugh, and Lenore would point out how senseless it was that the number-two man at one of America's fastest-growing companies would spend his weekend nights patrolling Kit Carson Park, making high school kids pour out their beer.

"Wallace, are you listening to me?" Lenore was snapping her fingers, trying to get his attention. "I said Peg Brown is livid. She wants a meeting. She's threatening to pull the contract."

This wrenched Wallace from his daydream. Peg Brown was the director of group systems at Cal Max. She was Merksamer Digital's conduit to the membership and operations side of the health plan, and like a third-world dictator she ruled her territory with a despotic hand. It was a serious threat; Cal Max had the contractual right to cancel for nonperformance at any time, without notice.

"Software problems?" Wallace asked.

"What else?"

"How bad?"

"They loaded the Meisenheimer tape and it cancelled almost a thousand members."

With a long sigh, Wallace meditated on this. He and Lenore became mirror images, sipping their coffee, staring straight ahead, contemplating the damage being done on an almost daily basis by Merksamer Digital's out-of-control, defiant engineers. The software *still* wasn't working. The company's celebrated cornerstone account was shaping up as a disaster of Hindenburg proportions. Wallace looked at his watch. The staff meeting was about to start.

"What's our excuse this time?" he asked.

"Who knows?" Lenore said. "Why even ask?"

In the conference room, for Wallace, there were handshakes and high fives all around. Michael realized it was hopeless to start the meeting until Wallace told the story for everyone in the room.

———•◦•———

The perpetrator was one Joshua Allan Trout. White male. Seventeen years of age. One hundred forty-nine pounds. The arresting officer talked to the boy's stepfather by phone. Josh started going bad in high school: blowing up mailboxes, burglarizing neighborhood garages. In his sophomore year, he quit the French club and stopped doing homework. By the end of his junior year, he was staying out nights and sleeping through most of his classes.

The stepfather suspected drugs.

Josh quit school early in his senior year. When his antics got too far out of control—after the cash kept disappearing, after the family van was implicated in a hit-and-run accident in the middle of the night, after one too many druggies showed up at the door looking for Josh—his stepfather kicked him out of the house. He heard a story going around Victorville about drug dealers murdering siblings to settle debts, and Josh had a twelve-year-old half sister. His stepfather guessed he was up to his eyeballs in drug debt.

"Got any drug debts, Josh?" the cop asked.

"Nope."

"Think your stepfather would lie?"

"I dunno'. Probably."

Banished from home, Josh went to the freeway on-ramp and stuck out his thumb. He had a duffel bag and about sixty dollars in cash. Two Latinos in a brown Ford sedan stopped. They may have been gang members or ex-cons. They had prison tattoos, Josh recalled. The men said they were headed to San Diego. Palm trees and an ocean sounded pretty good to Josh, so he opened the car door, threw in his duffle bag, and jumped in. The two men had a cooler of beer. By the time they reached Escondido, about thirty minutes north of San Diego, they were drunk, out of beer, and nearly out of gas. They exited the freeway at Valley Parkway and found a gas station and mini-mart. There, the two males strong-armed forty dollars from Josh to pay for the beer they said he drank, then sent him inside to pay for their now-full tank of gas. As Josh stood in line, the car sped off, leaving him with the clothes on his back, a knife tucked inside his belt, and just enough cash to settle the bill with the hulking Samoan behind the counter.

"Where'd you get the knife from, Josh?" the cop asked.

"My real dad."

"And where's your real dad now?"

"Dead."

"Think he'd be proud of you, knowing you used that knife to try and rob someone?"

"He don't know nuthin'. He's dead."

"Yeah?" said the cop. "What if he's up in heaven? What if he's looking down on you?"

"Them *beaners* took my stuff. I shoulda' killed 'em both while I had the chance."

"I don't know, Josh," the cop said. "Double homicide might be a tad ambitious, based on your track record and the fact you got piss in your pants."

Eventually Josh got around to telling the police officer everything he wanted to know.

"First thing I thought about was lifting a purse," Josh said. "But them redneck construction guys was around that mini-mart like ants. And I ain't stealing no purse in front a' no construction guys drinking Big Gulps. Them dudes'll run you down and beat the holy crap outta' you for lifting a lady's purse."

Josh walked the streets of Escondido, looking for a convenient purse to snatch. He took a wrong turn and ended up at a rock quarry. Then he followed the railroad tracks to a feed store that was across the street from the police station. Finally he came upon a ramshackle elementary school surrounded by a neighborhood of old Victorian homes, but the streets were as empty as the schoolyard was. Darkness was falling. The temperature was dropping ominously. Josh was hungry and running out of options. He decided to try his hand at crime: robbery-at-knifepoint. Earlier in the evening he had passed a bank. He returned to the bank and staked out the drive-through ATM.

"You intended to rob someone?" the cop asked.

"Yeah," Josh said. "I thought it would be easy. You know, get a hold of someone's bank card and get all the cash I wanted."

Watching the cars come and go at the bank, Josh realized it was impossible to squeeze between a car and the ATM, even for a skinny beanpole like himself. What he really needed was for someone to use the walk-up teller at the front of the bank.

"That's when you made the sign?" the cop asked.

"Yeah. From stuff I got out of the dumpster."

"Keep going."

"So this silver Cadillac come along. Like an old lady's car, you know? But then I seen it was this guy driving it. And he just sat there with his window down, talking on the phone. So I figured I'd take him while he was sitting in the car. No way I knew he was a police officer. No way!"

There was a thick bandage on his right shin where the car door had imposed a deep gash. Josh's first stop was the emergency room. The wound needed thirteen stitches.

"By the way, Josh, how's your leg?" the cop asked.

"It don't hurt none."

"Good," said the cop. "'Cause I threw away all your pain pills."

It was almost midnight by the time Wallace and his girls finally arrived home.

———◦◦———

"What a story!" Charlie Dye said, upstairs in the conference room.

"Thirteen stitches," Otto noted. "Unlucky number."

Wallace said, "It was stupid on my part. I should have just given him the card."

"At least we can be thankful you are safe," Sanjay Sangam said. He was Merksamer Digital's chief technology officer. Sanjay's skin was the color of Hershey's dark chocolate, and when he spoke his pink tongue flashed like a cat's.

"The moral is," Lenore said, "pity the poor fool who comes between Papa Bear and his cubs."

"All right," Michael said. "Enough about that. Let's get this thing started."

It wasn't long before the meeting degenerated into a lot of finger-pointing and shouting. Cal Max had a long list of technical issues. Sanjay was vague about what he could do to fix their problems. His only solution was for Cal Max to take a new release of the software, scheduled for somewhere around Christmastime.

"But, Sanjay, Cal Max doesn't want a new release," Lenore said. "They want us to fix the software they have."

"Impossible!" Sanjay said.

"Why?" Lenore asked. "Name one good reason."

Sanjay refused to answer. He crossed his arms and stared at a spot on the carpet.

"Answer her, Sanjay," Wallace said. "Why can't we build a simple patch?"

"Because we are already working twenty-four hours a day," Sanjay said. "My people, they will walk out. I am telling you. I cannot give them more work."

"We're kidding ourselves if we think this is going to fly," Lenore said. "Cal Max is not about to put their clients at risk by giving them buggy software."

Sanjay stared at her with hatred. "Give me five new resources and I will give you a patch."

"No way," Michael said quickly. "We are not hiring five more people—not until the venture money comes in."

So it was a stalemate: Sanjay needed more resources, and Michael wouldn't authorize it. The Cal Max account would suffer.

That was the problem with Merksamer Digital's company culture: it was engineer-driven. All anyone cared about was process and technology—whatever made it easiest to get a new release out the door. But the technicians, from Michael and Sanjay down, didn't comprehend *context*. They didn't understand how their customer *used* the software. Anyone who did would never ask a major insurance company to take a new release at Christmas. It was their busiest time of year.

When the meeting was over, Michael called Wallace into his office.

"Put a muzzle on your attack dog Lenore," Michael said. "And get off Sanjay's back. He takes it personally."

"I can't help it if he has thin skin."

"You're playing with dynamite. He comes from Silicon Valley, where engineers make all the decisions. They can put a company out of business just by walking out the door."

"So we're not supposed to call a bug a bug? Because our engineers might walk out?"

"Just tell her to back off. Let Sanjay do his job."

Julie knocked on the door.

"Sorry to disturb you," she said. "A police detective is in the lobby to see Wallace."

"Be right there." Wallace turned to Michael. "Anything else?"

"One last thing," Michael said. He sat slumped over his desk, his head buried in his hands—his usual position after a staff meeting. "Trek Reese thinks we have a big hole in our organization. He wants us to bring in someone on the sales side of the company, someone with industry experience and a good Rolodex."

"You mean replace Charlie?"

"Not replace him. Just put somebody over him."

"He won't like it."

"I don't give a damn what Charlie likes. Here's the thing: whoever we get is going to want a good title. I'll have to bring him in as an executive vice president, put him over sales and marketing."

Wallace turned to the window. It sounded like an expensive position to fill.

"He'll be a direct-report to me," Michael continued, "which means the two of you will be equals on the organization chart. I hope that's all right with you."

Wallace watched two squirrels wrangling in a tree branch. They chased down the knotty trunk.

"He'll want stock options," Michael added. "And probably an expense account and a company car."

"Whatever you think, Michael. I just want this thing to work."

"It's not so much what I think," Michael said. "It's what Jacaranda thinks. And Trek Reese all but said we won't get that money unless we find this guy."

CHAPTER FIVE

A clean-cut, broad-shouldered young man stood waiting for Wallace in the lobby. He showed his police identification and introduced himself as Detective Tetley. Peeking out from the right front panel of his woolen sportcoat, affixed to his belt, was a police shield. Behind the shield was a holstered gun. Like a census taker, he carried a heavy clipboard and wore black leather shoes.

"Is there somewhere we can talk?" Tetley asked.

"Nice little lunch place around the corner," Wallace said. "If you're hungry."

"I'm thinking somewhere more private."

"My office, then."

The receptionist buzzed them through the security door, and they made their way up the stairwell to the second floor. As he walked, the detective took in the environs of the executive hallway: the spacious offices, the conference rooms, the kitchen stations.

"Looks like you're in the computer business," he said.

"Insurance stuff," Wallace said. "Nothing very exciting." He smiled at the detective. "No car chases."

Wallace had spent a sleepless night working out in his mind an alternative scenario to the required service hours of a level-one reserve officer: he would be available to work closely with the chief and other top brass on long-term, strategic projects—a brand action plan, an officer recruiting and retention program, a project to *productize* the department's menu of services and market them proactively to the community. In his capacity as a special reserve officer, Wallace would carry a badge. He would qualify on the range to pack a gun. He would ride occasionally with a uniformed patrol officer—a full shift every third or fourth Friday night and on full moons, just to keep a pulse on the streets.

"I took some computer courses in college," Tetley said. "Mostly programming. I have to say I enjoyed it."

"You're lucky," Wallace said. "In my day we had punch cards. I hated the darn things."

"A good software application—you have to respect it," Tetley said. "Every routine has its function, no overlap."

"Human resources is right down the hall," Wallace said. "Based on my last meeting we could use you."

"Impressive," Tetley said, looking around.

Merksamer Digital had a formidable grapevine. Wallace knew it was probably all over the building that he was meeting with the police behind closed doors. He could imagine the speculation: Was the city going to present him with a hero's plaque? Make him guest of honor at a special luncheon? Nominate him for Citizen of the Year?

In Wallace's office, the detective was momentarily drawn to the bookcase, where there was a model of a diesel locomotive—a Burlington Northern Santa Fe DASH 9 44 CW painted in the railroad's distinctive red and yellow war-bonnet scheme.

"Train guy?" Tetley asked, looking at Wallace.

"One in a long list of bad habits," Wallace said. "At least that's what my wife would tell you." He showed the detective to a chair at the small conference table. "Please, make yourself at home."

Julie stood in the doorway. She had followed them in. "Can I get you anything? Water, coffee?"

The question seemed to take the detective by surprise.

"I'm sorry," he said, blinking up at Julie. "And who are you?"

"I work for Wallace—"

"This isn't a social occasion. You need to leave. And close the door on your way out."

Julie looked at Wallace.

"It's okay," Wallace said. "Standard operating procedure."

Tetley watched Julie pull the door shut. Satisfied, he opened his clipboard and removed a stack of papers. Wallace recognized the top page as the cover sheet to the police report from the night before.

"I'd like to clear up some things about last night," Tetley said. "Just a few quick questions." He reached inside his sportcoat and produced a pocket-sized cassette recorder. "Any objection if I turn this on?"

"Feel free," Wallace said.

"I'll be straight with you if you be straight with me."

"Goes without saying."

Tetley eyed Wallace cynically. He began combing through the pages of the report.

"Mr. Noe, you stated that you were seated in the vehicle when the suspect approached your car. Is that correct?"

"Yes."

"And when you first identified yourself as a police officer, were you still seated in the car? Or were you out?"

Wallace answered carefully. He wanted to come across as detail-oriented and a good communicator—a reliable witness. "Just getting out."

Tetley took a moment to write something down.

"Tell me about your cell phone," Tetley said. "You brandished it as if it were a loaded weapon?"

"Correct."

Last night this little tidbit had sent the cops into peals of laughter, but not this cop, not this day.

"And while you were pointing your cell phone in a gunlike, threatening manner, what else did you say, other than to identify yourself as a police officer?"

"Exact words?"

"As best as you can recollect. Did you say, 'Stop or I'll shoot' or 'Put your hands in the air,' anything like that?"

"I definitely told him to drop the knife. And I remember telling him to get on the ground."

"Did he do it? Did he drop the knife and get on the ground?"

"Almost right away."

"He submitted to your authority?"

"Boy did he ever." Wallace grinned. "I see now you guys have it easy."

Tetley glanced up at Wallace, as if offended. He narrowed his eyes. "What about the injury to his leg? How did he get that?"

Wallace looked back curiously at the detective. Surely he already knew the answer.

"The car door," Wallace said. "It swung and hit him."

"And what role did you play in making that happen?"

Wallace couldn't help but smile. "I kicked it."

"Intending to strike him?"

"What else?"

"How bad was he hurt? In your best judgment?"

"He was in pain."

"Was he incapacitated? Was he retreating?"

"I would say yes to both."

"And he was unarmed when you tackled him?"

Wallace thought for a moment. "Well, I never really tackled him. It's not like he was running away. I mean, he was already on the ground."

Tetley appeared surprised. "He had already surrendered when you attacked him?"

"No, you've got it wrong," Wallace said. "I never attacked him and he didn't surrender."

"I'm not talking about waving a white flag," Tetley said. "But you just told me he was incapacitated and complying with your verbal commands. He already dropped the knife, correct?"

"Yes."

"So you had the upper hand? At no point were you threatened in any way?"

"It was a tenuous situation. My kids were in the car."

"I understand where your children were. I'm talking about the suspect."

Wallace shifted uncomfortably in his chair. He had an ominous feeling about where this was going.

"Mr. Noe, did you ever tell the suspect he was under citizen's arrest?"

"I think I made it clear I wasn't there to buy him ice cream."

The detective raised his voice impatiently. "That wasn't the question. What is it you do for a living, Mr. Noe?"

"I told you. Software."

"You're not a police officer or a federal agent?"

"You know darn well—"

"Then I'm confused. Why would you identify yourself as a police officer?"

"Why the attitude, Detective? I haven't done anything wrong."

Tetley grunted contemptuously. He turned back to the police report.

"Let's talk for a minute about these other witnesses. Several said they actually addressed you as *officer*. Do you recall that happening?"

"I really don't remember." Wallace glanced at his wristwatch. "Look, I have a meeting in a few minutes—"

"Answer the question."

"Someone may have called me that, there were a lot of people, I had my mind on other things—"

"But at no time did you ever tell the witnesses you were not a real a police officer?"

Wallace hesitated before answering: "No, probably not."

"You kept this little vigilante thing going, even after the suspect was subdued—"

"I saw a snake and killed it."

"You're the snake, Mr. Noe. This was a kid. You choked him, you smashed his head in the ground, you pummeled him with your fists—"

"No, you're wrong—"

"Then you intentionally manipulated our response—"

"I didn't manipulate anything—"

"You were thinking we, meaning the Escondido Police Department, would respond sooner if we thought one of our own was involved—"

Wallace was embarrassed. He felt his face growing hot. Why was this such a big deal?

"Okay, I'm not stupid," Wallace said. "We all know how it works."

"How does it work, Mr. Noe? Tell me."

"You guys take care of your own," Wallace said. "Everyone knows that. It leaves the rest of us to fend for ourselves."

"You took the law into your own hands."

"I took a stand."

"That's not your job."

"It damn well better be somebody's job!"

The detective studied Wallace's face for a long moment, then asked, "Mr. Noe, is there any other reason you can think of? Any other reason you didn't tell the witnesses on the scene that you were not a real police officer?"

"You tell me. You have all the answers."

"I've got all day. Take all the time you need."

"Go to hell. Get out."

"I'll stay until you answer the question."

Wallace pushed back from the table. He marched to the door. "Have a nice day, Detective."

"Very well." Tetley looked down. His motions became self-conscious and deliberate: he put away his mechanical pencil, straightened his papers, and filed them inside the metal clipboard. "Mr. Noe, I am going to ask you to step away from that door. And please put both arms straight out to your sides where I can see them."

Wallace stared in disbelief.

Tetley stood. He leveled a commanding finger at Wallace. "Please step back, sir."

Wallace let go of the door handle.

Tetley stepped sideways, flung a chair, and grasped Wallace firmly at the shoulder, detaining him. Then he patted Wallace down and checked his pockets.

"Got any rockets or bazookas? Anything sharp that's going to stick me?"

"What is this?" Wallace said.

Tetley locked a pair of silver handcuffs over Wallace's wrists.

"You're under arrest for impersonating a police officer," Tetley said. "That is against the law in the state of California."

"Come on!"

"Is there a blanket we can use to cover your hands until we get to the car?"

"This is an office. We don't have blankets."

"I should warn you. Your colleagues might see you going out in handcuffs."

"I want to call an attorney."

"Later."

"I have meetings—"

Tetley pulled open the door. He led Wallace down the hallway.

"Julie, cancel my appointments," Wallace said. "Something's come up."

Julie was at her secretary's station. She looked up. She covered her mouth and burst out laughing.

"Oh, that is so priceless!" she called after them. "The oafish cop is taking away the hardened criminal in handcuffs!"

Wallace could hardly blame her for thinking it was a joke. That was the way things were between them—they were always looking for ways to get each other going.

CHAPTER SIX

"Tetley, Tetley, Tetley—" Escondido Police Sergeant Ernesto "Ernie" Fernandez put his head in his hands and groaned. They were massive hands and it was a mighty groan. Had he been Zeus, king of the gods, he would have launched every volcano, every ampere of lightning, every cataclysm at his disposal, if only it meant the inexorable Detective Lance Tetley would be vaporized, wiped off the map, annihilated into officious little Tetley molecules. Ernie Fernandez was less than two months from retirement, and more than anything that was the gift he wanted from the department: to see this young detective reduced to ash and fumes.

Holding the Olympian pose did little to relieve the situation. The second he opened his eyes, Ernie knew, Tetley would still be standing there. The old sergeant's heartburn roiled like wind-whipped flames up the pharynx, a regular October firestorm. Swear to Christ, there were days it seemed like Satan himself was down there, camping out in the lower esophageal sphincter, pouring lighter fluid on the blaze and stoking the inferno with a fiery pitchfork.

The drawers of Ernie's metal desk in the detective bureau—like his medicine cabinet at the ranch house north of town—were filled with drugs and tonics the quacks at the HMO thought might bring relief: Tums, Bromo-Seltzer, Zantac, Prilosec, Pepcid AC. Ernie ate the stuff like candy all day long, the same way he chewed spearmint gum. He drank water, too, and milk by the buckets, to stimulate saliva production. But ask a six-one, 245-pound cop, the son of a Mexican immigrant, to give up the alcohol, the cherry-flavored cigars, the greasy food he loved—beef enchiladas, chiles rellenos, cheese-stuffed jalapeños, carne asada chimichangas, barbecued baked beans—and you might as well be asking him to take out his Glock and shoot himself in the head.

Which, at that very moment, was what he felt like doing with Detective Tetley.

"You just ... " Even with his eyes closed, Ernie couldn't bring himself to say it, couldn't get the words out. "Tetley, what in God's name ... " A blowtorch flared suddenly—a blast strong enough to hoist a hot air balloon. It was that morning's chorizo breakfast burrito and four cups of coffee serving a no-knock warrant on the digestive tract of Ernie Fernandez. He gave up trying to speak, trying to make sense of the world. He reached for the Zantac, top right drawer, next to the crushed pack of cigarillos and the 1997 California paperback edition of the *Penal Code*, unabridged.

"He clearly copped to motive," Tetley pointed out.

"He's the victim, for chrissake!" Another pill in the mouth—that incorrigible food, vodka, and tequila intake hole below the walrus mustache that flopped like a dry, white mop—and again the outraged brown eyes fell closed, the big head dropped into the strapping hands. The younger cops called him *abuelo*—grandfather. The contrast of his white hair to his dark, leathery skin was so pronounced they referred to him as the human negative; on fishing trips to Cabo he was *The Old Man and the Sea*. The strained pose was reminiscent of Auguste Rodin's *The Thinker*. His white Western shirt made his broad back look like a drive-in movie screen.

"I'm telling you, Ernie, it's a good case," Tetley said. "The guy dimed to the whole thing—"

"Shut up. Let me think about this." Ernie rubbed his eyes and took a deep breath. "Who's the victim here?"

"The people of the state of California."

"Aw, bullshit."

"He willfully led witnesses to believe he was a cop. It went out as an officer down. Listen to the tape. We took a lot of men off the street to cover that call. So therefore the victims are the people of the state of California."

"That's crap."

"He kicked the tar out of that kid. That's assault under color of authority."

Ernie stared back with revulsion. "Tetley, the guy ain't even a cop."

"Which leads to false imprisonment—"

Ernie's telephone rang.

"Fernandez."

The report from the field was not good. Ernie's new quarter horse, a three-year-old show cutter prospect, was still missing. A few hours earlier it had bucked off Ernie's third wife, Colleen. The horse broke through a fence and legged it. Colleen was at home nursing a broken rib, a sprained wrist, and a sore foot. Ernie was called away as soon as it happened—that's why he wasn't at his desk earlier that morning to put the kibosh on Tetley when he went out the door to arrest Wallace Noe. It was shaping up to be that kind of a day.

The phone call was from a patrol sergeant, who, along with the sheriff's department and animal control, was searching for the runaway filly. A FedEx driver sighted the horse hoofing it westbound on Deer Springs Road, in the general direction of the Golden Door Spa.

"My god," Ernie said, hanging up the phone. For once the pained expression on his face was unrelated to a nasty burning sensation in his gullet. This torment was purely forward-looking and financial. He had allowed his umbrella liability insurance policy to lapse—Colleen's idea, to save a few extra bucks for retirement—and now Ernie's ticket to easy street, his service pension, was at risk. He formed a mask with his meaty hands and let his face sink into the dark abyss.

"Trouble?" Tetley asked.

"Do you have any idea the damage a runaway horse can do to a spa for the rich and famous?"

"Want me to go look for it?" Tetley asked.

Ernie peered out from behind the mask. He already had one unbridled rogue on the loose. He didn't need another.

"No, Tetley, you've done enough damage for one day," Ernie said. "Let's pay your prisoner a visit. Before I eat a bullet."

CHAPTER SEVEN

For nearly an hour Wallace sat in the Escondido police station, locked in a tiny holding room. The heavy wooden table was hacked with graffiti, its surface tacky with goo. The mismatched chairs were strewn about, as if whipped by a windstorm.

For Wallace, sitting alone in the windowless room magnified a jarring reality. Overnight he had gone from hero to prisoner, vanquisher to victim. From all four walls the questions kept flying at him like crows: How would Julie explain his sudden absence at the office? How would he get word to Hannah? What would happen to Addison and Tiffany if he had to spend the night in jail? He was loath to ask his mother-in-law to take the girls—he'd never hear the end of it.

And what about an attorney? Merksamer Digital worked with a slew of lawyers, but this was no matter for an army of pondering, pompous document jockeys. This was criminal. There was always his college roommate, Morty Schlegg, who was perhaps still licensed. Like most married men with children, Wallace rarely communicated with his single friends. Moreover, Morty dwelled in the depths of the underworld. His clients were prostitutes, drug dealers, murderers, and drunks. He got most of his business by way of a back-alley deal with a bail bondsman named One-Eyed Jack. Wallace imagined having to ask his mother-in-law to call One-Eyed Jack. She'd probably faint before she could finish writing down the name.

It was so dizzying, so depressing, that Wallace became determined not to think about anything at all. It was easier to presume it was a giant mistake. There was always the chance that one of the officers from last night would recognize him and set this hotshot detective straight. Wallace and those swing-shift cops had gotten along well; it wasn't often a citizen took down an armed robber with a cell phone. With luck he'd run into the patrol sergeant, that ex-marine who got the girls their hamburger meals.

Wallace slammed on the brakes. That kind of thinking was wrong-headed. It was relying on chance, like catching a flu bug. Wallace wasn't one to wait for something to happen. A man lays his own groundwork, he takes the bull by the horns.

Wallace took stock of his situation.

What was this tiny interrogation room but just another conference room?

Who was Detective Tetley but just another skeptical, low-level technician?

And what was a criminal charge but just another conceptual brick wall, a barrier ripe for a breakthrough?

Feeling a swell of confidence, Wallace vowed to turn the tables on the police, just as he had with the robber. *Psychological jujitsu.* He would handle the next encounter like it was just another business transaction—an initial consultation, a fact-finding mission for a new sale. Only his objective this time would be talk his way *out* of an organization rather than *in*.

So, when Ernie Fernandez stepped into the room, followed by Detective Tetley, Wallace took the initiative. He pushed back his chair and stood tall, extending a hand to the much older plainclothes investigator.

"Hi. Wallace Noe. Pleased to meet you."

"Sit down and shut up," Tetley said.

"Why don't we all sit down and shut up," Ernie said.

Tetley stationed himself at an angle blocking the door. He sat forward in his chair, poised on the balls of his feet, prepared to pounce.

"Mr. Noe, my name is Ernie Fernandez. I am a sergeant with the Escondido Police Department." Ernie champed an unlit cigarillo. He took a chair, spun it around, and sat backwards, cowboy-style, his arms draped over the back. "I am Detective Tetley's supervisor—"

"Look, Sergeant, I'm glad you're here," Wallace said. "There's been a terrible mistake—"

Ernie held a finger in the air, stopping Wallace short. "Before you say anything, the law necessitates that I ask a few questions."

"That means shut up and listen." Tetley's jackal eyes were boring into Wallace.

Wallace glanced at the young detective. He was by nature a peace-maker, and he couldn't comprehend this jerk, this sociopath with a badge, wanting to make trouble.

"Mr. Noe, do you understand your rights as Detective Tetley has read them to you?" Ernie asked.

"I'll just call my secretary," Wallace said. "She can pick me up."

"Hey," Tetley said, standing. "You a vigilante? A Bircher, maybe?"

Ernie warned, "Tetley—"

"Think your money puts you above the law?" Tetley asked. "Nice corner office—"

"Tetley, put a sock in it—"

"You crossed the line, mister!" Tetley said. "How big is your network?"

"Tetley, take a walk," Ernie said. "Now!"

Tetley was seeing red. He gave Wallace the stink-eye.

"And give me that report," Ernie said.

Tetley reluctantly handed his copy of the police report to Ernie. He left the room, slamming the door behind him.

"That kid goes after people like a wild dog," Ernie said. "Thank God for retirement and horse farms."

"If you can show me to a phone," Wallace said, "I really should check in with my office."

Ernie was flipping through the report. "We were talking about your rights. You understand you have the right to an attorney—"

"We're all reasonable people here."

"You being a businessman, Mr. Noe, I should think you could find a more lucrative occupation to impersonate."

"How is it against the law to protect myself?"

Ernie looked up. "You want to talk about what happened?"

"I don't even know what I did."

"You played cop. That's a deal we take pretty seriously around here. More often than not it's a precursor to bad stuff going down, like kidnapping and murder."

"Murder? I was taking my kids to Burger King."

Ernie turned back to the report. He spoke without looking at Wallace. "These rug rats—they in school? You a local in this outfit?"

"Edelweiss Christian. And I pay my taxes, if that's what you're asking."

"Says here you drive a late-model Cadillac. If I were to take a look at this car, would I see anything unusual? Spotlight on the door? Any red lights or sirens?"

"I use that car for business."

"Ever work as a security guard? Dress up like one for Halloween?"

"Are you serious?"

"Own a scanner, Mr. Noe? You familiar with the ten code?"

"Sorry. Jargon to me."

Ernie frowned. He took a short breath and swallowed hard, as if suppressing a scorching belch. "Lordy," he managed to say.

"If you don't mind, Sergeant, I've got a full calendar and a lot of people waiting—"

"You're under arrest, Mr. Noe. It's out of my hands. In a minute another supervisor is going to be taking over for me. I got some personal business on the north end of town—Man v. Horse. It's turning into quite a circus. But that's the way it is in this town, more and more."

Wallace thought back to his girls in the car that night. He was holding the robber on the ground when he became aware of a clownish ruckus coming from inside the Cadillac. Addison and Tiffany were mimicking their father, marching across the seats, laughing, shouting boisterous commands: "Police officer!" "Get on the ground!" "Hands where I can see 'em!" They led sheltered lives. They failed to recognize the face of evil, even when the spitting hydra was at their door.

Wallace said, "I did it for them you know."

Surprised, Ernie raised an eyebrow. "Did what for who?"

"That car door—it was like a shield. I could have driven off. But I had to finish the job."

"Sometimes it's better to go with the flow."

"Do you have children, Sergeant?"

Ernie studied Wallace's face for a long moment, then stood up to leave.

"Mr. Noe, I should warn you. There's a good chance Detective Tetley will be booking you into county jail today. How long you'll be there I cannot say. But however long it is, you're not going to like it much. Do as you're told and say as little as possible to the other inmates, and you should get through it okay. Police business aside, some of us appreciate what you did last night, settin' on that robber like that."

At the door he stopped and turned.

"We'll get you squared away with a telephone so you can call your attorney. Meanwhile, I'm going to recommend we buck this up to the captain. Maybe he'll have an answer to this goat rope we've caused you."

CHAPTER EIGHT

"My grievance with you people is the magnitude of your stupidity," Morty Schlegg fumed into the phone. He was trying simultaneously to monitor the results of a satellite horse race and retrieve his repossessed office furniture. He was talking to the owner of the furniture store, who was resistant.

"You're all a bunch of schmucks," Morty added. "If I had money to bring my account current I'd be in Vegas, making book on harness races."

He was in his usual negotiating position—leaning back in a Naugahyde imitation leather chair, stocking feet on the desk, chewing Demerol, or what he hoped was Demerol. They were pills his private investigator picked up in Tijuana while placing Morty's wagers at the offtrack betting parlor.

Morty wasn't one to keep his ear glued to the telephone, especially with a creditor on the other end of the line. At the first indication the other party was trying to speak, he held the receiver at arm's length and turned his attention to the four-legged competitors on the TV screen until the jabber stopped.

Why dignify their feeble posturing with a response? Looking back on thirteen years of solo practice, Morty was already the recipient of every threat known to man, pecuniary and corporal.

Receiving a multitude of visitors, on the other hand, was not a hallmark of the Law Offices of Mortimer Schlegg, LLC, since the larger part of its clientele was locked up in county jail or state prison, or dispensed to various mental institutions. This afforded Morty a certain latitude when it came to locating his place of business. The two-room building was a leaky stucco box, situated under a freeway on-ramp next to the railroad tracks. He didn't mind that it was located in a squalid part of San Diego known as Middletown, distinguished for its junkyards, adult bookstores, Port Authority infrastructure staging areas, and, on one corner near Pacific Highway, an enterprise that allowed you to take pictures of a completely naked woman. The rent was competitive.

Morty's windowless office was paneled with a timeworn walnut veneer that cast a pall over his days—an enduring melancholy that prescription painkillers were less and less able to quash. The walls were bare but for two framed Western prints, both by Frederic Remington and hung a little too high. The first was called *Dash for Timber*. It pictured eight horsemen at full gallop on the range, firing their rifles, trying to outrun a platoon of pursuing Indians. The second, titled *Scout: Friend or Foe*, depicted a lone rider on high ground, peering intently at a column advancing in the distance. In his early days as a lawyer, Morty identified with the galloping, gun-wielding cowboys. Lately, though, he empathized with the scout. He was a loner who strived to live life above the fray, a renaissance man who preferred the wind-swept meadows of independence to the regimented tree line of marriage. Being a criminal defense attorney afforded a stark view of the human condition. His was a profession of vigilance. Morty considered himself the protector of innocents, the champion of the downtrodden, the last line of defense for murderers and thieves. He was passionate about his cases, particularly when long prison sentences came into play. The unfavorable outcome of a single trial could stir torrents of angst, leading to an avalanche of depression. It made him consider, on an almost daily basis, getting out of the business and going into something easy—like restaurants or yoga.

Morty's paralegal stood in the doorway, motioning for his attention. She was slight in stature with raven-black hair, the Americanized progeny of a Vietnamese mother and a U.S.-infantry-soldier father. She was a determined twenty-seven-year-old, a third-year law student. Her name was Patience.

Morty covered the phone. "What?"

"You have a call. Line two."

"Who is it?"

"Some guy named Wallace Noe."

Morty returned to his phone conversation with the furniture dealer. "Listen to me. I'll say this once. My revenge is swift and final. You have one day." He slammed down the receiver.

The hold button blinked urgently.

Morty's eyes darted to the TV. The pack was headed down the backstretch. He watched his horse lose by a length.

"Crap," he said. "There's goes my perfecta."

"You're probably the worst gambler ever," Patience said.

The furniture crisis—the latest in a long string of financial setbacks to befall the Schlegg firm—was having the greatest impact on her, forcing her to type Morty's briefs perched on a milk crate. As a result, she was battling a ferocious neck ache. Sitting through evening classes at the Robert Morris School of Law, across the freeway in City Heights, was proving to be a challenge—but nothing compared to her ordeal as a child, locked for hours in the baggage compartment of a tiny, Cessna 0-1 *Bird Dog* during the fall of Saigon, circling over open ocean while the crewmen of the USS *Midway*, a 70,000-ton aircraft carrier, pushed Hueys over the side to make room for the single-engine plane to land. Refugees were, above all, survivors. Patience had sailed easily through Civil Procedure and Constitutional Law.

"I told you to bet the quinella," she said, sitting on the edge of Morty's desk. She had a penchant for tightly tailored suits and six-inch heels. Around the narrow-minded bigots of the San Diego legal community, it took a costly wardrobe to short-circuit the mistaken impression that she was eighteen and easy. "Can I have a Demerol?"

"One," Morty said.

"Three. Because it's your fault."

Morty watched her shake a handful of pills from the yellow vial. It was like being in the shadow of an exotic, deadly snake—the Malayan pit viper came to mind. They struck suddenly and without warning.

"Who's Wallace Noe?" Patience asked. "Is he rich?"

"He'd like to be," Morty said, tallying his losses. He rocked back in his chair, pushing it as far as it would go, until he was looking almost straight up at the ceiling tiles. They were gray with age and impaled with a decade's worth of Dixon Ticonderoga #2 soft pencils, launched by Morty tip-first in alternating fits of frustration and rage. "It's a sad story. He's trying to please his father's ghost."

"What are you, his psychiatrist?"

"I don't know why he's calling. I don't give money to the alumni association."

"You don't *have* money."

"I don't go to reunions, either."

"I think you'd better take this one. It sounds like he's in trouble."

CHAPTER NINE

Wallace sat immersed in the hot tub, knocking back tequila shooters, drinking scotch from a weighty tumbler, and puffing a cigar. He liked the look of his small, single-story tract house at night. The back yard was nothing but hard, flat loam. That was the beauty of the place after dark—you didn't see the dirt or notice the spartan rooms. All you saw were the lights ablaze in the evenly spaced windows, the clean line of the roof, the distant glow of town, and the stars overhead.

There was solace in the continuous thrum of the jets, serenity in the sight of ghostly steam rising against a cold night, comfort in the smell of cigar smoke fusing with chlorine. Two perfectly shaped volcanic islands thrust from a turbulent sea where Patience drifted on her back as effortlessly as a water strider. A few hours earlier, when she spied the hot tub, she asked Wallace to turn the temperature up as high as it would go. Then she stripped to her underwear and climbed in.

She slid in close to Wallace and presented her back.

"Check this out," she said, lifting her hair.

Wallace touched her neck. It felt like hard, hot rubber.

"Tight as a knot," Wallace said.

"Rub it."

Patience slowly rolled her head while Wallace massaged her neck. The black straps of her bra crossed over her back.

"Harder."

"Like this?"

"Mmm."

Their faces were emerald green, as if they were staring into a witch's cauldron.

From the vantage of the hot tub Wallace could see Morty in the kitchen, refilling his highball glass. He wore nothing but wet boxer shorts. He greedily topped his drink and took long sips, in alternating motions.

"Look at him," Wallace said. "He's found my best whiskey."

"Is that thing any good?" Patience reached for Wallace's cigar.

"Take it."

Patience smoked in silence, resting her head against Wallace's shoulder, contemplating Ursa Major.

Wallace turned his gaze to the heavens. Earth was an absurd place.

"Makes you feel small," he said.

"Not me," Patience said, exhaling cigar smoke. "Nothing makes me feel small."

"You're young and beautiful."

"Law's a joke. We can beat this thing." She offered Wallace a puff of his own cigar.

"Morty used to sound like that," Wallace said. "Why you? Why law?"

"Means to an end." Patience took the cigar back. "There's an orphanage in Ho Chi Minh City. I'm going to own a jet. Rescue kids."

Across the yard Wallace's dog, Scottie, had its nose planted firmly at a hole in the fence and was barking up a storm. Scottie was a small white dog with sharp ears and the narrow face of a fox—an American Eskimo, the runt of the litter. Wallace knew that bark. A car was in the driveway.

A moment later the doorbell rang. Morty ignored it.

The doorbell rang again.

Wallace looked at Patience. "What is he, deaf?"

"He's a liar. He promised me a BMW."

"Morty, would you get that!" Wallace called.

Morty grumbled about having to go to the door. He finally corked the Maker's Mark and padded in wet feet to the small foyer.

"Quite the guard dog you've got." The old man at the door was tall and silver-haired. He clutched a fedora that, in the shadows of the porch, could easily have been a Bible. The woman with him was clearly the instigator of this late-night intrusion. She was as old as, if not older than, her companion. She was stationed near the doorbell, and she had the pointed toes of her Gucci shoes planted firmly on the threshold.

Morty eyed the couple poisonously. "Go away. I don't talk to Jehovah's Witnesses."

"Where's the man of the house?" the old woman asked. She wore a silver brooch.

"Here but indisposed," Morty said. When he went to swing the door shut she blocked it with a quick foot.

"Indisposed how?" she demanded. "A sudden case of conscience?"

"He's in the hot tub with my Asian secretary and a fifth of scotch."

"Tell him his mother-in-law is at the door. And this is Pastor Maltby of the Hidden Valley Presbyterian Church. We've got his children in the car."

"Let me amend that," Morty said. "I don't know where he is."

"And I say you're a bold-faced liar!" Audrey Taylor forced her way inside. She knew the floor plan well. She headed straight for the sliding door to the yard.

Pastor Maltby dropped his amiable countenance. He glowered at Morty. "Good God, man, where's your sense of decency? Put some clothes on!"

He went in hot pursuit of the old woman.

"I wouldn't jump to conclusions," Morty called after him. "My client is despondent, and the girl's on the clock."

Patience was curled in Wallace's lap, and with interlocked arms they were tossing back shots of tequila.

Wallace blinked up at the matronly apparition that appeared over the spa. Audrey was bouncing around like a roulette ball, scooping up discarded clothing. She strained to make out Patience's features against the flashing pool light.

"I see that little fortune cookie, Wallace. Don't tell me she's nude!"

Wallace pointed to one ear. "Sorry, Audrey. The jets."

"No wonder the state's being overrun by hordes," Audrey said. "You stupid men keep breeding with mongrels. He's a married man, sister. I doubt you can show him anything he hasn't seen before."

"Is she for real?" Patience asked.

Pastor Maltby came to the edge of the hot tub and peered in.

"Congratulations, you horse's rear end," Audrey said to Wallace. "You just sinned in front of a man of God."

"Nobody sinned here," Wallace said.

Pastor Maltby followed Audrey around the hot tub. "Please don't torture yourself this way, Audrey. There's nothing for you here."

Audrey wasn't budging. She held open a beach towel for Patience. "Let's go, babycakes. His kids are home. And you, Romeo, I didn't bail you out of jail just so you could come here and—"

Wallace slid off the narrow ledge of the spa and sank to the bottom. As the water passed over his ears all he could hear were the thundering jets. He held his breath until he felt lightheaded and saw stars.

When he came up, Patience was standing outside the hot tub. She was backlit by the porch light. Steam rose from her silhouette. She was defiantly slow closing her towel.

"Take a picture, Ralph," she said to Pastor Maltby, flicking the cigar butt in the dirt. "It'll last longer."

Pastor Maltby steered Audrey toward the house. "Enough said. Let's give these people a chance to get decent."

"That's a tall order in this Sodom and Gomorrah," Audrey said.

CHAPTER TEN

"**A**re you listening to me?" Audrey was banging on the bedroom door. "Wallace, what are you doing in there?"

Wallace resisted the urge to climb into the disheveled bed, to burrow under the covers and pull the sheet over his head. He was buttoning an old Hawaiian shirt he picked up off the bathroom floor.

"Hannah's on the line," Audrey called. "Long distance from Kansas City."

"Okay, Audrey. I said I've got it." Wallace took the call at the nightstand. "Hannah—"

The door opened and Audrey barged in. Wallace glared at her. She gave the bed a once-over and backed out of the room, closing the door behind her.

"Mother left me this crazy voice mail message," Hannah was saying. "Wallace, what on earth's going on?"

What on earth's going on? When Hannah got worked up she sounded neurotic, just like her mother.

"Nothing on earth's going on," Wallace said. "Everything's fine."

"Mother had to bail you out of jail?"

"Don't worry. Morty thinks we can beat it."

"Not Morty Schlegg?"

"I needed a lawyer, Hannah, so I called Morty—"

"But I thought you said all his clients were wife beaters and drunks."

"Come on, Hannah. That's a gross exaggeration. You think Morty could make a living off nothing but wife beaters and drunks?"

"You sound like you've been drinking."

"I'm just not in the mood for your negativity."

The bedroom door opened an inch. Wallace could sense Audrey standing in the hallway, listening.

"Why were you arrested?" Hannah asked.

Wallace turned his back and lowered his voice. "We're having software issues."

"What does that have to do with—"

"The point is, Hannah, none of this would've happened if you were home."

Hannah went silent. "That's plain stupid. Don't make this a referendum on my career. And why weren't the girls in school?"

"Who told you that?"

"Mother."

"Don't believe everything you hear."

"I don't understand what's happening. Something seems very off, here."

"You need to get rid of that voice mail thing," Wallace said. "Your mother uses it as a wedge and it causes immense problems in our marriage—"

"I can't believe this. The police take you to jail and you accuse my mother of causing problems in our marriage—"

"I'm not accusing anybody of anything."

"Maybe you should see a doctor."

"It's a freak aberration."

"Did you have to call Mother? Wasn't there someone else?"

"Believe me, Hannah. I had no choice."

By all accounts the office was in a panic. At first there was shock, then a flurry of activity to find out where Wallace was, then pandemonium when it was learned he had been booked into county jail. Michael and Otto were meeting behind closed doors when the call came in. Would the company post bond? No. Michael wouldn't take the call. Julie was in tears. Wallace tried calling a second time. Again Michael refused. Julie was beside herself. Finally Michael asked Julie into his office. He and Otto explained that a corporation couldn't lend money to an officer without a formal board resolution. The problem was, Jeter at Jacaranda was asking for copies of the board minutes, and Michael didn't want to have to disclose, at the eleventh hour, that the company's founder and senior marketing executive had just been arrested for impersonating a police officer. "It would surely queer the deal," Michael said. Otto added, "Believe me, Julie, we're painted into a corner here." Both men wished she'd stop crying. "It's not the end of the world," Michael said. "Hannah's family has lots of money. They can post his bail. Worst case it'll cost him a couple extra hours in the slammer." As if Wallace couldn't wait to involve Hannah's side of the family in the matter; as if county jail were one of those goofy plastic alcoves in Mickey's Toontown.

"There's Newark," Hannah said. "They're calling my flight."

"Jesus, Hannah. Listen to yourself."

"What's that supposed to mean?"

"Figure it out."

"Don't talk to me like that. I'm not your secretary."

"The girls need a mother."

"That's a reprehensible thing to say. I have to go."

"Hannah, wait—"

The phone went dead.

Wallace caught his image in the mirror. His shorts were stained with red wine. He was as rumpled as the bed. He walked barefoot down the hallway to see his girls.

He found Addison and Tiffany sitting cross-legged on the family room floor, eating cereal and watching *Flipper* reruns on the VCR. Patience was passed out on the sofa, a beach towel wrapped around her like a sarong, her wet hair covering her face. She looked like a marooned refugee.

Wallace went to the kitchen and poured himself a scotch. He had an audience—Morty, Audrey, and Pastor Maltby sat at the table drinking wine.

Wallace glanced at his mother-in-law. "Has she calmed down any?"

"I think we've all calmed down," Pastor Maltby said.

Audrey turned to Pastor Maltby. "See now with your own eyes. That's more whisky than a man should drink."

"Don't start," Wallace said.

"Put down the alcohol, Wallace, and give Pastor Maltby a tour of the house," Audrey said. "I'm sure he'd like to see how you're raising your family."

Wallace stared menacingly at Audrey and brought the scotch to his lips. "The park's closed. The bears need sleep."

"My client has been traumatized by his day in jail," Morty said. "That's why I think we need to keep a suicide watch."

"I told you, I'm not suicidal," Wallace said. "I just want to have a drink and go to bed."

"Tell me, Mrs. Taylor, does he keep any guns in the house?" Morty asked. "Or neckties? I imagine a man in his position would have a substantial collection of neckties, any one of which he could use to hang himself."

"The only thing that would make me want to hang myself is having *you* for an attorney," Wallace said. "Bring me a gun with two bullets and I'll take you with me."

Morty looked at the others. "I don't know why I'd expect to have a rational conversation with a man who just got arrested for impersonating a police officer. That's a crazy person's crime."

"I've certainly learned my lesson," Audrey said. "I won't soon again bail him out of jail just so he can sneak home and drink like a fish and fool around with that tart on the sofa. He can break rocks, for all I care." She turned to Wallace. "What's Hannah ever done to you? She's been a good wife. You can't say she hasn't."

"That tart on the sofa bills about a hundred dollars an hour," Morty said.

"Hannah was certainly the apple of her father's eye," Pastor Maltby said. "I'll never forget the day Ed walked her down the aisle. You remember that, Audrey? He was bawling like a baby."

"Thank goodness he's not alive to see this day," Audrey said. "He never would have lived through it in his weakened condition."

"What did your husband die from, Mrs. Taylor?" Morty asked.

"Nobody knows," Audrey said. "It's a mystery."

Wallace said, "Oh, Audrey, he was mowing the lawn and had a heart attack—"

"Could've been rapture," Audrey said. "The lawn mower was still running. He was a good Christian, you know."

"It was an electric motor without a kill switch," Wallace said. "It ran to the end of its cord and did a helicopter job on the rhododendrons."

"Audrey, have you ever had a criminal in your family before?" Pastor Maltby asked. "Or is this your first time?"

"First time."

Morty poured more wine. "I will remind you that my client hasn't been convicted of anything yet. Merely charged."

Audrey couldn't take her eyes off Morty. "Jewish, right? I suppose he's lucky to have you for an attorney. You'll get him off on a technicality."

"What makes you so sure?"

"Your tribe's a clever lot. You always do."

"I'm starting to think our best defense might be a good offense."

Audrey narrowed her eyes at Morty. "Meaning what?"

"Meaning we sue the living shit out of the police department and the city," Morty said. "Right down to their bras and panties." He turned to Pastor Maltby. "Pardon my French, Monsignor."

"I suppose it would never occur to you to do the right thing," Audrey said. "I suppose you couldn't just forgive them."

Morty stared at her with disbelief.

"Good night," Wallace said. "Everybody out."

Pastor Maltby, gazing off in the distance and savoring his wine, jumped suddenly as if kicked under the table. He knit his eyebrows at Audrey, and then brightened.

"Say, I understand we have a model railroader in our midst," he said.

Audrey said, "My daughter has to pinch pennies, yet he'll waste hundreds of dollars on a thing that would fit in the palm of your hand. Be a good host, Wallace, and show Pastor your train."

"No, Audrey, I'm sure he doesn't—"

"On the contrary," Pastor Maltby said. "This old chap never met a model railroad he didn't like."

"Don't be a donkey, Wallace," Audrey said. "Your friend and I will watch after your wine." She turned to Morty. "Tell me, counselor, what's *your* billing rate?"

Morty reached for the bottle and poured more wine. "You can't put a price on freedom, Mrs. Taylor."

"Great," Wallace said. "I need a lawyer and I get Socrates."

"The garage is that way," Audrey said, pointing. "Go with Pastor, Wallace. At least show him where to turn on the light."

"Then promise me you'll leave," Wallace said.

"We promise," Audrey said.

Reluctantly Wallace led Pastor Maltby to the garage and flipped on the light switch.

"Oh, this is marvelous," Pastor Maltby said, going in for a closer look.

Wallace's model railroad was situated along one wall. The bench-work sat chest high; Wallace had once read that tall benches made the trains look more realistic. The track itself had the unmistakable appearance of a work in progress. Large sections of roadbed were shimmed with construction paper and masking tape—Wallace's effort to stem the ever-increasing tide of derailments. The backdrop was a single piece of half-inch Styrofoam cut in the shape of a mountain. It looked more like a volcano. Locomotives and railroad cars were strewn about the layout in what appeared to be a massive train wreck.

Pastor Maltby walked slowly down the length of the bench. He bent over and peered through a wooden truss bridge, squinting with one eye. "I like what you've done here—HO scale in the diesel era. I see by these orange and silver F3s you must be modeling the Western Pacific."

"Sounds like you know something about it."

"I grew up in Minnesota. We had a basement. The winters were long." He turned to Wallace. "Why the Western Pacific, might I ask?"

"My father took me once on the Zephyr," Wallace said. "When I was a kid."

"Ah, yes," Pastor Maltby said. "The train through the Feather River Canyon—Arthur Keddie's dream. Old C.P. Huntington told him no one would ever build a railroad through the Feather River Canyon. Can you imagine anyone being that capricious?"

Wallace didn't answer. He felt a moral lecture coming on.

Pastor Maltby stopped to finger the wheel of an Atlas turntable. "You know, Wallace, your mother-in-law was devastated today when she got your call. She worries about her daughter, about your marriage, about the finances. She hardly recognizes you anymore. She's troubled about her granddaughters, too—about the environment in which they're being brought up. From what I've seen I can hardly blame her. First, you spew a lot of agnostic nonsense and pull them out of school. Then the police cart you off to jail. Now we find you in a hot tub, playing footsie with another woman. There's no reference in your home to God, no overriding sense of moral decency. It's funny. You can tell a lot about a place just by looking around. In most homes I see smatterings of religious knickknacks and Scriptural framework. In yours I see a lot of empty booze bottles and Jewish attorneys with gutter mouths. What's the deal with you and the Asian girl, anyway?"

"She's working on my case. That's all."

"Still, it's cause for concern. Propinquity between a man and a woman can lead to a number of things: alienation of affection, illegitimate births. You wouldn't believe the problems adultery has caused in my congregations—"

"Forgive me, Reverend, but I don't recall inviting anyone here to discuss my personal life—"

"Listen, son," Pastor Maltby said. "Accusations of criminal wrongdoing can bring out deep feelings of humiliation and shame. Your mother-in-law asked me to come along tonight in case you felt the need for some Christian counseling."

"I've got legal counsel," Wallace said. "That should do me for now."

"Hannah can't possibly support your taking the girls out of school."

"That's not your business."

"My business is running a church. You should come sometime."

Wallace stared back coldly.

"Very well," Pastor Maltby said, forcing a smile. "This old preacher knows when to take no for an answer." He turned his gaze to the train wreck in front of him. "About this school thing. One thought. We go back to the old system. Just this one time. We'll grandfather you in—"

"Saying write a check?"

Pastor Maltby looked at Wallace. "Turns out the seminary could use a new copier."

"And the girls?"

"Back in school. First bell tomorrow morning.

"Not just any copier, mind you," Pastor Maltby added. "Sorting, stapling, color—the whole shooting match, as they say."

"I'll courier a check tomorrow."

"Maybe you could bring it by in person. Come to the church office—"

"Sorry," Wallace said. "Tell Audrey my calendar's full."

Pastor Maltby smiled ruefully. "Yes, I suppose these are busy times for a man in your position. About this thing tonight—no hard feelings, I hope."

"I'm just sorry you got dragged into it."

"Don't worry about me," Pastor Maltby said. "I liken my job to running a railroad. From time to time people lose their way. I do what I can to get them back on track. It's probably why you and I like these little toy trains so much. A car derails and we can just reach down and set things right. It gives us a world we can manage, the illusion we can play God." He put a friendly hand on Wallace's shoulder. "Now, what say we rejoin the others before they drink all the good wine?"

CHAPTER ELEVEN

It was just after seven o'clock on a Monday morning. Rain was in the forecast. Above the Park 'n Ride lot, black clouds were gathering. Wallace and Lenore sat in the car, watching papers blow across the parking lot. Lenore held a tall cup of coffee, a trace of lipstick gracing the lid.

"So tell me the truth," she said, shifting in her seat and leaning across the center console. "Why is Sanjay really coming along?"

Their elbows shared the armrest.

"You keep asking me that," Wallace said. "What's your problem with Sanjay?"

"I don't think he's as good as everyone says."

"I want him in the dialogue."

"They'll eat him alive."

"How's that coffee?"

"Don't change the subject." Lenore looked at Wallace. Her blue eyes flashed. "Want a sip?"

"Why not." Wallace tasted the coffee. Café au lait with a hint of *Chilly Berry,* by Estée Lauder.

He handed the cup back to Lenore. Her French manicure was pristine.

Lenore said, "I'm telling you, he's holding something back."

"You're paranoid. You've learned not to trust men."

"No, there's a reason the software isn't working." Lenore gazed off into the distance. "I just haven't figured out what it is, yet."

"There he is now," Wallace said.

Sanjay's green Honda picked its way tentatively up the first row of cars.

Just as Wallace was about to step on the brake and put the Cadillac in gear, a pickup came roaring into the lot. The truck had off-road tires and a load of lumber over its bed. It quickly overtook the Honda and veered sharply, cutting Sanjay off. The driver's window came down and a paper cup flew out, hitting Sanjay's windshield and leaving a big splash of mud-colored coffee. Two men yelled obscenities out the window of the truck. They raged and shouted taunts, calling Sanjay a *diaperhead*.

"My gosh," Lenore said. "Should we do something?"

"Not as long as they stay in the truck." Wallace watched from inside the car. Morty Schlegg had warned him to keep his nose clean, particularly in the city of Escondido. "Sometimes it's better just to let the cowboys shoot up the saloon."

Finally, thankfully, the truck sped off. The driver leaned on the horn while the passenger, a big-shouldered man with a Fu Manchu mustache, gave Sanjay the finger.

Sanjay calmly gathered his things and walked over to the Cadillac. He opened the rear passenger door.

"Hello, Lenore," he said. "You sure look beautiful for this early in the morning."

"Hardly."

Wallace was relieved to see that Sanjay would at least make a good first impression on the people at Cal Max. His wool suit was appropriately dark, and his white cotton shirt was starched and neatly pressed. His colorful tie projected confidence. He could have passed for a successful Calcutta banker.

"What happened back there, Sanjay?" Wallace asked.

"Rogues," Sanjay said. "They've been honking ever since I got on the freeway. I thought maybe their horn was stuck."

"Might be it," Wallace said, making dubious eyes at Lenore.

Once on the road, Lenore and Sanjay got down to business. Out came the file folders, legal pads, cell phones, and laptop computers, and Lenore began working her way down the log of software issues.

"Sanjay, what can we do about some of this stuff?" she asked.

"Good question. And on most of these things I have no idea."

Wallace always enjoyed the ride north to Cal Max. First there were the rolling fields of Camp Pendleton, where the views of the ocean were good. Then came the border checkpoint at San Onofre, where the line of trucks waiting to pass through the scales could sometimes back up for miles. Wallace always slowed for the speed traps in San Juan Capistrano—the highway patrolmen worked the stretch with fervor, as if locked in a tight sales contest or out to curry favor with a demanding boss. The toll road came next. Here Wallace could look down on all the finish-graded pads that were the future tract homes and superstore centers of Laguna Niguel. On the 405 freeway it was a dull ride all the way up to Century Boulevard and LAX, but Wallace used the carpool lane and the time passed quickly. At the Santa Monica Freeway, traffic slowed to a crawl all the way through Westwood and over the hill to Sherman Oaks. Then, in the San Fernando Valley, they'd turn west on the 101 toward Woodland Hills, where Cal Max had its headquarters.

Wallace enjoyed traveling with Lenore. He liked the way she worked the issues, prioritizing and bringing perspective to difficult problems—she had strong opinions, and she always had good arguments to support her positions. She was confident, polished, and savvy about business in a practical sort of way.

Lenore wasn't the only one who made interesting conversation on the trip to Cal Max. Sanjay spoke of growing up and going to school in India. The students in Bombay had to pass a succession of exams in order to continue their education, and Sanjay was good at taking tests. After getting into one of the best universities in India, he then came to America and worked for two well-respected firms in Silicon Valley. Nothing had been given to him—he achieved success all on his own. He was young to be a chief technology officer at a company like Merksamer Digital, but during the recruiting process Michael had liked Sanjay more than the older, more seasoned job candidates. "Trainable," Michael often said, when talking about his decision to hire Sanjay.

"I certainly appreciate the opportunity to come along," Sanjay said, putting away his laptop computer as the Cal Max tower loomed in the distance. "I am looking forward to meeting our client."

"Brace yourself, Sanjay," Lenore said. "These ladies can be pretty tough."

"Mainframers," Sanjay said. "Counting the days to retirement, most of them."

"I wouldn't be so sure."

"Let me ask you both something," Sanjay said. "What kind of a guy is Michael, really?"

"Why, Sanjay?" Wallace asked. "Having problems?"

"One day he tells me to do something one way, the next day he tells me to do it another way. Then he blows his top because I didn't do it a third way. Shameful!"

"Sounds like Michael," Wallace said.

"I think you call it bipolar disorder," Lenore said.

"He's under a lot of pressure," Wallace said. "This funding thing's taking its toll."

Lenore turned around in her seat. "So, Sanjay, why do we have so many problems with our software?"

Sanjay leaned forward, resting his boyish arms against the back of Lenore's headrest. "The truth?"

"Tell us."

"All right, but you must never tell Michael I told you."

Wallace glanced at Lenore.

"We built it wrong from the start," Sanjay said.

"Wrong how?" Lenore asked.

"It's a bastardized system," Sanjay said. "Motel reservations. Did you know this? Michael is recycling an old project to save money."

Wallace nearly drove the car off the road.

"I will tell you why this will never work," Sanjay continued. "A simple analogy: a Coke machine. All cans the same shape and size. They load in one place, at the top, and come out the bottom. Maybe a hundred cans a day. That is our motel reservation system. Now we are using this same machine for enrollment records. Each one a different shape and size—and we are trying to cram hundreds of thousands of cans, maybe millions one day, into this single machine, all through the little slot in the bottom. You see? Upside down. Big problem."

"Can this be fixed?" Lenore asked.

"We can keep building patches and adding servers. But that's the problem with store-and-forward architecture. Things keep getting worse. The only solution is to start from scratch. Build it on the Internet."

Lenore said, "That's a long way off."

"One year at least," Sanjay said.

Lenore put a hand on her forehead and stared out the window.

It was the first time Wallace had heard of an underlying, systemic flaw in the software.

"Does the system work?" Sanjay asked rhetorically. "Yes—much of the time. But is it scalable? No. Millions of enrollment records hitting all at once. Our database cannot handle this. Too much stress on the system. That is why I'm saying it is a disaster waiting to happen."

CHAPTER TWELVE

"**G**et out."

"What?" Sanjay seemed taken by surprise.

"I said get out."

They were in the city of Woodland Hills, a few blocks off the free-way, stopped at a red light. The street was flanked by trees: acacias, sycamores, Monterey pines. The light turned green.

"Out of my car, Sanjay. Now!"

"But Wallace—"

"Out!"

Sanjay opened the door and stepped to the curb. Wallace hit the gas. The Cal Max tower receded in the distance.

The distress on Lenore's face was unmistakable.

"What?" Wallace said, glancing over.

"You can't just leave him there."

"If he can find his way to America, he can find his way back to San Diego."

Wallace was gunning the car up the broad boulevard, driving like a madman. The trees flashed by. Luckily, the morning traffic was light.

Wallace felt a sense of hopelessness and rage at the stupidity around him—he drove erratically, he was all over the road. He couldn't get Peg Brown out of his mind. The way she pulled back her straw-colored hair in a sort of mullet, the way her lower jaw thrust out like an ape's. Peg always wore a Cal Max pin on her hideous scarves. She had no sense of fashion—her career was everything. She trusted Wallace. The more Wallace thought about it the angrier he got.

"Damn these stupid people," Wallace said. "They botch everything."

"It isn't that bad," Lenore said.

"We can't do this to Peg."

"She doesn't have to know."

Wallace hit the brakes. "You wanna' get out, too?"

"Don't be a jerk. Now turn around—"

Wallace stomped on the gas again. "We're pulling the business."

"Don't be rash," Lenore said. "We can buy time with a patch. But we need Sanjay."

"Not if I have anything to say about it."

"At least pick him up. He doesn't have to talk."

"He better not," Wallace said. "Not a single goddamn word."

"There's a light," Lenore said, pointing. "We can turn around there."

Wallace grudgingly moved into the left lane and flipped a U-turn.

They found Sanjay a few miles back, standing in the shelter of a bus stop. He seemed shaken.

"A bus came by. I didn't know what to do."

"Get in," Wallace said.

Sanjay climbed into the back seat. "Wallace, I am so sorry—"

Wallace snapped his head around. "Not a goddamn word, Sanjay."

Turning left onto Oxnard Street, Wallace tallied the cost of pulling the business. The first thing that came to mind was Jacaranda and the funding. Trek Reese would walk away from any deal that didn't include Cal Max. Worse, Merksamer Digital's revenue would be in a free fall. A company that was already losing money would be pitched even further into the red. Shutting the doors and putting everyone out on the street would be their only option. It was like signing your own death warrant.

Am I jinxed in business, doomed to be dragged down by blunderers and crooks? Wallace wondered.

"I wanted to tell you sooner," Sanjay said. "But Michael made me swear on my mother's grave."

Wallace said, "That's a very interesting story."

"Level heads for the meeting," Sanjay said. "Anger doesn't solve anything."

Wallace glared at Sanjay in the rearview mirror. "One more word, Sanjay, and you're fired."

Sanjay folded his arms and looked out the window, appearing stung. "If you insist."

"I insist," Wallace said. "Shut it."

Arriving at Cal Max used to give Wallace a thrill. In his mind, signing the colossal insurance company was the watershed of his career. On a palpable level, it was like gaining entrance to an exclusive country club—the wrought iron fence, the meandering drive, the vibrant waterfalls, the brightly colored flower beds. Now the tower that rose from the canopy of eucalyptus trees gave Wallace a headache. The very sight of it depressed him. He knew the rolling lawns were filled with the graves of vendors who had tried to force their agendas on Peg Brown and her systems team.

When they came to a stop at the guard shack, an armed guard with white hair stepped out holding a clipboard. The tight security had an obvious subtext: this place was a target for any loony with a station wagon full of dynamite.

"Appointment?" the security guard asked.

"With the roof," Wallace said. "I'm going to jump."

Lenore leaned across the center console. "Peg Brown. In systems. We're from Merksamer Digital."

"If you're not using that gun," Wallace said, "there's someone I'd like to shoot back in San Diego."

The security guard located their company name on his clipboard and sent them ahead.

It was a short walk from the visitors' parking lot to the glass office tower.

Peg Brown's systems team occupied the entire sixth floor. It was an expansive room, a maze of eerily silent gray cubicles where pale employees hunched over keyboards and stared into computer screens while breathing filtered air. Some huddled in groups, studying reports printed on wide green-bar paper. They spoke in hushed tones.

"Mainframers," Sanjay said in a low voice to Wallace and Lenore. "Checking the balances on their pensions, probably."

Peg Brown's secretary said, "You can go right in."

Inside the Desert Tortoise Conference Room, the supportive atmosphere of the enrollment project's early days had vanished. The modular Lucite tables were pushed to the back of the room, and the lightweight chrome chairs were arranged in rows theater style—or, more accurately, courtroom style. The room was filled with Cal Max employees, backs stiff with indignation, laps laden with error reports documenting mayhem, necks craning to see blood spilled.

Wallace, Lenore, and Sanjay took seats in the front row.

"Looks like the storm clouds have formed," Wallace whispered to Lenore.

"Good time for sun and sand," Lenore whispered back. "Want to come with?"

Wallace looked at her.

"Didn't I tell you? I'm counting the days to Lahaina."

"Hawaii?"

"I'm delivering the boat money. One last shot. Ricky's agreed to counseling."

"Which one is Peg?" Sanjay asked.

Before Wallace could answer, Peg Brown strode in and took a position behind the podium.

"It pains me to have to call this meeting," she said. Her eyes were fiery and she gripped the podium with white fingers. "But I am convinced you people at Merksamer Digital are never going to get things right."

"Miss Peggy," Sanjay said, raising his hand. "May I please?"

Wallace couldn't believe his eyes. He looked past Lenore and glared at Sanjay.

"This is a freak show of ineptitude—how you hope to stay in business is beyond me," Peg continued. "I can't decide if it's deception or stonewalling—"

"Miss Peggy," Sanjay said again.

Peg stopped mid-sentence. "Young man, is there something you wish to say?"

Here we go, Wallace thought, burying his head in his hands.

"There is. Yes. Thank you." Sanjay stood and buttoned his jacket. "Miss Peggy, you are using this very raw, emotional language, saying things are bad—" As he spoke his pink tongue darted like a glassy eel.

Peg said, "Excuse me—"

"And I tell you, Peggy, we have come here in good faith to discuss the issues. Already you are depleting our emotional bank account. Your staff is aggrieved, yes, this I can see plainly. But this is lose-lose, and this is not what people want. Everyone wants win-win. So I ask you, Peggy, please. Let us speak with restraint and respect."

The room grew painfully quiet. All eyes turned to Peg, who looked as if she'd just been struck on the back of the head with a two-by-four.

Peg said to Wallace, "I'm sorry, who is this?"

"Our chief technical officer."

"Here to sharpen the saw," Sanjay said.

"The what?"

"There is one thing you should know about me," Sanjay said, surveying the room. "I come from Silicon Valley, where people are very intelligent, very hardworking. And one thing we have learned is never to call a meeting without first identifying an objective. So this is my first recommendation. Before we do anything today, let us engage in a dialogue to define our objective most clearly." He turned full circle. "Yes, Miss Peggy. Suggestion?"

"Here's a suggestion, you pompous worm," Peg said. "How about we clearly define why in hell these idiotic things keep happening! Why you keep passing us group numbers that don't exist! Why your underwriting questions come up Greek! Why some guy named King Bed keeps enrolling for MaxCare Plus! Why, *you little turd from a dog*, you don't have the standing to tell *me* how to run a meeting! I was running meetings when your daddy was pulling rickshaws in Chinatown!"

"I am from Bombay," Sanjay said in a measured voice. "Bombay is in India."

"Well, this is L.A. Ask anyone in this room. I don't give a damn who you are or where you come from as long as you do your job. And that's my beef with Merksamer Digital. You people don't do your job. I don't know any other way to say it except that I am incredibly frustrated right now. And quite frankly, as a systems professional, I am appalled by your company's consistent failure to respond. You're either a bunch of liars or a bunch of dunderheads, I'm still trying to figure out which." Peg took a deep breath, sighed, then left the podium and slumped in a chair. She put a hand on her chest and closed her eyes. "Look, people, we've got an issues log that's bigger than a Manhattan phonebook. What in heaven's name are we going to do about it?"

"Let me address that," Sanjay said. "Early in the first quarter we are moving to a program of scheduled releases—"

"Stop right there," Peg said, holding up a hand. "I've told Lenore a thousand times, we're not interested in taking a new release. My people are doing enough as it is, just working the errors. I want you to fix our software."

"We will simply move you forward on the product road map—"

"Not a chance," Peg said.

Sanjay looked puzzled. "I don't understand."

Lenore spoke up. "Because, Sanjay, a new release takes a lot of extra man-hours. They have to certify it before they can put it in production."

"They do?" Sanjay had a stunned look on his face.

"Look, kids, we're going to do it my way from now on," Peg said. "I'm shutting you down, effective immediately. I'll give you one last chance. Fix our software or I'm pulling the contract."

Sanjay looked crestfallen. "Then I guess we will fix your software."

"Yes, I guess you will," Peg said.

Lenore smiled and gave Wallace's arm a squeeze. They'd live to see another day.

"Good, then it's settled," Wallace said, standing quickly. He pulled his car keys from his coat pocket and jangled them in front of Sanjay's face. "Tell you what, Sanjay. Lenore and I can finish up here. Why don't you run down and pull around the rickshaw?"

CHAPTER THIRTEEN

"Stop fretting," Hannah said. "I want this to be a nice holiday."

"What makes you think I'm fretting?" Wallace asked. The yard work was done. The walks were swept. The turkey was in the oven. Wallace and Hannah were in the bedroom, trading turns in the shower.

"You're assaulting that stack of mail."

"I'm looking for the Cadillac registration. I think it needs a smog check."

Earlier that day Wallace was parked outside his mother-in-law's hilltop, hacienda-style home when he noticed the tag was about to expire. He was picking up Audrey so she could join them for Thanksgiving dinner.

For Wallace, the long holiday weekend couldn't have come at a worse time.

Sanjay and his engineers were in the middle of thinking out a critical component in the software patch for Cal Max, Lenore was in Hawaii with Ricky, and Michael, point man on the search for venture capital, had just taken delivery of a Maserati and was driving up the coast to Santa Barbara with his new wife, Becka.

For Wallace, it was like riding a fast train that had been signaled suddenly to a siding. Everything had come to an unnerving halt.

The previous day, taking advantage of Michael's absence from the office, Otto met privately with Wallace to voice a concern: Michael, in anticipation of a funding event by Trek Reese, was ramping up his personal compensation. It wasn't exactly embezzlement, according to Otto, but Michael had nearly doubled his salary and the company was paying his personal credit card expenses—groceries, wine, haircuts, restaurant tabs, gifts for Becka.

"How do you think he paid for the Maserati?" Otto asked.

"That isn't possible," Wallace said. "There must be some mistake."

Otto had a file marked *Personal and Confidential*, which he opened on the desk in front of Wallace. It was all there—the payroll journal, the check register, the paid bills. Wallace felt sickened. He and Michael had a gentlemen's agreement that they would always take equal salaries.

"If it isn't embezzlement, then what is it?" Wallace asked.

"I'd call it *purloining*," Otto said. "It's a breach of trust and I thought it should be brought to your attention. Have a nice weekend."

In the kitchen Audrey scrutinized Wallace, who was topping off his glass with a heavy splash of scotch.

"A man shouldn't drink like that, especially on a day of prayer and thanksgiving," Audrey said. She watched Wallace put the glass to his lips. "Dad never drank much, only an occasional whiskey sour at the country club. He never drove drunk, either."

"I don't drive drunk," Wallace said.

"He was comfortable in his own skin," Audrey said. "He never pretended to be something he wasn't."

"That's very interesting. What's your point?"

"No one's ever erected a statue in honor of a man who imperson-ated a police officer."

Addison and Tiffany were planted in front of the television, eat-ing dry Cheerios from a bowl and watching *Flipper* reruns. Addison nursed a passion for dolphins. According to her it wasn't enough to have a career training them at Sea World—she wanted to be the first human being to communicate with them in their native language. On her bedroom wall she kept a chart of clicks, whirrs, and cheeps from the TV show and their approximate translations into English.

Audrey watched Wallace with stony eyes, tabulating his cocktails.

"That should be your last one," Audrey said. "You've still got that lovely free-range turkey to carve, and that involves sharp cutlery and a reasonable amount of dexterity."

"I'm fine to carve the turkey," Wallace said.

"That turkey came all the way from Paris, France."

"It's from Riverside County. I should know—Perris Farms uses our software."

"Dad never liked the French people," Audrey said. "He felt they'd intentionally steer you to the wrong subway train."

Wallace sensed he was being drawn into an argument. The irrefutable proof he needed—that Perris Farms was in California and not France—was as near at hand as the trash compactor; it was printed in plain English on the slick, plastic turkey bag he had discarded a few hours earlier. Wallace couldn't help himself; his desire to prove his mother-in-law wrong was overpowering and all consuming, like Nietzsche wanting to prove God was dead. Wallace set his drink on the kitchen counter, pulled open the trash compactor, and began sifting through the rank, soggy garbage. Audrey watched with mild disdain. For his trouble all Wallace came away with was a blood-soaked remnant of the turkey bag, which offered no printed evidence of a turkey farm in Perris, California. The only discernable wording was the Perris Farms motto: *"Making Your Turkey Dreams Come True!"* Fragments of broken eggshells and greasy, translucent squares of wax paper clung to the sleeves of his shirt.

"It's unbecoming of a man to root through the garbage like a hog," Audrey said. "You'll need those hands for handling the turkey."

Wallace felt slightly humiliated. His fruitless foray into the trash was a juvenile attempt to prove his mother-in-law wrong. What did he care if an old woman wanted to believe her Thanksgiving turkey came from Paris, France? As a gesture of contrition, he refilled her glass of wine and told her the cheap sauvignon blanc was a French Sancerre, carefully chosen to complement the French turkey. Audrey seemed appreciative. She praised the wine for its distinct nose.

Wallace fixed another scotch. He drank with his eyes closed. The truce was short-lived.

"Don't come running to me when you cut off your fingers and need a ride to the hospital," Audrey said.

"I'll call a cab."

"You can't afford a cab."

"What's that supposed to mean?"

"You think I don't know your financial condition?" Audrey asked. "You think I don't talk to my own daughter? Why you gave up a perfectly good job at the consulting firm I will never understand. Dad said you had a good future ahead of you."

"If you ain't the lead dog the scenery never changes."

"You've said that before. It means nothing to me."

"Something my father taught me."

"Your father once tried to have an affair with me."

"He asked you to dance at our wedding."

"He reeked of gin and said he thought we'd make a snappy couple. If that isn't a proposition I don't know what is."

"Okay, fine," Wallace said, giving up. He was concentrating instead on quartering a lime and squeezing the juice into his glass.

"You know, I had another visit from Dad last night. He said Satan was a big balding bird, like a vulture. He said it had you in its clutches."

It wasn't the first time Audrey had been visited in the night by her late husband.

"You don't find that alarming, communing with the dead in your sleep?" Wallace asked.

"That wasn't all he said, either."

"Give you any stock tips?" Wallace sampled the scotch critically. It was amazing how a squeeze of lime could take the bite out of a towering, peaty scotch.

"He said you're destitute, or soon will be, unless you get your moral house in order. By the way, I haven't breathed a word to Hannah about your tryst with the Oriental secretary, and I won't, either, if you hit your knees right this second and give your soul to the Lord."

"I can't hit my knees. I can barely get out of a chair." Wallace had smacked his right knee taking down the robber, and it had been bothering him ever since. His entire right leg had locked during the long ride home from Cal Max. He was having recurring, shooting pains that felt like sciatica.

"Make light of it all you want," Audrey said. "But your daughters need saving. They told Pastor Maltby they didn't even know who the Messiah was. I hope you've had that little fortune cookie tested for syphilis."

"Please."

"Blindness is no joke. And neither is insanity."

"You'd be in a position to know."

"Don't you dare throw that half lime in the garbage," Audrey said. "That's a perfectly good piece of fruit."

"I can afford it."

"Tell me. How much is in your savings account right this very minute?"

"None of your business."

"I hope you haven't touched Dad's inheritance. That was meant to be in trust for the girls' education."

The inheritance was already gone. Wallace hadn't told anyone, not even Hannah.

"I don't get it," Audrey said. "Why keep throwing good money after bad?"

"It's like poker," Wallace said. "You have to keep anteing up or you lose."

"Dad never liked gambling," Audrey said. "He always felt gamblers were of weak moral character."

Hannah came into the kitchen, fixing an earring. "How's it going, Mom?" Her hair was pulled away from her face. She wore a sleeveless black cocktail dress and a simple silver cross around her neck. She liked to dress well for the holidays, and she insisted her daughters do the same. Even Wallace went along, wearing slacks and a freshly laundered shirt—white, since that was all he owned.

"Going just fine," Audrey said. "That French turkey smells heavenly."

"Mom, I have a surprise for you. Someone's on the line." Hannah picked up the telephone receiver and handed it to Audrey, smiling as she watched her mother talk on the phone.

"Oh, that's wonderful!" Audrey said, beaming. "Just wonderful news!"

"What's the news?" Wallace asked Hannah.

"Dirk Junior and Baby are coming for Christmas," Hannah said. "Dirk wanted to be the first to tell Mother."

Wallace took a healthy pull of scotch. "Wonderful."

Dirk Junior was Hannah's brother—Audrey's only son. His parents had named him after his paternal grandfather, Eldridge "Dirk" Taylor. For a few dementia-ridden years, the grandfather's life had overlapped with the new baby's, under the same roof, so calling one Dirk *Senior* and the other Dirk *Junior* helped keep things straight around the house ("Dirk Junior needs his diaper changed"; "Hey, get that thing out of Dirk Senior's mouth!"). Now Dirk Junior was in his midthirties—he was a few years younger than Hannah—and he still hadn't shaken the nickname. His wife's name was Baby.

Audrey spoke on the phone with Dirk Junior while Wallace, under Hannah's direction, lifted the turkey from the oven and placed it on a cutting board. Audrey asked to speak briefly with Baby—just long enough to give Thanksgiving greetings and ask her to call later with a Christmas wish list "for you know who." When Dirk Junior got back on the line, the tone of the conversation turned serious. Wallace did his best to ignore what he couldn't help but overhear. He went to work on the turkey with a carving knife.

"No, I don't think much is happening with him," Audrey said, glancing once at Wallace and turning away. "No, he hasn't been back to prison yet. His attorney is a J.E.W.," she spelled this out, "quite nasty, and wouldn't you know he wants to sue everyone in sight. Of course it's expensive, it's terribly expensive! No, I know it isn't the Christian thing to do. Oh, she seems to be handling it all right. Hanging in there, considering. Yes, of course you'll see her at Christmas. For sure! Oh, it's such wonderful news you and Baby are coming out. We're looking forward to it, too. Right. Bye."

After Audrey hung up the phone, she reveled in the news of her son's upcoming visit. Hannah opened a bottle of champagne. She forced a glass into Wallace's hand. He was feeling the effects of the scotch. The turkey meat was coming off piecemeal and ragged.

Addison and Tiffany ran into the kitchen. "What! Who's coming?"

Audrey pressed her hands into her apron. "Girls, Grandma has a surprise for you. Guess who's coming for Christmas? Dirk Junior and Baby!"

The girls squealed and clapped their hands, jumping in circles. Even Scottie, the dog, got into the act. Dirk Junior and Baby always brought Addison and Tiffany presents from Arizona—kachina dolls, Indian turquoise jewelry, and beaded belts with their names on them. Dirk Junior and Baby had no children of their own.

"How long are they staying?" Hannah asked.

"I didn't even think to ask," Audrey said. "Probably not long. They're busy people."

"Like the rest of us aren't," Wallace said to the smoldering turkey.

Dirk Junior and Baby sold residential real estate in North Scottsdale.

"They're driving out?" Hannah asked.

"I think so. They always do."

An image flashed in Wallace's mind: Michael, wearing thin leather gloves, driving up the coast in his Maserati, top down, the ocean breeze whipping his hair, Becka urging him to pass on a blind curve. She was Michael's own deal with the devil; Becka was almost twenty years his junior.

"What's Dirk Junior driving these days?" Wallace asked.

"I can't keep up," Audrey said. "With him it's always something different."

Dirk Junior liked to drive expensive German automobiles. He once told Wallace he thought it furthered his career—buyers equated the caliber of a car with an agent's skill at selling real estate.

"A lot like a lawyer in that regard," Dirk Junior said.

The previous Easter, Dirk Junior and Baby had arrived in a four-door Mercedes with a sunroof and built-in car phone. Dirk Junior told Wallace it was the largest sedan Mercedes made, not counting the limousine. On both sides of the car were blue and white magnetic real estate signs that read *Team Dirk Junior and Baby*. The couple had their phone number and picture on the signs—he with his trademark blue blazer, bow tie, and *Promise Keeper's* baseball cap; she with her big Arizona hair. Dirk Junior and Baby were avid seminar takers. They once took a course on brand building, and as a result they were meticulous about cultivating their personal brand—meticulous to the point that Dirk Junior never left the Scottsdale Road townhouse without his blue blazer, bow tie, and *Promise Keeper's* cap, and Baby without her full face of makeup and her hair big.

"You want to sit in the car?" Dirk Junior had asked Wallace, holding open the driver's door. The back seat was filled with an assortment of Easter baskets and chocolate bunnies.

"Not really."

"Come on. Sit in it."

"Why would I want to sit in your car?" Wallace mistrusted a grown man who'd wear a baseball cap with a blue blazer.

"Just sit in it."

Wallace sat in Dirk Junior's Mercedes. The interior smelled of leather and Baby's perfume. On the walnut-burl center console was a stack of *Dirk Junior and Baby* business cards, same picture. Through the open sunroof, Wallace could see the tops of the Mexican palm trees that soared above Ed and Audrey Taylor's swimming pool.

"Very nice," Wallace said, looking around. "Very impressive."

"We lease it," Dirk Junior said.

"But that doesn't mean we can't afford it," Baby said, leaning through the open window on the passenger side. The way she stood Wallace could see more than a little of what was down her shirt. "A lease makes the government our partner in building an image."

"You should think about taking one of these seminars," Dirk Junior said. "It gives your life absolute focus."

"Two kids and the terror of losing everything I own gives me plenty of focus," Wallace said.

"What you need to understand," Baby said, "is God wants you to have it all."

"Absolutely," Dirk Junior said. He had his father's moon-shaped face and colorless skin. With his full Bavarian lips and ghostly eyebrows, he reminded Wallace of a panzer-division tank commander.

"Beautiful car," Wallace said, putting his hands on the heavy steering wheel. "Bet with this thing you could overrun Holland in a single day."

"Easily," Dirk Junior agreed.

From the open window, Baby eyed Wallace coolly.

Back in the kitchen Hannah was tying on an apron. "You want to put the turkey on a platter or just serve it here?" she asked Wallace.

"Platter." Sinewy and fatty, with bristly bones, the cooked turkey had proved a sizable foe for Wallace—the literal incarnation of the bald, satanic bird of Audrey's imaginings. Prone on the cutting board, it looked like it had been hacked with a machete. In his liquor Wallace took refuge from the misshapen carcass. Even absent the squirt of lime, he could no longer taste the scotch that had burned in his throat all afternoon. There was only numbness. *Good.*

Audrey was in the dining room putting salad plates on the table.

"What have you done to that poor turkey?" Hannah asked. "Are you insane?"

Wallace said, "Did you hear her just now on the phone?"

"Watch where you're pointing that knife. It's dripping."

Wallace's mood darkened. "Why does she have to drag him into this? And who's he to second-guess Morty Schlegg?"

"If you didn't want Dirk Junior to know about it you never should have called Mother in the first place."

"Great advice, Hannah. Maybe I should've called you."

Between angry gulps of scotch, Wallace piled the turkey meat on the platter. He used the long blade of the serrated carving knife and an oversized fork as a makeshift set of tongs. Every second or third chunk missed the platter.

"Dirk Junior and Baby," he grumbled. "It sounds like a law firm for dwarfs."

"He does her a lot of good. He watches after her affairs."

"I wouldn't trust my affairs to a grown man named Dirk Junior."

"Shhh. Mother will hear you."

"I don't care. He sounds like a mouse."

"He has a good mind for business."

"He's a real estate agent who lives in Phoenix. He hasn't had an original thought his whole life. And what's with a grown woman named Baby?"

"You're drunk. Maybe you should drink some coffee."

"Maybe I should drink some strychnine. To think I'm related to two human beings named Dirk Junior and Baby."

"Don't be nasty."

"Where are they staying? Not with us, I hope."

"They're staying at Mother's."

"Of course. Dumb question. He's a momma's boy. Women run his life."

Now the picture in Wallace's head changed: Becka was driving the Maserati, hell-bent for leather, Michael hanging on for dear life.

Hannah had to remind Wallace it was Thanksgiving. "Do try to sober up for dinner," she said. "And watch where you're waving that knife. You're spilling everywhere."

"I did that on purpose for the dog," Wallace said. Scottie was at his feet, wolfing down scraps as they rained from the countertop above.

Trustworthy team member, Wallace thought. No betrayal from this one.

"It's awfully cold in there," Audrey said, coming back into the kitchen. "Can't you turn up the heat?"

"No," Wallace said.

"Sure," Hannah said.

"Don't you dare turn up the heat," Wallace said to Hannah when Audrey was out of the kitchen. "You won't do it for your own children. She can put on a sweater."

"You're wearing that stupid barbecue apron and you've been working next to the hot oven," Hannah said. "It's a lot cooler in there."

"Ninety-five instead of a hundred is still hot. Give her one of your stolen airplane blankets." It was Hannah's one vice in life—she collected airline blankets. She had a closet full of them. She stubbornly maintained they came from charter flights and were paid for.

"I am not going to make my mother eat her Thanksgiving dinner wrapped up like some Egyptian mummy." Hannah went to the thermostat and turned up the heat.

"She may as well be a mummy, the way she drives."

"We'll need to get more chairs for the dining room," Hannah said, "if we're going to have all these people for Christmas."

Wallace hung his apron on the back of the pantry door. "Has anyone talked to her yet about her driving?"

"I told you. I'm going to talk to her."

"Make your lazy brother do it for once."

"I can't make him do anything. He's a grown man."

"A grown *mouse* more like it." Wallace picked a sliver of turkey off the platter and popped it into his mouth. The morsel was appropriately moist—dark meat, mainly fat. He licked his fingers. "What's she going to do about the house?"

"What's it to you?"

"I am stunned your father didn't have something arranged—he of all people."

"What are you talking about?"

"She can't stay there. She's demented."

"Wallace, hush! She'll hear you."

"It's too much."

"She loves that house. I am not going to ask her to leave it."

"I'm not saying you alone, Hannah. You and your brother together. Make her sell the house. And get her to stop driving."

"Quit picking the turkey fat. It's offensive."

Time was slowly marching on Hannah; she was turning into her mother. Wallace pictured her in old age: humorless and inflexible, bone thin and slightly hunched. Plastic surgery was the bane of modern medicine. In another twenty-five years the women of his generation would all look alike: frozen in time, hair frosted, tummies tucked, faces slick, smooth, and tightly trussed, like Perris Farms turkeys. The medical establishment would have to work on the *fun* chip next. Without it, Hannah would be a torment to Addison's and Tiffany's husbands just as Audrey was to him—counting their cocktails, accusing them of adultery, proclaiming ridiculous things to be French.

Wallace said, "Get her to stop driving and make her move into one of those places where you have your own apartment, where they take you around in a little bus—"

"I am not going to tell my mother to move into a nursing home," Hannah said. "Especially not in the middle of her Thanksgiving dinner."

Audrey came into the kitchen rubbing the tops of her arms. "Have you turned up the heat? I didn't hear anything come on."

"With your hearing you wouldn't," Wallace said.

"The furnace takes a minute to kick on, Mom." Hannah handed Audrey a basket of rolls. "Here, take these to the table."

"Not a nursing home, Hannah," Wallace said. "A place where you have your own kitchen—"

"You're dripping. It's all over your shirt."

"A contract for lifetime care—that's the critical thing. But you have to get in while your health is still good. Before you fall and break a hip. Or they figure out you're crazy."

"Are you calling my mother crazy?"

"I'm open to the possibility. She thinks Satan is a big, bald bird."

Hannah said, "You all ready for dinner, Mom?"

Audrey stood in the doorway. "Better believe I'm ready. I've been ready since supper time. That was two whole hours ago."

"Where are the kids?"

"You'll stunt their growth plates," Audrey said, "eating so late. Dirk Junior and Baby eat at five."

"Big deal," Wallace said. "They eat crap out of a can." He sucked his fingers—four in the mouth, like playing a harmonica.

Hannah sent Audrey to round up the girls while she served up the food. She had arranged her good china dishes in a line on the counter.

"Just promise me you and your brother will talk about it when you see him at Christmas," Wallace said.

"Do something productive and open wine."

"Promise me, Hannah. You'll talk to him—"

Hannah handed Wallace a bottle of wine. "Start with the merlot."

"Clock's ticking, Hannah. Think of it. A bird." Wallace used a waiter's wine opener to uncork the bottle as Audrey began shuttling heaping plates into the dining room. The food pitched precariously in her hands.

"Christmas at the latest, Hannah," Wallace said. "I'm seeing serious decline."

"This is supposed to be a holiday, not a conspiracy session."

"Prudent estate planning is hardly a conspiracy. If she has a fall or a stroke, guess what—you and I will have to take her in. Because you can bet your brother and his bossy wife won't do it."

"Enough."

"Be honest, Hannah. Is that what you want? To trade in your wings and be a live-in nurse to your mother?"

"Stop."

"The sad fact is, your father should have attended to this long before he died. You and I can't bankroll her. We've got Michael's Maserati to pay for."

Hannah turned in surprise. "Michael has a Maserati? How much did that cost?"

"Forget the Maserati, Hannah. The point is we're on thin ice here. It's a retirement home for her or bankruptcy for us."

"The only thing that's going to bankrupt us is your lame company." Hannah carried the platter of turkey into the dining room. "Wash your hands. It's time to eat."

Wallace stayed behind in the kitchen, picking at the carcass. He thought of Lenore as he last saw her: climbing into the back of an airport limousine, the white shirttail of her blouse hanging below the hemline of her roll-sleeve cardigan. As the car pulled away she gave Wallace a desultory wave and a determined smile.

"Bent shaft my ass," Wallace said, tearing back a turkey leg.

Hannah called from the dining room. Everyone was seated and ready to eat. Wallace ignored her. He would not be a party to a sham holiday dinner (celebrating what, Pilgrims and Indians and rampant disease?) while he teetered on the brink of bankruptcy and total ruin, thanks to his father-in-law's criminally negligent estate planning and Michael Merksamer's thievery—*purloining,* as Otto called it! The meat from the turkey carcass tasted just fine in the kitchen. Hannah kept calling from the dining room, but Wallace wanted nothing to do with the dinner. He would stay here and enjoy his scotch. Now both girls were in the kitchen. Addison was tugging at his shirtsleeves, trying to coax him into the dining room with dolphinlike clicks and whirrs. Wallace wouldn't budge. Tiffany backed up to the refrigerator, tears streaming down her face. "Daddy, we've been working on this for two whole days!" With a cold detachment he'd later regret, Wallace shook off Addison's hand and told his girls the same thing his father had once told him: "Life has its disappointments, kids. Sometimes there's not a goddamn thing you can do about it."

Stunned, Addison took a step back. Her eyes welled with tears. She took her sister by the hand and ran from the kitchen.

When Wallace finally set foot in the dining room, reeling, he hit a doorjamb and spilled most of his scotch. Momentum kept him going. With a considerable lurch he fell into his chair at the head of the table. He used a forefinger to stir what was left of his drink, then sucked it. The scotch tasted curiously salty.

Hannah, Audrey, and the girls stared.

"What in the world are you doing?" Hannah asked.

"I am still stunned he didn't line up a place before he died," Wallace said.

"Let's enjoy dinner."

"Honest to God, if that isn't gross negligence for an actuary, I don't know what is."

"Quit now," Hannah said.

Audrey stiffened in her chair. "Is he talking about Dad?"

"No, Mom, no one you know," Hannah said, glaring at Wallace. "Now who'd like to say grace?"

Addison finally said grace, but none of the adults heard her prayer. Each had his own reason.

CHAPTER FOURTEEN

Lenore came into the Monday morning staff meeting carrying a cup of coffee and a thick stack of file folders. She set her things on the table next to Wallace.

"Missed you in the courtyard," she said, taking a seat. Her face was tan and she wore a gold whale's tail pendant.

"I was trying to catch Michael early," Wallace said. "How was Hawaii?"

"Days were great. Nights a little stormy."

Otto chaired the meeting. The others streamed in and took places at the long table: Sanjay, Charlie Dye, Julie. When Michael finally walked in, late, the meeting started.

It was a familiar agenda: Lenore gave an update on Cal Max, Sanjay talked about his team's progress building the patch, Charlie reviewed his sales funnel, and Otto passed around the latest financials. Michael was his usual disgraceful self. He continually interrupted the presentations, becoming red in the face and working himself into an apoplectic frenzy, pinpointing root problems that were discernible only to him—Sanjay's engineers were lazy, Cal Max was walking all over Lenore, Charlie Dye lacked a sense of urgency, Otto's spreadsheet formulas had to be wrong.

The last item on the agenda was the Christmas tree.

Michael turned to Julie, who was taking notes.

"Get a noble fir. A big one, like you see in department stores."

"When should I schedule the tree trimming party?" Julie asked. The holiday potluck was a company tradition.

"Forget it," Michael said. "Drunk engineers hanging ornaments—that's a bad idea. Last year's tree was an embarrassment."

Otto was examining a line in Michael's handout. "Is this a typo?" he asked, putting on reading glasses. "Five thousand dollars for decorating?"

"I plugged a number," Michael said. "So what?"

"You're saying no party?" Julie asked.

"It's a distraction," Michael said. "There's bigger fish to fry."

Sanjay said, "Michael, we can surely afford one hour at lunch—"

"Forget it, cancel it," Michael said. "We're starting a new tradition. Becka's gonna' do the tree. She wants to make it her annual opus, have it covered in the press."

Otto glanced at Wallace.

Wallace stared at a spot on the floor.

That Becka was taking over the Christmas tree project should have neither surprised nor angered Wallace. She was a self-proclaimed interior design consultant—she carried cards and was beginning to hire herself out to friends—and, as a Merksamer Digital director, she increasingly inserted herself into the company's business, particularly as it pertained to aesthetics and image: the tropical chenille tapestry fabric on the conference room chairs, the vintage-looking cotton drapes in Michael's office, which operated via one of two foot pedals under his desk (the second pedal swung the door shut), the new Mediterranean paint scheme and cut-pile Berber wool carpeting in the executive suite. On a recent trip to New York, she spent a week acquiring artwork—sophomoric, socially-conscious oil paintings that now hung in the company lobby: men in business suits, rowing a Phoenician slave ship; an Edvard Munch rip-off of a cityscape populated with lost souls; a woman in a taxi chauffeured by a blind priest, driving over a street paved with people of color.

"Find us some velvet ropes, like in a bank," Michael told Julie. "Cordon off the tree. I don't want these damn people touching the glass balls. We're talking Chihuly."

Wallace interrupted. There was no disguising the anger in his voice. "Michael, we need to talk. The minute this meeting's over."

Surprised, Michael looked at Wallace. With extensive throat clearing and frequent glances in Wallace's direction, he quickly wrapped up the meeting. He ducked through the doorway and hurried back to his office.

"You son of a bitch," Wallace said, looming over Michael's desk.

Michael was seated in his black leather chair. He held up a finger. He was on the phone, checking voice mail.

"Hang up," Wallace said.

"What?"

"I said hang up."

"Wait. I'm getting—"

Wallace snatched the phone from Michael's hand and slammed it down in its cradle.

Michael licked his lips. "If this is about the Christmas tree I can explain—"

"Christmas tree, Maserati, pay raise—you tell me."

Michael glanced at the door. "This is unfortunate—"

"What in god's name were you thinking?"

"I meant to talk to you—"

"This is indefensible, Michael."

"What's your problem? I haven't done anything wrong."

"The hell you haven't!"

Michael's foot fumbled beneath the desk. There was the soft whirr of an electric motor as the drapes began to move. "Shit." He touched the other pedal. The door swung shut.

"What," Wallace said, "you didn't think I'd find out?"

Michael's face reddened. He pounded a fist on the desk. "You're way out of bounds. I am still the majority shareholder of this company—"

"We had an agreement."

"Show me. Show me the agreement in writing."

"Come on, Michael. You're better than that."

"You're naïve. What do you think we're in business for?"

"Not to loot the company!"

"Rule number one," Michael said. "Pay yourself first."

"I hate thieves."

"You're a fool. The bank would have covered your losses."

"I'm talking about you."

Michael's lower lip trembled. "I don't have to stand for this."

"What about Trek Reese? How will this look to him?"

"You think Trek Reese could live for one week on what you and I make in a year?"

"That's not the point."

"What's the point? The Maserati?" Michael picked up the phone. "I'll call Otto right now. Tell him to get you one, too."

"I don't want a car."

Michael hung up the phone. "A pay raise? Is that what this is about? Say the word. I'll give you a raise."

"This company can't afford it—"

"We'll reallocate resources, then. Roll some heads. Starting with Lenore."

Michael eyed Wallace intently, letting this sink in.

"That's ignorance talking," Wallace said. "She holds this place together."

"She gives away the store, anything they want. We're supposed to be selling software, not handing it out for free."

"It's a patch. We have no choice."

"That's crap! You've spent too much time in the consulting business. It's made your head soft. The customer pays for *everything*."

Wallace paced the floor. He didn't know what to say. "I can't believe you. It's like you're running a Mafia bust-out scam on your own company."

"How about this?" Michael said. "Starting today we're operating like a *real* company. We're going to pay the CEO what he's worth. And it's up to the goddamn management team, you included, to meet the bottom line. Otherwise you're fired."

Wallace stared at Michael with contempt. "Is that it? Is that our new agreement?"

"New? It's inherent in your job description. It's always been there."

"So I'm just another employee?"

"You serve at my pleasure, yes."

"Nice of you to clear that up." Wallace was stunned. He turned to leave.

"Wait a minute. I'm not finished." Michael stood. He pitched his meeting folder across the desk. Papers scattered. "This clown Charlie Dye—he's pathetic. I'm making a change, effective immediately. He reports to me."

"Michael, that's crazy—"

"It's clear you're incapable of managing him," Michael said. "We wouldn't be having this conversation if this company was making sales."

"No, Michael, we wouldn't be having this problem if you hadn't saddled us with a third-rate reservation system."

"That's cock-and-bull. Who told you—"

"A guy named King Bed. Ask him. He's a Cal Max subscriber."

Michael stared out the window. "Pathetic. No wonder this place is falling apart."

"You have a problem with my performance? Say it to my face."

"Here's my problem," Michael said, turning back to Wallace. "You coddle people. You won't fire someone who needs to be fired. The purpose of a business is to make money, not friends."

"Anything else?"

"Just this. Fix your legal problems. You're becoming a liability."

"You want me to resign?"

"I want you to start kicking people in the ass. We need customers, lots of them. Then we can raise serious money—fifty, a hundred million. A man in my position should be flying private. I should have a place in Aspen, a big yacht."

Wallace could only shake his head. "You're unbelievable. You never stop."

Michael mistook this for praise.

"That's the difference between you and me," Michael said. "You haven't learned to think big."

"Wrong, Michael. Our differences are a lot more significant than that."

"Don't be so sure." Michael picked up the phone and buzzed Julie. "Round up Otto and Sanjay. I don't care what they're doing. Tell 'em to drop it and get in here. It's time for a come-to-Jesus meeting."

"Anything I need to stay for?" Wallace asked.

"Believe me, for this you don't want to stay," Michael said. "Get with Lenore and Charlie. Make something happen. In case you haven't noticed, this company's dead in the water."

Wallace passed Otto and Sanjay in the corridor as they headed for Michael's office.

For the rest of the morning, through the thin walls of his office, Wallace could hear Michael's accusations. Executive compensation, choice of a software engine—the subject didn't matter; neither man could keep a secret. Michael's screaming continued through the lunch hour.

CHAPTER FIFTEEN

Charlie Dye reporting to Michael was a predictable disaster.
The next Friday, on the phone with Wallace, Charlie announced he was quitting.

"A guy could get a complex. You're the only one who's returned my call in two days."

"Try sitting on the toilet," Wallace said. "That always makes the telephone ring."

Charlie didn't laugh. "My generation went to war against this kind of tyranny."

"Don't quit, Charlie."

"There's another opportunity. They're offering a decent retirement plan."

"I'll clear my calendar. Where can we meet?"

Charlie lived in an old neighborhood on Point Loma, near the airport. It turned out he had a favorite spot on Harbor Island, overlooking the bay. From the road Charlie's Bonneville was easy to find—navy blue with a white front, the only hood he was willing to pay for after the Taco Bell accident.

"What, you've never seen a sailboat before?" Wallace asked.

Charlie sat on a bench, watching a trim white sloop pass. "I wish I was on it." He took in the view through a cheap pair of wraparound sunglasses. Wisps of hair blew across his knotty head. He wore a faded windbreaker.

Nearby, a shirtless man fished from the jetty.

"Mind?" Wallace sat on the bench.

"I'm convinced there's no such thing as justice in this world," Charlie said. "I'll be your character witness if you need one."

"I wouldn't want you," Wallace said. "Your gloom could sell cemetery plots."

"To hear Michael talk you wouldn't think I could sell anything at all. He's trying to force me out of the company."

"I doubt that."

"He won't let me set foot in the building. He cancelled my badge."

It sounded like Michael—one of his ass kickings. The company was housed in a secure building with doors that were computer controlled for keycard access.

"What's the point?" Wallace asked.

"He thinks I'd rather be loafing in the office than out making sales calls. Said the only way I'd get my badge back was to get him an appointment with a decision maker at a Blue Cross plan. You know how impossible that is. I'd stand a better chance scoring a meeting with the secretary of health."

"So what do you do all day?"

"What do you think? I lock myself in the bedroom and dial Blue Cross plans. Then at five o'clock we go over the call records, minute by minute. Then Michael bawls me out for calling this guy, for not calling that one. It's beyond hostile—it's like working with a damn blowtorch in my face." He looked at Wallace. "I thought you were supposed to be my supervisor."

"It's only temporary," Wallace said.

The fisherman moved farther down the jetty. He walked barefoot on the trimmed grass.

"Watch your back," Charlie said. "Michael wants to get rid of you, too."

"I don't believe that."

"He told me himself—he's recruiting someone to head up sales and marketing. That leaves you and me out in the cold."

Word travels fast, Wallace thought. "We'll still have a place."

"Can I get that in writing?"

An orange Coast Guard helicopter flew low over the water, heading toward open ocean. As it passed the noise was deafening.

"I should just quit," Charlie said.

"I wish you'd stop saying that."

"Look, Wallace, for all I know you're ready to put me out to pasture. If that's the case I wish you'd tell me."

"No, Charlie. Absolutely not."

"Here's how I see it. I believed in you, and I believed in this company. I took a pay cut for this job. I was supposed to make that up in commission. Now it's pretty clear the money isn't coming anytime soon, and I'm reporting to Michael. It's not the deal I signed up for."

"It's a long sales cycle. We know that."

"I've always sold tangible goods. Maybe that's my problem."

"Like they say, Charlie, it's darkest before the dawn."

"Baloney. Dark is when they tie the blindfold on and hand you a cigarette."

Charlie opened a pack of gum. He offered a piece to Wallace, who declined.

"Regional vice president of sales. That's the other opportunity." Charlie placed a stick of gum in his mouth and began to chew. "A major player in the pet accoutrements market. These guys have a killer rope monkey. Dogs go crazy over it. Plus it gets me health insurance."

"You've already got that."

"What I've got is a standoff with Cal Max and what feels like a surgical instrument sewn inside my chest."

"I thought it was scar tissue."

"That's a lie. Pain's worse than ever."

"You can't get it x-rayed?"

"I could if those bastards would authorize it. They say it's preexisting."

"So go over their heads."

"I can't. If I raise my voice or ask to speak to a supervisor they accuse me of having panic syndrome and cut me off. If I say I'm in pain they tell me to hang up and call 911."

"I'll call Peg Brown. See if she can pull some strings."

"Nothing personal, Wallace, but I've heard your promises before. Why'd you sell out, anyway? We had a good thing going."

"Survival, Charlie. Sometimes you have to put your fate in someone else's hands."

"Well, you're a terrible judge of character. I saw that guy coming from a mile away."

"Michael's just Michael."

"At your age I thought I was pretty smart, too. Trust me. When you're at the end of the line and your health is shot, it's hard to look back and admit you made a mistake."

"Patience and persistence, Charlie. You taught me that."

"Too late for conventional tactics. The serpents have taken our home and made it their den. What's wrong with our software, anyway?"

"Sanjay's on it."

Charlie turned back to the bay. "That's about as comforting as this ice ax inside my chest."

CHAPTER SIXTEEN

"**Y**ou're breaking a sweat," Audrey Taylor said. "I'll make you some lemonade."

She stood in the breezeway of her Escondido home, the double doors open to the sunshine. It was the first Saturday in December, a magical Southern California morning: warm, dry air; a cloudless sky; a faint offshore breeze. The rock-covered hills looked close enough to touch.

"You watch, Mrs. Taylor, this Santa Ana will break, and there'll be rain," Owen Andersen said. "You can count on it." He was trying to slide a heavy Christmas tree from the pickup bed of his new V8 Turbo Diesel Hummer H1, and the tree wasn't cooperating. Owen was a big man—his chest muscles strained the buttons of his golf shirt—but the tree branches were in a herringbone pattern, and they thwarted his progress. He was pulling from the wrong end.

"Gosh darn this thing is stubborn," Owen said, grinding his teeth.

He finally got the right angle on the tree and levered it out of the bed in an arc that brought to mind a tilt-a-whirl. The weight of the tree was more than Owen could handle. He staggered backward. The sharp branches swept the side of the truck, making a sound like dragging a bow across an out-of-tune violin.

The *f*-word formed on Owen's lips, but at the last possible moment he managed to soften it. "Fish sticks," he said.

There were spider veins in the gleaming black paint where the tree had traversed the side of the truck, like someone had taken steel wool to it. In anger Owen slapped the heat-treated, aluminum alloy fender, allowing himself a single transgression in the presence of Audrey Taylor. It stung his hand.

"God dammit," he said, in a voice meant to be a whisper.

"Owen?"

Owen turned and faced Audrey with a forced grin. In his capacity as a deacon at the Hidden Valley Presbyterian Church he was spending his day delivering Christmas trees to seniors and widows, and swearing wasn't in the script. Owen had a habit of always looking on the bright side, though: the scratched paint was one more thing in his favor, on the Big Ledger. Now God owed him a paint job.

"It's got a lovely shape," Audrey said, stepping aside as Owen carried the tree through the front door.

"I was there when the truck came in," Owen said. "I saved this one especially for you."

"You're spilling needles."

"The usual spot?"

"On the sheet. By the french doors."

"No problem." This came out sounding more like a grunt. Moving the tree was like handling a dead body. Owen managed to stagger into the living room without knocking anything over. He planted the base of the tree trunk more or less on the center of the bedsheet that had been laid out on the terra-cotta Spanish tile floor. He held the tree in a straight vertical line. "How's it look?"

"Wonderful."

"I always like a Doug fir." Owen caught his breath. He looked past Audrey to the portrait hanging on the wall: there was Hannah, much younger, but still the same Hannah—those eyes, that hair. With her were Ed and Audrey Taylor, and Dirk Junior, looking like a frat boy.

"If you've got a ladder," Owen said, "I can hang the lights while I'm here. And I bought some new Teflon hoses for your washing machine."

"You're too thoughtful."

"Nonsense. There's no such thing. Our morning men's group—we've had you in our prayers. How's she doing, anyway?"

"Hannah? Oh, you know. The best she can."

Indeed Owen knew. It was like shooting fish in a barrel—consoling a wife who had just awakened to the realization that her husband was a failure, a cheat, a liar, or a bore. Forget the seven-year itch—that was myth. In Owen's experience (and according to his ranking system) disillusioned, discontented wives were the easiest to bag, followed second by newlyweds—a young wife was still genetically imprinted with the sexual spontaneity of a coed. Third on the chart were middle-aged mothers whose children had just left the house—off to college in another state. Divorcees were a subdivision of this category. These were women who had lost confidence in their looks, who were emotionally vulnerable and craved affection. With minimal wooing they could be quickly persuaded to shed their inhibitions and turn wild. Thus did Owen Andersen bestow on the Hidden Valley Presbyterian Church the moniker Church of Shooting Fish in a Barrel. Owen's faith was the bedrock of his personal philosophy: chase your dreams with divine perseverance and God will reward you with prosperity. The congregation itself served as the proving ground for Owen's canon of demeanor: be utterly confident at all times, boast assertively about your successes, and celebrate conspicuous consumption. It makes the guys around you look like losers. Everyone knows women are attracted to the Neanderthal with the biggest cave.

People were always trying to make sense of the vanity plates on Owen's Hummer: *LDOL*. Through car windows, Owen could see the faces of sexy young mothers turn; in back seats their children's heads would swivel, lips mouthing, trying to sound it out.

"Le doll? Le dole?"

And temptresses of various ethnicities, saddled with ignorant, tattoo-laden boyfriends—ditchdiggers, all of them!—who looked up enviously at the Hummer—they, too, didn't have a clue.

LDOL. No one ever got it: Looking Down on Losers.

Because that's what it was like to drive around town in a Hummer. You were always looking down on losers—underachievers who craned their necks to see who was rich enough to be behind the wheel of that big black truck with the hood scoop, roof rack, fog lights, and premium-sound stereo.

"Goodness sakes, what did you run into, a tank?"

"A pole," Audrey said.

Owen and Audrey stood in the cool garage. Owen had just finished taking the last of the Christmas things down from the rafters when Audrey stopped to show him the deep crease in the door of her Buick.

"You can't rub that out," Owen said. "You'll have to take it to a body shop."

"Oh, dear," Audrey said. "Ed won't be happy."

Owen looked at her, worried. "Mrs. Taylor, Ed's gone. He went to be with the Lord some time ago."

Audrey touched him on the forearm.

"Of course I knew that," she said. "Come inside for something cold to drink."

"Business first. Let me hang these lights and take care of the tree."

When Owen finally quit working, Audrey was ready in the kitchen with a plate of cookies and a pitcher of lemonade.

"That hits the spot," Owen said, wiping his mouth with the back of a hand. All that was left now was to change out the hoses on the washing machine. He held out his glass. "All right, one more before I go."

Audrey poured lemonade. "Please, eat more cookies."

Owen picked a macaroon off the plate. "I've got good memories of this place, Mrs. Taylor. Tell Dirk Junior I've got a business opportunity for him."

"I doubt he'd be interested. He hardly has an extra minute—"

"The gift of prosperity," Owen said. "That'll be my testimony. Hannah, too. After all you and Mr. Taylor have done for me over the years."

"It wasn't that much."

"More than you'll ever know," Owen said. "My father used to beat me with a belt." There were stories he could tell about his father—

lots of them—but Owen didn't want to frighten Audrey with monster tales of an angry, ugly drunk. He let it drop.

"Don't judge him too harshly," Audrey said. "Ed had a strong hand, too. He used to give Dirk Junior what for. You'll understand if you ever have a family of your own."

"Not me," Owen said. "At least not for a long time." He downed his drink in one long, greedy gulp. Then: "You think Hannah would ever give up flying?"

"She can't afford to."

"Never say never," Owen said. "He works in mysterious ways."

Owen studied his empty glass. It seemed like just yesterday when he'd gotten the word: Hannah was really getting married. What followed for Owen was a three-day drunk.

"I hope you've forgiven him," Audrey said. "Your father, I mean."

"Oh, I've forgiven him all right," Owen said. "Hannah, too. I forgive her just about every day of my life."

Owen and Hannah had dated for a period of time, many years earlier. Their courtship was during Owen's turbulent, womanizing years, and Hannah had dumped him suddenly, cruelly, for a married airline pilot.

"I imagine she's evaluating her options," Owen said, "with respect to her domestic situation."

"It's frustrating," Audrey said. "He won't take counseling. He's shut the door on Pastor."

"I've seen the numbers for his business," Owen said. "I truly can't fathom why he persists. Too pigheaded to see reason, I guess."

"Dirk Junior thinks—" Audrey turned to the window. "Well, I shouldn't say."

"Divorce?"

"There's a fidelity issue," Audrey said. "I've witnessed it with my own eyes. That's between you and me and the lamppost."

"You don't say." Owen shook his head. "The irony is Hannah would probably be the one to pay alimony."

"As a practical matter, sometimes, you have to face these things head-on," Audrey said. "Dirk Junior thinks she'd be better off in the long run. That doesn't make him a bad Christian."

Good, Owen thought. It's started—God's hand.

Even better than a paint job.

"I pray she does something a lot sooner than that," Owen said, grabbing the last macaroon. "We have a saying in the mortgage business: in the long run everybody's dead."

CHAPTER SEVENTEEN

It was Monday evening, and Wallace stood in the dark parking lot, listening to a loud row just outside the lobby doors. Michael came over to his Range Rover, walking with angry steps.

"Get in," he said to Wallace. "Get Julie on your cell. Tell her our dinner reservation just changed from five to three."

Stumped, Wallace opened the passenger door and climbed in. The seat was pushed all the way forward. Wallace sat at an awkward angle, his long legs splayed. Wedged in the back seat was a large, terra-cotta horse.

Michael threw the Range Rover in gear and drove off, leaving Otto and Sanjay standing speechless on the sidewalk.

"What happened back there?" Wallace asked.

"I won't have my authority undermined by blatant insubordination," Michael said. He drove belligerently, fixing the cars ahead with a nasty stare, as if they were insolent employees. "There's too much at stake."

Wallace had to borrow Michael's cell phone to call Julie. Since this was a social occasion, he had left his phone behind at the office, zipped inside his computer bag. They were on their way to the airport. Michael had an acquaintance flying in from Boston. He was coming out to interview for the top marketing job.

"Michael, watch out!" Wallace braced as Michael slammed on the brakes. The Range Rover nearly collided with a truck.

"Are you guys all right?" Julie asked at the other end of the line.

"I've come to realize that Judas comes in pairs," Michael said.

"Maybe I should drive," Wallace said, lowering the phone from his ear.

The traffic light turned green, and Wallace signed off with Julie. The Range Rover began moving again, merging onto the freeway. It was a busy night on the roads.

"I told Sanjay he could get pizza for his people," Michael said. "I specifically said cheese only. No toppings until they finish the patch. Otto knew damn well. He signed the check anyway."

Whenever the engineers were planning to work through the night, it was standard practice to have pizzas brought in. That Michael had passed the pizza delivery guy in the lobby, and stopped to inspect the boxes, was everybody's bad luck.

Wallace asked, "Tell me again what's wrong with sausage and pepperoni?"

"They're the carrot to surpass the cheese. Otherwise these guys will never finish the job. You give a bunch of engineers pizza with all the toppings, and they'll drag this out till Kingdom Come. They'll burp and play games."

"You must have a well-trained dog at home," Wallace said.

"Not me. I don't have time for a dog."

In the passing light Wallace could see the rankled expression on Michael's face, the veins raging in his neck. His tie was tightly cinched. He did not speak again until they were off the freeway, coming down the hill toward the airport, the yellow lights of the harbor and the dark curve of the bay unfolding before them.

"The three of us can run this company," Michael said suddenly. "We'll be the inner sanctum."

Three? It seemed a funny number. Which three?

"How do you know this guy?" Wallace asked.

"We worked together at CPC, in El Segundo," Michael said. "Sold a lot of government business, raised a lot of hell, closed a lot of bars. Back before my first wife."

"His name's Carl?"

"Carroll," Michael corrected. "Carroll Quinn. He's exactly what we need. Has a Rolodex that won't quit."

The terra-cotta horse was poking Wallace in the back.

At the airport, Carroll Quinn stood waiting at the curb. He wore a dark suit and sported a neatly trimmed beard. He spotted the Range Rover and put a hand in the air. Michael saw him at the last second, swerved, and came to a quick stop. Carroll stepped out, opened the rear hatch, and sent his suitcase spilling over the tailgate. It was a sturdy, black, compact job with rollers—the kind of case favored by most well-traveled executives. With the hatch open, Wallace could smell the sea air, humid and slightly tropical, the unmistakable scent of jet fuel lingering. Carroll worked himself into the back seat. Close up, he looked older—Michael's age at least. His beard was streaked with gray, and his face was wan and overspread with worry lines. He sat eye-to-eye with the horse.

"Who's this?" Carroll asked.

"That damn thing belongs to Becka," Michael said. "It's a Tang Dynasty horse."

"Fellow seems a bit worse for the wear."

"I meant to take it out. Move it if you want. Carroll, meet Wallace Noe."

Wallace twisted in the seat to shake hands.

"Heard a lot about you," Carroll said.

"All good I hope."

"Oh yes."

Then Carroll clapped Michael on the shoulders, hard, with two hands. "And you, old boy. Great to see you. Where's the rest of the gang?"

"Working." Michael tramped the accelerator. Without looking back he steered across four lanes of traffic and out of the airport, eyeing Carroll in the rearview mirror. "What happened? Your plane must have come in early."

Carroll pulled back a monogrammed shirtsleeve and glanced at his watch. It was a heavy gold timepiece. "Were we? I didn't notice." He tried shifting the horse to make more room, but the horse wouldn't budge.

"Because you said six thirty-five," Michael said. "It takes a good eight minutes to unload the plane, then another three to walk out. Unless you were first class. Then you'd have saved yourself about seven minutes."

"That's it," Carroll said. "Rode first. Talked the girl into bumping me up. Lovely thing." His breath had the whiff of sour wine.

"Some things never change," Michael said. He turned to Wallace. "This guy could talk the lava back inside a volcano."

Carroll leaned forward. He clamped a hand on Wallace's shoulder. He had big hands. "Can't wait to go to work. We're going to hit the ground running."

Wallace turned in the seat. "What are you doing now?"

Carroll chuckled. "Good one."

Michael said, "He's working for us."

"Didn't you know?" Carroll asked.

Michael glanced at Wallace, then turned back to the road.

Wallace said to Carroll, "Fine by me. We can use all the help we can get."

Carroll put his arm over the terra-cotta horse. "Yes, friends, the cavalry has arrived. And I've got the nag to prove it." He couldn't take his eyes off the view: the skyline at night, the reflections of the buildings shimmering on the black surface of the bay. He let out a whistle. "What a dream of a place to fly into. Did I mention Boston was about thirty-one degrees?"

CHAPTER EIGHTEEN

The Range Rover pulled beneath the brightly lit entrance canopy of the upscale chop house, stopping short of the valet podium. When it came to letting his gaze fall on minimum-wage service workers, Michael had a particular aversion. He let the uniformed attendant come to him and took his time opening the door.

The attendant had a ticket waiting. "Good evening, sir. Welcome to Sire Beef's."

"How safe is your parking lot?"

"We have excellent insurance."

"That's it," Michael said to the others. "The horse comes with us."

It took Wallace, Carroll, Michael, and the valet working together to spring the gangly statuette from the back seat of the Range Rover.

Inside the restaurant Carroll stood with the horse under one arm while Michael checked in with the hostess.

"Hold the table," Michael told her. "We're going to start with a drink in the bar."

The cocktail lounge was decorated in a vocabulary of dark wood, recessed lighting, and black leather booths. On the walls were paintings of reclining nudes. The terra-cotta horse stood on the banquette, its long nose gazing over the miniature cocktail lamp. At the next table, two women in tailored suits, one a redhead and the other a brunette, asked if it was a real Chinese Tang.

"Better be, for what I paid," Michael said.

The bartender, a burly enforcer type in a red vest and bow tie, noticed the horse and came out from behind the bar.

"You can't have that thing here."

Michael made a face. "Says who?"

"No packages of any kind."

"This isn't a package. It's a priceless antique."

"Owner's policy."

Damiano Giuliano was the well-known proprietor of Sire Beef's. It was rumored he had ties with the mob. It was also said the federal government spent so much time watching the place they kept a permanent room on the top floor of the limited service hotel across the way.

"We're here for an important business dinner and this horse belongs to my wife," Michael said. "If you think I'm leaving it outside you're crazy."

Carroll pulled a gold money clip from his pocket. He peeled off a twenty. "How about a one-time exception to your policy?"

The bartender said, "How about you shove your small change?"

"You don't know what you're talking about," Michael said. "Where's your manager?"

Even the ladies from the next table got into the act.

"It's a terra-cotta Chinese Tang, you dumb lummox," the redhead said to the bartender.

The general manager came over, soft-spoken and pale. He steepled his fingers. "Surely you can appreciate the policy. It stems from Mr. Giuliano's concern for his clients' privacy."

"You think this is a surveillance device?" Carroll asked.

"Don't you know who I am?" Michael said. "I eat here all the time."

"I'll have to ask you to leave," the general manager said.

"I'm not going anywhere," Michael said. "I demand to speak to the owner."

Damiano was summoned. He was a short, balding man with owl glasses and a raspy voice. He spoke with his hands, swatting at the air like he was chasing away low-flying bats. "I can make you guys from a mile. Ditch the camera."

The bartender set his jaw and clenched his fists.

"Camera?" Michael said. "This is the focal point for my wife's boudoir."

"Hey, it's a decorator item," said the redhead at the next table. "Think really fancy sawhorse."

"You damn people busted up my family," Damiano said. "You put my kids in jail."

"I don't know about the rest of you, but I'm ready to see a wine list," Carroll said.

Michael pulled a business card from his wallet and showed it to Damiano. "My wife and I ate here last week. Your early-bird prime rib. The metallic silver Maserati—you parked it out front."

"What if we let you keep the horse behind the bar?" Wallace asked.

Damiano looked at Michael. He looked at Wallace. A lightbulb seemed to come on in his head.

Carroll said, "We'll take a bottle of Dom. Make sure it's properly chilled."

Damiano turned to his burly enforcer. "All right. They can stay. Park the horse behind the bar."

"Fine," Michael said. "Keep it behind the bar."

Damiano snapped his fingers. A Mexican busboy came over. He was respectful about touching the horse. "Please, I take it?"

"Be careful," Michael said. "*Mucho dinero.*"

A cocktail waitress followed. She was a typical Sire Beef's server: reed thin, chemical blond hair, a pretty face. She wore high heels and a sheer, short dress.

"Bottle of Dom for the gentlemen," Damiano said.

Across the room the bartender combed over the terra-cotta horse with a small flashlight, looking for pinholes.

The waitress brought the Dom Perignon cooling in an ice bucket.

"Cocktail?" Her green eyes were striking.

"Vodka martini," Michael said.

Carroll studied the top of the wine list. "I'll stick to champagne."

"Scotch and soda," Wallace said.

"Appetizers?"

Michael was eyeing a plate of food at another table. "What's that seafood thing you got?"

"Seafood Sampler."

"That's the one you're famous for?"

"Pretty famous."

"Bring one of those."

The cocktail waitress wrote the order with a flourish and was gone.

Carroll eyed her departure closely.

"There's a dish I wouldn't mind sampling."

Fifteen minutes later the table was brimming with champagne flutes, cocktail tumblers, highball glasses, and the tiered tower of ice that was the restaurant's signature dish, the Seafood Sampler: Dungeness crab legs, oysters on the half shell, prawns, clams, scallops, and three different dipping sauces. Garnishing the tower were lemon slices, edible flowers, and lobster heads with their antennae still intact.

"You guys doctors?" It was the redhead at the next table.

Carroll turned. "How did you guess?"

"Because you drink like doctors. You must be here for the pain management conference."

"Just flew in from Kalamazoo. Allow me to introduce myself. I'm Doctor Carroll. These are my colleagues, Dr. Michael and Dr. Wallace. We've come seeking cures to the common appetite, starting with the grape."

"You know Valvular?"

"Stuff that keeps your heart clean?" added her friend.

"We sell it," said the redhead.

"Affairs of the heart," Carroll said. "My specialty."

"You guys cardiologists?" The ladies pulled their chairs over.

"Except him." Carroll indicated Wallace. "He's an imposter. Plays one on TV."

Carroll put a hand in the air and called for two more champagne flutes.

"Really?" the redhead said to Wallace. "You're on TV?"

"Try some of this," Carroll said, pouring champagne. "This should manage your pain nicely."

"You look familiar," the redhead said to Wallace. "I think I've seen your show."

Her friend was trying to make conversation with Michael. "Hypertrophic cardiomyopathy? HCM?"

Michael's eyes were glassy. He was already on his second vodka martini.

"Atrial fibrillation?" the girl tried again. "Angina pectoris?"

Michael finally looked at her. "Sounds serious."

"Duh, like, it's a heart attack." She turned to the redhead. "I don't think they're doctors."

"You guys are hilarious," the redhead said to Carroll. "Who are you?"

"I'm the one your mother warned you about," Carroll said.

More plates of hors d'oeuvres materialized out of thin air: calamari, beef carpaccio, grilled artichokes.

"You're surprised," Michael said to Wallace.

"I just didn't realize he was already on the payroll."

"Think of it as bringing in a hired gun. I had to move fast. He had another offer on the table."

Wallace studied the lobster heads on ice. Carroll Quinn had their same eyes—beady, black, and furtive. A man with an agenda. He told Wallace he'd held senior management positions with prominent life insurance companies around the country, but to Wallace they all sounded second-tier and suspect: Bankers and Farmers This, Life and Casualty That, Scoundrels Running Amok in the South. The Boston insurer Carroll had just left was large but bleeding. In his rush to bring his friend aboard, Michael had dispensed with reference checks.

Carroll called for the cocktail waitress to bring more champagne. Wallace pictured him as a lobster of considerable weight, a crustacean with a Rolodex, directing the lowly coelenterate to fetch him a canister of frothy sea foam. He was surrounded by two sultry sea stars, his sharp antennae swaying above his head, a pink claw clutching the wine list.

"Wait and see," Michael was saying. "He's going to make a huge difference in this company."

"You said a Maserati?" the brunette interrupted, striking up a conversation with Michael.

Carroll invited the two pharmaceutical reps to stay for dinner. He was doing well with the redhead. He asked the name of her hotel. She laughed and gave him her card.

Wallace got up and went to the bar.

"Your nag's asleep," the bartender said. The horse's back was dressed with chef's towels.

"Scotch and soda," Wallace said. "Make it a double."

Wallace sat alone at the bar, nursing his drink. It seemed the more he drank, the glummer he got. There was a time in his life he would have mocked the restaurant owner's insanity. He kept staring at the dimly lit painting on the wall. The nude in the picture could have been Lenore: wheat-colored hair, seductive eyes, a graceful neck.

"Got a pay phone?" he asked the bartender.

"Next to the restrooms."

Wallace's only thought was that he had to talk to Lenore. He wanted to tell her everything: that the job offer was a fait accompli; the personal dirt he'd gleaned on Carroll Quinn: three-times divorced, estranged from his children, a dinosaur on the technology front. Wallace fleetingly imagined Lenore would agree to meet him later, for a drink.

The pay phone was in a dark alcove. The walls were cluttered with black-and-white photos of ancient celebrities. Wallace dialed Lenore at home. The line was ringing when Carroll, drunk, came around the corner. He was on his way to the men's room.

"There you are, old boy. Take this." He was inexplicably trying to pass Wallace a salt shaker.

"Why would I want that?"

"Put it on your desk—"

Lenore picked up. "Hello?"

Carroll was pressing the salt shaker into Wallace's palm.

"You and me. We're going to work together like salt and pepper."

"Hello?" Lenore said again.

"You're the fountainhead, the visionary," Carroll said, gripping Wallace's hand. "I'm your bricklayer. We're gonna' do great things here … "

Wallace hung up the phone.

In the cocktail lounge the Seafood Sampler had dwindled to ice and flowers. The lobster heads, willing spectators in front-row seats, listened as the conversation ebbed and flowed, from sales strategy to venture capital, from alcohol-fueled double entendres to bawdy jokes, from software architecture problems at Cal Max to the long list of open-bar events at the pain management conference. It turned into a good party. With their come-ons, the Valvular girls pulled at the men like a steady rip current.

The lobsters on the seafood tower kept an especially close eye on Carroll Quinn.

He was their brother who'd made it to the other side.

CHAPTER NINETEEN

Sanjay and his engineering group finally delivered the software patch to Cal Max on the night of December 9, twenty days after the infamous meeting known to company insiders as, simply, the *rickshaw* meeting. Peg Brown was appeased, Lenore was hopeful, and Michael was in good spirits.

Magnanimity was in the air.

Carroll Quinn bought a Peugeot road bike, aspiring to assimilate to the California lifestyle. He used it to commute from his rented hotel room to the office. He ditched his expensive, double-breasted suits in favor of black, snug-fitting cycling shorts and luminescent jerseys imprinted with bold graphics of European brands: Nokia, Perrier, Porsche, Gucci. "Can you get one in Asti Spumanti?" Wallace asked, smiling as he closed the door on Carroll's meeting with Charlie Dye, who looked like he wanted to jump out of his skin.

In the end everything worked out: Carroll ordered Charlie's badge reinstated, and Charlie went about cold-calling Blue Cross plans with a newfound enthusiasm.

The only cloud hanging over the company was the money situation. According to Otto, they were quickly running out of cash. Trek Reese, their best hope for an infusion of capital, was being nonresponsive. A payroll was right around the corner, year-end bonuses were coming due, and Otto still didn't know how they were going to pay for the Christmas party, less than ten days away. It took some doing for Otto to convince Wallace and Michael that the company was on the brink of a crisis. The only solution, he maintained, was for the owners to go back to the well—that is, to put in more cash.

Michael had a big position in equities, and, for him, that meant having to sell off some of his blue-chip stocks. The consequence of a stock sale was that it triggered a host of taxable, and therefore objectionable, events. For Wallace it meant having to borrow against his house again, and he was loath to do this, not because borrowing against the house to feed a start-up company could ultimately lead to personal financial ruin, but because it meant having to meet and sign papers with his mortgage broker, the insufferable Owen Andersen.

On the second Saturday in December, the storms were lined up one after the other over the Pacific Ocean. A torrent of rain fell on Hannah as she ran from the car to the cover of Dee Dee's Daily Egg to put in her name for a table. It was the rare Saturday morning that Wallace and Hannah didn't have breakfast at Dee Dee's. Addison and Tiffany had grown up in the shabby Naugahyde booths, beneath the wagon wheel chandelier lamps, among the restaurant's mixed bag of customers: eccentric widows, on-call contractors, municipal employees, food-crazed fatties. The portions were generous. A heaping avocado, bacon, and cheese omelet for Wallace, a bran muffin and a bowl of fruit for Hannah, pancakes and sausages for the girls—the family's breakfast order was all but carved in stone.

For Addison and Tiffany, the extended downpour had transformed the strip-center parking lot into a playground of running water and puddles. The girls wore bright yellow rain slickers buttoned to the neck, hoods up, and carried plastic see-through umbrellas stenciled with cartoon characters—presents from Dirk Junior and Baby. Wallace stood under the overhang, watching his daughters. They marched in circles, then up and down the covered walk, their flimsy parasols raised against the waterfalls that flowed from the clogged rain gutters above. Spying an especially deep puddle, they jumped in with both feet and stood looking down, captivated, delighted, as water soaked through their Velcro-fastened sneakers and into their pink socks.

In an effort to coax his girls out of the rain, Wallace gave them a handful of coins and sent them next door to Alice's Liquor to buy a newspaper. It took several tries before they were finally able to drop the right combination of coins into the machine and hold open the heavy glass door long enough to pull out a single copy of the *Escondido News-Journal*. It was the only newspaper Wallace would read all week; he'd terminated his home subscription years earlier, exasperated with the trickle of hard news versus the massive, weekly effort of recycling an avalanche of newsprint. He didn't need back problems at forty. He could get the state of the world from radio.

Hannah came out of the restaurant and called to Wallace that their table was ready. She saw the girls' wet shoes and made a face— the correlation between damp feet and catching cold was an ongoing disagreement in their marriage—but for once she let it pass.

"Let's just go inside and eat," she said.

The restaurant was packed with people. The windows were fogged. The air was thick with the smell of bacon cooking. Wallace helped the girls hang their rain gear on the wooden coat rack. The waitress, one of Dee Dee's daughters—this one had purple hair and piercings in her eyebrows—looked hungover and took a long time getting to their table. She seemed mildly perturbed when Hannah asked her to bring two hot teas, with lemon and cinnamon, for the girls, to stave off flu.

Wallace ripped through the newspaper, discarding whole sections at a time.

"What are you doing to that poor paper?" Hannah asked.

"I want to see if it's going to keep raining."

"What do you care if it keeps raining?"

Wallace was trying to concentrate on the paper. "It's of interest to me."

"It's not like you're a farmer. It's not like you go outside."

"I go outside," Wallace said. "By the way, what was your mother doing last night? Was she shopping?"

"I don't think so. Why?"

Wallace showed Hannah a picture in the newspaper. A car had plunged backward into the San Diego River. "Look. Right in the river."

"Very funny." Hannah was headed to Mission Valley to do some shopping of her own. She needed a dress for the Merksamer Digital Christmas party. It was a formal affair. Wallace was taking the girls for the day.

"Whoever it was," Wallace said, "she must've been in a shopping frenzy."

"What makes you so sure it was a *she?*"

"Because it's always a she. Haven't you noticed? Every Christmas some woman gets in a shopping frenzy and backs her car into the river."

Wallace finally found the weather report. *Good.* More rain was expected, heavy at times through the weekend. Winter storm warnings were in effect. A small-craft advisory had been posted for the open ocean. Wallace read the weather report aloud even though Hannah said she didn't want to hear it. Memories of furious Northern California storms fueled Wallace's love of winter weather—pelting rain, windows rattling against a howling wind, trees down, power outages.

"You sure you want to go to Mission Valley?" Wallace asked. "Shopping's going to be treacherous."

"Shopping's always treacherous." Hannah was stirring sugar into her coffee, leafing casually through a garden wares catalog.

Wallace turned to the *Business* section. Things were on a roll. Economic indicators were positive. Stocks were up. The business editor had unmasked a local Ponzi scheme.

"Ever notice San Diego has more than its share of swindlers?" Wallace said. "I wonder why that is. Must have something to do with the climate."

The girls were coloring on paper place mats.

"Daddy, why do you like the rain so much?" Addison asked.

"Yes, Daddy," Tiffany said. "Why do you always talk about the rain?" She was up on her knees in the booth, her face pressed close to the table, intent on the tip of her crayon.

"Your mom and I had our first kiss in the rain," Wallace said. "At least I think it was your mom."

"Oh my goodness," Hannah said. "Look who just walked in the door."

Owen Andersen was stripping off the hood of his rain-soaked poncho. Were it not for his clean-shaven face and milky complexion, you'd have thought a baboon had walked into the restaurant, if baboons wore sandals and silk slacks and walked stiffly, shoulders slightly behind heels, carrying thick mailing envelopes stuffed with loan documents.

"There you guys are," Owen said, finding Wallace and Hannah in the booth. "Mind if I sit?" He shed the poncho, pulling it over his head.

"What's with the Birkenstocks, Owen?" Wallace asked. "I always thought you were a die-hard saddle shoe guy."

"I'm trying not to restrict my circulation too much."

"In that case the Sansabelts are probably a good choice."

"Armani," Owen said. "Without the belt. Hello, Hannah."

"You might try going a little longer on the inseam," Wallace said to Owen. "I could see your ankles from across the restaurant."

"I'll be sure and mention it to my tailor next time I'm in Little Hong Kong." With his right foot Owen worked the poncho under the booth. "Ouch. That's hell on the big toe. Scoot over, girls."

Addison and Tiffany shifted obligingly in the booth. Owen slid in next to them. He placed the thick envelope on the table.

"Don't you want to know why I'm smiling?" Owen asked.

"You don't look to me like you're smiling," Wallace said.

"Trust me. On the inside."

"What's wrong with your toe?" Hannah asked, glancing under the table.

Owen winced, as if visited suddenly by a stabbing pain. "Fact is, I've got some health issues."

"If it's about your teeth Hannah can recommend a good dentist," Wallace said.

Owen drummed his knuckles on the table and looked distractedly across the dining room. "I wrenched my back delivering Christmas trees, went in for a muscle relaxant, Doc didn't like what he saw. He's running some tests." Owen appeared unnerved by Dee Dee's clientele—at the next table was a fat one in overalls, eating biscuits and gravy. "Is this place safe?"

"Perfectly," Wallace said.

"My doctor thinks it's either gout or Lyme disease."

"Sounds serious," Hannah said.

Owen abruptly perked up—one who didn't want to let on to the world that he felt supremely sorry for himself. "What the hell," he said, forcing a smile. "We're all gonna' die. Here, girls. Take these." He laid two green suckers on the table.

Addison and Tiffany glanced at the candy and went back to drawing.

"You wouldn't believe the morons they got ringing bells in front of grocery stores these days," Owen said. "Give 'em a penny and they give you back a five-cent sucker. No wonder they call it a not-for-profit."

"You ripped off the Salvation Army for two suckers?" Wallace asked.

"Hey, the Lord helps those who help themselves." Owen looked down at Tiffany's place mat. "That's a very scary picture you're drawing. Is it people caught in a storm?"

"It's Jesus getting even with liars," Tiffany said.

Owen blinked once at the picture and looked quickly away.

"I thought you could cure gout just by taking vitamin C," Hannah said.

"That's scurvy," Owen said. "Gout's a lifestyle affliction. Too much rich food—surf 'n' turf and expensive cabernets."

"Tell me, Owen," Wallace asked, "how would a bon vivant like you get Lyme disease?"

"I was bow hunting near Weaverville," Owen said. "The deer up there are infested with black-legged ticks."

"Bow hunting?" Wallace asked. "What's a deer ever done to you?"

"Check out Leviticus," Owen said, smiling at Hannah. "It's all the moral authority I need."

"Only forest rangers should be allowed to kill animals," Addison said.

Owen looked at her. "Hey, I eat what I kill."

"Yuck!" Addison said.

Hannah looked up from her catalog. "Nice breakfast conversation. Can we change the subject?"

The waitress brought tea. When she saw Owen she did a double take. "You staying? You eating?"

Owen seemed insulted. "I'll stay but I won't eat. Bring me bottled water, with gas."

"Bottled gas water?" The waitress looked at Wallace. "Is he making a joke?"

"Just bring him regular tap water," Wallace said.

Owen groused at having to drink local water. "You know, fish crap in that stuff all day long."

Tiffany was coloring with a crayon called Fire Engine Red. She was firmly filling in the face of a liar. "Two hells and a crap. You owe us three dollars."

"Sweetheart, I just gave you a nice sucker."

"Five cents. Big deal."

"Are any of these diseases contagious?" Wallace asked. "Shouldn't a guy like you be in quarantine?"

"Nothing to worry about," Owen said. He couldn't take his eyes off Hannah sipping her coffee. "Worst case, my extremities will puff up and I'll start to bleed from every orifice. Then my heart will seize and I'll die with bulging eyes."

Hannah pulled the coffee cup away from her mouth and swallowed hard.

"Hear that, girls?" Wallace said. "If you see something start to happen, eat fast."

Owen futzed impatiently with the envelope. "So folks, what's it going to be? Take care of today first or take care of tomorrow?"

"Let's start with today," Wallace said.

Hannah looked suspiciously from Wallace to Owen.

"Didn't he tell you?" Owen asked. "Your husband and I had an appointment this morning."

"Owen said he had something he wanted to run past us," Wallace said.

"That's right, you both strike me as smart business people," Owen said. "Also I need you to sign some papers."

"What kind of papers?" Hannah asked.

"All I can say is you're lucky I specialize in bad credit," Owen said.

"What papers?" Hannah asked, turning to Wallace.

"Your husband's refinancing the house again," Owen said. "I don't know if it's because his business is out of cash or because he got arrested and has an expensive defense to mount—"

Hannah interrupted. "Owen!"

"Because in this day and age you pretty much get the justice you pay for."

"Owen, stop." Hannah widened her eyes and glanced at Addison and Tiffany.

"Oh, don't worry about them," Owen said. "Kids don't pay any attention to adult conversation, do you girls?"

Neither child answered; each was lost in her own world, coloring.

"By the way, is impersonating a police officer a felony or a misdemeanor?" Owen asked, turning to Wallace. "Because if it's a felony and you get sent up the river for a long time, I might consider asking out your wife. Strictly platonic, of course."

"That would be up to her," Wallace said. "But to answer your question it's a misdemeanor."

"I can't say as I understand the thrill of writing old ladies parking tickets," Owen said. "But oh well."

"I wasn't writing old ladies parking tickets," Wallace said. "My lawyer wants to file a lawsuit. He thinks we have cause for a civil action."

"I despise lawyers," Owen said.

Hannah turned to Wallace. "Why are we refinancing the house again?"

"A bridge loan," Wallace said. "Until the venture money comes through."

"Is this smart?" Hannah looked at Owen.

"I wouldn't do it," Owen said. "I like a good solid mutual fund, myself."

He watched Hannah closely. She put a hand to her forehead and sighed.

"I asked for a loan, not an opinion," Wallace said. "What does it take to make this thing happen?"

"You still haven't asked me why I'm smiling," Owen said.

"I really don't care," Wallace said.

"For the first time in my life I can look forward to being financially secure. Did you know home-based businesses are the fastest-growing segment of the U.S. economy?"

"Oh, god," Wallace said. "Owen's got a pyramid scheme."

"Not a pyramid scheme," Owen said. "A system with which to gain complete financial independence. A business opportunity unlike anything I've ever seen."

"What's wrong, Owen? Brokering mortgages ain't what it used to be?"

"Hey, I was treading water just like the two of you. Then I came across this opportunity and realized there really can be a light at the end of the tunnel. And it doesn't have to be from an oncoming train."

Owen was interrupted by the arrival of the food. He eyed Wallace's eggs skeptically.

"Sure you won't eat?" Hannah asked.

"You kidding?" Owen said. "I wouldn't touch that stuff any more than I'd be drawing down the equity on my home. These dumps are breeding grounds for salmonella."

Hannah picked tentatively at her fruit with the tip of her fork. She found browning around the edges of her cantaloupe and mold on her strawberries. She pushed the fruit bowl away.

Wallace said, "Do me a favor, Owen, and pass the salt."

"The favor is getting you in on the ground floor," Owen said. "Picture the downstream marketing organization you could build simply by daisy-chaining every Presbyterian congregation in the country. Church leaders are standing behind it, and it's already passed a series of strict government tests so it's perfectly legal. You watch. These guys'll make Amway look like pikers."

"Sounds to me like money-changing in the Temple," Wallace said.

"You must not have gotten the word: prosperity is your divine right."

"I'm not interested."

"I was thinking more of Hannah," Owen said. "The bylaws of this company are very strict. We'd have a hard time getting you in, with your criminal background and all."

"You're saying they wouldn't take me?"

"I'm saying your wife is perfect," Owen said. "Flying all over the country, always meeting new people. A beautiful smile—"

"She works too much as it is," Wallace said.

"A little extra income can take the pressure off a struggling household," Owen said.

"Who says we're struggling?" Wallace asked.

"Don't look at me," Hannah said.

Owen spilled out the contents of the envelope. "Your corpus is going in financial reverse, and I've got the papers to prove it." He held up a piece of paper and made a disapproving face. "By the way, three thousand dollars to the Four Gospels Theological Seminary? Is that wise for a man in your financial condition?"

Hannah looked at Wallace.

"Forget it," Wallace said. "It's not important."

"Wallace, tell me—"

"I bought a copier."

"A very expensive copier," Owen said.

Hannah had an incredulous look on her face. "Three thousand dollars?"

"It's a long story," Wallace said.

"Proves my point," Owen said to Hannah. "You need to control your own financial destiny. Here's the pitch: It's called Acres of Money, a discount buying club. They're in the process of building direct relationships with every major manufacturer in the country. Furniture, flooring, prime meats, exercise equipment. People I know are already replacing their full-time incomes, making five, ten grand their first month—"

"That's bull," Wallace said.

"They're adding new lines every week," Owen continued. "What manufacturer would say no to what in essence is a religious charity?"

"I don't know about the manufacturers," Wallace said, "but I'm saying no."

"Hannah was right," Owen said. "You are hostile and quick to judge."

"Why, you already talked to her about this?"

"I may have mentioned it the other day," Owen said, "while I was reformatting her hard drive."

"It does sound intriguing," Hannah said. "If you can really make that kind of money."

"It's phony-baloney," Wallace said. "Smoke and mirrors."

"There's a sales rally and induction meeting in Mission Valley this afternoon," Owen said to Hannah. "I was hoping you could come. I'll get a free microwave."

"You're shameless," Wallace said.

"I happen to be headed that way," Hannah said.

"Look, Owen, Hannah can do whatever she wants," Wallace said. "But we're not joining your multilevel marketing club."

Owen took a sip of water and winced. "In that case I hope you saved room to eat crow. Because no lender wanted to touch this one."

"What are you saying? We didn't get the loan?"

Owen picked out another sheet of paper from the stack of documents—a letter. "I'm saying your equity is tapped out, the financials on your company are upside down, and Hannah's airline is on the brink of bankruptcy. It took a miracle to get a loan commitment, but here it is." He presented the letter to Wallace. "Meet your new lender: Acres of Money. So happens second mortgages is their newest line of business—low interest rate to start, fully adjustable. The catch is you have to be a member to qualify."

"In other words you're extorting us into joining your pyramid scheme?"

"One day when your wife is grocery shopping in a mink and pearls, you'll thank me."

Hannah said, "If I'm ever grocery shopping in a mink and pearls just shoot me."

Owen turned his attention to another document in the stack, this one a long, preprinted form. He held it up like a lawyer presenting an exhibit in a courtroom. Wallace recognized the legal-size page as a crude summary of assets and liabilities—a hack's version of a personal balance sheet.

"A question," Owen said. "The Able Quaker Money Market fund—what happened to it?"

Here we go, Wallace thought. *The genie's out of the bottle.*

It was too late to kill Owen with a butter knife, and the heavy silver napkin holder was out of reach. Wallace couldn't use it to bludgeon Owen's skull.

Hannah turned to Wallace. "Dad's college fund for the girls?"

"So where'd it go?" Owen asked. "You don't show it anywhere on this current statement."

Wallace pointed to a line on the balance sheet. "Right there. The Merksamer Digital note."

"A promissory note?" Owen asked. "Oh my dear Lord. Don't tell me you lent the kids' college money to your own company!"

Wallace took a sip of coffee. "The important thing is it's still an asset."

He was unprepared for Hannah's sudden hand slap, which hit him hard and sharp across the face. It sent his coffee flying. He saw white. For a moment the scene in the restaurant was a surreal haze.

When Wallace's vision cleared, he discovered he was still seated in the booth, but everything seemed to be moving in slow motion. Owen faced him, holding the paper, his mouth twisted in a self-satisfied smirk. Addison and Tiffany looked on, stunned. People in the restaurant were staring.

Hannah stood, tears gathering in her eyes. "I don't ... I can't believe this—"

"Hannah—"

"I'm finished. I need air." She grabbed her purse and hurried for the door.

Somewhere a utensil hit a plate—it was the only sound in the restaurant.

Tiffany wanted to go with her mother, but Wallace ordered her to stay put. She put her head down and sobbed into the sleeve of her knitted wool sweater—a handmade gift from her grandmother.

Addison reached over and pinched a sausage from her sister's plate. "Don't worry, Dad. I can skip college and go straight to work at Sea World."

"I'm curious about that Cadillac you drive," Owen said to Wallace. "That thing leak a lot of oil?"

"Shut up, Owen. Pass the ketchup."

It was a different Hannah, composed and collected, who returned to the table. Her hair was tangled from walking in the rain.

"I've been thinking, Owen," she said. "I'd like to keep my daughters in private school, no matter what. And I'd be a fool not to control my own fate. When you get right down to it, one really doesn't know what's around the corner, does one?"

"Nope," Owen said, "one does not."

"Maybe after the meeting we could grab a decent bite to eat. There's that little place on Coronado, with the view of the bay. Surely, Owen, you remember that place?"

"I remember the room service," Owen said.

"All right, that's enough," Wallace said. "Can we just deal with the papers?"

It was an imposing stack of documents. Hardly a word was spoken. Owen seemed relieved when the last page was signed; he quickly took the papers and forced them back into the envelope.

"My office will be in touch about the notary thing," he said, climbing out of the booth. "Girls, would one of you be so kind as to hand me my rain jacket off the floor? I'm in no condition to bend over."

As Owen wriggled into his poncho, Hannah stood and kissed Addison and Tiffany good-bye on the tops of their heads.

"Don't wait up," Hannah said to Wallace.

She left with Owen.

The waitress came by with a coffee pot. She stared at the red welt on Wallace's cheekbone.

"You want ice for that?"

"No," Wallace said, "but I'll take another shot of coffee."

The girls were busy coloring again.

"I don't like Uncle Owen," Tiffany said. "He uses bad language."

"He brags," Addison said. "All he talks about is money."

"Some men are like that, girls," Wallace said. "They're scavengers by nature, and they're always looking for a shipwreck."

"If he's so rich he should buy his own ship," Addison said.

"Exactly," Wallace agreed.

CHAPTER TWENTY

The sound of rain pelting the roof of the shadowy garage; the dank smell of the wood that undergirded the layout; the picture in his mind of the Northern Sierra Nevada rail line crossing the granite faces of the Feather River Canyon; the details of the orange and silver diesel locomotives that took you back in time, back aboard the California Zephyr, riding in the hushed luxury of a vista-dome lounge—these were the things that brought Wallace comfort, and for several hours he was lost laying track for a mountain loop.

"Dad, Grandma called," Addison said, standing in the doorway. "She left a message on the answering machine."

Wallace hadn't even heard the phone ring. "What did she say?"

"She needs Mom's Crock-Pot for the ladies' auxiliary lunch. She's coming by to pick it up."

Suddenly Wallace had the irresistible urge to add a string of stainless steel passenger cars, some with dome lounges, to his collection. He left the Crock-Pot on the porch, loaded Addison and Tiffany into the car, and headed for the train store across town.

Wallace bought most of his model railroad things at Duncan's Junction, a poor man's hobby shop with inadequate lighting, irregular flooring, and a second-rate inventory. The store was located in the industrial part of town, in the north-facing suite of a tin-roofed building that had once housed an ice factory. Donald Duncan was the store's sole proprietor. He was gangly, middle-aged, and had a distinct overbite—a self-avowed railfan who wore an engineer's cap and spent most of his days perched behind the counter like a rangy bird.

In the teeming rain, Wallace and his girls picked their way through the muddy parking lot. A red wrecker was parked blocking the entrance to the store, and Wallace and his girls had to circumnavigate the old truck to reach the door—no easy task given the magnitude of the puddles and the depth of the slop. The spokes of Addison's and Tiffany's cartoon umbrellas caught in the rusted chains and crossbars of the wrecker.

"I've already called the police on that truck," Donald Duncan said when Wallace and his girls entered the store. "Those *amigos* next door need to be taught a lesson."

"That's all right," Wallace said, directing Addison and Tiffany to set their wet things on the floor. "But if this rain keeps up you might want to dredge the parking lot for customers."

"Why? You have to park a long way out?"

"El Centro, I think," Wallace said.

Donald blanched. He was a co-tenant in the old ice factory building with Gonzalez Brothers Street Rods, and the still-life parade of junk cars in the gravel lot—stripped, on blocks, hoods up, windows accumulating grime—was a constant source of irritation to him. Wallace couldn't remember a time he had been in the store when Donald Duncan hadn't complained about the auto shop.

"I see you brought a couple modelers with you," Donald said to Wallace. "This hobby could use some new blood."

A fat man was leaning against the counter, having a solemn conversation with Donald. Wallace had seen the man in Duncan's Junction before. He had thinning hair, a meager mustache, and the alert stare of a small game animal. His ragged wool sweater hung like a tarpaulin over his hips. He eyed Wallace and the girls closely, wiping the back of his neck with a soggy handkerchief.

Addison and Tiffany had become enthralled with a life-size crossing signal that alerted whenever they stood in front of it and waved
their arms. The warning lights flashed and the bells sounded. After
several iterations of this, Wallace put a stop to it.

"Please, girls. You'll give these poor people headaches."

"Oh, they're all right," Donald said. "They can't hurt anything.
What is it you're looking for? Anything in particular?"

"Just browsing," Wallace said. "Hiding out, actually. I like the
crossbuck. Is it real?"

"Real but not for sale," said Donald. "If it was, I could have sold
it ten times over by now. That's a motion detector it's got in there."

"Very slick."

The fat one at the counter continued to stare numbly at Wallace.

"If you get serious about anything, let me know," Donald said.

Wallace and his girls had to step around plastic buckets strategi-
cally placed in the aisles to catch rain that dripped from the clerestory
windows in the roof high above the old warehouse.

Duncan's Junction was arranged like most of the model train
stores Wallace had been in: stacked boxes of rolling stock in the center
shelves; tracks and turnouts along one wall; paint, scenery, and plastic building kits along the other. Across the back wall were shelves of
dust-covered train literature and modeling how-to books. The power
packs, specialty tools, and locomotives were locked under glass at the
front of the store.

First, Wallace took Addison and Tiffany to look at building kits.
It was standard practice on trips to the train store that each girl got to
add something new to the layout. Addison chose a rural hospital with
a helipad, reasoning that mountain railroading was a dangerous profession and there would be a need for medical services. Wallace scrutinized the unoccupied helipad in the picture on the box.

"Don't worry, Dad," Addison said. "We'll get the kind of helicopter that doesn't crash."

Tiffany picked out a country church, saying she wanted to make
certain all the little plastic townspeople could get to heaven.

"You think going to church is the only way to get to heaven?"
Wallace asked.

"Yes. Unless you go to college."

There was a sudden flash of lightning, an earsplitting clap of thunder, and then the unmistakable drum of hailstones on the roof. The intensity of the storm frightened Addison and Tiffany into holding hands and staying close to their father.

"Don't worry, girls," Wallace said. "Nothing can hurt you."

They moved next to the rolling-stock aisle, where Wallace began pulling coach, sleeper, and vista-dome observation cars—all painted in the distinctive silver California Zephyr scheme—from the shelves. Duncan's Junction didn't have shopping carts, and Wallace had to stack the boxes on the floor.

Tiffany plopped down in the middle of the aisle and intently studied the picture on the front of her building kit. It was the kind of church found in small New England towns—narrow with white clapboard siding and a high steeple.

"Daddy, if a bad man goes to church, will he still go to heaven?"

"I don't know, Tiff," Wallace said. "Why do you ask?" With his daughters he had learned to buy time where religious issues were concerned; the teachers at the Christian school would often arm them with biblical questions that would snare him like bear traps.

"Because people who kill animals are mean."

"It's not like God's a schoolteacher who takes attendance," Wallace said. "He sees inside your heart."

"I thought you didn't believe in God," Tiffany said.

"What makes you say that?"

"Grandma says you don't."

"Of course I believe in God," Wallace said. "How could I not believe in someone who's given me such perfect gifts as you and your sister?" His words were drowned out by the prolonged blast of a car engine racing.

As the noise subsided, Wallace heard someone call his name.

"Wallace Noe! I thought that was you!" Pastor Maltby from the Hidden Valley Presbyterian Church came up the aisle with an outstretched hand. "What brings you out on a day like this?"

Wallace hated running into people he knew in train stores. It was embarrassing to be associated with the hobby of model railroading—the odd ducks and misfits.

"Been one of those weeks," Wallace said. "I needed a break."

"I know what you mean," Pastor Maltby said. "I needed a little sanctuary myself. My organ has a short and my choir director's being a pill." He turned to Addison and Tiffany. "Aren't you girls lucky to be out with your father today? Do you remember me? I was with your grandmother the day she picked you up from school. Do you remember that?"

The girls clung to Wallace and didn't answer.

"Oh, they're just being shy," Pastor Maltby said. "Or maybe it's the storm. Did you girls hear the thunder?"

"I think we all did," Wallace said.

"Yes we did, didn't we?" Pastor Maltby said, still looking at Addison and Tiffany. "It was very loud, wasn't it? Yes it was. Which one of you girls likes trains?"

"I like horses," Tiffany said.

Pastor Maltby said, "You like *horses!* Yes. Horses are nice animals, aren't they?" He put on his reading glasses and peered at the boxes the girls were holding. "And what have you got there, can you show me?"

Addison and Tiffany showed him their building kits.

"Ah, yes. Even in our perfect little railroad towns there's always the need for healing. Did you know God is sometimes called the *Great Physician?*"

"This morning our mom slapped our dad for stealing our college money," Tiffany said.

Pastor Maltby looked at Wallace gravely.

Wallace said, "Who'd expect a flight attendant to interpret a balance sheet?"

"Oh, but your mom is a nice lady," Pastor Maltby said, turning back to the girls. "Where is she today?"

"She went with Uncle Owen," Addison said.

"She's going to be rich," Tiffany said.

"Don't tell me." Pastor Maltby turned to Wallace and made a sour face. "That Acres of Money thing?"

"You don't approve?" Wallace asked.

"God's interested in character, not shameless cash. No wonder the whole country's turning Baptist. Listen to me. I sound like my choir director. I have a confession to make. Would you like to hear it?"

"Maybe not with the children—"

"I'm hopelessly in love. I sent poor Mrs. Maltby shopping just so I could come over and sneak a peek at her."

"Her?"

"I'm talking about that Big Boy up front. I'd take her home with me but I'm afraid Mrs. Maltby would have my head."

Wallace looked at the Presbyterian minister, shocked.

"The Rivarossi," Pastor Maltby said. "Don't tell me you haven't seen it?"

Wallace had no idea what a Rivarossi was.

Pastor Maltby said, "Come. Take a look."

With arms full of merchandise, Wallace and the girls followed the Presbyterian minister to the front of the store, where the fat one was still having his guarded exchange with Donald Duncan. Their conversation ended abruptly as Wallace and Pastor Maltby approached the counter.

"There she is," Pastor Maltby said, pointing out a model steam locomotive locked under glass. It was a magnificent model—a black and silver Rivarossi with a Union Pacific shield beneath the headlight.

"What say you, Pastor?" Donald asked. "This the day you're finally gonna' do it?"

"Oh no, not me. I have absolutely no right to have her."

"Here, let me at least take her out for you."

"Don't bother."

"I insist. For you, I'm taking her out." Donald unlocked the glass door and took out the model. He set it ceremoniously on the counter. "There she is. The Big Boy in all her splendor."

Pastor Maltby leaned toward the model. "She's a jim-dandy. Just a jim-dandy."

The fat one swabbed the back of his neck with the handkerchief. "That one there? That's a superb model. Very accurate. Nice grab irons and piping."

"I have a feeling today just might be the day," Donald winked. "How about it, Pastor? Treat yourself to an early Christmas present?"

"No," Pastor Maltby said. "I can't do it, not this time of year. That buys a lot of clothes for the orphanage."

Donald turned to Wallace with a hint of impatience. "What about you? Don't tell me you're saving it for the orphans, too?"

"Now I'm feeling guilty," Wallace said, looking at all his train cars.

"I've got my own charity to worry about," Donald said. "Put that stuff up here."

When Wallace stacked his Zephyr cars next to the cash register, the fat one crinkled his eyes and shook his head.

"Bad idea."

Wallace looked at him. "It is?"

"Carson, I'll thank you to mind your own beeswax," Donald said.

"I'm talking car swing," the fat one said. "You kidding? Those couplers? Unless your curves have a radius the size of Texas."

"What do you suggest?" Pastor Maltby asked.

"An exorcist. You'll need him for the derailments."

"Now Carson, there's nothing wrong with those couplers," Donald said. "Maybe Pastor and his friend, here, would like to hear about the new model railroading club. Why don't you tell them while I ring up the sale?"

Already Wallace didn't like where this was headed—two membership pitches in one day.

"No thanks." Wallace was taking out a credit card.

The fat one, named Carson, looked at Wallace. "Is that an extra?" He reached brazenly into the fold of Wallace's open wallet and helped himself to a business card. "Wow. Merksamer Digital. We could use a computer expert."

"Not me. I'm on the marketing side."

"Better yet. When's a good time to call?"

"I travel a lot."

They were interrupted by another blast of a car engine—the throaty roar of a hot rod running at full throttle without a muffler. The walls shook. Carson mopped his forehead with the handkerchief, waiting for the noise to subside.

"Well, here's about the club," he said. "Donald's giving us space in back for a thirty-five by one hundred bench. Santa Fe. El Cajon Pass. Number eight minimum turnouts on the mains, one percent grade, max. That's in stone. No traction. No high-speed electric. No other gauges without a supermajority vote from membership." Carson shut his eyes tightly, as if trying to suppress a painful memory. "I won't make that mistake again." He turned to Wallace. "You've got voice mail? You'll get my message if I call?"

"I'm really not interested."

"Here's what I'm thinking. Maybe I could stop by sometime. Pick your brain about marketing. I'm thinking one-color tri-fold, fit in a number ten envelope. Maybe borrow a meeting room while Donald gets his sublease agreement worked out with the *Cinco de Mayo* parade next door."

"Our conference rooms are pretty busy."

"Just an organizational meeting or two. We promise not to lay any track."

The crossing signal sprang to life as two Escondido policemen walked in the door. Wallace immediately recognized the older of the two: Sergeant Fernandez. A bulletproof vest bulged conspicuously under his uniform shirt, making him look like a walking armadillo. He hung near the door, taking in the sights of the store's peculiar inventory.

The second officer, much younger, approached the counter.

"You called about the tow truck?" he asked. The wire of a radio earpiece wriggled up the back of his ear. He pulled a notepad and a pen from his shirt pocket.

"Yes," said Donald. "He's an impertinent Taco who refuses to respect my side of the property line. He parked that truck blocking my door with malice and aforethought, and he needs to be put in jail."

"Hold it, hold it," the policeman said, opening his notepad. "You said *Taco?*"

Across the store, Ernie Fernandez fixed his curious gaze on Wallace.

Donald Duncan gave the younger officer a detailed account of his running dispute with the Gonzalez Brothers, starting with the junkers taking over the parking lot and the recurring, unbearable noise. Now there was the defiantly-parked tow truck. As if on cue, a car engine revved.

"See what I mean?" Donald asked. "A plague on my commerce. We're having a civil war and he means to drive me out of business."

"Say he parked that truck there on purpose?"

"He's a sociopath who needs to be put in his place."

The younger officer stepped away from the counter. He conferred in a low voice with Ernie Fernandez, who shook his head.

"Here's the deal," said the younger officer, returning to the counter. "We can't make him move that truck. It's private property. There's no vehicle code violation, no public sidewalk."

"You've got to be joking," Donald said. "He's blocking my door!"

"It's a civil issue. Try getting a restraining order. Or ask your landlord to build you a fence."

Ernie took a step toward the counter. "Look, we can draw an imaginary line in the dirt, but that don't mean he'll respect it."

Carson said to Donald, "He respects it any less and you'll be selling tamales instead of tank cars."

"We can try talking to him, if you want," Ernie said.

"I want you to beat him with a rubber hose," Donald said. "I want you to put him in the gas chamber."

"What's this character's name again?" Ernie asked.

"Refugio."

Ernie said to the younger officer, "Go next door and talk to this bandit Refugio. See if you can get him to move the truck."

The crossbuck alerted as the younger officer left the store.

Ernie sidled up to Wallace, this thumbs hooked in his gun belt. "Innocent bystander, or do you play a role in this nefarious tow truck caper?"

"Just getting out of the rain," Wallace said. "Girls, say hello to Sergeant Fernandez."

"These your daughters? Thought maybe they were two supermodels passing through on their way to Hollywood."

Addison and Tiffany hid behind their father's legs.

Ernie said, "I spent a lifetime collecting wives and horses, and it's brought me nothing but grief. Maybe I should try electric trains."

Tiffany said, "One time my dad fell asleep and burned all the meat on the barbecue."

Ernie grinned at Wallace. "Always a pleasure to see them at this age before they sprout the fangs and claws."

"Been with the department long?" Pastor Maltby asked, making small talk.

"I been with this department too long."

"Your chief and I are in Rotary together," Pastor Maltby said. "We've had some interesting conversations on the challenges of juvenile reform. All these flavor-of-the-month programs, all this talk of self-esteem. It's unnecessary, like teaching a Chinese how to run a restaurant. These kids today are more self-absorbed than a pack of wild coyotes."

"Gang bangers and graffiti artists," Ernie said. "Little bastards should be horsewhipped in the public square, if you ask me."

Pastor Maltby said, "I've got my own idea for a program. I'd put them to work building model railroads. Consider the psychic benefits of soldering and making dioramas. The capacity to heal is every bit as valid as punching a pillow or painting a sad clown. I say forget rolling old ladies in the parking lot. Let's give 'em Burlington rolling across the heartland!"

The crossing signal came to life as the younger officer returned. With him was a mechanic with long black hair, a flattened nose, and a scar across his face. His forearms were covered with axle grease.

"This is Leobardo," the younger officer announced. "He says Refugio isn't there."

"That true?" Ernie asked the mechanic. "Refugio is gone?"

"Yes."

"You say your name is Leobardo?"

"Yes."

Ernie looked at him mistrustfully. "Then how come your coveralls say Dave?"

"They all say Dave."

"Can you move that truck?"

"Only Refugio has the keys."

"He carry a cell phone?"

"No. I don't think so."

Ernie gave the mechanic an angry stare. "Next time you talk to Refugio, you tell him I want that truck moved. This man is trying to run a business here, and there's an implied property line that needs to be respected. I see that truck parked there again, someone's gonna' regret it, and it's probably gonna' be Refugio, understand?"

"Yes."

"You tell him that."

"Yes."

Ernie sent the mechanic back to work.

"You can keep complaining to your landlord," Ernie said to Donald. "But there's really nothing we can do."

"Appalling," Donald said. He finally finished totaling Wallace's sale. It came to almost three hundred dollars.

Pastor Maltby saw the figure and gasped.

"Something wrong, Pastor?" Donald asked.

"That's a lot of socks and underwear." He turned to Carson. "About these club meetings—what's your policy on women and drinking?"

"I can honestly say we have no prospects for women at this time," Carson said. "And the drinking's all BYOMD."

"BYOMD?"

"Bring your own Mountain Dew."

"Sensible," Pastor Maltby said.

At the door, Wallace held two brown bags brimming with Zephyr cars while Addison and Tiffany collected their rain gear. The crossing signal prattled like a mental patient.

"I'll give you a call at the office," Carson promised Wallace.

Outside, darkness had fallen. On the narrow stoop, Pastor Maltby pinched the collar of his coat closed and prepared to run for his Lincoln Continental. The bright lights in the yard illuminated the falling rain.

"You know, joining that fellow's model railroad club could be a great opportunity to hone your skills," Pastor Maltby said to Wallace. "I have yet to meet the man who can't benefit from fellowship and the pursuit of a good, honest hobby."

"You may be looking at him," Wallace said.

"I wouldn't be so sure. God can still hit a long ball with a crooked bat."

He skirted the old wrecker and ran for his car.

Ernie stepped from the shadows outside the auto shop, where he had been standing under a tattered awning. The black-and-white patrol car was idling in the yard, its parking lots on.

"Kid's in training," Ernie said. "He'll do all right."

"I didn't expect to see you here," Wallace said.

"I'm working overtime to support three wives, a farrier, and a large-animal vet who thinks she's a horse whisperer. This rain's got us running."

Addison and Tiffany were zigzagging their way around the wrecked cars, pretending to be drum majors, making their way to the Cadillac. They used their umbrellas as batons.

"I still work for this department, but I'll give you some friendly advice," Ernie said. "This district attorney's a number one prick. If he offers a deal, take it."

CHAPTER TWENTY-ONE

The return trip home was everything Wallace could have hoped for: rain pounded the windshield, roads were closed, streets were flooded. There were signs of power outages—whole blocks were dark and traffic signals flashed red.

"Girls, I hope you learned a lesson this afternoon," Wallace said.

In the back seat of the car, Addison and Tiffany didn't appear to be listening to him. They were in their own world, making up stories about their unopened building kits.

"What if a dolphin washed up on the beach," Addison was saying, "and they brought it to this hospital and asked the doctor to perform surgery. I was the doctor. I go into the waiting room and ask all the kids to help. They're in chairs, waiting for pink medicine—"

Tiffany said, "I could be one of the kids."

"I tell you to come quickly. We need everyone to help hold down the dolphin for the operation. We have to hurry because she's almost out of breath."

"Uh-oh," Tiffany said.

"Dolphins breathe air just like people," Addison said. "Did you know that?"

"Then what happens?" Tiffany asked.

"The operation is a success, so we rush the dolphin back to the helicopter. I ride with her back to the beach. I'm the only one who can talk to her, in her own language, to tell her everything will be okay."

"Mmm," Tiffany said.

"She tells me all about her family, how she got separated in a storm and hit her head on a rock. We both stay friends, even after I'm famous. We do shows together at Sea World."

"I could hold the fish bucket," Tiffany said.

"Girls, are you even listening to me?" Wallace asked.

"I'm sorry, Dad," Addison said. "What was the lesson?"

"That man with the train store is a renter. He has no power. Even the policemen couldn't help him. But if he owned that building, he could have forced that other man to move the tow truck. That's why we tell you to work hard in school and get good grades. Then you can go to college and get a good job. You can earn enough money to own your own building."

"Do you own the building you work in?"

"I am speaking metaphorically, Addison. I'm talking about taking ownership of your life."

"Why did Pastor Maltby say money isn't important?"

"He was talking about character."

"He said God doesn't care if you're rich."

"Because most people fall short of their full potential," Wallace said. "That's why they need someone like Pastor Maltby. He helps them feel better about their lives, especially when they're disappointed with what they've accomplished or haven't made a lot of money."

"Does that man who owns the train store make a lot of money?"

"I don't think so, Addison. That's probably why they're starting that model railroad club. If I'm reading the tea leaves right, it's a last-ditch effort to keep their store from dying."

"That's sad."

"It's his own fault," Wallace said. "He made a classic mistake: he took something he loved and tried to make it a business."

"I won't be sad when you die, Dad," Tiffany said.

"Why is that, Tiff?"

"Because I'll see you in heaven."

"*I'll* be sad when you die," Addison said.

"Both comforting thoughts, girls," Wallace said. "But the real lesson is that we need to make the most of every single day here on earth. You'd hate to look back when you're on your deathbed and regret all the things you didn't do."

That night Wallace nearly gave up the hobby of model railroading for good. Carson was right. The Zephyr cars couldn't handle the radius of the new mountain loop. They derailed every time. There were cars in the river, cars in the tunnel, cars in the canyon—the place was a true train wreck. For Wallace it was frustrating, it was maddening, it was depressing.

He tried bolstering the roadbed with shims made of construction paper and masking tape, but the more he did the worse things got. Soon the trains were derailing engine first, still on the straightaway, before the curves. In frustration Wallace tore out a long section of track, then the entire mountain loop, then most of the mountain itself (this after launching a Zephyr sleeper through the mountain shell, like a Tomahawk missile).

Tiffany was having an equally bad time assembling her country church. She came into the garage, in tears, holding pieces of the building kit. She had mistakenly superglued the townspeople to an outside wall panel. Even working with his sharpest penknife Wallace couldn't pry the victims loose. The rural church looked like a glue trap for worshippers.

Only Addison's rural hospital project was going well, but she soon lost interest, put on her pajamas, poured a bowl of Honey Nut Cheerios, and turned on the Disney Channel.

Back in the garage, surveying his model railroad—what was left of it—Wallace found himself weighing the merits of taking a chain saw to the whole thing. There was no denying the wasted time, the squandered money, the lack of forward progress.

There was still no sign of Hannah.

"Don't worry, Dad," Addison said, coming to say good night, seeing the layout in ruins. "There must be something you're good at."

CHAPTER TWENTY-TWO

Carroll Quinn was in his second week working for the company when he tapped Wallace on the shoulder and dropped a bombshell. They were in the conference room, wrapping up a product development meeting with Lenore, Sanjay, and some of the senior engineers.

"Got a minute?" Carroll's cyber metallic cycling jersey said Krups. His bike shorts were black, with extra-thick chamois padding under the seat.

Wallace followed Carroll into his office. The backs of his cycling shoes were bright orange.

"Kangaroo leather," Carroll said. "Don't sweat the carpet—they're walk-on cleats. You might want to close the door for this."

Wallace took a chair at Carroll's desk. The furniture in his office was new—Early American, medium cherry, a style favored by most insurance company executives. The desk was a special rush order, along with a conference table, a framed Bierstadt print, and an oversize hutch.

"Tell me about Lenore," Carroll said.

"What do you want to know?"

"Anything. Everything."

Wallace took his time answering. He wasn't sure where to start. "She was born in Texas. Has a master's degree in public policy. Swears she was a wallflower in high school on account of being a military brat—her father was an admiral. When she feels like getting drunk she likes a Tanqueray martini."

"I wouldn't know about getting drunk," Carroll said. "But I find her very poised, very impressive. What about her husband?"

"Runs a tuna boat out of American Samoa. Home less than half the time."

Carroll smiled knowingly. "She married the dustman."

"She was young."

"Kids?"

"No. What's this about?"

"Travel constraints—anything you know of?"

Wallace bit his lip. "I don't think so. Why?"

"I was wondering. How bad do you really need her?"

"How bad do *I* need her?"

Carroll grazed his beard with a calculating hand. "Let me put it another way. How bad does Cal Max need her?"

"She's probably the only reason they haven't thrown us out."

"But we could replace her?"

"If we had to, yes."

"Understand she's still your direct report," Carroll said. "I want to be sensitive to that."

"What's going on?"

Carroll sat forward. He put his fists together, forming a ball—a wrecking ball. "What if I told you I was on the verge of signing a deal with a major client, but I needed help from you and Lenore to seal it? Think we could steal her away from Cal Max for a few days?"

"Who's the client?"

"Asbury Care, out of Boston."

"You're serious? Asbury Care?"

Asbury Care was New England's premier health plan, a venerable institution in the health care industry. According to its own publicity, it claimed nearly three million members across five states.

"Just got a voice mail message before our last meeting," Carroll said. "My friend confirmed a meeting on Thursday. Actually it's a lot more than a meeting—it's a working session with their senior staff, predicated on the expectation they'll sign a letter of intent. Think we can pull it together to go to Boston in two days?"

"Boy, Michael wasn't kidding when he said you worked fast."

"I was thinking you, me, and Lenore would make the trip. You've got a good grasp of the big picture and I'm tight with the decision maker. But my friend wants to put us in front of the worker bees, and you know what that means—they'll want all the gory details. Lenore would be just the gal for that. She's pretty, she's polished, and she's been down this road before. I have a feeling she'd be dynamite in a sales position."

"You're saying pull her out of Cal Max permanently?"

"Think she'd be interested?"

"I don't know," Wallace said. "You'd have to ask her."

"Unless you two have something going. I won't force the issue if you'd rather keep her at Cal Max."

"Don't be stupid. We don't have anything going."

"No need to get hot. I was just saying I'll drop it right now if you want to keep her working under you."

Wallace felt his face burning.

Was it that obvious?

"And I'm saying you'd have to ask her," Wallace said. "She can do anything she wants as far as I'm concerned."

"Look, let's just take her to Boston and consider it a test-drive, if she's interested."

Wallace managed a smile. There was no need to begrudge Carroll his interest in Lenore—she was clearly the future of the company. Besides, to sign Asbury Care would put Merksamer Digital on the map.

"Does Michael know?" Wallace asked.

"Not yet. You're the first."

"He's going to want to go."

"That absolutely cannot happen," Carroll said. "Those days are over—Michael personally flying to every meeting with a prospect. It makes us look small and pissant. He shouldn't be showing his face unless it's a scripted event with a client. Now, who's going to talk to Lenore? I'd be glad to do it."

"I'm going that way," Wallace said. "I can do it."

"You sure? I don't mind."

"You say the meeting's Thursday in Boston?"

"Starts at nine. The three of us can fly out Wednesday and come back Friday. We'll stay at the Park Plaza. I'll get Julie working on the tickets."

"And Friday night's the Christmas party."

Carroll knocked twice on his desktop. "Let's hope we'll have something to celebrate."

"Are you kidding?" Lenore said. "Of course I can do it!" She marked off the days in her calendar book. "I'll have to move some things around, but that won't be a problem."

"Hey, and just so you know," Wallace said, "Carroll's got his eye on you for carrier sales."

"I know. He told me."

"You already talked about it?"

"He called me at home last night. We talked for about an hour."

Wallace wanted to impress her as being a string-puller in the company. Now he was embarrassed. It made him look out of the loop.

"So what do you think?" Lenore asked.

Wallace walked the few steps across the office and took a seat in Lenore's visitor's chair. He was surprised at the starkness of the space. On the floor was a scrubby houseplant, and on the wall hung a small, framed photograph of a black cat—other than that, no obvious signs of a home life or other interrelations. Wallace remembered Lenore used to have a framed photograph of her husband, Ricky, hanging prominently on what was now a blank wall. It was an aerial shot: the Marlborough man at the prow of his tuna trawler in heavy seas.

"What are you, a renter?" Wallace asked. "What happened to the tuna boat picture?"

Lenore seemed amused. "I'm not one to clutter my workspace with my personal life. So tell me, Wallace, am I crazy to want to do this?"

"The downside is there'd be lots of travel."

"Yes, and dinners out and trips to great cities and conferences at fabulous resorts." With a hand she brushed a loose strand of hair behind one ear. Her eyes were bright with anticipation.

"Carroll's right," Wallace said. "They'll love you."

"He said that?"

"In so many words."

The telephone rang.

"This is Lenore." She looked at the papers on her desk. "Hi, Julie, he's right here." She handed Wallace the phone. "One of your daughters. Julie's putting her through."

Wallace took the receiver. "Hello."

"Dad, I need to go to Santa Barbara." It was Addison.

"Why, Addison, what's in Santa Barbara?"

"The dolphins are washing up on the beach. It's all over the news—"

Wallace glanced at Lenore. She sat with her arms folded across her chest, staring impassively at the floor. Her wedding ring shone.

"Addison, I can't take you to Santa Barbara—"

"Please, Dad, they're dying!"

"That's a six- or seven-hour drive."

"But they're everywhere!"

"I'm sure it happens all the time—"

"No, they don't know why it's happening."

"Ask your mother."

"She said to ask *you*."

"I'm sorry, Addison. The answer is no. I'm having a busy day. I'll see you tonight."

Wallace hung up the phone.

"Crisis?" Lenore asked.

Wallace told her about the dolphins.

"Don't let her know about my husband's tuna nets," Lenore said. "Snaring cute little Flippers by the thousands." She looked at Wallace like there was something else she wanted to say.

"Where were we?" Wallace asked.

"We were talking about the future."

"Cal Max would miss you."

"We can always find someone to manage the account."

"No one as good as you."

"Don't look at me like that. You're making me feel guilty."

"Do whatever you want," Wallace said. "In fact, I think you should take it. You'd be moving up in the organization, and that's good for everyone."

"I think I'd miss our working together most of all."

"Look at it this way," Wallace said. "In two days we'll be going to Boston together. After that, who knows?"

CHAPTER TWENTY-THREE

It was not the prospect of signing Asbury Care that excited Wallace, but rather the sense of vindication, the incontrovertible proof of concept that signing the health plan would confer. With Asbury Care and Cal Max as clients, Merksamer Digital would assume a coast-to-coast presence. It would become a magnet for talent, industry attention, and customers—not to mention venture capital. Success would be in the fabric; if they could sign two insurance companies they could sign twenty, and if they could sign twenty they could sign two hundred. Wallace's gamble would pay off. He and Michael would get their IPO.

Between meetings, Wallace huddled in the hallway with Carroll and Lenore. There were handout materials to pull together, PowerPoint presentations to be written. Carroll had taken to wearing black-rimmed reading glasses, and the lines on his forehead deepened as he pondered strategy. He was confident about the working session with Asbury Care's senior staff—his friend was high up in the organization and had the inside track—but, as he saw it, the line managers' presentation was a potential minefield. At Asbury Care, as most insurance companies, paper enrollment forms were keyed manually into the membership system. Automating the process was an attack on the status quo, a potential job killer, and Carroll was afraid the middle managers might counterattack to protect their turf. Asbury Care was not a streamlined tower of West Coast modernity like Cal Max, a company that could ingest new technology and reorganize on a dime; it was backward-looking, paper-intensive, and corrupt as only an old East Coast insurance company could be. It was *smokestack*.

"We're ultimately asking them to cut jobs," Carroll said, worrying. "It's like asking a general to decimate his ranks."

In the end, Carroll ordered the marketing consultants to be brought in. In his mind, the situation warranted big guns and big ideas. In addition to the complexities of selling a software system, there were social and psychological issues at play, and Carroll wanted the input of objective outsiders.

"Those two fat ticks?" Wallace asked.

The marketing consultants were community theater acquaintances of Becka's—she had done a brief summer stint on Mt. Helix playing Winnie Tate in *Annie Get Your Gun*. At her insistence Merksamer Digital had engaged the two men as brand-image consultants. Harry was a frustrated stage actor, and Oswald an unpublished playwright. What began innocently as a corporate brand review soon mushroomed into a litany of questionable—and expensive—projects: a revamped corporate logo, employee focus groups, a web site, customer satisfaction surveys, and a monthly newsletter (atrociously titled *Rock Enroll!*).

Hard as Wallace tried, there was no talking Carroll out of it; he was determined Harry and Oswald should be in on the brainstorming session. Everyone cleared his calendar to meet the next morning.

Exhilarated, Wallace ended the day in Lenore's office. It was late, and on a whim he brought a bottle of champagne—a dusty, room-temperature souvenir that had been on his bookshelf since the day they signed Cal Max. Lenore was already proving her mettle as a member of the sales team; she had gone through the long afternoon enthusiastic, energetic, and nearly as optimistic as Carroll, all the while juggling some sticky technical issues with Cal Max. The champagne was in recognition of this baptism by fire.

Lenore eyed the bottle of champagne. "Are you trying to get me drunk?"

"I'm hoping to see you dance on this desk," Wallace said.

"At least let me close the door." Lenore took two Merksamer Digital coffee mugs from a bookcase. "We can drink from these."

She sat at her desk and gazed at Wallace with what he sensed were inviting eyes.

"What's your cat's name?" Wallace asked, turning awkwardly in his chair and looking at the grainy photograph on the wall.

Two yellow eyes, pointed ears, and a red collar—the cat was curled on a pillow and appeared put out at having its picture taken.

"That's Hank," Lenore said. "Hank's a she." Then: "Why are you smiling? She's the only true friend I've got."

"Me," Wallace said. "I'm a true friend."

The phone rang. It was Carroll. He was nervous about the dwindling time. Their flight to Boston was first thing Wednesday morning, and he was calling to ask Lenore if she could start work even earlier the next day.

"I've got Wallace here with me," Lenore said. "Let me put you on speaker."

She touched a button on the console and hung up the receiver.

"Working late, I'm impressed," Carroll said over the speakerphone, in a disembodied voice.

Wallace leaned toward the phone. "Something like that."

"I was just explaining to Lenore, there's a lot to do and a short time to do it. I've asked the marketing guys to be there at seven sharp. Can you both make that?"

"Sure," Lenore said.

Wallace shook his head no. "I'm on kid duty. It'll be more like eight-thirty for me."

"No harm," Carroll said. "Hopefully we'll have something to show you by then. Lenore, can I call you at home tonight? I'd like to go over some notes before morning. I'm at the gym, here, until nine, so it'll be sometime after that."

"That's fine." While she listened, Lenore absentmindedly stroked a Cal Max pen—a health fair giveaway.

"And you'd better start thinking about your replacement," Carroll added. "I have a feeling this sales role's going to fit you like a silver satin glove."

Lenore raised her eyebrows.

"Okay, Carroll, I'll start thinking."

"Signing off now. Stairmaster's free."

"Later." Lenore ended the call with the touch of a button.

"That's an odd thing to say," Wallace said. "Who wears silver satin gloves unless it's in a sex movie?"

"You might be surprised at what some of us will wear for good sex," Lenore said. "Especially if it's been awhile."

Wallace was taken aback. He had the champagne bottle resting on the edge of the desk and was stripping away the foil capsule. Lenore was watching. Wallace had the sudden sense he was undressing her.

"I thought we'd toast to your future," Wallace said. "Truth is, we're lucky to have you in any position."

"Either that's obscene or it's the most romantic thing you've ever said to me."

Wallace had brought the bottle because he felt like celebrating. Now it seemed Lenore was opening a door to him, and he didn't know what to make of it.

"This might've already turned. If it's bad, feel free to spit it on the floor."

"Also very high on the romantic scale."

Wallace separated the wire hood from the cork. He glanced at Lenore, who looked on expectantly. Before Wallace could get back to the business at hand, there was a pop, a crash, then a shower of spray as champagne erupted from the bottle. Wallace did his best to stem the flow with his thumb.

The cat photo lay broken on the floor. The unleashed cork had flown across the room, hit the picture, and knocked it off the wall.

The unlikely shot commanded a brief moment of reverential silence.

"There goes your only friend," Wallace said. "Sorry."

"It's just a picture," Lenore said. "Pour."

Wallace filled Lenore's coffee mug, then his own.

"Can you believe this is really happening?" Lenore asked. "I feel like I should be asking you to pinch me."

Wallace paused, trying to think of something clever to say—a retort that would cast him in the light of a thoughtful, seasoned leader.

"I've learned not to count my chickens before they're hatched," he said. Not very profound or leaderlike, he realized too late.

"Whatever happens, happens," he added.

"Does that mean you believe in destiny?"

"The Great Beard Upstairs who controls our every move? No. I'm more of a free-will guy. You shape your destiny with your own hands. Mine just happen to be a little slippery at the moment."

"Be serious. I'm talking about fate, like when two people are meant to be together."

"I wouldn't know about that," Wallace said. "I do believe in irreconcilable differences, though. Sometimes two people just *can't* live together."

"I know what you mean. My single friends have no idea how suffocating a marriage can be."

"Wait until you have children," Wallace said. "It's like being buried alive and consumed by fire ants. You can't imagine what it's like until you actually experience it."

"Sounds appealing. I'll stick to birth control."

"Cheers," Wallace said. "To Asbury Care."

They touched mugs.

"To Boston," Lenore said.

CHAPTER TWENTY-FOUR

In the electronics superstore, open till midnight, the video cameras for sale were lined up like filets mignons in a high-end market. Wallace couldn't tell one model from another; he realized too late he should have consulted Sanjay. The man with the crew cut from the appliances aisle helped Wallace pick out a suitable one: digital tape, auto focus, low-light capability, two hours of recording time at normal speed. The man said a tripod would help steady the zoom shots, so Wallace bought one of those, too.

Wallace arrived home at ten minutes past nine, arms full of camera equipment, optimism unflagging. Addison and Tiffany were wrapped in airline blankets, kneeling on kitchen chairs, busy with paper and pencils. Hannah was on the floor in the family room, collating cardboard boxes, surrounded by stacks of shrink-wrapped books and videotapes. It was like coming home to Santa's workshop; the place was chilly and the elves were fully engaged. Wallace felt like a trespasser. He barely got a grunt from his daughters when he kissed their hair, which smelled faintly of lavender baby shampoo, except to complain that they were both dying of hunger—Tiffany was starved nearly to the point of tears.

Only Scottie seemed happy to see Wallace. He barked until Wallace finally relented, went to the pantry, and gave him a Milk Bone.

"A dolphin is five times smarter than a dog," Addison said.

"What makes you say that?" Wallace often found himself defending his American Eskimo. What other breed could be trained to wear circus hats and walk tightropes on hind legs?

Addison counted four words in Scottie's vocabulary: the plaintive bark when he was locked outside the house and wanted in; the piercing bark in anticipation of a car ride; the alerting bark when the doorbell rang; and, finally, the clipped bark when shown either his dinner or a fatty prime rib bone. By contrast there were twenty words in a dolphin's vocabulary—twenty-one if you counted *quickly!* and *emergency!* as two separate words.

"You really think a dolphin knows the difference between an ambulance and a fire truck?" Wallace asked, hovering over Addison's shoulder.

"Yes, you can hear it clearly on the tape." She was busy writing out words that corresponded to a list of sounds.

"She's been running those stupid *Flipper* tapes back and forth all afternoon," Hannah said, pushing a wisp of hair from her face. "She's going to wear out the VCR."

Wallace stepped into the family room. "I doubt a kid can wreck a VCR watching *Flipper* reruns. What is all this stuff?"

"College money." Hannah was sealing cardboard flaps with packing tape.

The boxes contained Acres of Money membership kits. The Stonehenge around her was all the inserts: glossy product catalogs; *Deal Blaster! Daily Devotionals; Everlasting Success!* videotapes; *Just Say Money! Business Development Manuals*; four-part enrollment forms.

"Were you planning on feeding your children?" Wallace asked. "Or were you going to wait until they lapsed into a coma?"

"This is taking longer than I thought," Hannah said. "I need a hundred by morning."

"Owen's got you brainwashed. I don't see him stuffing boxes."

"He was only here all day. What about you? It's late."

"I made a stop."

"Your cell phone was off."

"I was in conference. I didn't tell you. I've got a trip to Boston."

"Morty Schlegg called. He said it was urgent."

"What's so urgent?"

"How should I know? He was incoherent, calling from a bar. The telephone number is next to the phone."

Wallace went to the kitchen. He emptied his pockets and glanced at the number. Morty could wait. Wallace opened a can of chicken noodle soup and started two hot dogs boiling for Addison and Tiffany. He poured himself a drink.

"Dad, can you take this to your office tomorrow and fax it to Santa Barbara?" It was Addison, handing over her neatly lettered page of dolphin words.

"Don't fret, Addison. I'm sure it's nature taking its course," Wallace said.

"No, they can save them if they try."

"Not always."

"Please, Dad. Just fax it."

"Okay, I'll ask Julie to get it to the lifeguards."

"Not the lifeguards. Sea World is there. It needs to go to their chief scientist."

"All right, then. The chief scientist."

Wallace was peeling bananas when something hit him on the backs of his legs.

"Tiffany, what are you doing?"

"Practicing. It's homework." She was inverted, doing the crab-walk around the kitchen island. She had recently been enrolled in a preteen gymnastics program designed to enhance self-esteem.

"The people running this school are certifiable nut jobs," Wallace called to Hannah. "For this we pay tuition?"

He lifted Tiffany off the floor and placed her on the far side of the kitchen. It was a quick trip; she weighed little more than a spider. She went scrabbling down the hallway. Scottie followed, barking. Even to a dog, a human doing the crabwalk was alarming behavior.

When the wieners were thoroughly boiled, Wallace fished them out with tongs and dropped them into buns. He put the hot dogs on plates, added the bananas, ladled the soup into bowls, and called the girls to the table.

Having mastered the crabwalk, Tiffany did somersaults back to the kitchen. She came up dizzy. Addison had to press her against the back of her chair to keep her from falling to the floor.

Wallace poured two milks and set a bottle of ketchup on the table. "Bon appétit, ladies."

While Addison and Tiffany ate, Wallace topped off his scotch. He carried his drink to the family room, where he stood for a moment watching Hannah build membership kits. She was a diligent, determined worker, especially when she put her mind to something.

"Why a hundred?" Wallace asked.

"Our national sales conference starts tomorrow," Hannah said. "In Las Vegas."

"Figures," Wallace said. "Hustlers."

"When do you go to Boston?"

"Day after tomorrow."

Hannah's hands went still. She looked up. "You can't watch the kids, then, Wednesday night?"

"No, we don't come back until Friday."

"Vegas is two nights," Hannah said.

"Sorry, Hannah. This is a major insurance company. Carroll just got the meeting."

"He didn't ask you first?"

"It's not like he needs my permission."

"That means you're going to miss the kids' Christmas program."

"Not altogether—"

"Daddy, you're not coming to our show?" Addison was listening attentively from her chair at the kitchen table. She had a speaking role in the school Christmas program. She was memorizing lines. Tiffany was in the chorus. She would be wearing mittens and doing hand motions.

Both girls were looking at their father with wounded eyes.

Wallace said brightly, "I'll still see it, girls, because Mom's going to videotape it."

Hannah looked at Wallace balefully.

"I bought you a camera," Wallace said.

"I can't work those things."

"It's easy. It does everything for you."

"Forget it. Take it back."

"What do you mean, take it back? Try, Hannah."

"I'm not going to waste my time fooling with a camera."

"Just try."

"You scheduled this. Don't make it my problem."

Wallace put his hands on his hips. "My god, Hannah, could you be any less accommodating?"

"Accommodating?" Hannah said. "Now it's my fault?"

"This is a big trip, a career-maker, and what help do I get from you? Nothing but grief."

"What other surprises are there, Wallace? What else are you going to spring on us?"

"I'm the transparent one here," Wallace said. "You're the one with all these people skulking around the house."

"No one's skulking."

Addison said, "Dad, why are you always so angry all the time?"

"Yes, Daddy," Tiffany said. "Why are you so mad at everything?"

"Not mad, girls. Just tired."

Hannah said, "Time for bed, you two. It's late."

Addison and Tiffany kissed Wallace goodnight. Hannah took them down the hallway, turning out lights.

Alone in the kitchen, Wallace found a package of chicken in the refrigerator. He thought he'd cook the pieces on the grill, after a basic marinade of beer, lemon juice, garlic, and a pinch of salt. He opened a can of beer and quartered a lemon. He took one of the quarters and squeezed hard, drizzling the juice over the surface of his scotch.

The sight of Wallace staring into space, holding a beer in one hand and a cocktail in the other, the chicken sitting untouched on the counter, seemed to infuriate Hannah.

"You haven't started cooking yet?" she demanded.

"I don't want you going to Las Vegas."

"I have no choice, thanks to you."

"Those girls need a mother. They can't take care of themselves any more than that dog can open his own can of dog food—"

"They need a college education."

"They're still children!"

"I won't put my life on hold just so you can tool around this country flogging faulty software."

"Really, Hannah? Is that what you think I'm doing? Flogging faulty software?"

"You never should have quit your job. By the way, I don't suggest ultimatums. It makes you sound insecure and pathetic."

"This whole thing's a joke, Hannah. You're naïve about business."

"And you're such a pillar in the community."

"I've done a lot more than serve coffee at thirty thousand feet."

Hannah's face hardened. "Such a perfect husband, isn't it a shame about the wife: she has to work for a regular paycheck."

"Fine, go to Las Vegas with that putz. I couldn't care less."

"Good, because he's picking me up at six sharp," Hannah said. "We have to trailer all these boxes to airfreight."

"Paper enrollment forms?" Wallace said, glancing at the membership kits. "Don't make me laugh. Tell Owen those guys should stick to saving souls."

He took a pack of matches and went outside to the grill. Scottie followed him out. The night was clear and cold. As the burners came on, the dog began licking at the grease spots on the concrete under the barbecue.

"Really, Hannah," Wallace said, returning to the kitchen, "I hope you go to Vegas and sign a ton of people, make a lot of money, truly, I do—"

Hannah shook her head. "You're so full of it—"

"I'd love to be a man of leisure. I could tell Michael to shove it."

"You'd love nothing more than to see us fail."

"I'll join a country club and play golf. Be a stay-at-home dad, manage the household—"

"You're so full of shit—"

"—pick up the dry cleaning, whatever you want. Just promise me one thing: when the bottom drops out of your pyramid scheme and your own kids hate you for the kind of mother you've been, don't complain to me. I won't be in the mood to hear it."

"You care more about that damn company than you care about me."

"That's really what you think?"

"Choose right now, Wallace. Me or the company."

"Don't tempt me, Hannah. You might not like my answer."

"Choose!"

"Go to hell, Hannah. This company is who I am."

"Then this marriage is over. I want a divorce."

"Fine, let's get a divorce."

Wallace ate dinner that night in front of the TV, surrounded by a stadium of Acres of Money membership boxes. He watched the eleven o'clock news. The coverage on the Santa Barbara dolphin story was extensive. An on-scene reporter, a pretty young woman about Lenore's age, wondered aloud to the camera how such a friendly, sociable animal—one that seemingly goes through life with a smile—could possibly want to kill itself.

"Ask me," Wallace said. "I'll tell you how."

CHAPTER TWENTY-FIVE

At eight thirty the next morning, Wallace entered the darkened conference room. He spotted Lenore and slipped quietly into the chair beside her. The image of a blank PowerPoint screen was projected against a far wall.

"Welcome to the Asbury Care Cabaret," Lenore whispered. "I think Carroll's about to have a stroke."

As Wallace's eyes adjusted to the light, the players in the room took shape. Carroll sat with his chair turned sharply away from the long table, his head in his hands. Oswald, the playwright, studied an open binder, chewing an earpiece of his tortoise shell glasses. Dora, from word processing, manned the computer keyboard. She sat ramrod stiff, staring at the screen, awaiting instructions. The clutter on the table—paper wadded into balls, platters of mangled fruit, open pastry boxes cocked at oblique angles, resting on tangled power cords—suggested a pivotal project in disarray.

No one uttered a word.

Curious, Wallace glanced at Lenore. Her eyes were intent on Carroll.

Oswald finally spoke. He had the bourbon-cured voice of a smoker. "I think we are very, very close."

"Close?" Carroll looked up. "This is pitiable. We've got absolutely nothing."

"Harry, let's try it once more from the top, less dark this time," Oswald said. "You are a gargoyle, yes, but a dangerously romantic one."

Only then did Wallace realize that Harry, the second marketing consultant, was lurking in the shadows at the front of the room. He was the actor: small in stature, fair hair, a shapely mouth that gave him the crestfallen expression of a sickly little boy.

"This is the damnedest thing I ever saw," Carroll said, shaking his head.

Wallace leaned toward Lenore. "What is this?"

"Shh. Listen."

Harry stepped to the center of the room, where the beam of the projector lit him like a spotlight. He read his lyrics from a legal pad. The tune was vaguely Broadway:

"Asbury Care, Asbury Care, you're always there.
Pearls before swine, this was to be my time.
Imprisoned in a workplace jail, my life, my love, is a living hell ... "

Oswald's pen was made from a long black ostrich feather. He used it as a pointer. "Now cut to the hospital. A saucy nurse on a stark white gurney—"

Harry flipped the page. He sang the part of the nurse, falsetto:

"From the chasm in my heart, aortic dreams take flight.
Longing for a start.
Rules are for fools.
Fools are for jewels.
My cafeteria dollars can't buy coconut cream pie ... "

Lenore turned to Wallace, delight in her eyes. "Check out Carroll's face."

Carroll looked like he wanted to vomit.

"Back to the gargoyle upstage," Oswald commanded. "Darkly, now, with a bitter subtext—"

"Our tortured souls, no rock and roll.
Adrift *sans* coverage,
Slaves of the working day.
A pandemic of duplicity.
Save me from the city ... "

"Chorus, now! Chorus!" Oswald implored Dora to join in. She mouthed the words obediently, pretending to sing:

"Asbury Care, Asbury Care, you're always there.
Pearls before swine.
This was to be my time ... "

Carroll leaned across the table and said to Wallace, "My mistake. I'd have thrown them out hours ago, but they're having lunch with Becka."

Wallace reached into his computer bag for aspirin. He hadn't slept well; the family room sofa was rutted and lumpy, and for much of the night he had lain awake, rehashing his argument with Hannah. At six o'clock the doorbell had rung. As dawn broke, Wallace found himself loading Acres of Money membership kits into a rented trailer, hitched to Owen's Hummer.

"Looks like you could use some coffee," Lenore said.

"Please," Wallace said.

Lenore reached for the silver thermos at the center of the table. Wallace's gaze settled on her narrow haunches. He imagined unzipping her out of the blue felt skirt she wore.

"Explain this to me again," Carroll said.

"The lament of the human spirit," Oswald said. "Our little hospital of horrors is ultimately about hope. So what do you think?"

Carroll pulled his reading glasses away from his face. "It's all so off-putting I don't know what to say. It strikes me as antagonistic."

"The grittiness is deliberate," Oswald said. "Good theater demands a certain amount of tension—"

Carroll cut him short. "To be brutally honest, I don't understand a thing you're saying and I wish you'd stick to the topic at hand. Why must it be sung? What's wrong with a straightforward PowerPoint presentation?"

Oswald made a testy face. "Picture dining in a five-star restaurant, the *amuse-bouche* that the chef sends out. We need to serve up something exciting, something gripping, because when you get right down to it this stuff's just drier than petrified dog shit."

Carroll said, "It may be dry, gentlemen, but it's the business we're in."

After months of consulting with Merksamer Digital, Wallace knew, Harry and Oswald still didn't have a clue what the company did. They often said computers were distasteful and disturbing—tools of torture foisted on an unsuspecting public by remorseless nerds. They dismissed the insurance industry as contemptible.

"So tell me the truth," Oswald said to Carroll. "If a meteorite were headed for Earth, and was certain to hit in the next hour, would you really waste another minute of your life on this tripe?"

"No, I'd be having sex under this table," Carroll said. "And it wouldn't be with either one of you."

Instinctively, all eyes turned to Lenore.

"Don't look at me," Lenore said quickly.

Oswald had a wolfish grin. Whenever he laughed he self-consciously put a hand over his mouth to mask tobacco-stained teeth. He looked at Lenore and said, "Sweetheart, if there's a meteorite headed this way, you'd better get ready because I have a feeling there's gonna' be one helluva dog pile."

Lenore sank in her chair. Wallace put a fatherly arm around her shoulders and pulled her close.

"Hold on," he said. "No one's gonna' dog pile Lenore."

Lenore's hair tickled his ear.

"Come on, guys," Carroll said. "We're losing valuable time here. We need ideas."

"Maybe a Rastafarian-reggae theme," Harry said, shielding his brow from the light of the projector. "Does this software have anything to do with the trip cancellation insurance you buy for a Caribbean cruise?"

"Not even close," Carroll said, his voice edgy.

"Or a tragedy," Oswald said. "The reconciliation of a rebellious daughter with her transvestite insurance-executive father—a dark comedy of patricide and mistaken identity."

"Absolutely not," said Carroll.

Wallace looked at Lenore. She raised an eyebrow.

"What's Boston known for?" Harry asked rhetorically. "Fishing and beans, right? We'll dress the gargoyle in a yellow slicker and a nor'easter Cape Cod hat. He'll be the flatulent fisherman of Worcester, your tour guide to the future. The set would evoke a tall-mast sailing ship. The musical numbers would be upbeat, an ode to the past."

He demonstrated a quick soft-shoe time step on the carpet, singing:

"Yankee Clipper,
Think I'll keep her.
She's my Asbury gal from Katmandu—"

Carroll slammed a fist on the table. "Dammit, people, we're talking software here! It's a scalable system of discrete modules designed to handle standard enrollments in the theater of managed care: group numbers, family coverage category, and primary care physicians. That's all. It has nothing to do with flatulent fishermen or transvestite fathers or saucy nurses on stark gurneys. It's a software engine for the insurance industry, we leave for Boston first thing in the morning, and we need to have this thing locked and loaded by close of business today. The clock is ticking."

The room went silent.

Wallace found himself enjoying the scene—Carroll trying to extract a rational result from Harry and Oswald, whose relationship with Becka, until now, had always afforded them a certain immunity to deadlines and deliverables. Discreet as a court reporter, Dora stared straight ahead. She hadn't put a word on the screen since Wallace had set foot in the room.

"You're looking unspeakably angry," Harry said to Carroll.

Carroll said in a measured tone, "No, I am trying to comprehend the magnitude of incompetence in this room."

"Guess we need to know more about the software," Oswald said.

"Then ask away," Carroll said. "What can I tell you?"

Harry stared glumly at his notepad.

Oswald scratched his head with the ostrich feather and looked toward the door.

Lenore poured more coffee.

"It saves time and money and gives our clients a competitive edge," Carroll said impatiently. "What else do you want to know?"

"If my friend Pierre were HIV positive, would your software cover *him?*" Oswald asked, after a long pause.

"It doesn't give a fig about your friend one way or the other."

Piratelike and menacing, Oswald pointed the feather at Carroll.

"Then you should fix that," he said.

"What about union members and corporate whistle-blowers?" Harry asked. "Do the flying monkeys in your software automatically spit them out, too?"

"Guys, it's bits and bytes," Carroll said. "There's no moral compass. It just puts people in the system."

"Like an iron maiden," Oswald said.

"These people in Boston sound like sadists," Harry said. "Tell me, do they still burn witches and wear Pilgrim outfits?"

"They should be indicted on racketeering laws," Oswald said. "For all the coverage they've probably denied."

"I wonder if Michael could be charged with aiding and abetting," Harry said. "Becka would so die."

Carroll tossed up his hands. "I give up."

"Maybe we should just use the presentation we have," Wallace said.

"I take it you haven't bumped into your friend Charlie this morning?" Carroll asked.

"No. Why?"

Lenore turned to Wallace.

"Major problem," she said. "He's locked himself in his office. Says if *he* isn't going to Boston, then his sales presentation isn't going either."

"No one has a copy?"

"No," said Lenore. "Hence the problem."

Carroll looked gravely at Wallace. "It's time we stop pussyfooting around. This is insubordination of the highest order. This guy needs to be fired."

"No one's firing anyone," Wallace said.

"We've got an appointment to hunt an elephant in two days. We can't show up with an empty quiver." Carroll made a head nod in the direction of Harry and Oswald. "I can't say as I'm encouraged by what I've seen so far."

"Ouch," said Harry.

"Woof," said Oswald.

"I'll talk to Charlie," Wallace said.

"He needs to be terminated for cause."

"All right, Carroll. I said I'd talk to him."

"Two Frisian widows live alone in a ramshackle Southern plantation," Oswald said. "They come home from a premiere of *To Sir, With Love* to find a doted-upon house monkey dead and their health insurance lapsed."

"Listen, you," Carroll said, turning angrily to Oswald. "I've had it to here with your storybook crap! We asked you in this morning because we're up against a make-or-break situation, and we need a crisp, comprehensive theme for our sales presentation. Now, what in blazes are we going to do?"

Again, silence.

"Who's the audience?" Harry asked. "Are we talking male or female?"

"Insurance executives are primarily male," Carroll said.

"They sponsor golf tournaments," Oswald interjected. "They drive Cadillacs and wear blue blazers to Ruth's Chris Steakhouse on Saturday nights."

"At least they don't wear rouge," Wallace said, taking a potshot at Oswald. The remark about the Cadillac had left him feeling stung.

Harry looked at Lenore. "We'll have you do a striptease. Call it *Merksamer Bares All.*"

Oswald smiled lecherously. "We'll request a conference room with a pole."

"Or better yet bus them to a *real* strip joint," Harry said. "We'll rent one—an intentional dive."

Carroll had long since pushed back from the table. He sat with his arms crossed, stewing.

Julie interrupted with a knock on the door.

"Excuse me, but we have some issues with the trip." She was backlit by the doorway. The tone of her voice told Wallace there was something he needed to know.

"What's up?"

"On the first leg, to Dallas, the plane is completely full," Julie said. "The best I can do is three center seats, all coach, with Michael the only one in first."

"What's this?" Carroll looked up, alarmed. "Michael?"

Michael stepped into the conference room and turned on the lights.

"Nice try, guys, but you aren't doing this one without me." He sat heavily in his usual chair at the head of the table. He looked haggard and on edge.

"I figured your order of the day was working the venture guys," Carroll said.

"You're wrong, Carroll. A start-up company has to play by a different set of rules. I'd hate to have to explain to Trek Reese why I didn't make the trip. He's a hands-on guy himself."

"Then come," Carroll said. "Whatever you think."

"As long as my name's on this building, I'm as accountable as anyone for making sales."

"Goes without saying," Carroll said.

Wallace looked at Carroll.

So much for you and your stand against looking small and pissant.

Carroll had a dire expression on his face, and for good reason: in sales situations Michael came across as arrogant and argumentative. He lied about almost everything. Boston would be a disaster.

A pall settled over the room.

Michael sat back in his chair. He turned to Harry and Oswald.

"Okay, guys," he said. "Show me what we've got."

CHAPTER TWENTY-SIX

Wallace bolted from the conference room and headed down the stairs, two at a time, to Charlie Dye's office. He had a sudden impulse to strangle his salesman. The door was locked.

Wallace pounded on the door. "Charlie, open up."

Curious employees—mostly members of Sanjay's engineering staff—leaned out from their cubicles to witness the spectacle.

"Charlie, I'm not leaving."

Charlie finally spoke from behind the door. "Here for the final clip?"

"I need those presentations."

"That bastard sold me down the river."

"Who?"

"Carroll. He wants to shoot me. Michael, too."

"No one's going to fire you, Charlie. Now open this door."

"All right, but it's against my better judgment." The latch turned. The door opened a crack. Charlie peeked out, glassy-eyed. His reading glasses were pushed up on his head. "Wait a second."

The door slammed shut.

Wallace stewed, pacing. He glanced at the onlookers and rolled his eyes. For a stage effect he blew an impatient sigh.

When the door finally opened, this time a little wider, Wallace gave it a shove. A bookcase lay on its side, blocking the door. Wallace pushed harder until the bookcase finally gave way, allowing him to step inside. Charlie's tie was askew, his shirttail was out. He reeked of alcohol.

"This place smells like a sewer," Wallace said.

"I'm sick of the paperwork," Charlie said. "What's the point, anyway?"

It looked like a tornado had touched down in the small office. The blinds were drawn at demented angles. File drawers were pulled open, their contents strewn across the floor. A bottle of Old Overholt— straight rye whiskey—stood planted like a trophy on the desk, surrounded by vials of prescription drugs.

"Are you drunk, or crazy, or both?" Wallace asked.

"I get a commission if we sign Asbury Care," Charlie said.

Wallace pointed to the laptop computer on the desk. "Is that thing turned on?"

"I won't let you and Michael screw me on this," Charlie said.

"E-mail me your presentations—everything you have."

"What about protecting my lead?"

"What lead is that?"

"Asbury Care. I've got a foot in the door. I sent a brochure."

"I doubt it."

"Her name's Tabitha. It's in the prospect file—"

"The presentations, Charlie. You're wasting my time."

Charlie sat heavily behind his desk. His fingers were clumsy on the keyboard. The mouse was a brick in his hand.

"And while you're at it," Wallace said, "send copies to Carroll and Lenore, too."

"This is a big mistake."

"Do it," Wallace said.

"You're taking Lenore?"

"Yes."

"And Michael, too?"

"So happens we are."

"What does he think? He thinks he can waltz into a place like Asbury Care and bullshit 'em to death? You can't bullshit a company like Asbury Care. They're in the business."

"That's why we're taking Lenore."

"The purge has started."

"It's one trip, Charlie. You're blowing this way out of proportion."

"You're next. Maybe you'd realize it if you weren't so involved fawning and sucking up."

"No one's fawning and sucking up."

"Fine," Charlie said. "Why should I care?" He worked the computer with his nose tilted in the air, peering through bifocals. "Here's what I hope. I hope you go to Boston and fall flat on your face."

Wallace looked at him. "Actually I'd rather have you pulling for us on this one, since I just mortgaged my house to pay your salary."

"I'm the friggin' vice president of sales. I should be going."

"Get sober. Get this place cleaned up."

"We were friends, Wallace. I thought I could trust you."

"Nothing's changed."

"Everything's changed. You included." Charlie pushed the whiskey bottle toward Wallace. "Have a drink. To old times."

"No thanks."

"You sure about this?" Charlie asked.

"I'm sure."

Charlie hit the send button. "That's it, there goes our leverage. I'm holding you responsible for whatever happens next with these jackals."

"I have some advice for you, Charlie. You work for Carroll now. You better give him anything he asks for."

"Listen, Wallace, I've slaved for two years on this sales funnel. If he thinks he can ride in at the last second and take all the credit, he's wrong. I won't let it happen. Same for Lenore. I'll sue you, first."

"Sue me?"

"You think I don't know what's going on? I've seen the way you look at her."

"I don't know what you're talking about."

"No?" Charlie grabbed the bottle by the neck and took a hit of whiskey. "Tell me you wouldn't do anything to have a crack at a piece like that, including sell me out."

Wallace glared. "Sell you out?"

"Her job offer. I know all about it."

Wallace snatched the bottle away. "You're blind. I'm taking you home."

"I should've gone with the pet toys. At least I could've hanged myself with a rope monkey."

Wallace stepped around the desk and took Charlie by the arm. "Come on, before I throw you out for good."

Charlie howled. Wallace had him by his bad arm.

"Don't touch me!" Charlie shouted. "I am still the vice president of sales for this company!"

In the hallway Wallace faced a crowd of startled employees.

"Reaction to medication," Wallace said, hauling Charlie toward the lobby.

CHAPTER TWENTY-SEVEN

A h, Las Vegas.

For the first time that morning, Owen Andersen took his eyes off Hannah. He settled into his seat in the middle row of the van taxi for the short ride to the Strip. Looking out the window, he drew in—*inhaled*—the electric skyline, this mecca for high rollers. Ahead were all the glistening shrines to big money: Caesars Palace, MGM Grand, New York-New York, Bellagio, Mirage. Playground to the rich and famous. Everywhere you went, nudity galore and Heineken for a buck.

"First time in Vegas?" the taxi driver asked. He had oily, black skin, and his shirt was a rag. His ivory teeth reminded Owen of a talking skull.

Owen stared sourly at the impudent driver. "Do I look like it's my first time?"

"I think maybe you come for a honeymoon." The taxi driver leered in Hannah's direction and showed his purple grin.

Owen said, "I'll say this: I wouldn't kick her out of bed for eating coconuts."

"Owen!" Hannah said.

Owen leaned forward. "Tell me, driver, you have that saying in your third-world country?"

"Yes, Father—what happens behind the closed door." The taxi driver laughed his skeleton laugh.

"You might as well have left your coconuts at home," Hannah said, crossing her arms and turning to the window. "This trip's strictly business."

"I hear that, Mother." The taxi driver laughed again. "What is your business?"

"Ever heard of Acres of Money?" Owen asked.

The taxi driver scratched his head. "Pawnshop downtown?"

"A juggernaut of commerce. Check it out. Maybe someday you won't have to drive a cab."

"This taxi's a juggernaut of commerce. Except for chiropractors. Chiropractors don't tip."

Owen was irked by the numbers on the meter—they kept turning, even when the van wasn't moving. He peered at the cabdriver's license, displayed on the dash.

"Mohammed. Is that Arabic for Mike?"

"Mohammed means Mohammed."

"Tell me something, Mike. Does your monkey eat a lot of bananas?"

The taxi driver looked confused. Owen pointed to the timeworn photograph that was fastened with rubber bands to the visor—a bushy-haired little boy in a soccer uniform, kneeling beside a soccer ball.

"Joking," Owen said. "Cute kid."

It was a short ride from the airport to the hotel.

"The Petropolis, this is a nice resort," the taxi driver said, steering the van past iron gates. "Only for rich people."

"Shut off the meter," Owen said curtly.

The Petropolis was a hotel-within-a-hotel, a micro-resort designed for a discriminating clientele. Acres of Money had bought out the place for the national sales conference.

"Checking in?" The muscle-bound men of the Petropolis bell staff were dressed in Brazilian slave costumes: scanty loincloths, weighty Mapuche necklaces, colorful Amazonian cuff bracelets.

A bronzed young man named Levi helped Hannah out of the van.

Owen paid the fare and made a show of giving the taxi driver a two-dollar tip.

"I'll need a receipt."

"Yes, Father," the taxi driver laughed. "Big boss coming in."

A second bellman was loading Owen's and Hannah's bags onto a luggage cart.

"I have a metabolic condition," Owen said to the bellman. "It prohibits me from lifting heavy objects."

For his work bringing in the bags, the bellman earned a handful of coins.

"These fancy hotels are worse than one-armed bandits," Owen said to Hannah. "They'll nickel and dime you every chance they get."

In the cavernous lobby, a Brazilian slave girl delivered mai tais on a tray while the attractive female desk clerk checked Owen and Hannah into rooms. Owen had booked a junior suite. The details of his reservation, priced at the Acres of Money preferred corporate rate, were painstakingly noted in Owen's mobile office organizer.

"And, Mr. Andersen, how many room keys for your stay with us?" the desk clerk asked.

"Two," Owen said. With downcast eyes he glanced at Hannah. "Whirlpool tub and complimentary cable. Sure you wouldn't rather crash at my pad?"

"Positive," Hannah said. She passed her credit card to the desk clerk. "Reservation is for Hannah Noe."

"Of course, Mrs. Noe," said the desk clerk. She tapped her keyboard with manicured fingernails, concentrating on the monitor mounted low behind the counter. Her dark hair was pulled back in a long braid.

"What time does your room service stop?" Owen asked.

"Room service is available twenty-four hours," the desk clerk said, without looking up.

"I've got front-row tickets to the midnight review. Is it any good?"

Hannah looked at Owen. "A midnight show?"

"Rio Burlesque is very popular with couples," the desk clerk said.

"Couples?" Hannah said.

Owen said, "Go with the flow. Vegas, baby."

"I need sleep."

"What do you think your husband does on business trips?" Owen asked. "He doesn't sleep, I can guarantee you that."

The first bellman showed Hannah to her standard room in the adjacent tower.

"We'll take this elevator, Mr. Andersen." The second bellman had Owen's bag on a luggage cart. He led Owen up to the junior suite and unlocked the double doors. The suite was an expansive corner room with a sweeping view, a gaudy place that oozed lust and money. The king-sized bed was against one wall; it was two steps up a marble pedestal to the giant whirlpool tub in the center of the room.

"Ain't this the cat's meow?" Owen said.

He could see that the view at night, with the drapes open wide, would be breathtaking. A Vulcan Mind Probe, a few White Russians, and the boundaries of a rocky marriage would dissolve like aromatic crystals in a hot bath.

The bellman was trying to show Owen how to operate the thermostat, but Owen cut him short. He sent the bronzed slave away without a tip. "Yeah, yeah, thanks, man. I've got a brain. I'll figure it out."

Owen washed, donned a clean Tommy Bahama shirt, and took the express elevator to the grand ballroom.

Hannah was waiting for him. The airy foyer was full of people—soccer moms in athletic warm-ups; Evangelicals in long, shapeless dresses; and real estate types with tailored suits, suntans, and exaggerated smiles. Owen and Hannah checked in at the registration table. Because of the gold star on his name badge, Owen was directed across the foyer to a second table where a conference hostess loaded him down with presentation materials.

"What is all this?"

"Change in the program. We need you to speak."

"I don't think so."

The hostess double-checked her roster. "Yes. Owen Andersen. Tomorrow morning at ten. *Recipe for Success.*"

Owen's heart raced. "But no one—"

"The syllabus is in your presenter's binder," the hostess said. "Just put it in your own words. Breakout room six. We're expecting about four hundred."

"Four hundred *people?*" Owen's palms turned clammy and he broke out in a sweat.

"Get there early. We'll fit you with a lapel mic."

Owen took the binder, feeling like he wanted to puke. He was dizzy. His legs trembled and he couldn't speak for the knot in his throat.

"Owen, you're hyperventilating. Try to relax." Hannah helped him to a chair. It was her flight attendant training kicking in.

"No, I can't," Owen said. He felt like something heavy was sitting on his chest—a floor freezer came to mind. His extremities began to tingle. The familiar symptoms of gout were like old friends compared to this. He was losing consciousness.

"You're having a panic attack," Hannah said. "Just take a breath—"

Owen lashed out angrily. "I can't make a speech!"

Hannah took a step back. She looked at him with disbelief. "Stage fright? You?"

Owen's eyes filled with tears. He dropped his head in shame.

"Hannah, I am so sorry. But oh, god, all these people—"

"Really?"

"Don't make me do it."

Hannah sat with Owen. She cradled his head in her hands and rocked him, waiting for the dizziness, the faintness, the nausea to pass.

"I thought I was safe," Owen moaned.

"Shh. You're safe."

"I'm not a public speaker."

"No one's going to make you give a speech."

Owen managed to raise his head. "It's a recruiting session for our business, Hannah—to build our downline. You'll have to do it."

"Me? I can't do it!"

"Please, Hannah. It's now or never. We can't go home empty-handed."

With an exasperated look on her face, Hannah stared across the foyer, where, unfathomable for a fine resort, a pack of shrieking children streamed by. Under normal circumstances Owen would have gone over and told them to shut up, but he felt too faint to bother. The sight of a young mother stopping to lift one of the grubby crumb-crunchers up to a drinking fountain—this little girl had a balloon tied to her wrist—seemed to trigger something in Hannah.

"All right, I'll do it," she said, turning back to Owen. "Hand me the binder."

There was a writing desk in the sitting area of Owen's suite. Hannah went to work while Owen stretched out on a nearby sofa, making suggestions.

For Hannah the false starts just kept coming. The presentation materials were of little help.

"I can't do this."

"That's your first mistake," Owen said. "Never say can't."

Hannah left the suite and took a long walk around the hotel grounds.

Owen got on the phone and ordered a club sandwich and fries. Darkness came.

"This is impossible," Hannah said, leafing through the binder for the umpteenth time.

"You're the strongest woman I know," Owen said. "You can do this. Think of all the single mothers trapped in financial free fall and stuck with grimy kids."

"You're a lot of help." Hannah stood at the window, staring at the lights.

"Use your flight attendant training," Owen suggested. "Approach it like an in-flight emergency. Talk to them like they're your passengers."

It was the catalyst that would forever frame the voice of Hannah's *Recipe for Success* seminar.

Suddenly the words flowed effortlessly. Hannah penned the seminar script in longhand, and then set about committing it to memory. Owen had a good ear. He coached her on delivery: the timing of dramatic pauses, where to stress certain words, when to repeat key phrases.

They worked together into the night, perfecting a seamless presentation.

Instead of taking in the midnight burlesque show—Hannah wouldn't even consider it—they adjourned downstairs to the hotel's formal restaurant, where they had a lavish dinner of spring rolls, cranberry crab Rangoon, and double-cut prime rib. The rich food was pushing it with Owen's gout, but in his mind he justified it as a worthy gamble—his goal was to consume more than what was on his dinner plate.

It seemed to be working. With the second bottle of wine, an expensive Château Margaux, Owen had the sense he was beginning to see cracks in the Mount Rushmore that was seated across from him.

"It's almost unimaginable," Hannah said, gazing into her wine goblet, twirling a strand of hair. "To think I'm about to lose a marriage over money."

CHAPTER TWENTY-EIGHT

The telephone could not possibly be ringing again.

After a woman's voice answered in the middle of the night, Lenore had yanked the cord, giving Pago Pago a permanent busy signal. Lenore opened her eyes and saw by the clock it was morning. With a nimble hand she doused the clamor of the alarm, and then lay in bed for a long moment, her mind racing.

Simultaneously apprehensive and exhilarated, she pushed off the floral duvet that had been a gift from her mother and swung her legs to the floor. In bikini panties and a white camisole, she padded barefoot to the bathroom, where she flicked on the lights and looked in the mirror, swiping the hair out of her eyes. This was the spacious master bathroom of the most popular three-bedroom, three-story floor plan of a master-planned condominium project in the San Diego suburb of Linda Vista, where the interior streets were European-narrow and the exterior walls rose up like cliffs in a river gorge; where neighbors lived on top of neighbors but the views overlooking Mission Valley were commanding. The bathroom evoked a Roman-era decadence: it was a surfeit of glass, chrome, and contrasting Travertine tiles. The fixtures were unmistakably modern—each a sleek, stirring *objet d'art* made from polished chrome. The glass around the shower was nearly an inch thick, and the showerhead inside was as big around as a sunflower, with a flexible arm and settings for spray, massage, or a drenching rain shower (Lenore's favorite).

The irony of the bacchanalian master bath was that, for nine months out of the year, Lenore used it alone.

Ricky hated everything about the Linda Vista condominium complex—the *rip-off bird perch,* he called it. He hated the tininess of it; he hated the luxury. He despised the busybodies who enforced the sweep of homeowner's association rules, who could cite parking regulations verbatim when all he wanted to do was to patch a fishing net or temporarily park a Zodiac in the RV lot at the back corner of the property while he worked on the motor. The meddlesome old busybodies, he told Lenore, reminded him of the dolphin observers who rode the *Katherine Jo,* his father's tuna clipper, in the 1970s, at the height of the environmental craziness. They were kooks who preached saving whales, rescuing baby harp seals, and eating dolphin-safe tuna. Collectively their efforts led to Congress passing the Marine Mammal Protection Act, thereby decimating San Diego's tuna fleet. When the *Katherine Jo* left her Grape Street berth for the final time in 1981, the die was cast. Ricky Terry would follow his father to a sea that was halfway around the world. Ricky was a chip off the old block, too: he drank vodka like it was water, smoked like a chimney, and resented being told what to do, whether by a congressman, an environmentalist, or the hammer at home.

Lenore's excuse was that she married young.

With the day's first light little more than a spectral gray in the window, Lenore performed the same early-morning choreography she had performed thousands of times and too often alone: she pulled off her camisole and stripped off her panties. Standing nude on the Travertine floor, in the spot where the canned lighting created a perfect halo around her head, where the rose-colored rays embraced the soft curves of her body, she contemplated the future. This body would have to get her there. She had no doubt that it could. It was a deal closer—the ultimate hostile takeover weapon, if necessary.

With a determined burst of energy, she stiffened her legs and bent over at the waist—down, down, down, until her hair nearly touched the floor. Then, in a sweeping motion, she stood erect, shook out her hair, and took inventory in the mirror. What she saw was what any man would want: the body of a serious woman, a woman accountable. Her fair skin was free of telltale tan lines. Her breasts were not the big, gross bowling balls of flighty temperament but rather were compact and symmetrical, proportional to the lithe body type, an affirmation of solid character. Her hips were wider than she would have preferred—there was no denying that her body was first and foremost a machine made for childbirth—but there was consolation in the shape of her legs. They were the legs of a runner—strong and gazelle-like. Her gaze was serene and self-assured.

She pulled open the heavy glass door and unleashed the monsoonal rain shower, contemplating her momentous conclusion: it was high time the organization made a change.

Thank you ever so much, tuna captain Ricky Terry. Effective immediately, your services are no longer required.

CHAPTER TWENTY-NINE

Per-thwock, per-thwock, per-thwock.

The steering wheel pulled hard to the right.

"No, God, not now—"

Wallace glanced instinctively at the digital clock in the center of the dash. He had less than thirty minutes to make his flight. To the sounds of horns honking, he managed to get the Cadillac off the busy thoroughfare.

He got out of the car, inspected the flat tire, and considered his options. It was a short distance to the airport terminal—maybe a mile—but the car was undriveable; the right front tire was completely blown. He thought about locking the doors and walking, but the section of asphalt on which the Cadillac sat marooned was technically an active taxiway, used from time to time by Falcon Jets from the Coast Guard station across the street to access the runway at Lindbergh Field. According to the warning signs posted on the perimeter fence, the penalties for abandoning a car on this hallowed ground were severe.

There was only one thing for Wallace to do: he removed his tie, rolled up his white shirtsleeves, and went to work changing the tire.

Fifteen minutes later he was limping into the airport on a toy tire, hazard lights flashing, steering with smudged hands. The rental car buses were blowing past him like trucks on a highway.

The cell phone rang. Wallace answered it, assuming it was Lenore.

"Why haven't you called me back?" It was Morty Schlegg, sounding anxious.

"Can we talk later—I'm racing." Wallace was at the entrance to the parking lot. He pulled a ticket.

"I've spent the last twenty-four hours in the emergency room," Morty said. "And it's all your fault."

"Why's that?"

"I got the shit kicked out of me at a cop bar," Morty said. "I was defending your honor."

"Morty, I really don't have time—" Wallace could hear Patience chattering excitedly in the background.

"She's copping an attitude," Morty said, "because I still don't have office furniture."

"Pig bastard!" Patience was shouting. "I can't work sitting on a milk crate!"

"You've sat on worse," Morty said. "And so has your mother."

Patience berated him in Vietnamese.

Wallace found a parking space close to the sky bridge. "Morty, I'm about to catch a plane. I'll call you from Boston."

"Why, what's in Boston?"

Wallace told him about the meeting with Asbury Care.

"And I'm telling you, you cannot go to Boston right now," Morty said.

"I have no choice—"

"—because you and I have a settlement conference tomorrow morning. Are you listening to me? Yes! We're due at the courthouse. They want you to plead guilty to a misdemeanor."

Wallace grabbed his bags, locked the car, and started walking toward the terminal. "I thought we agreed. I'm not pleading guilty to anything."

"They're offering a deal, minimal jail time. Thirty days. It comes off your record if you stay clean."

"I sit on an armed robber and they want me to do thirty days in jail?"

"I think it's a fair offer."

"What happened to the best defense is a good offense? What about fighting fire with fire?"

"Maybe the severe head clobbering took the fight out of me, but as your attorney I'd advise you to take it."

"No way."

Patience's voice cut in. "Don't listen to him. We can win this."

There was a commotion as Morty and Patience wrestled for control of the telephone receiver.

"You suck," Patience said. "You're a disgrace to your profession."

Morty said, "Go back to your rice paddy, you impudent scrod."

"Morty, listen to me," Wallace said. "A guilty plea is not an option."

"Then maybe you should get another lawyer. I can dissolve my practice and enroll in truck driving school with a clear conscience."

"I learned something this morning," Wallace said. "One small nail can bring down a two-ton automobile. That's what I need from you—be a nail."

"I know this prosecutor," Morty said. "He means to try you as a vigilante. He'll sensationalize the facts and impugn your character. It'll be like David against Goliath."

"As I recall David came out all right."

"Spare me your right-wing Christian fables. Spurning their offer will be perceived as a declaration of war, and that's a fact."

"Then let's go to the mattresses. I'm ready."

"There is one other idea," Morty said. "I have a friend who works for the newspaper. Maybe I can get her to do a story."

"Let's keep the press out of it," Wallace said.

"Don't be so quick to judge," Morty said. "A sympathetic article could pressure them into dropping the charges. We'll portray you as a bold crackpot who's been rendered impotent by the stresses of life."

"Please don't. I'd hate to give my enemies the satisfaction." Wallace was entering the terminal. Waiting for him was Sanjay.

Wallace did a double take. Sanjay?

"I should warn you," Morty said. "She's a woman of large appetites. You may have to sleep with her."

"I'm not sleeping with anyone," Wallace said. "Morty, I need to go."

"I'll have to think about it," Morty said. "Call me when you get back."

Wallace hit the end call button.

"All set for Boston?" Sanjay asked.

"If I ever get there."

"Wallace, did you fall? Your face—"

"Flat tire." Wallace showed Sanjay his hands. "I need to wash."

The public address system was announcing Wallace's flight. It was the final boarding call.

Sanjay followed Wallace into the men's restroom. Wallace went to the first washbasin and looked in the mirror. His face was blackened with grime. His knuckles were bloody from stripping lug nuts. His shirt was streaked with soot, as if someone had brushed it with a paint roller.

"What's up, Sanjay?" Wallace ran the water and began scrubbing his hands.

"I have been thinking. This Internet thing is going to be very, very big."

"You came all the way to the airport—"

"So why not postpone the Boston meeting. Become a development company again."

"Don't go negative on me, Sanjay."

"I have friends in the Bay Area. They can tie all these things together—enrollment, insurance companies, physicians."

"So can we."

"No, we are broken beyond repair."

"I don't believe that."

"At least say you will talk to him."

"Talk to who, Sanjay? I don't even know what you're asking."

"Trek Reese. Ask him to redeploy the capital. Fund a restart."

"No."

"I am telling you, Wallace. These people in San Jose, they are very smart. They call these virtual communities."

"We already have e-mail, Sanjay. What more does a guy need?" Wallace wiped his face and hands with a paper towel.

Now they were calling his name on the public address system.

"Please, Wallace. I am trying to stop a mutiny here. My engineers, they are slaves working for Peg Brown and your girlfriend Lenore. And for what—basic salary and a little Christmas bonus? They will not continue to do this. They are already planting bombs in the software—"

"Bombs?"

"Yes, bombs. If they do not get equity they will all quit, and the bombs will go off. Then we will have a true disaster on our hands."

"It's an old scare tactic, Sanjay. Don't believe it."

"But they are serious."

"Here's how you handle it—fire the next guy who mentions it."

"At least say you will talk to him."

"No, Sanjay, we're sticking to the plan." Wallace realized he was as clean as he would get. He collected his bags off the floor. "And by the way, Lenore is not my girlfriend. She's a colleague who plays a key role in this company, and I happen to have immense respect for her. Now if you don't mind, I'm about to miss my flight."

Wallace hurried for the gate. Waiting for him at the entrance to the security line were Donald Duncan and Carson, from the train store.

"Your secretary told us we'd find you here, if we hurried," Carson said. "Hope we're not catching you at an inopportune time."

"I'm a little pressed," Wallace said. Out of the corner of his eye he could see Sanjay leaving the terminal building.

"Then I won't beat around the bush," Carson said. "Tonight's the big organizational meeting for our model railroad club, and we've lost our room."

"Ruined by eminent domain," Donald Duncan said. "Retribution for calling the cops—*Taco Time* next door occupied the expansion space." He wore his engineer's cap and a black windbreaker with a Southern Pacific logo.

"We tried getting a meeting room at the local hotel but there seems to be an issue with my credit card," Carson said.

"He maxed it out the other night at HomeTown Buffet," Donald said.

Carson cut him short. "How it happened is beside the point. Fact is, we're in a pickle."

"Carson, I can't give you my credit card," Wallace said.

"No, no, certainly not," Carson said. "I thought perhaps you could lend us a conference room, just for this evening."

Wallace felt sorry for the two men. He had empathy for anyone with an entrepreneurial dream and a maxed-out credit card.

"How many people are we talking about?"

"Anywhere from fifty to a hundred," Carson said. "As you can imagine, interest in a club of this caliber is considerable."

"We have a training room, but any more than fifty and we'll have the fire marshal on our case."

"Not to worry," Carson said. "I'll post my boy Paul on the perimeter of the parking lot. Two blasts of the car horn will signal the fire marshal is approaching. We'll halt the meeting and stash the overflow bodies in the antechamber."

"Nice plan."

"You'll find when I'm on task I'm like Hannibal crossing the Alps," Carson said.

"Or Hitler," Donald added.

They were paging Wallace again. The aircraft door was about to close.

"All right," Wallace said. "Call my secretary. Tell her I said you could have the training room for tonight."

"My fine friend, this is above and beyond," Carson said, shaking Wallace's hand. "At the very least it's worthy of a plank holder membership *in absentia.*"

"Don't bother," Wallace said, running for the plane. "You wouldn't want me in your club, anyway."

CHAPTER THIRTY

The plane touched down in Boston more than an hour late. Wallace ducked his head to exit the MD-80. He trudged up the jetway, lugging his bags.

"Slowpoke," Lenore said. She stood waiting with Michael and Carroll inside the terminal.

"How was the flight?" Wallace asked.

"Spoiled me for life," Lenore said.

"We tried sending you back a drink, old boy, but the flight attendant wouldn't hear it," Carroll said. On the last leg of the trip he had managed to finagle two seats in first class—one for himself and one for Lenore—thanks to a complicated formula of miles accumulated, upgrades purchased, and charisma with the gate agent.

Wallace wanted to say something nasty, but he managed a smile. He was just thankful to be off the crowded plane.

An incoming snowstorm had the airport bustling. Planes were backed up at the gates. Carroll trooped toward baggage claim like a wrangler cutting through the herd. Logan International was familiar territory. He wielded his knowledge like a weapon. Wallace and Lenore trailed behind, walking together.

"Bring me that dirty shirt when we get to the hotel," Lenore said.

"Sorry, not in your job description."

"Nonsense. I'll hand-wash it in my sink."

People stood four-deep at the baggage carousel.

"What a madhouse," Lenore said, looking around.

Outside the terminal the black sky sputtered snow. The air smelled of exhaust.

"Cabs are this way," Carroll said.

Lenore drew stares from sullen business travelers as she made her way down the long taxi line, pulling her roller bag.

With Michael joining the trip at the last minute, and with the holiday season in full swing, Julie was unable to book them into the Park Plaza, Carroll's first choice for a hotel. She exhausted a long list of alternatives before landing them at the Paraguay Arms, an aging boutique hotel near Boston Common. The lobby was small, and the staff was surly. There was no bellman to take their bags.

Wallace felt like a Russian henchman, standing near the registration desk in his heavy overcoat, watching Carroll check everyone in. The desk clerk, a small man in a green Bavarian jacket, kept glancing nervously at Wallace.

"This form is an acknowledgement," the clerk said, sliding a piece of paper across the counter to Carroll. "Your Platinum card will be charged for any missing bath mats or towels."

"Jesus God." Carroll turned his eyes to the ceiling and quickly signed the form.

The elevator car was cramped. It shuddered like a carnival ride, causing everyone's eyes to widen. When the car dipped suddenly, Lenore clenched Wallace hard on the forearm. She wasn't wearing her wedding ring.

"This would be a hell of a way to lose the company," Carroll said.

"It's like we've been granted a stay of execution," Wallace said when the doors finally opened on the tenth floor. Carroll and Lenore stepped out first. Michael stood alone in the elevator. He had the Patriot suite, top floor.

"There's a nice restaurant around the corner," Carroll said. "If we hustle we can make it."

"Nix," Michael said. "Work before pleasure." He checked his watch. "We'll meet in my room in, say, fifteen minutes. Do a walk-through of the new presentation."

"Wait, what's happening?" Carroll asked.

"What you had was passable as a first draft," Michael said, "but as a final product it lacked a lot of critical information. I gave it a tune-up on the plane while you two had your party."

The doors closed, leaving Carroll with a baffled look.

"Vintage Michael," Wallace said.

"So much for dinner," Lenore said.

Carroll started down the acrid-smelling hallway toward his room. "Well, no sense in fighting city hall. See you both in fifteen."

Wallace's hotel room was the size of a large closet, with a high ceiling and shabby furniture. It smelled of disinfectant—as if housekeeping had recently removed a cadaver found lying in the badly sunken bed. The view was of a brick wall. There was a clawfoot tub in the bathroom and the labyrinth of exposed plumbing made getting hot water seem unlikely.

Wallace hung his last clean shirt, his suit jacket, and his overcoat in the freestanding antique wardrobe. A sign warned in multiple languages against stealing the wooden coat hangers. A silverfish scurried along the baseboard.

"Paul Revere slept here," Wallace said, mashing the insect with a shoe.

Wallace went into the cryptlike bathroom and tried once again to scrub the black grime from his fingernails. Satisfied, he took the elevator to Michael's room.

The Patriot suite was newly renovated—fresh paint, sturdy furniture, new carpet. The room was insufferably hot. Lenore and Carroll were already there, working to prop open a window. With nightfall the snow had turned heavy. Snowflakes whirled in the silver light; they blew in and alighted on the windowsill. People and cars on the street sounded clear and close, as if on a bandstand.

Michael was hooking up his laptop computer to the portable projector.

To make room for the projector image, Wallace helped Carroll clear a picture off the wall.

"Somebody man the lights," Michael said.

Wallace turned out the lights.

Lenore stood near the open window. When Wallace caught her eye she smirked and made a face, and then crossed her arms and stared out into the white haze.

"Don't jump," Wallace said.

"I hear there's some fabulous places to eat in this town," Lenore said.

"That's right, and they all stopped serving about an hour ago," Michael said. "Call room service. Have them send up Cokes and sandwiches."

"For dinner?"

"Tomorrow night, Lenore—that's when you'll get your big night on the town," Michael said.

While Lenore was on the phone with room service, Michael began to page through the presentation. He had rewritten most of what Wallace, Carroll, and Lenore had finalized only the day before, and he took his time with each screen, expanding on the bullet points, organizing his thoughts, working on his phrasing.

Carroll sat in an armchair, chewing a pencil, a legal pad in his lap. He made wide eyes as each new slide appeared. Finally he stopped Michael.

"I'm worried about the audience," Carroll said. "Your CV will put the room to sleep."

"I'm establishing my credentials up front," Michael said. "It needs to be done."

"Why all the different type fonts?"

"It looks like a ransom note," Wallace said.

"You're talking cosmetics," Michael said. "Focus on substance."

Michael put up the next slide: *About Merksamer Digital! Who we are! What we do! We have experience! We have references!*

"What's with all the exclamation marks?" Lenore asked. "Doesn't that violate a basic rule?"

"Nitpick like this and we'll be here all night," Michael said. "And by the way, Lenore, you're wrong. Exclamation marks create a sense of excitement. We're elevating their pulse."

Chastened, Lenore turned back to the window. She narrowed her eyes at something across the way and motioned to Wallace.

"What?"

"That window over there," Lenore whispered. "Two people were about to have sex in front of a camera. The guy just pulled the shade."

Michael stopped talking midsentence and turned. "What did you say?"

"I think we're checked in to the porn capital of New England," Lenore said.

Carroll peered over his reading glasses and eyed Lenore intently.

"Pay attention to the presentation, people," Michael insisted. "This is important."

As Michael droned on, the screens became increasingly crowded with shadowy, insectlike figures—generic humanoids from a clip-art library. Some of the figures appeared to be clever and acting out schemes.

"I don't get it," Wallace said. "Are we implying that we're actually insects?"

"Graphics humanize the story," Michael said. "They connect on a subliminal level."

"How do bugs connect?" Lenore asked.

Michael stared at her.

Carroll interrupted Michael in the middle of the next slide. "I'm still not copacetic with the doodlebugs. Might I ask, what are they intended to signify?"

"The stick men are helpers," Michael said stubbornly. "Helpers who help."

Carroll gnawed his pencil. "I guess that's all right, then."

Wallace found Michael's facts increasingly preposterous. The text made bold assertions that were patently untrue. Wallace was accustomed to Michael's embellishments, but this was off the charts.

"Michael, your numbers are way off," Wallace said.

"I'm feeding the fantasy."

"A thousand sites at Cal Max? The system generates a list bill and makes your doctor's appointments for you? Any monkey could debunk this with a single phone call."

"We're visionary, painting the future."

Wallace turned to Carroll. Intentionally lying to a client struck him as idiotic. "Tell him, Carroll. We can't say this. It's suicidal—"

"We can say anything we want," Michael said. "It's software. That's why we have Sanjay—to backfill our promises with code."

Lenore guffawed.

Wallace said, "Michael, listen to yourself. Why don't we just hypnotize them and pick their pockets."

Michael thought for a moment. "That's the smartest thing I've heard you say."

Wallace said, "We can't use any of this—"

"The hell we can't." Michael eyed Wallace with contempt. "Watch me."

"Wait now, everyone take a breath," Carroll said, his gaze focused on the image on the wall. He sucked his pencil and stewed for a moment. "Let's not throw the baby out with the bathwater."

Lenore watched the scene coolly.

"The more I think about it, the more I think Michael's right," Carroll said. "We're talking worker bees here. They'll expect a rosy picture, a robust system. I say we go with it as is."

Wallace returned to his hotel room, wondering why he even bothered making the trip. The telephone rang. It was Lenore.

"I'm still hoping you'll bring me that dirty shirt."

She met Wallace at the door to her room.

"Help yourself to a drink. I'm running some hot water."

She disappeared into the bathroom. She had filled the ice bucket and set out drinking glasses.

"Can I pour you something?" Wallace asked.

"In a minute."

Wallace opened the minibar and inspected the line of miniature bottles. It was one thing the Paraguay Arms had gotten right: the bar was well stocked. Wallace picked out a bottle of Dewar's and filled a glass with ice cubes.

"Okay, give me your shirt." Lenore's arm was reaching out the bathroom door.

Wallace hesitated a moment, then unbuttoned his shirt and delivered it to her waiting hand. He felt almost naked, standing in his dark suit trousers and white undershirt. He could hear water sloshing as Lenore worked the fabric with her hands.

"You really did a job on this," she said.

Wallace finished fixing his drink—he gave the scotch a splash of soda. "That's what happens when they throw you under the bus."

"Forget about work. See if you can find us a good movie."

Wallace turned on the television. He stood beside the bed with the remote in his hand, surfing channels.

"How's it going in there?" he asked.

"I think I've about got it." Lenore was running more water.

"Ready for a martini?"

"Give me another minute. I want to get out of these clothes."

When Lenore emerged from the bathroom she wore a terrycloth robe and what looked to be nothing else.

"How does a guy like that get to be CEO?" she said, pouring straight gin into a glass.

"I'll be damned." Wallace was peering at the image on the TV screen—a submarine surfacing on a raging sea.

"What?"

"*Ice Station Zebra.* It's an old movie. They're trapped—no way out."

Lenore sat cross-legged on the bed, heedful not to spill her drink. "Listen, I have something important to tell you."

"You shrank my shirt."

"I'm leaving Ricky."

Leaving Ricky. Wallace dreamed of the day he would hear these words from Lenore's lips; he had a well-worn fantasy in which she left Ricky and became his mistress. He would whisk her off to a Caribbean island or put her up in a secret apartment—the story line was never more concrete than that. Now, for all his dreams, she might as well have thrown him a live grenade. The casualness of the remark, the smugness on her face, the aplomb with which she sat on the bed and balanced her drink—Wallace felt like shaking her. He wanted to tell her marriage wasn't a game, that you had to take the bad with the good, that they were all stewards of an equilibrium that needed to be maintained, jointly and severally, by everyone who had taken the vows. Instead of admonishing her, he turned back to the TV.

"Wallace, did you hear what I said? I'm getting a divorce." The tone of her voice was distinctly impatient. "That generally warrants a response."

"What do you want me to do, applaud?"

"You don't approve."

"I didn't say that." Wallace found himself staring at Lenore's feet. He was surprised to see she wore a silver ankle bracelet and a toe ring.

"I might've known," Lenore said.

"What's that supposed to mean?"

Lenore fingered the rim of her glass. She eyed Wallace coyly. "The staunch family man, perfect marriage, kids in a religious school—"

"Hey, the church stuff is all Hannah."

"I thought you'd at least be on my side."

"I'd hate to see you make a mistake, that's all."

"Mistake?"

"Ricky's a good guy. What's wrong with Ricky?"

"Ricky's a jughead."

Wallace glanced at the TV screen. A team of huskies was eating blubber.

"Come now," Lenore said, patting the mattress. "Keep me company on this big bed."

Wallace was no prude. Where was the crime in lying on a bed and watching TV with a woman who was not your wife? He slipped off his shoes and stretched out on the bed, legs crossed at the ankles, black sock over black sock. Instinctively he took a mouthful of scotch and began to gargle. He imagined he could do it subtly and that it would make his breath somewhat more tolerable.

"What in the world are you doing?" Lenore asked.

Wallace swallowed hard. "A method. To discern the peat."

The hemline of Lenore's robe rode seductively up her thighs.

Lenore said, "I'll show you how to discern peat."

It was over in a matter of seconds.

The rest of the night passed in an alternating sequence of events: deep sleep interrupted by frantic sessions of lovemaking—Lenore had a wicked crocodile move—followed by trips to the bathroom and long drinks of cold water. On her way back to bed, Lenore kept stopping at the window to part the blackout curtains and report to Wallace on the pace of the blizzard.

The phone rang in what seemed like the middle of the night. When Lenore failed to stir—asleep, she appeared almost childlike—Wallace reached across the bed and fumbled for the receiver.

"Wallace?"

"Yes."

"I thought this was Lenore's room." It was Carroll.

Wallace propped up on one elbow. "It is."

"Well. That's interesting."

"What time is it?"

"You've missed the appointed rendezvous."

Wallace glanced at the clock. It was after eight.

"Christ, I don't believe this," Carroll was saying. "You're sleeping with her. Of all the days—"

"Just tell me what you want us to do—"

"Michael and I need to head over now. Meet us at Asbury Care as soon as you can get there."

Carroll hung up.

Wallace sprang from the bed and pushed back the curtains. The sky was gray. Ten floors below, the alleyway was blanketed with snow.

"Get up. Get dressed." Wallace paced animatedly around the bed, picking up clothes. His head was swimming.

Lenore sat up in bed. She followed Wallace around the room with her eyes, smiling. The look on her face was one of unflappable self-possession—a look that said things were going her way.

CHAPTER THIRTY-ONE

"No entry! No visitors! Closed to all personnel!"

Owen Andersen was a man under siege. It was almost noon in Las Vegas, but it could easily have been midnight—there wasn't a clock or window to be found. He was barricaded in the catacombs of the resort Petropolis, in the opulently furnished, technically advanced business center, sitting on a high proctor's stool, playing traffic cop to an army of Brazilian slaves commandeered from the hotel's obliging bell staff. A few hours earlier, in the Carnaval Ballroom, Hannah's presentation had precipitated a near riot.

"Stand back!" Owen said. "Make way for the forms!"

The crowd standing in the wide, marble hallway had been whipped into an entrepreneurial frenzy. They cleared a path to let through the bellhop who bore above his head a banker's box brimming with Acres of Money enrollment forms. Like the hard-bodied young men before him, he trod barefoot, beating a path between the ballroom and the expropriated business center, remitting to Hannah and Owen the currency that could make them rich beyond their dreams.

For Owen, the vibrant parade of Sherpas capped two extraordinary days in Sin City. Hannah's *Recipe for Success* seminar was more than a home run—it was a grand slam! Owen had imbibed lavishly, running up his credit cards, aggravating his gout. Still, the acute pain in his big toe—not to mention the burning in his ankle joint—was no match for the exhilaration he felt at seeing yet another box of forms coming through the double glass doors. He leapt off the chair, winced as his bad foot hit the wide-plank hardwood flooring, and limped in his Birkenstocks after the bellhop who carried the box.

"That's what I'm talking about," Owen said, his voice resonating through the business center. "Ask and ye shall receive! The Bible spits cash!"

He rubbed his hands gleefully. Their downline was growing exponentially—as fast as a slave named Ferdinand could feed forms into side-by-side Toshiba fax machines and send them off to Acres corporate headquarters. In all likelihood, without lifting another finger, Owen had surpassed his income as a mortgage broker. Hannah had more than doubled her pay at the airline.

"Check this out, we're off the charts," Owen said, waving a reference table from the *Just Say Money! Business Development Manual* under Hannah's nose.

"Forget it, Owen. I can't think about that now." Hannah sat sequestered in a cubicle in a quiet corner of the business center, concentrating on the mission at hand: systematically removing the forms from the boxes, checking the fields for accuracy, giving each cover sheet a date and time stamp, then passing it off to Ferdinand, who fed the pages into the fax machine and pressed the redial and fax-start buttons.

"That's as fast as you can go?" Owen asked, looking over Ferdinand's shoulder.

"You're being a nuisance," Hannah said. "Leave Ferdinand alone."

Owen favored expediency over accuracy—blasting the forms to headquarters in whatever random order they could be snatched from the boxes and stuffed into the intake slots of the fax machines. Hannah wouldn't allow it. She insisted the forms be numbered and sent in the exact order in which they were received. Fortunes were at stake. In a multilevel marketing business, hierarchy was everything.

The point was not lost on the crowd that thronged to the business center in hopes of a tête-à-tête with Hannah. These were the ambitious ones, dissatisfied with mere membership confirmations, eager to get to work building their own downstream organizations as quickly as possible. They carried calendar books and PDAs, and they were champing at the bit to schedule Hannah and her seminar into the fellowship halls of their hometown churches.

"Hannah, you should see all those people out there," Owen said. "You're like a goddess. Stay. Just one more day—"

"Absolutely not, Owen. I'm getting on that plane."

"A kiddies' Christmas program. I can take you to Siegfried and Roy."

"Forget it. Go back to your stool."

A vibrant pair of cuff bracelets propping up a box caught Owen's eye—another bellman was coming through the door. The crowd poured in behind him.

"Out! Get away! Off limits!" Owen turned back the throng. He sealed the doors and said through the thick glass, "We'll get her on your calendars, I promise."

Though Owen regarded the mob with disdain, he saw their collective clamor for Hannah's time as vindication. He was Svengali, she was his siren.

And what a performance! The *Recipe for Success* seminar had already catapulted Owen and Hannah to senior executive director level; the Acres marketing staff was contemplating putting Hannah on a ten-city tour. Her talk the previous day was so popular that a second *Recipe for Success* session was added to the Thursday morning, closing program.

A few hours earlier, Owen and Hannah had been standing in near pitch-black, at the edge of the brightly lit stage.

"Picture everyone naked," Owen said, giving his virtuoso one last piece of advice before she went on. The ballroom was packed—standing room only. For good luck Owen meant to give her a peck on the cheek. He kissed nothing but hair.

An assistant took Hannah by the arm and led her with a flashlight to the steps of the stage. The applause swelled as she strode to the podium. Owen watched spellbound from the wings. With a warm smile and a determined gaze Hannah took command of the room. Her crisp blue suit brought to mind a flight attendant's uniform. The stage lights made her jet-black hair shine. She spoke without notes, first introducing herself to the audience ("a working mother and a soccer mom, just like many of you ... "), then drawing them in with a frank version of her personal story ("Yes, we've lost practically everything due to neglect and reckless investment decisions, in which I played far too subservient a role ... "), and, finally, shocking them with a blunt reality: "Your plane is going down. Your seat belt will *not* save you, no matter how low and tight you have it pulled across your lap. The time has come to take matters into your own hands, to exit the aircraft ... "

They sat in rapt attention: the disgruntled real estate agents, the stay-at-home moms, the PTA presidents, the executive secretaries, the retail managers, the high school coaches.

"You're treading water, drowning in debt," Hannah continued. "Here, take this business development manual. It can be used as a flotation device. Take this financial lifeline we're offering. It is nothing less than the oxygen mask that drops from the ceiling, the lights in the floor that illuminate your way to the nearest exit ... "

Sitting in the bowels of the Petropolis, listening to the endless churn of pages queuing through fax machines, Owen found himself staring at Hannah, scrutinizing her ears, thinking about the future. Despite the big dinner bills, his attempts at intimacy had fizzled. She wasn't ready to let go, not yet, she claimed. The burning pain in Owen's big toe had moved to his heart. Oh, what he would give to nibble those ears!

Patience, he told himself.

As business partners they were now welded at the hip. The rest would come in time.

Owen closed his eyes and whispered a short prayer, putting it all in God's hands.

CHAPTER THIRTY-TWO

It was a cold night on San Diego Bay. The yachts in the downtown marina were trimmed with holiday lights. Their hulls lifted with the waves; their halyards clattered against their masts. High above the water, the hotel towers cast a luminous glow on the swirling fog, and the brightly lit flags snapped in the wind. The motor entrance was snarled with traffic—taxis, limousines, and revelers trying to valet their cars.

It was the third Friday in December. The Merksamer Digital Christmas party was about to begin.

In a hotel room on the twenty-first floor, Wallace was putting the finishing touches on his Santa Claus costume, strapping on the layer of stomach padding and zipping his coat. At the last minute, Becka Merksamer had conscripted him to play the role; she needed a tall extrovert to fill the rented costume, and by process of elimination Wallace was it. In the same hotel room, Hannah was under the gun, dressing for the party. She had arrived late at the hotel after a hectic afternoon: first a *Recipe for Success* seminar for the mothers at Edelweiss Christian; then driving north to drop off Addison and Tiffany, with their pink suitcases and aquamarine sleeping bags, at Audrey's house; then fighting the southbound holiday traffic through Mission Valley and into downtown.

"One of these days we're going to have to talk," Wallace said, jockeying for position in front of the mirror.

"Let's just get through Christmas."

"Does this look all right?" Wallace showed Hannah his beard.

"It's lopsided," she said.

"Shoot." Wallace tugged at the beard. It was the color of dirty snow.

"This is ridiculous," Hannah said. "What am I supposed to do with my hair?"

"I don't know, Hannah. Make something up."

"I hate theme parties. Doesn't anyone ever tell this woman no?" Wallace studied his reflection in the mirror. The Santa Claus staring back at him looked fatigued and indifferent. "Let me borrow some rouge."

"Here, I'll do it." Hannah used makeup to redden Wallace's cheeks. "Wait." She lifted the beard and brushed his lips with lipstick.

"How was the school Christmas program?" Wallace asked, dulling the lipstick with the knuckle of his right index finger.

"You mean aside from Mother's interminable complaining?"

"What this time?"

"She thinks we're taking advantage. We're not parenting our children."

"She said that?"

"In so many words."

"Let's take her to brunch at Lawrence Welk's. That'll get us back in her graces." Wallace straightened his hat in the mirror. Santa was starting to look himself. "How'd the kids do? How was the performance?"

"I'm sorry you missed it. They took my breath away. Up or down?"

"What?"

"My hair."

"Whatever you want." Wallace checked his watch. "I should get downstairs." He put on his wire eyeglasses and grabbed the pair of white gloves off the counter. "Need anything before I go?"

"A wife."

Wallace laughed. "You and me both."

Wallace took the elevator to the mezzanine. He quickly found the Coronado Ballroom.

The theme for the party was *Casino Royale*. It was Becka's idea—black tie for the men; the women were told to come as Bond girls, dressed to the nines. Near the door Harry and Oswald were giving instructions to a portrait photographer, who was arranging his camera equipment around a red velvet throne. Tonight everyone would be a spy and have his picture taken with Santa. The backdrop was an oversize photograph of the Italian Riviera—a full moon rising over a harbor packed with megayachts. The potted palms and blackjack tables were intended to evoke the mystique of Monte Carlo. The band was gathering on the makeshift stage and the woodwinds and brass were already warming up with *Rudolph the Red-Nosed Reindeer*.

When Harry saw Wallace, he shrieked and put his hands to his face.

Oswald came scuttling over like a crab in his big tuxedo shoes. "Oh, god, it's a Nordic Charlie Chan."

"Look at that shape," Harry said, giving Wallace a once-over. "Like a boa constrictor swallowed a cow."

Wallace did not appreciate these theater people criticizing his costume. It was the best he could do under the circumstances. He was determined to play a convincing Santa Claus, but the thick padding was already oppressively hot, the wig itched, and the glasses kept sliding down his nose.

Becka dropped what she was doing and hurried over ostensibly to inspect Wallace's outfit. Her hair was up and she wore Versace.

"I hear Santa's been very naughty," she said, narrowing her eyes. "Where's your wife?"

"Beats me."

"Do me a favor. Dance with her tonight."

"My sciatica's flaring. It was a long plane ride."

Becka forced a smile. "Yes, I imagine it was." She spotted a banquet worker across the ballroom and made a beeline for him. "You! Hotel guy! Tell your boss I've got *Pacific Coast Monarchy* and twenty pounds of fresh strawberries coming, and I expect a goddamned chocolate fountain!"

Oswald looked at Harry and rolled his eyes. "It's Hats Off for Horses all over again."

Pacific Coast Monarchy was a glossy Southern California society magazine. Harry and Oswald were charged with getting Becka's name in the magazine's Seen 'Round Town column. Their first effort, a summer charity function called Hats Off for Horses, was a bust. Although a photographer had shown up for a brief period of time to graze on the seared filet of beef, the event never made the magazine and only a small amount of money was raised to benefit the wild horses of the Anza-Borrego desert. Michael had to write a check to cover the catering costs.

"The band will be playing *Santa Baby*," Oswald was telling Wallace. "Make your entrance from stage left. Ham it up with the showgirls. Come in doing a little rumba."

Oswald and Harry had hired Ziegfeld-style showgirls to play Santa's helpers.

"Where's stage left?" Wallace asked.

"You're kidding, right? Lay low and keep your cell phone handy. I'll give you a five-minute call."

"Wait, what's a rumba?"

Wallace had time to kill. Having a short vodka, he decided, would jolly up old St. Nick. He took the escalator down to the first floor, keeping an eye peeled for Lenore. The hotel was busy with partygoers, and Wallace responded to their catcalls with a warm smile and the wave of a gloved hand. A whoop came up from the crowd as he entered the lobby bar.

"Vodka martini," he told the bartender.

Wallace was halfway through his drink when he realized someone was pelting him with goldfish crackers. Pulling the small crackers from his wig was like combing orange spiders from their web. He'd had enough of this boorish behavior when a cracker finally landed in his drink. He climbed off the barstool and found Charlie Dye sitting at the back of the room. Charlie was dressed in a black tuxedo. He looked pained.

"The disguise didn't fool me for one second," Charlie said. "What other Santa Claus is big as a house and drinks a Grey Goose martini?"

Wallace joined him at the table—wedging his padded hips into a Verona armchair.

Charlie was drinking bourbon. On the edge of the table was a crystal tumbler filled with goldfish crackers. "So. Asbury Care signed."

"Amazing what happens when you go in at the top."

"I wouldn't know. I'm just a low-level grunt."

"Michael's got a call in to Trek Reese. Things are going to move now, you watch."

Charlie took a gulp of bourbon. "What about Lenore?"

Wallace wondered how much Charlie knew. "What about her?"

"You're giving her the job?"

"She's good, Charlie—"

"In other words I'm cooked—"

"Their CEO loved her. He hosted us at his private club."

"Great to hear. Kid's got a future." Charlie took a handful of crackers and lobbed them in the general direction of the bar. They showered a gray-haired accountant-type sitting on a barstool.

"My tough luck, guess that's the way the cookie crumbles." Charlie hit the bar with another salvo of crackers. The bartender looked up.

"Charlie, stop," Wallace said.

"What really pisses me off is you made a sale and didn't have the decency to call." Charlie reached for another handful of crackers. Wallace grabbed him by the wrist.

"Charlie, enough."

Charlie tried to wriggle free, but the Santa glove had him like a vice. He made a fist with his free hand and swung on Wallace. His first punch—a wild roundhouse—caught Wallace on the side of the face, driving his beard askew and sending his glasses flying. Charlie fought to get his hand back; he kicked at Wallace's black boots. The bar table went over, sending their drinks crashing to the floor. A woman screamed. People stood. Wallace got behind Charlie and forced him into a bear hug. Together they fell onto the leather banquette. Two Good Samaritans jumped in. One took a cheap shot and bloodied Charlie's nose.

Hotel security arrived. They hauled Charlie, screaming obscenities, through a door to a harshly lit hallway, then through a series of corridors to the security office.

Wallace declined to press charges. It took some doing to convince the hotel manager not to call the police.

"Okay, Santa," the manager said. "But your crazy grandpa leaves this hotel, I don't care who he is."

Charlie sat handcuffed and dazed in a glass-enclosed holding cell. The blood on his white tuxedo shirt made him look like a gunshot victim.

"Want a steak for your eye?" the manager asked.

"I'll be all right." Wallace shrugged off the black eye that was forming. In the same vein, he ignored the cell phone that kept ringing deep in the cartoon pocket of his red coat.

As Charlie and Wallace made their way to the front of the hotel, under the escort of two security guards, Wallace finally answered his phone. It was Oswald, in great distress that Wallace had gone missing. The Ziegfeld girls were waiting in the hallway, the band was repeating songs, and Becka was standing on her head. The party was in near ruins.

Wallace explained the situation, saying he'd get there as soon as he could.

"First things first," Wallace said. "I need to get this guy into a cab."

Outside, under the high roof of the hotel entrance, there were no taxis to be found. The doorman wore a top hat and a long overcoat. He saw the blood on Charlie's shirt and put him at the front of the line. A cab finally pulled up. Wallace went to the driver's window, peeled off some twenties, and told the driver to take Charlie straight home.

By the time Wallace reached the second-floor ballroom the party was in full swing. The band was playing, people were dancing, and the hors d'oeuvre stations were bustling. A silver fountain was spilling over with liquefied chocolate, to the delight of a captivated throng. Michael and Becka were working their way around the room, shaking hands. Wallace was uneasy in his costume. He had thrown the party off-script, and he didn't know where he was supposed to be. He moved in the shadows, making his way to the nearest bar.

He was having the first sip of another vodka martini when somebody gripped his arm. It was Becka.

"Is there nothing you take seriously? Get on your throne!"

There was a long line of people waiting to have their picture taken with Santa.

When Oswald saw Wallace's black eye he made a face. "Great. Now Santa Claus is a hooligan." He fished a pair of black Ray Ban sunglasses from inside his tuxedo jacket. "Here, put these on."

They were prescription sunglasses. From his place sitting on the throne, Wallace saw the world through one eye, underwater.

Oswald presided over the portrait line. He offered each couple two pistols as props—a Walther PPK and a Smith & Wesson .38 revolver—and demonstrated Bond poses. Under his breath he had catty comments for the women: "Love the gown, sweetie. It's so *Thunderball*." The Ziegfeld girls, playing Mata Hari elves, flanked Wallace, their long legs covered in fishnet stockings. They wore identical Santa hats and red velveteen jackets trimmed with fur. They took turns bringing Wallace martinis. Though Oswald assured him the guns were only replicas, Wallace became increasingly disconcerted by the many ways his drunken employees could mishandle even a fake firearm. Like chimpanzees they tried to one-up their friends. Many eschewed the classic pistol-pointed-to-the-sky Bond pose. Instead they aimed the guns at Wallace's head, à la Bonnie and Clyde, and demanded pay raises and more vacation time. What annoyed Wallace most was that, in light of the programming staff's extortive past, the hostile poses should have been anticipated and the guns left locked in the props closet. Making Santa Claus the target of terror detracted from the Christmas spirit, Wallace thought.

Wallace's first glimpse of Lenore was her distorted image in the lens of his Ray Bans. She stood with Carroll in line. She wore a diamond choker necklace and a red formal gown with a long slit up the side. When it was her turn to be photographed with Santa, she came at Wallace wielding the Walther PPK.

"Lenore! Have you been a good girl?" By this time Wallace had developed a booming Santa voice, thanks to a sound vodka buzz. He put a gloved hand to the small of Lenore's back and guided her onto his lap.

She spoke breathlessly. "You have to ask?"

"What can Santa bring you," Wallace asked, "besides more gin?"

Lenore whispered in his ear, "I want to get laid."

"Ho, ho—whoa!'"

"Come to my room tonight."

The Ziegfeld girls were looking on, smiling. Oswald was working with Carroll, helping him to strike a proper pose.

"How sweet," Wallace said, raising his voice for the benefit of onlookers. "A pony! Or a bicycle!"

Lenore pointed the pistol at Wallace's groin.

"Promise me a dance," she said. "A slow one."

"Everyone, look this way," the photographer said.

Lenore lifted the pistol and gave the camera a sultry pose. The strobes flashed.

"One more—" the photographer said.

"Shame about our friend," Carroll said, smiling stiffly, looking straight ahead. "Deep-rooted mental illness, I suspect."

"He's a worthless nut who needs to be fired," Michael said. It was after dinner and they were all settled around the reserved table nearest the stage: Michael and Becka, Wallace and Hannah, Otto and his wife. Carroll and Lenore were just sitting down after a dance. The band was playing *Midnight at the Oasis*.

"Terminate him first thing Monday morning," Michael said, turning to Otto. "That's an order."

"Have someone walk him out," Becka said. "I don't want him taking my balls."

An awkward silence fell over the table.

Julie walked up behind Becka and touched her on the shoulder. "The photographer from *Pacific Coast Monarchy* is here. He's in the dessert line."

Becka made a face. "It's about time."

She left the table.

Michael watched her go, shaking his head. "Every time she opens that damn magazine it costs me twenty grand."

"We need to talk about severance," Carroll said.

Michael still had his eye on Becka. "Screw it. What's there to talk about?"

The women at the table were having a separate conversation. Word was out about Lenore's divorce.

"Any plans for Christmas Eve?" Hannah asked Lenore.

"None yet," Lenore said.

"Then you should come over," Hannah said. "It's family, mostly, but we always like to collect a few strays."

Wallace nearly spit his drink.

The conversation about Charlie Dye continued outdoors, on a balcony outside the ballroom, after port and brandy. The men stood in the cold night air smoking victory cigars—Hoyo de Monterreys smuggled in by a friend from Cuba, according to Carroll. Wallace slipped his cigar into his pocket after he realized he couldn't take it between his lips without ingesting stray hairs from the beard. Inside the music was loud. People were dancing and playing blackjack. Becka was leading the magazine photographer around the room. His camera flashed on the band, the singers, the food, and the people.

"Are we serious about firing Charlie?" Otto asked Michael.

"Oh, we're serious," Carroll said, stepping in. "Serious as a heart attack."

"Terminate him for cause," Michael said. He puffed regally on his Hoyo de Monterrey.

"What's the cause?" Wallace asked. Through the glass door he could see Hannah and Lenore talking.

"Insubordination and sabotage."

Wallace groaned.

"He wouldn't give Carroll a copy of his sales presentation," Michael said. "I'd call that insubordination and sabotage."

Otto said, "Michael, if this is about not paying a commission on Asbury Care—"

"It's got nothing to do with Asbury Care," Michael said. "We're at a turning point. It's a statement about who we are."

"We're playing in the big leagues now." Carroll had the lighter. He was relighting his cigar, trying to get a consistent burn on the ash. "No more shenanigans."

"But the matter of a commission is clearly stated in his employment letter—"

"Forget it, Otto," Michael said, growing angry, spitting a speck of tobacco leaf on the concrete deck. "I am not paying him a commission on Asbury Care. He's negative energy—drinking on the job, bad-mouthing a client. That stuff gets around."

"Speaking of getting around—" Carroll pulled the cigar from his mouth. He was looking in at the ballroom.

The band had stopped playing. Charlie Dye was on stage and had taken a microphone from one of the singers. He still wore his bloody tuxedo shirt and he was making a speech.

"Guy's out of his mind," Otto said.

Michael turned to Wallace. "Your crackpot friend is going to ruin Becka's party, and it's all your fault."

"I'll call security," Otto said.

Hannah and Lenore stared raptly at the stage. Hannah turned in her chair and looked back anxiously at Wallace.

Michael, Carroll, and Otto quickly extinguished their cigars and filed in the door.

Wallace stayed outside for one last, peaceful moment—a breath of fresh air, a look at the lights across the bay. He opened the door and stepped inside.

"I don't know why the Feds are so intent on tracking me down for a good asskicking," Charlie was saying. "I'm a secret colonel in the CIA—"

The lead singer, a tenor with a thick Italian accent, followed Charlie around the stage, urging him to give up the microphone. Charlie only turned away and talked faster.

"Firebase Rocket Box. This is Whiskey Tower, do you copy—"

Carroll spoke to Charlie from the dance floor. "Okay, old boy. Game's over."

Charlie crouched and went the other way, cupping his hands around the microphone. "Joker Patrol, Joker Patrol. Come in, Savannah. Do you read me?"

Wallace got up on the stage. "Hey, Charlie, how's it going?"

Charlie looked at Wallace with mad, frantic eyes.

Three security guards entered the ballroom through the main doors.

"Come on, I'll take that." Wallace reached for the microphone.

Charlie's eyes grew wide. He threw the microphone at Wallace and ran from the stage.

Wallace and Carroll followed after him, walking with determined steps, dodging blackjack tables, cutting through the crowd on the dance floor.

They cornered Charlie behind the chocolate fountain.

Wallace held up his hands, showing the palms of his gloves. "We're not gonna' hurt you, Charlie. We're gonna' get you help."

Charlie peered intently at Wallace. A surge of anger seemed to jolt through his body.

"Liar!" Charlie turned over the table. The avalanche of flatware rang as it hit the floor. Glass shattered. Plates broke. The fountain split into pieces and molten chocolate flowed onto the dance floor.

Becka leveled an angry finger. "You are *so* fired!"

The magazine photographer snapped pictures.

In the ensuing commotion, Charlie made a break for the door. As he passed the props table he seized the Walther PPK.

"Gun!" shouted a security guard. He and the other two guards dove behind a row of potted palms.

People screamed. Some ducked under tables.

"Charlie, stop!" Guided by his one good eye, Wallace leaped the river of chocolate and chased after Charlie, who disappeared through the main doors.

Wallace lost him going down the escalator.

"No use," Carroll said, catching up. "He's long gone."

First the empty streets, the deserted sidewalks, the massive parking structure; then the inky lawns of the bayside park, the quiet docks of the marina, and the vacant paths of Seaport Village—Wallace searched everywhere. Charlie had vanished into the night.

Wallace sat on the white stucco seawall and stared back at the lights of the city. He didn't feel like going inside.

The shadowy figure that approached him was too tall to be Charlie. The man reeked of alcohol and wore a tattered coat.

"Hey, Santa, got any spare change?"

"Here," Wallace said, reaching into his pocket. "Have a cigar."

CHAPTER THIRTY-THREE

"Out where?" Julie asked. She eyed Wallace suspiciously.
"A lunch meeting." Wallace was flipping through phone messages, being intentionally vague—a defense against Julie's sudden appetite for prying.

"It's not on your calendar," Julie said.

"It just came up."

"When will you be back?"

"Can't say."

Julie raised an eyebrow.

Wallace started to walk away, then came back to her desk. "Did I do something to make you angry?"

"How would I know." She wouldn't look at Wallace. She slammed a drawer shut.

"Go clean your ditto machine," Wallace said.

It was only Monday morning, and already the bad news was mounting. The transit police had tased Charlie Dye early Saturday morning, at the Gaslamp Quarter trolley station, when he failed to drop the Walther PPK, and now he was in the psychiatric ward, under arrest, on a seventy-two hour hold. Otto Foreman was in the human resources office drawing up Charlie's termination papers. Then Morty Schlegg called. The district attorney was upping the charges. Morty was vague about the details. He insisted Wallace meet him for lunch.

Morty was waiting for Wallace in the reception area of his Middletown office. Except for a few milk crates and a computer, the room was bare. The outline of a secretarial desk in the carpet was all that remained of Morty's repossessed office furniture. The telephone was on the floor.

Morty wore a cervical collar neck brace, the result of his barroom brawl.

"Speaking of a good fight, that's a nice shiner," Morty said, looking at Wallace's eye. "What happened to you?"

"Goldfish crackers," Wallace said. "What do you mean they're upping the charges?"

"You rejected their offer, and now they want blood. Assault and battery, false imprisonment, something else I can't remember—"

"False imprisonment?"

"Technically when you held down that boy—"

"That's baloney."

"That's why we're taking it to the newspaper."

"Morty, I told you. Absolutely not."

Outside a car horn honked.

"That's Patience," Morty said. "I have to go."

"You called me all the way down here and now you're leaving?"

"I'm due in court. I've arranged for you to tell your story to Babette."

"Who's Babette?"

"The *Escondido News-Journal*. She's a reporter."

"I told you, Morty. I don't want this in the paper."

"Listen, meathead. This is legal brinksmanship of the highest order. We need public sentiment on our side. She can save your bacon. At least talk to her."

Wallace cooled his heels in Morty's office, waiting for the newspaper reporter to arrive. He sat at Morty's desk, thumbing through a book on evidence, trying to make sense of the legal gobbledygook. Credibility of witnesses, privileges of defendants, confessions—the chapter headings made Wallace's eyes glaze over. The very thought of courtroom procedures made his stomach sink. He closed the evidence manual and studied Morty's bookcase for something else to read. There was a framed black-and-white photo of Morty and Patience sitting at a courtroom table, looking grave—probably a newspaper shot. The books were mostly law books. On the bottom shelf were two stacks of magazines: *Red Herring* and the *Economist*. Wallace was flipping through an issue of *Red Herring* when he heard the door open.

"Hello?" called a woman's voice.

"In here."

She stepped inside the office. "You must be Wallace. I'm Babette."

She was in her thirties, overweight, with dark glasses and a tangled mass of brown hair held in place by brightly colored picks. She wore tight green pants and a flowery top. Her handshake was strong—she was all business, Wallace could see, by the way she parked her sunglasses on her forehead and looked him in the eye.

Babette said, "Pardon me, this is a little awkward. I've, like, never done this."

"No?"

"Well, a couple times."

"Please, have a seat."

"Sure, why not." Babette dropped her oversize handbag on the floor and sat in the visitor's chair.

"Well," said Wallace.

Babette laughed nervously. "It's almost like an interview. Did something happen to your eye?"

"An accident," Wallace said. "Do you think this is such a good idea?"

"Maybe not," Babette said. "But on the other hand you never know."

"Morty's convinced."

"Adamant," Babette agreed.

"He's given you the basics?"

"You have two young children, you're divorced or legally separated. You're some kind of executive—"

"Wait," Wallace said. "That's not entirely true. I'm still married."

"I see." Babette looked down a moment.

"Does that really matter?" Wallace asked.

Babette glanced at the ceiling and said, "It ... What should I say? It complicates things. But I don't want to give you the wrong impression. I'm willing to work around it."

"The emotional realm. That's your department."

"Guilty as charged," Babette said. "I'm a sucker for romance—long walks on the beach, dancing in the rain."

"It always comes down to the heart."

"That's refreshing to hear from a man."

Wallace smiled. "I'm in marketing."

Babette leaned in to Wallace. "What else should I know about you?"

"For starters I'm no vigilante."

"Let's hope not."

"I don't just take out teenage boys for sport."

"Has that been an issue?"

"To be honest, my biggest concern is that my in-laws will freak out about this. They're overprotective of the family name. My father-in-law was on the hospital board."

"Discretion," Babette said, nodding. "On the other hand you can't spend your life worrying about what other people think. Sometimes you just have to damn the torpedoes and go full steam ahead." She grazed her breastbone with a fist and stared back at Wallace with yearning eyes. "So what do you say?"

"I'm still not convinced," Wallace said. "Can I feel you out and get back to you later?"

Babette flinched. "That's somewhat insulting, I must tell you. Dinner and a show—that's usually how I start."

"Maybe this time we could make it lunch," Wallace said. "Or just skip the meal altogether and do it right here. That'd be fine with me."

"Boy, Wilbur, you get right to the point."

"Wallace."

"Sorry, this is progressing faster than I expected. You could at least pretend to be interested in my side of the bed."

Wallace looked at Babette with surprise. "I didn't realize it was necessary."

"You're wicked," Babette said. "And since you're asking, I like farmers markets and walking the flower fields. Evenings I like jazz.

Sundays I often take a picnic lunch to the zoo and commune with the baboons."

"There's something in common," Wallace said. "I spend most of my week communing with baboons."

Babette did not laugh. "Business has made you cynical."

"People have made me cynical."

"I prefer a man with a sense of humor. And I don't french."

Wallace studied Babette sitting across the desk, the corners of his eyes tautening. He thought he was acquainted with newsgathering techniques, but this breed of reporter was a horse of another color.

"It's in your court," Wallace said. "How would you like to proceed?"

"Have you spent much time in Old Town?" Babette asked. "It's a wonderful first date if you like a big, salty margarita."

Wallace cocked his head at a slight angle. It was obvious he and Babette were not on the same page.

"Babette, why are you here?"

"Oh dear." Babette's face dropped. "Why are you asking?"

"What did Morty tell you?"

"He said you were looking for a girlfriend. Why, what did he tell you?"

"He said you could do us a favor, that you worked for the paper."

"You're in legal trouble."

Wallace nodded.

Babette's eyes darkened. "Listen, I may write Accolades and Onions, but I'm no press whore."

"Accolades and Onions?"

"My newspaper column. I'm a freelance critic."

"Not a reporter?"

"No," Babette said, "and I gather you aren't here for a blind date?"

"This is a little awkward," Wallace said.

Babette stood and collected her bag. "I'm gonna' kill that double-dealing twerp."

Wallace got Morty on the phone later that day.

"What did you do to screw things up?" Morty said. "You were supposed to take her to lunch."

"You're out of your mind."

"I warned you, you might have to spend a little time doing the bouncy-bouncy."

"Morty!"

"Don't worry," Morty said. "It took some doing, but I brought her around with a gift certificate—a hundred dollars to Victoria's Secret. She'll do the story. I'll add it to your bill."

"Are you sure we want this?"

"I am one hundred percent certain," Morty said. "Patience concurs. We'll hope for a ripple effect—first Babette's column, then a feature article on the front page, then the wire services, maybe some TV and radio."

Wallace felt sick. "Hope isn't a plan."

"This has nothing to do with hope," Morty said. "Babette's going to give the district attorney an onion, and she'll do it before Christmas."

Wallace started to laugh.

"What's so funny?" Morty asked.

"Legal brinksmanship of the highest order," Wallace said. "What's next, Clarence Darrow? FedEx 'em a pile of dog shit?"

CHAPTER THIRTY-FOUR

The cardboard box was badly bowed and shored up with packing tape, a repository for the few things that mattered: some old coffee mugs, a deck of cards, the community college course catalog. The rolling desk chair groaned as it carried its overweight traveler for the last time, from here to there and back again, the smudged track on the plastic chair mat worn in the pattern of a fleur-de-lis and to the thickness of a dollar bill. The trash can parked next to the cardboard box was spilling over with a career's worth of junk, enough odds and ends to fill a garbage truck. Every desk drawer was open, the case files long since dispersed, the antacids consumed, the Mardi Gras beads passed along to that new girl, the cute little blonde in patrol. Ernie Fernandez remained undecided as to what he should do with the plastic toy pony impaled in the mouth of a Coors Light can—an anonymous gift that had appeared on his desk the previous month. It was typical cop humor, a reminder of Ernie's runaway filly, the show cutter prospect that had threatened to wreak havoc on the Golden Door Spa. The horse had been put down after being struck head-on by a beer truck. Ernie was tempted to take the doohickey home, but he knew

Colleen would squawk at the sight of it. She continued to nurse her affection for the departed horse as if it were another healing rib.

That morning, the parking lot at Dee Dee's Daily Egg looked like a damn cop shop, with all the black-and-whites out front. What unfolded in the restaurant's back room was a scene reminiscent of the Last Supper: standing room only, all the dicks and brass and guys from SWAT, the civilian clerks, the CSOs, the motors—hell, most of the midnight shift had hung over, and the entire day shift was there.

"Ernie, you are a monument to your profession, a cop's cop, and we're gonna' miss you around here." Burly and balding, with a face like a prizefighter, in his dark blue uniform shirt sporting silver stars on the collar, Chief Dexter Thomas was playing emcee, presiding over Ernie Fernandez's last breakfast as a cop. As his eyes welled, Chief Thomas picked up a plaque and managed to flash his city hall grin. "Now get up here, you cockroach, and take this thing."

To raucous applause and a standing ovation, Ernie reluctantly tore himself away from his breakfast—a heaping chili-cheese omelet, butter-soaked hash browns, a side of bacon, and one of Dee Dee's signature sticky buns, big as a city bus and slathered with icing—and half-limped to the front of the room to accept the token award. With mirthful eyes he took in the beaming faces, his mustache twitching, his Western shirt spotted with salsa. Chief Thomas handed Ernie the plaque, shook his hand forcefully, and gave him a hearty hug. Cameras flashed. They looked like two bears dancing.

The crowd wanted to hear from Ernie.

"Guess this might come in handy in retirement," Ernie said, holding up the plaque. "If Colleen and I decide to eat wood."

The place cracked up.

And then the stories began. It seemed everybody had one.

Joe Duttweiler stood up first. He and Ernie went back forever. "Guy takes a bank manager hostage and makes her open the bank early. This is back in the '70s. We didn't have hostage negotiators, of course. Everyone's all long hair and Dirty Harry, carrying these oversize revolvers. Ernie's no different. Strolls into the bank. Guy says, 'Whaddya' want?' and Ernie says, 'I'd like to make a deposit.' At which time he busts this goddamn .45 Long Colt over the guy's head—actually bent the barrel!"

The whoops and hollers came like rounds from a Gatling gun.

Another old-timer, Carl Depascale, stood and said, "We didn't have many Mexicans on the force, naturally, in the early days when Ernie first joined. Somehow he gets in this shoot-out up on the Indian reservation. He's in plainclothes. The call comes in from witnesses as shots fired, a Mexican against two Indians. The dispatcher, he don't know what to do—all he heard was *Mexican*. So he calls Border Patrol!"

Hilarious! The place was in stitches!

Grover Trunk took a turn. "One day Ernie's at this intersection, directing traffic. Guy comes along in a pickup truck, has low blood sugar. He's slumped at the wheel. Ernie sees him just in time. Jumps on the hood of this goddamn truck, somehow winds up standing in back, in the truck bed. He's banging on the roof, hollering at this guy to pull over. Finally the guy stops. And the minute Ernie jumps outta' that truck, some country-club dude in an Oldsmobile honks, rolls down his window, and asks how much to build a block wall. Thinks Ernie's a day laborer!"

The people in the restaurant were howling!

Phil Cardelli took the floor. "One afternoon this guy sets himself on fire. Crazy guy, right in front of the police station. Protesting something or other. Next day ol' Ernie, he don't say a word. Just comes in with this big ol' raw hot dog on the end of a long stick and sets it by the door."

They were rolling in the aisles, falling out of their chairs!

Stan Gooding said, "Hell, we all know Ernie changes wives like most of us change socks. He's just back from his honeymoon with his first wife, and they've had this huge fight so she makes him sleep on the couch—" Laughter rippled through the room; everyone knew what was coming. "It's not a real comfortable couch, Ernie comes to realize. So he goes to buy himself a new couch. Ends up divorcing his wife and marrying the gal who sells him the couch!"

Mike Bragg said, "We were fishing at this camp in Cabo, and one night Ernie's had a little too much to drink. Next day he wakes up dead to the world, alone in this camp. Rest of us, we're out on the boats, fishing all day. Come back to find Ernie sittin' in the lobby. He's got his bags packed—thinks it's Saturday morning!"

They were *crying*, they were laughing so hard! Even Ernie had to wipe away tears. Thirty years had passed in the blink of an eye. And despite the fact that cops were an ignorant bunch of sons of bitches to spend that kind of time with, he had loved every minute of it.

A shaft of afternoon sunlight angled through the vertical blinds in Ernie's office, illuminating a calendar and a clock on a section of discolored wall, as if to underscore the day, the hour that had finally arrived. Ernie's sense of time slipping away was so acute that he felt paralyzed sitting at his empty desk. At this rate he'd be home before Colleen—she worked as an elementary school secretary—and he wasn't prepared for that. In the back of a drawer he had found a CD. He wistfully studied the jewel case. This one was a keeper: Don José, the singing Mexican cowboy. As Ernie studied the song list, the tunes played in his head: *My Broken-hearted Road; Truth is a Lyin' Woman; Adios Cruel World*. To him, nothing was more magnificent than a clear night in the desert, listening to a Western ballad, a campfire roaring, the horses stirring at the breeze, the coyotes yip-yipping in the canyons. He wondered if it was too late to take up the twelve-string guitar.

Ernie retrieved the course catalog from the moving box and flipped through the pages, contemplating his future. The classes that only yesterday had galvanized him as a veritable feast for the mind now numbed his senses: history, philosophy, psychology, comparative literature, political science. It seemed so far-fetched. He wondered if he had the fortitude to be a student again. So far Colleen had signed him up for square dancing lessons.

"Thinking about the one that got away?" Tetley stood in the doorway. He held a long pair of stainless steel kitchen tongs.

Ernie grunted. "The life, more like it."

"Sorry I missed the party. It was my day in the gym, doing curls."

If I ever write my life story, Ernie thought, I'll call it *Demise of Law and Order*. In the old days you knew who the bad guys were.

"What's with the barbecue tongs, Tetley? Gonna' pull somebody's tongue out?"

The young detective kept a ball python in a 20-gallon aquarium next to his desk. Feeding the snake was a disconcerting process for Ernie to watch. Tetley would grasp a live mouse with the kitchen tongs, wiggle the cowering rodent in front of the python's face, and then wait for the snake to take the mouse in its yawning jaws. Ernie had ordered Tetley to get rid of the python, but the young detective appealed to a higher authority and won. Chief Thomas had a thing for snakes. When he wasn't tied up doing performance reviews or preparing for a city council meeting, he often made it a point to come upstairs to watch the feedings.

Tetley stepped inside the office and offered Ernie his hand. "Guess this is it—"

Ernie lay back in his chair, his arms folded. "Lance, you scare me for the future of this department."

"Bury the hatchet."

Ernie glanced at the hand and stared back at Tetley. "Think I'd prefer to keep my options open."

"Come on, my way of saying good luck."

"Better go feed that snake. Before I flush it down the toilet."

Tetley eyed Ernie with disbelief. He pulled back his hand. "What's your problem, old man?"

"You're no centurion, Tetley. You're a thug."

"Go to hell." Tetley began to walk away. "I tried."

"Hey, Tetley."

The young detective turned.

Ernie tossed him the toy horse. Tetley caught it with one hand.

"What do I want with this?"

"From me to you," Ernie said. "Sooner or later a beer truck comes along with your name on it. Remember that."

CHAPTER THIRTY-FIVE

"Trek didn't tip his hand?" Wallace asked.

"Not a word," Michael said. "Just said to sharpen our pencils and meet his plane at noon."

Wallace checked his watch. It was five minutes to twelve. He and Michael stood behind a low cyclone fence at Palomar Airport, their matching black loafers leaving soft impressions in the Bermuda grass. It was much too warm to be wearing dark suits. The concrete runway shimmered in the distance. The Santa Ana winds were blowing. A thick stripe of brownish smog hung over the ocean.

The Cessna Citation V *Ultra* arrived from the west. The sleek jet touched down precisely at noon. It took several minutes for the Citation to taxi back to the one-room terminal. As soon as the engines quieted, the door opened and a white-shirted pilot let down a short stack of stairs. Trek Reese emerged from the cabin. He bounded down the steps and strode across the tarmac, like it was perfectly normal to be arriving at a small airport in northern San Diego County two days before Christmas on your own private jet. Behind him in the Citation's open doorway, Jeter stood blinking into the bright sun. He carried a brown leather satchel.

Michael greeted Trek with an eager handshake. "Beautiful jet, Trek. First-class all the way."

"Shit, that thing?" Trek said. "I usually have the Hawker, but a partner took it to Snowmass. I had to settle for the Volkswagen." He set his mighty jaw and walked past Wallace. "Tallyho, gents. Sittin' on your thumbs might make you famous, but it won't make you rich."

"Hah!" Jeter brushed past Wallace. His attempt at a callous laugh came out instead as a bucktoothed snort.

"The Range Rover is us," Michael called after them. It was parked in a red zone with its engine running and the air conditioner set to high.

"Like I told you on the phone, Asbury Care makes all the difference in the world," Michael said, steering the Range Rover out of the airport. "The universe is definitely galvanized."

"I'm equivocating," Trek said.

"We had them eating out of our hand," Michael said.

"Michael, everything you say is a lie," Trek said. "This transaction totally stinks."

"They've committed to a thousand sites."

"I personally hate your business model."

"Wait till you see the new numbers. This thing's a hockey stick."

"The only reason to do this is your CTO," Trek said.

Michael glanced over. "Sanjay?"

"And this new guy who landed Asbury Care," Trek said. "Sounds like he's got some know-how, domain-wise. But I'm losing steam."

Michael looked distressed. "We're definitely over the hump. The second carrier is traditionally the long pole in the tent—"

"It's not a huge category and there's no game-over strategy," Trek said. "Your web site sucks."

"I need an East Coast account executive," Michael said. "I need to field a national sales force."

"It's a brick, it's all smoke," Trek said. "Nothing's been developed, nothing's been accomplished. You're puttin' up an air ball and telling me it's a layup."

They were stopped at a traffic light, waiting to make a right turn onto the freeway on-ramp.

"The plan is padded," Michael said, stepping on the gas. "We can do this for five million."

Jeter spoke from the back seat. "Moving the goalposts. Fire sale!"

"We can slow-boat it," Michael said. "Start from both coasts and push in."

"My rejoinder to that," Trek said, turning to look at a stunning woman in a convertible Jaguar, "is skimming cream is not building mindshare."

"You said so yourself," Michael said. "The market is talking."

"Here's where I am on that," Trek said. "Don't confuse *disinter-mediation* with fragmentation. Your economics are terrifying. I think you're going to need more runway."

"I need someone to pay my taxes," Michael said. "The landlord just posted a three-day notice."

Jeter said, "Maybe you should move."

"I can't afford to move," Michael said.

Trek shook his head. "I personally think it's a gargantuan mistake that you're in a 7-Eleven city like San Diego. You wanna' get your clock cleaned as a VC, stake a nichey mom and pop."

"But we're about to bust this thing wide open," Michael said. "We've got momentum."

"Bullshit, Michael. You don't have market share. You don't have revenue. It's all in your head."

Michael drove in silence, chewing his lip. He was out of arguments. He made eye contact with Wallace in the mirror, who turned and pretended to be interested in something out the window.

They were on Highway 78, merging onto southbound I-15, when Trek suddenly stared at Michael, recoiled in the leather seat, and made bug eyes. "Turn around. Net-net I think this is a huge mistake."

Michael took his gaze off the road. "Now?"

"Take us back to the airport."

"But we've got sandwiches."

"Get off this freeway," Trek said, looking ashen. "I think I'm about to throw up."

They pulled off the freeway. Trek Reese had the dry heaves in a Target parking lot.

"It's all the takeoffs and landings," Jeter said. "This is our third stop of the day."

"I think I got some bad grapes—E. coli," Trek said, doubled over, hands on knees, licking his lips, casting spittle over a dormant flower bed. "We need to be fully invested by year-end."

Trek finished retching—he seemed disappointed nothing ever came up—and as he straightened he scanned the stores on the perimeter of the parking lot: LensCrafters, Barbecues Galore, a Starbucks. The Target center was bustling with Christmas shoppers.

"Look at all this friction," Trek said. "They're busting down my doors, giving me hundreds of millions of dollars to kill this ecosystem, and these people don't even know it."

"Bricks and mortar," Jeter said. "Insanity!"

"Can we please get back in the car," Michael said. "There must be some way to salvage this deal."

"Your data points blow," Trek said, going to the Range Rover. "Too many red flags. Truth be told, my take on you, Michael, is you're a pain in the ass to work with. I shouldn't even be talking to you." He reached for the door handle. "What's your valuation?"

Michael glanced at Wallace, then looked back at Trek. "Fifty."

"Mil?" Trek scowled. "Bullshit, back to the airport." He climbed into the front seat.

"Okay," Michael said, "ten."

Trek said, "Five."

Michael looked crestfallen.

"Plus I'll pay your rent current," Trek said. "And loan you money for your payroll taxes."

Michael perked up.

"We control the board," Trek added. "Your wife has to go."

"Becka?" Michael said. "No way. She'd kill me."

"Come on, Michael. You're bigger than that. Be a man," Trek said. "*Disintermediate* the wife."

The drafting of the term sheet took place at the Merksamer Digital offices, upstairs in the conference room, over bottled water, turkey sandwiches, and mustard potato salad. Trek Reese agreed to invest $5 million in exchange for half the equity in the company. Jacaranda's CFO could wire the money in a matter of days, Trek promised. Both Wallace and Michael would remain directors. Jacaranda would control the other three seats on the board. Their directors would be Trek, Jeter, and someone to be named later—in all likelihood a Dr. William

Ricketts, psychiatrist and professor emeritus at Stanford's Graduate School of Business, who already sat on a number of Jacaranda boards. Trek walked everyone through the mind-numbing details of the term sheet: liquidation preferences, registration rights, antidilution protection, preemptive rights. Wallace was thankful when Julie slipped into the conference room and handed him a note.

The note was from Lenore. Cal Max was experiencing a major crisis. Wallace excused himself.

"Where is she?" Wallace asked Julie.

"In your office."

Lenore was seated at the small conference table, leafing through a trade magazine: *Fall Anthology: Benefits Enrollment Digest.*

"What's up?" Wallace asked.

Lenore put the magazine down. "Better close the door."

Wallace swung the door shut. "I'm afraid to ask."

Lenore stood and wrapped her arms around Wallace's neck.

"I had to see you."

"What are you doing?"

Lenore was unbuttoning her blouse. "Let's go. On the desk. Like in the movies."

"Lenore, stop!"

Her fingers quit working and she frowned. "Spoilsport."

"I need to get back to the conference room."

"Then meet me at the Park 'n Ride. First thing tomorrow morning. I've got a motel room in Laguna Beach."

Wallace stared back blankly. He didn't know what to say. As keen as he was to sleep with Lenore again—they hadn't been together since Boston—tomorrow was Christmas Eve day. Addison and Tiffany were out of school, Hannah would be home cooking dinner, and Dirk Junior and Baby were coming to town. The office would be working a half day, tops. It was no time to be holed up in a sleazy motel.

"Julie's got it on her calendar," Lenore added. "I told her Peg Brown called an emergency meeting at Cal Max."

Wallace gave Lenore a cool kiss on the forehead. "Sorry, babe. Any day but tomorrow."

Lenore made a face. "Pooh. I hate the holidays."

Wallace gave her another peck, this time on the part of her hair. "Good plan. Just bad timing."

"So how much are they putting in?" Lenore asked, closing her blouse.

"Five million."

"What's the valuation?"

"Five," Wallace said.

"Pre-money?"

Wallace nodded.

Lenore looked at the ceiling and crinkled her nose—she was doing the math in her head. Her face brightened. "For you that's a million dollars."

"Not bad, huh?"

Lenore took Wallace's hand and placed it on her chest. "Feel my heart. It's racing."

Julie caught Wallace as he was going back into the conference room. She lifted the telephone receiver and held it to her ear. "Want me to confirm your meeting with Peg Brown?"

Wallace looked at her without blinking. "Change of plans. We're not going."

As he reached for the conference room door he heard Julie put down the phone and snicker.

Before leaving for the airport Trek and Jeter had one-on-ones with the rest of the management team.

"I like that guy Carroll," Trek said in the Range Rover, on the way back to Palomar. "Socked him in the jaw and found him compelling."

"What about Otto?" Michael asked.

"In way over his head," Trek said. "We need a heavy hitter, a talent of huge proportions. We'll start a search."

"What about Sanjay?"

"Sanjay's a total stud," Trek said.

At the airport Trek let it be known he had one more deal to fund before the day was over. He and Jeter boarded the jet quickly. The Citation ran up its engines and taxied to the end of the runway. It dipped its nose once in salute to the business acumen of the Merksamer Digital principals and hurtled noisily down the runway.

CHAPTER THIRTY-SIX

At this late hour, and with every passing minute, Wallace Noe—father, entrepreneur, millionaire, cheater—was less and less inclined to expend the effort necessary to bask in the hot tub, though it remained a seductive offer: the stars were out, the jets were pounding away, and the water temperature was in excess of one hundred degrees. On the other hand, the house was quiet, the girls were asleep, the dog was curled up on the floor, and Wallace was momentarily enthralled with his tract-home fireplace, where a row of flames danced a devil's merengue over the exposed gas log lighter. A Christmas tree glowed supernally in the corner. The scotch, too, was having its intended effect—casting its own radiance over the dark room. Wallace felt deliriously drunk, though he couldn't say he was happy. He was morose over a woman, and it didn't sit well that a lowlife like Michael Merksamer had lectured him on moral grounds.

It would be easy, Wallace knew, to fault Lenore for her forwardness, but things were much more complicated than that. That a pair of cobalt blue eyes, a falling wisp of straight blond hair, and a few square inches of anatomy could transform an accomplished, educated man into a lowly, humping dog was a miracle of biology, a testament to the tentacular nature of the female species.

God, what a pitiful lot.

Some six hours earlier, at Palomar Airport, Wallace had ignored Michael's call for high fives. He could only stare after the ascending jet, his head flooded with memories of the long road traveled: the decision to go out on his own, the sleepless nights, the debt, the travel, the fights. He had been so thwarted at every turn, had faced such adversity from outside forces, that his newfound sense of redemption moved him nearly to tears. The setting sun made him think of his father. With this latest turn of events, Wendell Noe III might have been pleased on the economic front, but he would have been horrified on the home front. Adultery was not in his vocabulary.

"Hannah, I am so sorry," Wallace said, his eyes brimming with tears, when he noticed her standing over the sofa, the firelight casting her face in an orangish, flickering glow. Wallace was always amazed by his wife's stealth. She could come and go like a cat burglar. She wore a black satin micro-chemise. Her feet were bare.

She went to the corner and grasped the rocker switch for the Christmas tree lights, mistaking his apology to be energy-related.

"Just turn it off," she said, as the tree went dark. Next she seized on the fireplace, turning the gas key counterclockwise, killing the flames. "What about the hot tub? Using it or not?"

"At this point, possibly not."

"Then I'm turning it off." Like an officer of the law, she pulled open the kitchen slider and braved the chilly night to kill the wanton spa. It, too, went dark.

"Parity with public companies in our sector," Wallace called over his shoulder, when he heard Hannah come back inside and lock the sliding door. "That's Michael's new motto. Pay raises, liberal stock options, everything effective retroactive." Wallace purposely kept the tone of his voice upbeat. He was taking the high road, paying little heed to the rage that was mounting in his brain stem at the underlying insult of his wife's totalitarian tactics—unilaterally shutting everything down, cutting off the power, forcing him to call it a night. These were *his* things, this was *his* house, it was *his* life.

"You're repeating yourself," Hannah said. "Did you remember to walk the dog?"

"Yes I have walked the dog," Wallace said. "I am merely pointing out to you that the situation, *our situation,* has materially changed. Believe me, Hannah. We can afford the utility bill."

"The receipt for the bicycles is next to the phone."

"Bicycles?" Wallace drew a mental blank.

"Wallace!" Hannah glanced at the almost-empty bottle of scotch on the coffee table. She looked at Wallace like she wanted to strangle him.

Determined to countermand the impression implied by his wife's hostile reaction—that in his inebriated state he has failed to retain some crucial shard of information—Wallace assumed the persona of Winston S. Churchill. He perched forward precariously on the edge of the couch, took a healthy swig of scotch, held it in his mouth for maximum effect, and cast a worldly gaze in the general direction of the now-lifeless fireplace. He thought about the perilous state of the universe. Behind every bush was a suit-happy lawyer, get things right with your constituencies, there's an IPO in our future—these were the overarching themes of Michael's rant against Wallace earlier that evening, as they sat in the Range Rover parked in the company parking lot, and for most of the night Michael's words had been swirling like killer tornadoes in the back of Wallace's head. Bicycles had not been foremost on his mind.

"Wallace, wake up!" Hannah shook him on the shoulder.

Perhaps he had dozed off a moment.

"Even fools are right sometimes," Wallace muttered, affecting a curmudgeonly British accent, taking another hit of scotch.

"I told you," Hannah said. "We're getting the girls bicycles."

The veil of fog lifted and Wallace remembered. Two bicycles: one pink and one purple. They were already paid for. Wallace was to pick them up, assemble them, attach the horns and bells to the handlebars, and hide them in the garage, preferably under one of Owen Andersen's old tarps. Tomorrow night they were expecting a houseful. Hannah would be in no position to deal with bicycles.

The implicit agreement between Wallace and Hannah was that they would stay married for the benefit of all concerned—at least through the holidays. This was somewhat problematic for Wallace and his subordinate employee-girlfriend, who was intent on feeding lies about their whereabouts to the secretarial staff and booking motel rooms in out-of-the-way beach towns.

"Michael wants me to get a new car," Wallace said, speaking with a sense of irony worthy of Churchill. "Something with a little more panache."

Wallace stumbled when he tried to stand.

Hannah caught him and took away his drink.

"Enough for one day," she said, leading him by the hand down the hallway. "Come to bed."

CHAPTER THIRTY-SEVEN

On Christmas Eve morning, Wallace arrived at the office to find the employees having a party. They were giddy, wandering the hallways, popping tops off beer cans, swilling champagne from bottles. Wallace stopped Carroll, who was dressed in bright, tight-fitting cycling garb and wheeling his Peugeot toward the lobby doors.

"Hey, what's going on?"

"Michael called a holiday."

Wallace stepped aside to let a group of Sanjay's programmers pass. They stormed the double doors and scattered for their cars.

Wallace said, "What about our budget meeting?"

"Right now I intend to tackle the grade at Torrey Pines," Carroll said. "Merry Christmas, old boy."

Upstairs, Julie's secretarial station was dark.

"Are we sending the right message here?" Wallace asked Michael, who was just turning out the lights in his office.

"I'm cultivating loyalty," Michael said. "Come Monday we'll hit it hard."

Wallace went to his office and dropped his computer bag behind his desk.

Michael followed as far as the door. "Everyone's asking if the gloves are off with respect to hiring. Do me a favor before you leave. Write up some parameters for the department heads. I don't want to show up a year from now and find we've burned through all the cash."

Wallace had a dull headache. He thought he'd start with a cup of coffee. In the kitchen he found the pot empty. He made a new one. He took a bottled water from the refrigerator and swallowed some aspirin while he waited for the coffee to brew.

He walked back to his office, down a dark hallway, carrying his coffee mug.

Wallace's window looked over the parking lot. Lenore's car—a white Mazda Miata—was one of the last cars left in the lot. It was parked directly beneath Wallace's window.

Wallace got busy disassembling the departmental budgets from the latest business plan. He spent several hours on the task, coming up with revised headcount targets and composing the memo to department heads. When he was satisfied with the numbers in the budgets and the wording of his memo, he went around the corner to word processing and ran off copies in quantity.

Wallace checked the parking lot again. Lenore's car was still there.

Is she waiting for me? Wallace wondered.

He was up against the clock—he still had to swing by the bicycle shop—but the sight of the small white car made him feel powerless to leave. He paced the floor of his office, annoyed at his own vacillation, irritated with Lenore. He had always viewed her through the lens of blind adoration, but in the days since their trip to Boston he had come to see another side of her: she was rash and impetuous to a fault. Also, he had recently pinpointed a flaw in her beauty: the shape of her mouth was somewhat reptilian.

Walking around distributing a memo was a ridiculous use of Wallace's time—he could have asked Julie to do it Monday morning—but he had a reason for wanting to play mailman: it allowed him to confirm that no one else was in the building. He crisscrossed the hallways, both floors, leaving copies of the memo atop the in-baskets on the deserted desks of department heads. His last stop was down a long corridor and through a series of security doors to the systems area—Sanjay's domain—a cavernous, nominally built-out room, home to an ever-expanding bull pen of cubicles that housed the software programmers. The lights were out and the chairs were empty. The monitors glowed. Wallace dropped a copy of the memo on Sanjay's desk. On the way out he took a detour.

It was time to nip this thing in the bud, Wallace decided.

The doorway to Lenore's office was brightly lit.

"Still working?"

Lenore was intent on her computer screen and typing. She turned and put a hand to her chest. "Gosh, you scared me. I thought I was the last one here."

"You pretty much are," Wallace said. "What're you working on?"

"This particular insidious animal is the RFI from Coast PrimeCare," Lenore said. She listed in her chair to give Wallace a full view of her computer screen, which displayed a dense-looking document. "Guess who I just talked to?" Lenore's eyes were teasing. "Your wife."

"Hannah?"

"Following up on her dinner invitation," Lenore said. "Told her I'd love to come."

"Please say you're joking."

"Don't be a grump. I want to observe the beast in his native habitat. Besides, it'll be fun."

"Lenore, this is not a smart thing to do."

"We're adults. I think we can manage one dinner."

"You could have any man you want."

"Few men interest me."

"You deserve a lot better."

Lenore stood. Her eyes widened and her chest heaved. "I'm a dirty fishwife." She tore open her silk blouse. "Treat me like I'm hourly, not salaried."

Wallace couldn't help himself. He kissed her fervently; he ran his hands over her face, over her perfectly sculpted collarbones, across the narrow frame of her shoulders. He parted her blouse.

Lenore's eyes were downcast. Her hands were working. Wallace felt his belt give way. He lifted her by the haunches and was working her onto the desk when a voice called from the darkened bull pen.

"Hello? Lenore? Are you here?" It was Sanjay.

Wallace and Lenore uncoupled quickly. Lenore sat hard in her chair. She planted both elbows on the desk and faced the computer screen just as Sanjay appeared in the doorway.

"Oh, Wallace, there you are," he said. "I have been looking all over for you. You have visitors in the lobby."

"Me?"

"I hope I am not interrupting anything important."

Lenore sucked a cheek and kept her gaze on the computer monitor. She clasped her torn blouse closed with one hand.

"Just working through some sticky issues," Wallace said, pointing lamely to the screen.

"Anything I can do to help?" Sanjay asked.

Go away, Wallace thought.

"It's the Coast PrimeCare RFI," Lenore said, taking a cue from Wallace. "A question I'm not really sure about."

"The health plan?" Sanjay eagerly joined Wallace standing behind Lenore's chair. "What do they want to know?"

"Cross-product selection under a single subscriber," Lenore said. She glanced at Sanjay. "We don't do that, do we?"

Wallace took a step back. It gave him a chance to buckle his belt.

Sanjay peered at the screen. Without his glasses he was slightly nearsighted. "Definitely not. We would have to change our entire database structure."

"I'll tell them it's a future feature." With her free hand Lenore clicked the mouse. Her French-manicured nails went rat-a-tat-tat on the keys.

"Very distant future," Sanjay said.

"Next release," Lenore said, continuing to type.

"No, not next release!"

"Sanjay, it's only an RFI."

Sanjay turned to Wallace. "She cannot say this. Next release is already locked down." Then: "Wallace, do you need to use the bathroom?"

"I think my belt just broke," Wallace said.

Sanjay made a skeptical face. "Just now? How could it break?"

Lenore snorted.

Wallace turned to Sanjay. "You said I had visitors?"

"Two men in the lobby," Sanjay said. "They want to give you a present. One is very fat."

"Maybe it's Santa bringing you a new belt," Lenore said.

"As long as it's not a subpoena." Wallace stopped at the door. "By the way, Sanjay, what are you doing tonight?"

"Working."

"Working's not allowed," Wallace said. "It's Christmas Eve. You're coming to my house for dinner. You can be Lenore's date."

"Truly?" Sanjay looked at Lenore and his face brightened.

Wallace ditched his broken belt in the wastebasket. "This is for you, Lenore. Don't say I never gave you anything."

Carson and Donald Duncan were waiting for Wallace in the lobby. Carson wore a bright red Christmas sweater. His hair was slicked back and his mustache was neatly trimmed.

"Glad we caught you," Carson said. "Indian gentleman who opened the door said everyone was knocking off early."

Donald was gaping openmouthed at Becka's Christmas tree. "Are these balls acrylic?"

"Handblown glass," Wallace said.

"Darn tree's probably worth more than my entire inventory," Donald said.

"We brought you a gift," Carson said. With stiff arms he offered Wallace a small box. "It isn't much, but Merry Christmas."

"Beats a death warrant," Donald grumbled.

Wallace glanced at him.

"You'll have to forgive my friend," Carson said. "It's been a horrific day."

"Most Mexicans are happy digging ditches," Donald said. "Mine has to amass a real estate empire."

"What's he talking about?" Wallace asked.

"*Los hermanos* Gonzalez bought the old ice factory," Carson said. "Donald just got his eviction notice. Duncan's Junction is out of business."

Donald said, "Have him open the present, Carson, so I can go put my head in a gas oven."

"The man's a superb technician," Carson said to Wallace, "but he handles adversity with the mettle of a wet tissue."

The wrapping paper on the gift was holiday train motif—holly leaves, red berries, and sleek, old-fashioned Lionel streamliners. Wallace pulled the paper off the box and lifted the lid. Inside was an HO-scale model locomotive, painted in the distinctive dark green and orange color scheme of the Western Pacific.

"All the boys kicked in," Carson said, "as thanks for letting us use the room."

"It's beautiful. I love it," Wallace said.

"It was hand painted by Redmond French," Donald added. "You'd never in a million years guess he has prosthetic arms."

"Oh, no, you sure wouldn't," Carson agreed.

"Notice the Blount trucks and low hood design," Donald said. "The spotting feature is the relatively short radiator."

Wallace stared blankly at the model locomotive, trying to locate the radiator. The small engine looked to him about as thoughtfully designed as a milk carton.

"That's an Alco S-1, a yard switcher," Carson said. "I presume your layout depicts the major hump yard at Oroville."

Wallace had a sense of being cast down a dark well. He could feel Carson's eyes boring down on him.

"My layout's pretty basic," Wallace said. "A dogbone with a figure eight, I think you'd call it."

"Good god, man, you can't sustain the hobby on figure eights and dogbones," Carson said, running a soggy handkerchief over his face. "You'll go stark raving mad."

"Through trains are pointless without meaningful switching movements," Donald said.

Both men chewed their lower lips and nodded solemnly, letting this sink in with Wallace.

"Point taken," Wallace said, glancing at his watch. "Good advice." He took a step in the direction of the double doors, hoping to move things along. The bicycle store would soon be closing.

"Let me guess," Carson said to Wallace. "It's Christmas Eve and you've got someplace to be: a standing prime rib roast, an expensive single-malt scotch, and more beautiful women than you know what to do with. Am I right?"

"More right than you know," Wallace said.

"All you high-powered executive types are cut from the same cloth," Carson said, running the rag across the back of his neck. "Before we go may I run something past you?"

"Can it be quick?"

Carson leaned in toward Wallace. "She's called the Ruby Ridge."

"Why are you whispering?"

Carson glanced furtively around the lobby. "She's been red-tagged by the city fathers as an eyesore. We can have her as is, for the cost of moving. See where I'm going with this?"

"Not really."

"She's private varnish—a 1923, Pullman-built baggage car, gutted and sitting on a siding in San Clemente. We'll move her down and park her on a spur—Mission Avenue under the freeway interchange."

"An old baggage car?"

"More than a baggage car—a sanctuary of the art form. Freedom from the despotism of third-world immigrants, a permanent home for Duncan's Junction and our model railroading club."

"All it takes is money," Donald said, looking glum. "Like everything else in this stupid world."

"So do it, Carson," Wallace said. "Why are you asking me?"

"Because you're experienced with this sort of thing," Carson said. "It's a complicated business decision fraught with traps."

Wallace thought about it. "Are you sure you want to do this? You've already gone out of business once."

"Tell me about it," Donald said. "I've lost my life savings."

"That's why we need your opinion," Carson said to Wallace. "You're a respected businessman. You know about these things."

"Some would challenge your assumptions—"

"So what do you think?"

"You never want to throw good money after bad," Wallace said. "You'd have to change your business model."

"Offer more products?"

"Either that or expand your market. Have you ever thought of doing business on the Internet?"

"Hmm," Carson said, narrowing his eyes.

"Computers?" Donald said. "Get real. We could barely afford that cruddy little switch engine."

"Talk to Sanjay," Wallace said. "He'd love to get involved with an Internet start-up."

Carson's face brightened. "I see what you're getting at. A virtual hobby shop. We could buy, sell, and trade all over the country ... heck, all over the world!"

"Global retail?" Donald said. "Who're you kidding? I'm not fit to push a hot dog cart."

"Start with a business plan," Wallace said.

"Outside investors?" Carson asked. "Think they'd go for it?"

"Look, I don't know the first thing about your business," Wallace said. "But to listen to venture capitalists talk, those hot rod guys might've done you a big favor, getting you out of bricks and mortar."

Wallace could see the wheels turning in Carson's head. Donald seemed less certain. His knees were wobbly.

"And this business plan you're talking about," Carson said. "Where could we get a template?"

"Any bookstore," Wallace said.

"Let's go, Donald," Carson said, pushing his friend out the doors. "We've got our marching orders. Cancel Christmas! To the bookstore! Prepare to work through New Year's Day!"

As Wallace crossed the empty parking lot on the way to his car, he noticed Lenore's Miata was gone.

It reminded him to call Hannah and tell her about the extra dinner guest.

CHAPTER THIRTY-EIGHT

Lenore kept making the same sequence of right-hand turns, circling the block. The streets were dark. The tract houses were indistinguishable. Parked cars obscured the curbs where the addresses were stenciled in bold numbers. Sanjay was laughing, deploring Lenore's sense of direction, mocking the city's primitive algorithm for assigning street numbers. Lenore was dismissive of the addresses per se; she was determined to find Wallace's house by sheer willpower. She had the sound system cranked—Bach's *Christmas Oratorio*.

"That's it!" Sanjay shouted, pointing.

"Don't think so," Lenore said. She took her eyes off the road momentarily to turn up the volume of the CD even louder. "Listen," she said, getting Sanjay's attention with her finger. "Perfectly informed baroque." At Texas Christian University she had majored in English and minored in classical studies. Having mentally put Ricky behind her—he was no man of letters—she was determined to resurrect her intellectual life with forays into art, literature, music, and theater. In a single week she subscribed to the *New Yorker*, *Fortune*, the San Diego Symphony, and the Old Globe Theatre.

"Maybe that one," Lenore said, slowing. She scrutinized the single-story house like a math problem. Little Tikes playhouse, windows brightly lit, Christmas wreath on the door—this looked like it.

"With the Hummer?" Sanjay asked.

"Has to be." Lenore accelerated up the street, searching now for a place to park. She handled the Miata like a toy, shifting gears with authority. She spotted a gap, told Sanjay to hang on, and threw the sports car in reverse. She shut off the engine. She found her purse, dabbed perfume in the V of her halter top, and fixed her lipstick in the mirror.

"Ready," she said, tucking a loose strand of hair behind one ear. "Should be a hoot."

Sanjay carried a great bouquet of flowers that covered his face. He studied the smallish house with an air of disappointment. "I pictured a mansion on a hill."

Lenore rang the bell. Inside the house a dog barked fiercely. Hannah finally answered the door, hair down, breezy peasant skirt, forced smile—a working mother pulling off the hat trick of a sit-down dinner party.

"You made it! Come in!" With a deft foot Hannah nudged the snarling, football-sized dog away from the door. She traded air kisses with Lenore.

"So nice of you for having us," Sanjay said.

The house was warm and smelled of a roast cooking in the oven. The entry was cramped—there was hardly enough room for the three of them to stand. Lenore could see through the kitchen to the family room. The Christmas tree was lit, a fire burned in the fireplace, and people were chatting amiably around the sofa.

"Love what you've done with the place," Lenore said.

"That's a sore subject," Hannah said. "Wallace promised to hang lights."

Lenore spied two small faces peeking around the corner, in the shadows. "Here, girls, look what I brought."

Wide-eyed and curious, Addison and Tiffany stepped tentatively forward, clasping hands. They wore matching Christmas dresses and black Mary Janes.

Lenore produced two snow globes from a plastic drugstore bag.

"Wasn't time to wrap them," she said. "Aren't they just darling? Now watch." She shook the globes. Cataclysmic blizzards engulfed the miniature scenes—cowboys scrambling to rope a wild horse, a family building a snowman. "Okay, your turn."

The girls said thank you and ran off to make storms.

"Beautiful children," Lenore said, watching after them.

The kitchen was small, with dated cabinetry and an out-of-fashion color scheme. The shelf above the built-in desk was lined with cookbooks. While Hannah put the flowers in a vase, Lenore took a step toward the refrigerator and studied the homemade chore chart. She smiled. Wallace's jobs were to do the grocery shopping, pick up the girls from school every other day, and vacuum the house on weekends.

"He's impossible," Hannah said. "Even when I have it in writing."

A broody weight-lifter type lurked in the corner. He perked up at the sight of Lenore and Sanjay, stopping them before they could pass through to the next room.

"Owen Andersen," he said, offering his hand.

"Lenore. This is Sanjay."

"You two an item?" Owen managed to shake Sanjay's hand but couldn't take his eyes off Lenore.

"Coworkers," Lenore said. "With Wallace."

"That company's still in business?"

"Barely." Lenore regarded him coolly.

"Bet your paychecks bounce."

"Absolutely. All the time."

"God helps those who help themselves," Owen said. "Know what I mean, Jake?" He cuffed Sanjay on the shoulder.

"It's Sanjay."

"Here's something, Sanjay. Would you believe home-based businesses are the fastest-growing segment of the U.S. economy—"

"Off limits," Hannah said, steering Lenore and Sanjay away by their arms. "The party's in the other room. We've got tons of hors d'oeuvres."

Owen called to Lenore. "Here's a tip. Go for the filet-and-mushroom puffs." He winked and made a smooching sound out the side of his mouth.

In the family room Audrey was ensconced like a museum mastodon on the old sofa. Baby sat next to her, balancing a teacup on a saucer. Dirk Junior stood with his back to the fireplace.

"I don't understand the thinking," Baby was saying. "When you could so easily put the whole thing behind you."

"I'll tell you what it is," Dirk Junior said. "It's that dog-bite lawyer, milking it for fees."

Baby said, "Pride goeth before the fall. That's what Pastor says."

Hannah interrupted to make introductions. Audrey stared back at Lenore with vacant eyes.

"Are those things real?" Baby asked, looking at Lenore's pricey necklace. Her frosted, swirling hair reminded Lenore of a flushing toilet.

"Hope so," Lenore laughed, fingering the black pearls self-consciously. "Better be. God knows my husband has gone down with enough pearl divers."

Lenore felt her face flush.

"Ex-husband," she added.

"Where does that one come from?" Audrey asked, pointing.

"Mom, Sanjay is from India," Hannah said. "He and Lenore were orphans tonight."

Audrey frowned. "Dad and I had dinner once with a man from India. He wasn't so black as him."

"Mother!"

"Tell me," Dirk Junior said, "do people in India really charm snakes?"

Sanjay smiled. "Yes, they truly do."

"I wouldn't put my life in the hands of a snake."

"You wouldn't worship a cow, either," Baby said.

No, but he's married to one, Lenore thought. She shifted her gaze to the bar. The martini shaker was there, the ice bucket was full, and a liter of gin stood among the open wine bottles.

"Dad never had any interest in going to India," Audrey said. "Poverty and dead bodies in the streets—he thought it would be too depressing. We went to Scottsdale instead."

"Scottsdale," Dirk Junior said. "Don't tell me about Scottsdale." He handed Lenore a business card.

The picture was corny—*Team Dirk Junior and Baby*. A gold embossed crest laid it on thick about all the real estate they'd sold.

Lenore looked at Baby. "Must be interesting working together as a couple."

"Not once you realize you're the one doing all the work," Baby said. "Dirk Junior has a tendency to skate."

"Tendency to skate?" Dirk Junior said. "When was the last time you went on a caravan?"

"Caravans are for fools," Baby said. "You get all the dope you need at chamber mixers." She turned to Audrey. "Mom, did you hear the news? Dirk Junior's giving me a bus bench for Christmas."

"A bus bench!"

"One of the best intersections in North Scottsdale—twenty-one thousand cars pass by every day."

"Twenty-*seven* thousand," Dirk Junior said, leaning toward Lenore. "But who's counting."

"Is this really a gift?" Sanjay asked.

"He can't give me children so he makes up for it in these oddball ways," Baby said. "Still, I can't imagine a better way to market our business."

"I'll tell you a better way," Dirk Junior said to Lenore. "Stadium signage would be better."

"Dirk, you're drunk," Baby said. "Get some coffee." She turned to the others. "Wallace is going to kill somebody with those stupid little drinks."

Dirk Junior spoke with a thick tongue. "They're called martinis."

Hannah was passing a plate of hors d'oeuvres. "Dirk, play bartender for our guests. I need to check on the roast."

Owen was a step behind Hannah going into the kitchen. He snatched a mushroom puff off the serving tray. "Strike while the iron's hot," he said, giving Lenore a wink.

"Specialty of the house is a martini," Dirk Junior said.

"Perfect," Lenore said.

"Good to me," Sanjay said.

"Dirk, you stick with wine," Baby said. "I don't want to have to carry you out vomiting like the last time."

Dirk Junior was a hesitant bartender. He handled the martini shaker like a bomb. He filled it with ice, poured gin, added a jigger of dry vermouth, and seated the cap like a detonating device. He fussed with colored toothpicks, trying to skewer Spanish olives from a jar. Lenore had to help him.

"Where is Wallace, anyway?" she asked.

"In the garage," Dirk Junior said. He poured the gin into two martini glasses. "Hannah's fit to be tied. He waited till the last minute to work on the bikes."

Sanjay reached for a glass. "Bottoms are up."

"Cheers," Lenore said.

Dirk Junior stared openmouthed at Lenore, unabashedly studying her profile.

Owen was at the bar, filling a balloon glass with red wine. "To be honest I think your boss is too humiliated to show his face."

Lenore grimaced at the moldy taste of her martini—too much vermouth. "Why, did something bad happen?"

"Don't tell me you haven't seen it?" Owen asked.

"Secular stupidity," Dirk Junior said. "In law school they don't teach turning the other cheek, apparently. Check this out." He went around the room, searching for a section of newspaper. He finally found it tucked beneath Audrey's massive purse. He showed it to Lenore and Sanjay.

ACCOLADES AND ONIONS
A Clear Instance of Self-Defense

This case calls for two putrid onions: one to the district attorney and one to the Escondido Police Department, who have conspired to throw the book at local businessman Wallace Noe.

While most law-abiding citizens would applaud Noe for his actions—he courageously turned the tables on an armed robber—the DA is charging him with an escalating list of crimes.

We're all in favor of effective law enforcement, but this case has nothing to do with vigilantism, as the DA claims. It has everything to do with self-defense— and common sense.

We call on the decision makers at City Hall to rethink this one. Winning at all costs is no strategy when a man's good reputation is on the line. More importantly, Noe's wrongful-arrest lawsuit could cost the city millions.

"Millions," Lenore said. "Nice ring to it."

"Very good," Sanjay said.

"I disagree," Dirk Junior said. "Any lawyer who planted that thing should have his head examined. Mother's sick with embarrassment. Her telephone's been ringing off the hook."

Wallace came up behind Dirk Junior. He had grease on his shirtsleeves and an angry look on his face. "Do me a favor, Dirk. Turn down the gas in that fireplace before it melts those Christmas stockings."

"No can do," Dirk Junior said. "Mother's cold."

Wallace turned to Sanjay and Lenore. "Hear that? He'd rather burn down my house than ask his own mother to put on an extra sweater."

"You owe her an apology," Dirk Junior said. "What's she supposed to tell her church friends?"

"She doesn't have to tell them anything," Wallace said. "They don't know me from Adam." He eyed the drink in Lenore's hand. "Who made those?"

Dirk Junior said, "I did."

Wallace snatched the martini out of Lenore's hand, sniffed it, and dumped it in the sink.

"It's all wrong. Here, Sanjay, gimme' that thing."

Wallace threw out Sanjay's martini, too. The skewered olives lay in the stainless steel bar sink, looking up like eyeballs. Wallace reached for the liter of gin and found it empty. He glowered at Dirk Junior.

"It's your mess," Dirk Junior said. "Don't blame me."

As Wallace searched the cabinet for another bottle of gin, a child's short-tempered scream reverberated through the hallway. Tiffany came running into the family room with Addison on her heels. They bowled into a wall and spilled to the floor, a howling mass of gangly limbs, Christmas plaid, and hair.

Wallace called out, "Girls!"

Tiffany protected her snow globe like a basketball. Addison made a desperate grab for the toy.

"Stop!" Tiffany foiled her sister with a body check.

"I just want to show you—"

"No!" Tiffany hunkered down in a corner. "I told you! Beatrice hates snow!"

Wallace physically separated his children. "Please, girls! Addison, stop tormenting your sister."

"But—"

"Just leave her alone."

Addison retreated to a corner, looking defeated.

Tiffany gasped for breath, choking on tears. She clutched the snow globe and refused to look at her sister. Lenore marveled at the willful child. It was as if she were watching herself.

Wallace removed the crying child from the room.

Lenore approached Addison and knelt down next to her.

"I bet you like tea parties," Lenore said. When Addison nodded, Lenore took her by the hand. "Come on. Let's make nice with your sister."

In the kitchen Wallace was cleaning Tiffany's face with a dishcloth. The snow globe was set aside, next to the toaster. Tiffany sat on the counter, her frilly white socks dangling.

"Out of the way, Dad," Lenore said. "We've come to make atonement."

Hannah was working at the stove. She glanced at Lenore with smiling eyes.

"The girls and I are going to have a quick tea party," Lenore said. She snapped her fingers at Tiffany and offered a hand. "Come on. Beatrice, too."

Hannah said, "You know about Beatrice?"

"Hitching a ride on the cosmic snow globe," Lenore said. "Aliens and I go way back."

Tiffany looked up at Lenore with amazement.

"Off we go," Lenore said. Tiffany scooted forward far enough to let Lenore swing her to the floor.

Wallace said, "Play nicely, girls, or poor Lenore will never want to have children."

"My fault," Lenore said to Wallace, looking over her shoulder. "Next time I'll bring two boxes of Cracker Jack."

The girls led Lenore down the hallway, past walls decorated with family photos.

"Who's this handsome couple?" Lenore asked, stopping at one of the pictures. The man was a dead ringer for Wallace, but he was older and had a thick shock of white hair.

"That's Papa and Nana," Addison said.

"Our father murdered them," Tiffany said.

"Oh, dear," Lenore said. She was familiar with the story. "And who are these two beautiful creatures?"

"Us," Tiffany said. "When we were babies."

Lenore paused in front of Wallace and Hannah's wedding picture. Wallace wore a white tuxedo. He was much thinner. His hair was long and he had a mustache.

"This picture of your mother could've been taken yesterday," Lenore said.

"She saved her dress," Tiffany said. "It's under the bed."

Addison, Tiffany, Lenore, and Beatrice had tea in Tiffany's bedroom, at a miniature table stenciled with flowers. Everyone got a small teacup on a saucer and a plate for make-believe cakes. Lenore sat on the floor. Tiffany served from a plastic kitchen in the corner. Her trundle bed was draped with a billowing purple spread.

"These are my baby teeth," Tiffany said, showing Lenore a miniature jewelry case. With a small hand she shielded the case from the empty chair to Lenore's right. "I can't let Beatrice see this. Bloody teeth make her sick."

Addison leaned forward in her chair, her legs crossed at her knees, the saucer perched in her lap. "Do you have any animals?"

"One cat," Lenore said, "named Hank."

"What color is he?"

"She," Lenore said. "To look at her you'd think she was black, but in the sunshine you can see she's actually a very chocolaty brown. She's a mouser. She likes to catch mice coming up from the canyon."

"Hmm," said Addison, taking a sip of imaginary tea.

"One time our dad caught a lizard in the house," Tiffany said.

"Tell me more about your dad," Lenore said. "What makes him special?"

Tiffany said, "He reads us stories."

"And takes us shopping," Addison added.

"What does Beatrice think of him?"

"He took her to the 1915 World's Fair," Tiffany said. "He bought her cotton candy."

Lenore feigned surprise. "They knew each other way back when?"

"We've all been here before," Tiffany said. "We just trade places."

"Did Beatrice tell you that?"

"Yes."

"I think she's very wise," Lenore said. "I believe that myself— we're all recycled old souls."

"One time a robber tried to steal our dad's money," Tiffany said.

"I think your dad still has plenty of money."

Tiffany said, "No. Because if he did, he'd buy a motorhome."

"Why that?"

"He makes us go look at them on weekends, even when we don't want to. Grandma says we should be in church."

Lenore asked, "What else would your dad get if he had lots of money?"

"A train set that works," Addison said.

"Train?" Lenore made a face. Trains and motorhomes—what was it with men and these lowbrow afflictions? "What about a big house or nice clothes?"

"He'd buy neckties," Tiffany said.

"I'll bet he has lots of neckties," Lenore said. "Does he keep them in his closet?"

"There's a safe in his closet," Tiffany said. "It has our birth certificates in it."

Lenore stood. "Goodness, all this tea. I think I need to use the bathroom."

"You can use ours," Addison said.

"No, I think I'd rather use your mom and dad's. Which way?"

"That way," Tiffany said, pointing.

Lenore went down the hallway to Wallace and Hannah's bedroom. She wanted to see the lair, to browse the peripheral clutter, to take measure of her rival. The centerpiece of the room was a plantation poster bed piled high with embroidered pillows. Hannah's nightstand was cluttered: ointments, a jar of cold cream, *Vogue*, *Vanity Fair*, a paperback romance novel. On Wallace's nightstand, a biogra-

phy of Theodore Roosevelt weighted down a stack of—god help us!—
Model Railroader magazines. The furniture in the room—a leather
ottoman, a bench at the foot of the bed, an Indonesian dresser—had
a faux import, Oriental flair, which Lenore recognized as the unmistakable sign of a woman making do on a tight budget. The curtains
were light and airy, as if bolts of mosquito netting had drifted from
the bedposts.

The mirrored dressing area led to a walk-in closet. Lenore couldn't
help herself. She found the light switch and browsed through Hannah's
clothes. Tweed suits, cashmere sweaters, wool jackets—Hannah had
impeccable taste. On Wallace's side of the closet were the familiar dark
suits, black shoes, and a row of white shirts. His bright ties hung like
streamers on two wooden organizers. Lenore lifted one of the ties and
pressed it to the side of her face. The silk was cool against her cheek.

She heard the water come on in the bathroom.

Wallace was at the sink, washing his hands. When he saw Lenore
in the mirror he started, then smiled.

"Hide and seek? Or just snooping?"

"You want to know a man," Lenore said, "check out his
closet."

Wallace dried his hands on a towel. "How was the tea party?"

"Illuminating." Lenore came up behind Wallace and put her arms
around his waist. "I have something to show you." She drew him into
the closet.

"I think I've already seen it—"

Lenore produced a small jewelry box from her pocket. "Here."

"What is it?"

"Open it."

Wallace opened the box. Inside were two onyx cufflinks.

"Carroll wears such beautiful French cuff shirts," Lenore said. "I
thought it was time to introduce you to Turnbull and Asser."

"Who?"

"Never mind," Lenore said. "Kiss me or I'll scream."

They kissed.

When Wallace tried to pull away Lenore bit his lip. "No, not yet."
She hugged his neck and nuzzled her head against his chest. "Can't we
please run away together? I can't stand it any longer."

Lenore suddenly had a sense they were being watched.

"Now that's what I call employee relations," Owen said. He stood with Hannah in the dressing room, staring into the closet. He had a little smile.

For a moment Hannah appeared stunned. She cut Lenore a cold glance, as if to say: How could you? *How dare you!* She shifted her gaze back to Wallace. Her dark eyes flashed poisonously.

"Whenever you two are finished," she said, lifting her face scornfully. "Dinner's ready."

CHAPTER THIRTY-NINE

It was pitch dark outside.

Wallace checked the time: four fifty-five. The dreaded morning, Thursday, January 7, had arrived. Wallace's hair was dripping from a quick rinse under a cold shower. He still hadn't figured out the hot water; it had something to do with turning a propane valve in the forward basement bay on the passenger side. He pulled on a pair of jeans and a golf shirt—he didn't know what color; he couldn't find the closet light switch, either.

Wallace was on his second day living in a motorhome.

It was exactly four steps from the bedroom to the compact, wooden dinette table, where Wallace could look out the window and see a camera crew from San Diego's most watched television news channel setting up for a remote broadcast. The crew was doing a test. Their floodlights illuminated the white clapboard exterior of the campground bathhouse, the tops of distant trees, and the disparate noses of a row of RVs, which were lined up like aged, private aircraft on a runway tarmac. The bulky camera was mounted on a tripod. Its lens was pointed at two high director's chairs—a cannon doing the work of a firing squad. The backdrop for the shot was Mission Bay—a vast black semicircle of nothingness surrounded by twinkling yellow lights.

The TV producer, a lean, self-assured girl in her twenties, had already knocked on Wallace's door once that morning—it was another four steps from the dinette table to the entry door at the front of the bus-style coach—and Wallace had been fool enough to answer the knock. Now he couldn't credibly claim to have slept through the appointed call time. He considered backing out of the interview, citing flu symptoms. The knots in his stomach and the vague sense of dread that had settled in his occipital lobes told him appearing on live television was something he was not cut out to do. The night before, while driving back to space one hundred at HappyCamp on the Bay, he had been sorely tempted to swerve his car into a freeway abutment. He had one last chance at the Balboa Avenue off-ramp, but the way things were going he knew he'd probably be rendered a quadriplegic, lose a lot of blood, and still have to do this television thing.

Morty Schlegg insisted on it.

The story of Wallace's legal fight gained traction when the *San Diego Union-Tribune* did a follow-up on the "Accolades and Onions" column from the *Escondido News-Journal*. That story, in turn, was picked up by the *Los Angeles Times*. It went national when the Associated Press put it on the wire service. Wallace heard from relatives and friends who had read about his legal predicament in the *San Francisco Chronicle*, the *Washington Post*, and the *New York Times*. Now Wallace and Morty had been invited to appear on a morning network news show. The show's executive producers in New York were notorious for going out of their way to schedule powder-keg interviews. Sharing the segment with Wallace and Morty would be Chief Dexter Thomas of the Escondido Police Department.

A pair of headlights swung in behind the TV van and cut. The correct term for the ensuing engine noise made by the pea green Pinto after its ignition was switched off, Wallace knew, was dieseling.

A minute later Morty Schlegg knocked on the door.

"Let me see this Winnebago," Morty said. He was dressed in a white linen suit with a vest and a black string tie. He looked like Colonel Sanders.

"You look ridiculous," Wallace said.

"Shut up," Morty said. "It intimidates the enemy."

"If he's a chicken, maybe."

Morty didn't wait for an invitation. He walked through the motor-home, nearly stepping out of his new black loafers, casting a critical eye over the posh interior: the his and hers captain's chairs, the mauve leather love seat, the long sleeper sofa. Overhead, handcrafted wooden cabinets ran the length of the coach. There was a full kitchen: refrigerator, icemaker, Corian countertops, convection oven, and a gas stove.

Morty stepped through the bathroom to the bedroom, where there was a queen-size bed. "You're licensed to drive this thing?"

"It's a Monaco Dynasty," Wallace said. "Buy it and they throw you the keys. It beats living in a hotel."

"What are you going to do if Hannah takes you back?"

"I'll keep it and use it for family vacations," Wallace said. "Make memories for my old age. If I live that long." He glanced out the window. The producer was approaching the motorhome. The sight of her long strides filled Wallace with a renewed sense of panic. "You sure we need to do this?"

"The key is to get sympathy and show damages," Morty said. "Just look woebegone and let me do the talking."

Most of the HappyCamp tenants were retirees—many were ancient and on canes. They were an early-morning bunch with a keen eye for anything unusual happening in their park. Not surprisingly, a sizeable crowd of them—they were equally divided between men and women—had gathered around the TV equipment. They wore colorful jackets with furry collars and socialized in carefree voices, clutching steaming cups of coffee. They kept a respectful distance from Wallace, but they clearly regarded him as a local celebrity.

"I could use a drink," Wallace said, as he and Morty took their assigned seats in the director's chairs. A technician affixed tiny microphones to their shirts while the producer fitted them with earpieces. Chief Thomas would be interviewed live via satellite link, standing in front of the Escondido Police Department.

"The first voice you hear will be Kelly," the producer said, meaning, of course, Kelly Starr, the famous network anchorwoman. "Keep your answers short and to the point. Look at the camera. I'll give you a countdown. We've still got a few minutes."

Off to the side was a large TV monitor. On it Wallace and Morty could watch a live feed of the show.

Morty leaned toward Wallace. "I meant to ask—what are you doing Saturday night?"

"Why?"

"Babette's calling in her marker. I need you to take her to the Indian casino."

"No way."

"You could get a nice room in the tower—"

"I thought I bought her a gift certificate for lingerie."

"The fourth paragraph in the column was an extra," Morty said. "I'd take her myself, but I have a conflict. Don't you want to know what it is?"

"Nope." Wallace turned to the monitor, pretending to be interested in the on-air segment. It was something to do with women's health.

"Things have, shall we say, evolved in a rather interesting way between Patience and myself," Morty said. "She's made it clear I'm no longer to see other women."

The health story ended. The show went to commercials.

Morty continued, "I thought since you were legally separated—"

Wallace turned sharply. "Morty, I said forget it."

"Get ready," the producer said.

"You picked a fine time to be faithful," Morty said. "When can I meet this other woman?"

The producer began counting down. "Five, four, three ... "

She pointed to Wallace. They were on. Wallace's heart began to pound. In his earpiece he heard the familiar voice of Kelly Starr. Her image filled the screen on the monitor.

"When is a hero not a hero but, in fact, a criminal?" Kelly asked rhetorically. "That's the question being asked in the town of Escondido, California, where businessman Wallace Noe confronted an armed robber outside a bank. Noe was able to subdue the suspect and hand him over to police. But now he finds himself in hot water: he's been charged with a number of crimes, including impersonating a police officer, assault and battery, and child endangerment—"

Wallace looked at Morty, surprised.

Child endangerment?

Morty shushed him.

"Joining us from our local affiliate in San Diego," Kelly said, "is Wallace Noe and his attorney, Morton Schlegg. Gentlemen, good morning."

Wallace's voice failed him. His mouth was too dry to speak.

"Good morning," Morty said.

"Mr. Noe," Kelly said, "let's start with you. That's some story. One minute you're hailed as a hero and the next thing you know the police are charging you with all these crimes—and these are some pretty serious charges, I might add. How does that make you feel?"

It was all surreal: the geriatric mob in the campground in the middle of the night, the bright lights, Kelly Starr's voice in his ear speaking his name and asking him a question. Wallace tried to come up with something witty to say, but his mouth seemed to be disengaged from his brain. He heard himself say, "Well, not so good."

Morty interrupted. "Let me tell you something about my client—"

"Go ahead, Mr. Schlegg," Kelly said. "I'm listening."

"He did what he thought was the right thing," Morty said. "He stood up for himself and he protected his children. Now he's facing these trumped-up charges. This is not a prosecution. This is a *persecution* by a ruthless and intimidating legal system."

"Before we get into that," Kelly said, "Mr. Noe, can you tell us in your own words what happened that night?"

"What happened never should have happened," Wallace managed to say. "Something snapped."

Again, Morty interrupted.

"Miss Starr, with all due respect I am going to ask my client to stop talking. It's only a matter of time until he says something stupid and self-incriminating. As I said, he found himself in a life-threatening situation, and he defended himself with a reasonable amount of force. We don't know what kind of mayhem this attacker had in mind."

"What about this charge of impersonating an officer?" Kelly asked. "Where does that come from?"

"That is a foundationless charge," Morty said. "Simply bogus. My client was no more impersonating a police officer than he was the man in the moon. It simply did not happen."

"But there must be some—"

"What you have here is a vindictive district attorney whom everyone hates, who's angry we won't take his deal, who runs the worst office in the entire state—"

"But Mr. Schlegg, the police—"

"Let me tell you about the police," Morty said. "This department is harboring a psychotic, baby-faced detective who can't get along with his own mother, let alone these law-abiding citizens he's been sworn to serve. He has a history of jacking up old ladies, kicking dogs, and harassing retarded people. His personnel file's going to get a thorough review in this trial, I assure you. The guy's name is Tetley, by the way, and he's a certified mental case."

Kelly cut Morty short. "Also joining us this morning is the chief of the Escondido Police Department, Dexter Thomas. Chief Thomas, what do you make of this brouhaha in your little town? I understand this is even dividing your rank and file."

Wallace caught a glimpse of Chief Thomas on the monitor. His balding head gleamed pink in the night. He was impressively at ease in front of the camera. He chuckled jocularly, impudently, at Morty's inflammatory rhetoric. His breath showed in the brisk morning air.

"Well, first let me tell you the men and women of the Escondido Police Department are consummate professionals," Chief Thomas said. "We have absolute confidence in the judgment and police work of our Detective Tetley. He's a fine young man with a promising career ahead, and we're lucky to have him."

"He's a two-bit sociopath," Morty said.

"So, Chief Thomas, you stand by the merits of your case?" Kelly asked.

"Yes, Kelly, we certainly do."

"Let's talk more about the case," Kelly continued. "Mr. Noe by all accounts thwarted a legitimate robbery attempt, and now your department is going after him with both barrels. Why is that?"

"Look, Kelly, you need to understand," Chief Thomas said. "This so-called robber was a slight-built, minor child who'd been kicked out of his house and was in desperate need of food and shelter on a cold, cold night in our town. This was a hapless attempt at a robbery using a small fishing knife—the only remaining memento of his dead father, by the way. It was really more like a nail file."

"Nail file!" Morty said.

"This boy was immediately incapacitated by Mr. Noe," Chief Thomas continued. "Then, when he was down on the ground and offering no resistance, Mr. Noe pummeled him with his fists. This was long after he had complied with verbal commands to surrender, I might add. The hospital report shows there were contusions on the back of the boy's skull, which leads us to conclude that Mr. Noe repeatedly slammed the boy's head into the asphalt parking lot. We wouldn't stand for such conduct by one of our officers, and we certainly won't stand for it from an ordinary citizen."

Wallace turned to Morty. "I'm screwed."

"I'm sorry," Kelly said. "Mr. Noe, was there something you wanted to say?"

"That was attorney-client privileged communication," Morty said. "He said he was screwed."

"He certainly is," Chief Thomas agreed.

Kelly made a face at the camera. "Be that as it may, Chief Thomas, I'm curious. Why impersonating a police officer?"

"We have witnesses on the scene who will testify to the fact that Mr. Noe falsely identified himself as a police officer. This contributed to an elevated response on our part. It took a lot of officers off the street."

"And what about child endangerment? We understand that's a new charge?"

"The child endangerment occurred when Mr. Noe exited his vehicle to confront the perpetrator. He became so focused on taking the law into his own hands, on administering a healthy dose of street justice, that he left his two young children unattended in that car. For all we know it could've slipped into gear and gone down a hole."

Morty said, "Down a hole?"

"Yes, down a hole!" Chief Thomas said, showing a hint of temper. "Mr. Noe's duty as a parent was to stay in that vehicle and protect his children."

"Listen to Heinrich Himmler from the Gestapo," Morty said, barging in. "My client is a wonderful father. Just because he doesn't spend his days shaking down speeders for bribes."

Chief Thomas was visibly indignant. "Sir, I am not the Gestapo and in the state of California we police officers do not shake people down for bribes."

"I can't take this bohunk," Morty said. "Get him out of my ear."

"I am a duly sworn police officer," Chief Thomas said, talking over Morty. "We protect good people like you from evildoers like your client, and we do it honorably every single day."

"My client saw that knife blade and blacked out," Morty said. "He has amnesia. He can't remember diddly-squat."

"I might add," Chief Thomas said, "that Mr. Noe is well over six feet tall and outweighs that boy by about a hundred pounds."

"Which brings up a good question," Kelly said. "Chief, what should Mr. Noe have done, under the circumstances?"

"Our advice to citizens is never, ever to confront an armed suspect. Simply comply with the perpetrator's wishes, whatever they may be. The fact is, we had officers in the area, we had dogs. Had Mr. Noe simply surrendered his ATM card, he then could have driven himself and his children to a safe, well-lighted place and used his cellular telephone to call 911—"

"Somebody unplug this Frankenstein."

"Mr. Schlegg," Kelly admonished, "let the chief finish."

"That kid was on foot," Chief Thomas continued. "We would have responded, we'd have set a perimeter, we'd have taken him into custody. Mr. Noe would've got his ATM card back, probably that same night, and most importantly he wouldn't be looking at hard-core jail time."

"And I understand the district attorney has dropped all charges against the would-be robber?" Kelly asked.

"That is correct," Chief Thomas said.

"That doesn't seem fair," Kelly said. "Why is that?"

"Kelly, there is a simple, logical reason for that," Chief Thomas said. "We need to call this young man as a prosecution witness against Mr. Noe, and it would be an obvious conflict if at the same time we were prosecuting a criminal case against him."

"Utter bullshit," Morty said.

"We were able to edit that, Mr. Schlegg," Kelly said. "But let me remind you. This is live television."

"And I expect to hear an apology for that Heinrich Himmler-Gestapo remark," Chief Thomas said.

"Mr. Schlegg," Kelly said, "I'll give you your say, but I'm warning you, keep it clean."

"The right to self-defense is indisputable law," Morty said. "My client did a brave and honorable thing. He stood up for this community. And now he's being railroaded by a justice system that consumes its citizens, that wants to deny us this basic, fundamental right. I'll tell you what's really going on. This rookie, psychotic detective Tetley made a horrible judgment call in arresting my client, and this is a cover-up by his jackbooted fascist friends in brown shirts—"

"Let me point out my shirt is blue," Chief Thomas said, smiling.

"They'd rather punish an innocent man than admit they were wrong," Morty said. "These charges are preposterous. My client is a hero."

"Chief, a response?" Kelly asked.

"We stand by our case," Chief Thomas said. "Mr. Noe took the law into his own hands. He acted as a vigilante would act, and vigilante-type behavior will not be condoned in our town."

"Mr. Schlegg, these are some very serious charges," Kelly said. "How's your client handling all this?"

"I'll tell you how he's handling it," Morty said. "His life is a shambles. His wife kicked him out of the house the day after Christmas. She wants a divorce. He lives in this dumpy trailer park, surrounded by gun-toting, survivalist kooks. He doesn't see his own children, he can't even visit his own dog. His software company, Merksamer Digital, is on the verge of collapse. It's hanging by a thread—"

Wallace turned to Morty. "That isn't true—"

"It's a company that cannot meet its obligations, that will soon have to close its doors and seek protection of the bankruptcy court—"

Wallace looked at the camera. "Kelly, we're fine. We're venture-backed."

"On a personal level my client walks around in a fog. He's clinically depressed, he abuses prescription drugs—"

Wallace turned to Morty. "Huh?"

"He's being stalked by the Mafia for massive gambling debts, he's impecunious, he's addicted to Internet pornography—"

Wallace looked back at the camera. "Kelly, don't believe a word he says. He's making it all up."

Morty looked angrily at Wallace. "Oh will you shut the hell up! I'm talking damages here."

"Yikes!" Kelly said. "Such potty mouths in San Diego."

"I told you last month to plead guilty," Morty said.

"Too late for that," Chief Thomas said, having a good chuckle. "He can rot in jail."

Wallace shook his head. National television. He felt like murdering Morty. He glared at him.

"One last question, Mr. Schlegg," Kelly said. "Does your client intend to sue the city?"

"Let me put it this way," Morty said. "I've instructed him to rent a big garage and hire a good mechanic because he's soon going to own a fleet of city fire trucks, water trucks, and police vehicles—right down to the meter maid's little golf car, which I intend to personally drive into Dixon Lake as payback for an incident that happened last month in front of the courthouse."

"I'll take that as a yes," Kelly said. "Chief, you've got the last word."

"Well, I can't comment on someone wanting to drive a city golf car into a lake," Chief Thomas said. "But suffice it to say no citizen should take the law into their own hands. If you have an incident call 911. Leave it to the professionals."

Morty raged at the camera. "Tell that to Sarita Aguilar, who was shot in the head for her Honda! Tell that to little Roberto Rodriguez, who was killed by gang cross fire in his mother's living room!"

"Gentlemen, I'm sorry," Kelly said. "But that'll have to be the last word—"

"Tell that to the Korean shop owners who were abandoned by the LAPD in the South Central riots!"

"Well, I can't speak for the LAPD," Chief Thomas said, casting his gaze to the ground and touching his earpiece. "These are all incidents that happened outside my jurisdiction. I'd just ask Mr. Schlegg to leave our golf cars alone."

"We really are out of time," Kelly said. "Chief Dexter Thomas from Escondido, Wallace Noe and his attorney Morton Schlegg, in San Diego. Thank you all." She raised her eyebrows. "Whew, that was interesting. And coming up next: how changing what you eat can lower your metabolism ... "

The producer told Wallace and Morty they were clear.

Wallace tore off his earpiece and turned angrily to Morty. "You grandstanding son of a bitch!"

Morty didn't wait to unhook. He sprang like a rabbit from the director's chair, pushed through the crowd of onlookers, and took off running in the general direction of Mission Bay Park.

"It was for your own good," he called to Wallace over his shoulder. "One day you'll thank me."

CHAPTER FORTY

Wallace arrived at the office later that morning not knowing what to expect. Still, he was unprepared for what he found: Julie was in the lobby, waiting for him. Behind her was a security guard.

"That bad?" Wallace asked.

Julie's face hardened. "You're to come with me."

"Blood drive today?"

"Do me a favor. Dispense with the cuteness."

Wallace followed Julie through the lobby. The security guard, an osteoarthritic casino-type with tattoos on his scraggy forearms, fell in behind Wallace and followed him up the stairs.

On the second floor, Julie traversed the long hallway, marching like a jailer. She wouldn't look at Wallace.

"Julie?"

She walked even faster.

The security guard lagged.

"Is this it?" Wallace asked. "Is this how it ends?"

"I'm not talking to you." Julie's eyes glistened with tears.

Wallace made the turn for his door.

"Not there," she said. "You're to see Michael."

Wallace caught a brief glimpse of his office. The walls were bare. His books were missing from the credenza.

"What've you done with them this time?" he asked.

"Wait here," Julie said, knocking on Michael's closed door.

The security guard lurked near a potted palm, keeping an eye on Wallace.

Michael swung his door open. When he saw Wallace his face turned white.

"Wallace."

"Michael."

"I've been on the phone. Helluva' morning." Michael retreated to his desk and began rearranging papers. "Please, sit."

The security guard followed Wallace into Michael's office. Wallace half expected him to sit down at the desk. Instead he stood near a bookcase, craning his neck when Michael touched the foot pedal, closing the door.

"Don't mind the rent-a-cop," Michael said. "Trek's policy." He smiled grimly. "Someone must've once bloodied his nose."

"That's what it's down to? Trek's calling the shots?"

Michael closed his eyes and massaged his temples. "In a nutshell, yes. Except it was Carroll's idea that he and Lenore should go to Boston. Asbury Care wants to pull the plug."

"Julie said you wanted to see me."

"I want to make this clear. This isn't my idea. You and I always made a good team. We balance each other out. As for the hullabaloo ... " Michael raised a hand dismissively. "Auditors, lawyers, some expensive dinners, a few rounds of golf—two weeks and it'll be water under the bridge. I've survived a lot worse."

Michael's telephone rang. It was Julie.

"Trek Reese for you, line one."

Michael hit the conference button on his telephone console. "Trek, I'm putting you on speaker."

"Tell me it's done," Trek said.

Michael licked his lips and glanced at Wallace. "In fact he's sitting right here—"

"Goddamn you, Michael. Your competence is totally illusory."

"I was working up to it—"

"I'm close to pissed off about this whole thing," Trek said. "What's the mystery? Wallace, buddy, we love you, but you need to resign. You're an embarrassment to this company. You're a detriment to its future. That bullshit this morning was inexcusable."

"I was considering the possibility of keeping him on as a consultant," Michael said.

"Grow a spine, Michael. The guy's toxic. He has a serious credibility issue."

Michael looked at Wallace and mouthed, "Sabbatical?"

Wallace leaned toward the speaker. "Trek, it's your company. I'll do whatever you want."

"A pleasure doing business with you," Trek said. "We need your resignation from the board, as well."

"I think we should talk terms, first," Wallace said.

"C'mon, partner. Just give us the letter."

"Buck up, Trek. You said so yourself. In five years this company's going to be worth a billion dollars."

"Not if you're within a thousand miles," Trek said. "This is non-negotiable. I want you gone yesterday."

"Here's where I am on that," Wallace said. "Buy me out. Personally. Right now. You'll never hear from me again."

"You know I can't do that."

Wallace said, "Come on, Trek. Show me what you're made of. Prove you're more than just a mouth."

Trek was silent a moment.

"Michael, what's your fax number there?" Trek asked.

An hour later Wallace was on the road, his personal effects consolidated into a single cardboard box. He started for the RV park but soon changed his mind. He got off the freeway in Mission Valley, circled around, and took the highway north to Escondido.

Wallace arrived home to find the sprinklers running, a landscape crew working in the yard, and a new white Hummer parked in the driveway.

Hannah met Wallace at the front door, wearing her flight attendant's uniform and pulling a roller bag.

"You're early," Hannah said.

Wallace looked around. "What is all this?"

"I'm tired of dealing with dirt clods."

Wallace watched her load the suitcase into the back seat of the Hummer.

"Don't tell me that thing's yours," Wallace said.

"It paints a picture. I'll see you Sunday."

"I don't like what I'm seeing, Hannah. These sprinklers shouldn't even be on."

"Gonzalo's afraid we'll lose the lambs ears and veronicas."

"Gonzalo?"

"My landscape consultant. Design and build."

There was no mistaking Gonzalo's pickup. It was an old Ford Ranger, loaded with gardening tools. It smelled of grass clippings and gasoline, and it pulled a trailer made from the cannibalized bed of another pickup.

Some consultant.

"Just so you know," Hannah said, "I'm not paying you alimony."

Wallace was taken aback. "What makes you think—"

"I caught the segment," Hannah said with a smirk. "I didn't realize things were so dire."

Hannah climbed behind the wheel of the truck and started the engine. She lowered her window.

"Addison has a birthday sleepover tomorrow night. The invitation's on the counter. You'll need to get a gift."

"Wait, Hannah, let's talk about this—"

"Talk to my lawyer," she said, raising the window. She threw the truck in reverse, backed out of the driveway, and drove off.

As Wallace turned to go inside the house, he heard men shouting commands in Spanish. Gonzalo's men were working at a gaping hole in the fence. They were rolling out the dismantled hot tub.

"Hey," Wallace said. "Where are you going with that?"

"*Basura*," Gonzalo said. "Trash." He spoke in broken English.

"Who says so?"

"Your wife. Sorry, mister. She is the boss."

CHAPTER FORTY-ONE

Wallace awoke Friday morning to a six o'clock alarm—his first full day unemployed. Had he been in bed in his Monaco Dynasty at HappyCamp on the Bay, he would have rolled over and gone back to sleep, but he was at home with his girls, and there were lunches to make, uniform shirts to iron, and breakfast things to set out.

He got busy, turning on lights in the kitchen, waking the girls, and letting the dog out.

By seven thirty Addison and Tiffany were dressed and fed and had their hair arranged to their liking. It was time to leave for school.

"Let's go, girls," Wallace said, doing his best to get them out the door. As usual there were unforeseen complications: a forgotten back-pack, a paper Wallace needed to sign, a jacket left behind.

While the girls went to retrieve the rest of their things, Wallace stepped out onto the porch. It was a cool, clear morning. The trees were bare, and all down the street the matching lawns were a wintry brownish green.

The landscape contractor, Gonzalo, was leaning against the front fender of his pickup. Looking over the roof of Wallace's house, his soiled hat shading his dark eyes from the rising sun, he flashed Wallace a gold-toothed grin.

"*Hola,*" he said softly. His men sat on the curb eating breakfast sandwiches and drinking coffee.

"I have a bone to pick with you," Wallace said, "about the way you mow the lawn."

"Where is your wife?" Gonzalo asked. His right eye was permanently bloodshot—Wallace suspected it was the result of having taken a rock while whacking weeds.

"Gone to the airport," Wallace said. He flapped his arms. "Flying on a trip."

"*Aeropuerto,*" Gonzalo said.

"*Sí.*"

"You tell your wife be *careful* in *aeropuerto.*" Gonzalo punctuated his words by jabbing the air with a dirt-encrusted finger.

"I don't worry too much about her," Wallace said. "She's pretty safe. This isn't Mexico, you know."

"You should go with her," Gonzalo said.

"Right now someone needs to be with these girls," Wallace said. "They need to get to school."

"Then you go to work?"

"Then I'm headed to a restaurant."

Wallace had already decided he wouldn't spend the day hanging around the house. With the commotion of rototillers and men working with shovels just outside the windows, he wouldn't be able to read, think, or take a nap.

"*Restaurante?*" Gonzalo asked. "You work in *restaurante?*"

"No, I eat in *restaurante,*" Wallace said. He pantomimed lifting a forkful of food to his mouth. "I'm a guy who likes his breakfast."

Gonzalo asked, "But Señor, what work for you?"

For the first time in years Wallace had to think about it.

"Nothing," he said finally. "Taking a break."

Gonzalo wagged a scolding finger. "Is no good. No work, no money."

Wallace glanced over his shoulder. The girls were coming out of the house, their arms loaded with gear. They were running to the car.

"My partners bought me out," Wallace said. "Paying me not to work."

Gonzalo shook his head.

"You don't like that?" Wallace asked.

"A man should work." Gonzalo regarded Wallace gravely with his one red eye. Wallace took exception to the landscaper's tone. It felt like he was being reprimanded.

"What if I gave you a hundred thousand dollars for this truck and all your tools?" Wallace said. "I bet you'd take it."

Gonzalo shook his head. "No, Señor." He solemnly touched a fist to his heart. "I must work. I am very proud."

"That's a lie, Gonzalo," Wallace said. "You could go back to Mexico and live like a king."

"No good," Gonzalo said. "Money is not happy."

"I'd rather be rich than poor."

"You're wrong," Gonzalo said. "Happiness lives here." Again, he touched his heart.

Wallace was peeved at himself for getting drawn into an argument with Hannah's gardener. Pulling a trailer made from the bed of an old pickup was hardly the mark of a world-class thinker.

"Explain this lawn mowing business," Wallace said. "Why do you go 'round and 'round and not back and forth?"

"I go 'round and 'round."

"I know. Why is that?"

"I no step on 'ronicas," Gonzalo said. "Go round and round, no step on 'ronicas. You understand?"

"Dad, we need to go!" The girls were sitting in the car. The doors were open.

"I understand you don't want to step on the veronicas," Wallace said. "But a lawn should go back and forth." He gesticulated broadly, showing Gonzalo how the lines of a lawn should go straight across the grass. "Not in a swirl. This isn't dang Fontainebleu."

"Dad!"

Gonzalo said to Wallace, "Fifty dollars."

"Fifty dollars for what?"

"Go back and forth."

"That's ridiculous."

"More gas. More money."

"*Bandito, robo,*" Wallace said. "If that's the case, I'll mow the friggin' thing myself."

Gonzalo stared impassively at the sky. He wasn't budging.

"How much are you charging for this whole job?" Wallace asked.

"Fifteen thousand dollars."

"To do what?"

"Your wife wants grass. And a gazebo."

"I'd like to see the plan."

Gonzalo pointed to his head. "The plan is here."

"That's dangerous."

"I trust your wife."

"I meant dangerous for her," Wallace said. "For me."

Gonzalo studied the top of a chimney at the end of the street.

"Let me ask you this, Gonzalo," Wallace said. "How much to add a bunker to the back lawn?"

"A bucket?"

"A bunker," Wallace said. "For golf. A little sand trap next to the grass."

"Bunker's no good," Gonzalo said. "Your wife wants fruit trees."

"Maybe kidney shaped, the size of a wading pool with powdery white sand," Wallace said. "For pitching golf balls."

Again the chimney at the end of the street came under scrutiny. "I think a thousand dollars."

"Come on, Gonzalo. It's a dirt hole and sand."

"Next to the grass?"

"Adjacent to it. To work on my short game."

"Maybe two hundred."

It must be a cultural thing, Wallace decided. It was like negotiating with a mariachi band.

"I want you to make it nice and deep," Wallace said. "Money's no object."

"Five hundred," Gonzalo said. "Nice and deep. And for that price I go back and forth. Every week."

"Deal," Wallace said, shaking Gonzalo's hand. "Make sure I get the bill. Got that, Gonzalo? I don't want my wife to pay."

"You tell your wife be careful."

———

At the Edelweiss Christian School, there was a strict protocol for dropping off children. Traffic flowed one way. Bossy women in fluorescent vests supervised the drop area. They worked in teams, rushing kids from the backs of cars and urging them inside the building, as if the parking lot were under sniper fire.

"Halt right there," Mrs. Hogan said, holding up a stop sign, stepping in front of Wallace's Cadillac.

Wallace sat with his foot on the brake pedal, waiting while the children unloaded from the van ahead of him. With all the kids running around, opening and closing doors, it looked like a Chinese fire drill. The last bell rang.

"Just jump out here, girls," Wallace said, throwing the car in park.

As Addison opened the car door, Mrs. Hogan blew her whistle, and as the girls ran for the school building she sounded her whistle again and directed Wallace to pull off to the side.

"My fault," Wallace said, lowering the window. "I got into it with the gardener and lost track of time."

Mrs. Hogan was taking down his license number.

"One hour," she said, handing him a slip of paper through the window. "That's illegal unloading."

———

Late that night Wallace was systematically making his way through the house, turning out lights and checking doors, on his way to bed, when he caught the faint sound of ... something. He stopped at Tiffany's bedroom door and listened. He had tucked her in some hours earlier and expected her to be asleep. He opened the door an inch.

"Tiff? Are you okay?"

At first Wallace couldn't see anything—the room was pitch-black. He could hear his daughter sobbing in her bed.

"What is it, honey? What's wrong?"

"I don't have any friends."

"That isn't true—"

"Is so."

As Wallace stepped into the room, he could make out the shape of Tiffany's head on the pillow. He sat next to her on the bed. Overhead, glow-in-the-dark stars slowly revealed themselves.

"You have me," Wallace said. "You have your sister and Scottie."

"That doesn't count."

"What about school? Not a single kid—"

"No."

"You have Beatrice."

With a wail like a wounded animal, Tiffany rolled over and buried her face in the pillow.

"Hey," Wallace said, stroking her hair. "Why so sad?"

"I don't know. I just am."

"Oh, Tiff. Come here." Wallace put an arm around her. He could feel her convulsing. She was gasping for breath and sobbing.

The curse of a broken home, Wallace thought. Children pay the ultimate price.

"Sometimes I get sad, too," he said.

They sat together in the dark, Wallace holding Tiffany, letting her work through her tears.

Then: "Daddy, what happened?"

Wallace chose not to answer right away.

"Mrs. Hogan said the whole world is mad at you," Tiffany said. "The police and Jesus."

"Don't believe everything you hear."

"That's what Beatrice said. She said Mrs. Hogan is a terrible liar—"

Wallace waited out another squall of tears.

"Is that what's got you worried, sweetheart? Your teacher?"

"Beatrice says Mrs. Hogan cursed you."

"No, darling. She doesn't have that kind of power. We can only curse ourselves."

"But you have to believe with a full heart—"

"What does that mean, honey? Believe what?"

"Everything," Tiffany said. "In yourself and God. Or the bad angels get into your aurora."

"You mean aura."

"No. *Aurora.* The bad angels are like nasty birds. They make wicked things happen."

Wallace brushed the tears from his daughter's cheek. "I don't think there's any such thing as bad angels."

"Then why did all this happen? Why did Mommy have to send you away?"

"It's all my fault," Wallace said. "I can fix it, I promise."

"You can't fix it. Beatrice says she'll have to fix it herself. She has to go away."

"She'll come back."

"No, she'll be gone forever. I'll never see her again." Tiffany's voice choked. Tears streamed down her face.

Wallace held his daughter and rocked her gently. He could feel her quaking and sobbing.

"When we lose someone we love, we still keep them in our hearts," Wallace said. "That's how people live forever. Beatrice will be with you always, I promise."

After a few minutes Tiffany grew still. They sat in silence, mourning the loss of their imaginary friend.

"Dad, can I take karate lessons?"

CHAPTER FORTY-TWO

Life at HappyCamp on the Bay was not the four-star experience Wallace had hoped for. For starters, a day at the swimming pool was unbearable. There were just enough toddlers living in the park—children being raised by grandparents, mostly—that it was impossible to sit quietly on a chaise lounge and read a book, or nap in the sun, without being splashed or bonked on the head with a rubber ball or awakened by ceaseless, prepubescent cries of "Marco!" and "Polo!" The day Wallace noticed a diapered child floating around the pool in an inner tube was his last day in the water.

After a few weeks, the knocks at the motorhome door finally tapered off, probably because Wallace hadn't accepted a single invitation to join the residents for a game of bingo at the clubhouse, or gin rummy in a neighboring fifth wheel, or horseshoes at the barbecue area.

As time passed, Wallace found himself becoming something of an ill-tempered recluse. He avoided the bathhouse altogether. A de facto men's club was in operation there, and its members took shaving in the mirror or toweling off after a shower as an opportunity to pry.

Most of Wallace's days were spent alone within the confines of space one hundred, under the awning, in a very comfortable lawn chair. As Morty Schlegg pointed out, Wallace could have pled guilty to the misdemeanor, taken house arrest, and got the same result: he'd still be out of work and sitting alone in a trailer park, confined to a very nice motorhome, with a honeysuckle hedge and a view of the bay. He just wouldn't be looking at hard-core prison time, as Chief Thomas had put it.

Wallace spent most of his days reading books, most of them about great men accomplishing great things—for the better part of a week he savored Morris's *The Rise of Theodore Roosevelt* cover to cover without interruption. He learned to ignore the din of speedboats and personal watercraft turning endless circles on Mission Bay, though in the first few days it made him want to scream. He realized the things over which he was most short-tempered—sounds of children playing and the notion of perfectly competent adults spinning in chaotic circles— were the things most awry in his life: he missed his girls and he was ambivalent about his future with Lenore.

Was he consciously avoiding her, or was she consciously avoiding him? The question perplexed him night after night, even though she was out of town much of the time. They rarely spoke by phone. She had a pressing schedule, and her telephone demeanor had become increasingly businesslike, even brusque.

The night was January 20. Despite the doom and gloom swirling like the fog over space one hundred at HappyCamp on the Bay, Wallace was optimistic he could at least hammer out a workable relationship with Lenore. She was just back from Boston, and she was coming to the RV park for dinner.

Wallace checked his watch against the display on his cell phone.

Nine thirty-five.

More than two hours late.

Wallace paced the length of the coach, stopping at the bar to freshen his drink. The motorhome door was propped open, the stairwell was lit, and the yellow porch light was on. Wallace didn't mind the raw, damp air coming in; he was fortified with a heavy sweatshirt and had a goodly number of scotches under his belt.

He sat at the dinette table and tried to focus on the camp newsletter. It was a grim collection of predictable, illiterate paragraphs: the need to clean up after your dog, tips for recycling trash, the importance of locking up your kitsch crap when the weekend loonies descended on the park. There was even a local crime blotter—the police were actively searching for the culprits who had recently submerged a stolen Bob's Big Boy statue in the park swimming pool.

For Wallace, living even part-time at HappyCamp on the Bay was a dismal existence—enough to make him want to pull chocks and run for the nearest Holiday Inn Express.

Wallace checked the time again. In the back of his mind he worried about the dark night and the camp's circuitous roads. The gate guard would give Lenore a map, Wallace knew, but with her sense of direction Wallace pictured her unconscious and slumped behind the wheel, her Miata stuck like a cow in the tidelands at the edge of the park, sinking into oblivion.

"Hello! Here I am!" Lenore said, bounding up the stairs. She was still in her business suit, and she carried her high heels.

She came in so breezily that Wallace stiffened.

"Wow," she said. "It's enormous. Do I get a tour?"

"Help yourself," Wallace said.

Lenore walked through the motorhome. "Call this camping? It's borderline decadent. It's like a house."

"That's the idea."

"So how are you?"

Wallace didn't answer.

Lenore came up behind him and put her arms around his neck. "I have big news. And some juicy gossip. Oh, and some of the ladies at the office want to give you a going-away potluck. I promised I'd mention it."

"Tell them I've left the country," Wallace said. "Tell them I've been eaten by wild dogs."

Lenore studied Wallace's highball glass. "How many of those have you had?"

"Not enough."

Lenore looked disappointed. "I wish you'd waited."

Wallace shrugged her off. What do you think I've been doing?

"Listen to this," Lenore said, taking a chair across the table from Wallace. She didn't entirely sit—she was up on both elbows. "They walked Otto out the door today." She spoke with a gleam in her eye.

"Security guard and the whole nine yards. Quite the scene. Ever heard anything about a bribe to Asbury Care?"

Wallace looked at her blankly.

"Otto swears it's true," Lenore said. "A kickback—ten grand. Carroll paid off his friend. That's the scuttlebutt, anyway. Of course Carroll denies it, and Michael isn't saying a word."

She was intent on Wallace's face, waiting for a reaction.

Wallace was expressionless. The business no longer mattered. Couldn't she see that?

"I think it's hilarious," Lenore said. "Who's surprised, right, with this felonious lot?"

"What else?" Wallace asked, interrupting.

"All right, here's the news. They're offering me a vice presidency. Throwing me in the wolf's den, literally. They want me to run the Boston office. Carroll was going to do it, but now they've decided he should stay with Michael, in corporate. He's going to be chief operating officer, fill your shoes. Hah, that's a laugh, I said."

Wallace looked at her with a fixed smile.

"Me running my own office," Lenore continued. "How amazing is that? I mean, there's no way I can turn it down. I'd hate to look back when I'm fifty—" She froze. "Oh, darling, please don't look at me like that. I've got the cutest little Beacon Hill apartment, and I'll be in Massachusetts carrying on all the work you started, full circle." Her mood suddenly turned somber. "I can't believe this whole chain of events. I feel terrible."

"Want anything?" Wallace pushed back his chair and went to the bar. In the tight quarters he stumbled momentarily.

"Maybe you should slow down," Lenore said.

"I've opened a bottle of red."

"Good. I'll have some of that."

Wallace filled a Collins glass with red wine.

"That's a heavy-handed pour," Lenore said.

"Is that a complaint?"

"Michael took us for drinks," Lenore said. "He wanted to pow-wow with Carroll and me about taking the tiger by the tail. We ended up at a place called Sire Beef's. Ever heard of it?"

"Yep." Wallace banged the glass on the table in front of her.

Silence.

"Here I thought you'd be happy for me," Lenore said.

"Boston isn't exactly across the street," Wallace said, sitting down again, wrapping his hands around his glass.

Lenore asked, "So what's next for you?"

"Who knows?" Wallace turned to the camp newsletter:

Quiet Hours

Please remember not to run generators, allow pesky dogs to bark, play loud music, etc., during quiet hours. Many of us are attempting to get some well-deserved shuteye!

"You're a man of ideas," Lenore said. "You must have something up your sleeve."

Wallace looked up. "You could've called."

Lenore's face flushed. "Get here whenever—that's what you said."

"Dinner means dinner."

"I couldn't just walk out."

"Damn you, Lenore. Whose side are you on?"

"I didn't know I was supposed to choose."

Wallace went back to the newsletter.

"How are the girls?" Lenore asked.

Wallace kept his eyes on the page. "What?"

"Your daughters. How are they?"

"Fine."

"Maybe I should go."

"I'll start the barbecue."

"Don't," Lenore said. "I've already eaten."

Wallace gave Lenore a cold stare. "I bought steaks."

"We picked at a seafood tower," Lenore said. "Michael wants us back at seven."

"You could stay here," Wallace said.

Lenore shook her head. She stood and found her shoes. "We're reorganizing. I need sleep."

A kernel of sadness welled up inside Wallace.

"I'm leaving for New England day after tomorrow," Lenore said, balancing herself with a hand on the refrigerator, slipping on her high heels. "I expect I won't be back for a while."

"Lenore, please—"

"I have to go."

"We could get married."

"I'd make a terrible mother."

"I don't want to lose you—" A lump formed in Wallace's throat. His eyes welled with tears. He hung his head.

"It's me being selfish," Lenore said. "I couldn't sustain another long-distance relationship—not with this job to do."

Wallace kept looking at the floor.

"Good bye, lover," Lenore said. "Take care of those little girls."

When Wallace looked up she was gone.

CHAPTER FORTY-THREE

The morning had a quiet, summery feel. The sun was shining, the bay was devoid of speedboats, and the bees were working the honeysuckle hedge. Automatic sprinklers soaked the strip of green grass that separated Wallace's dirt pad from the adjacent campsite. Wallace sat in his favorite lawn chair, under the motorhome awning, leafing through a new issue of *Model Railroader*, considering the merits of changing over to a high-tech layout. Detection circuitry, actuators, decoders—computer technology was hitting the hobby in a big way. The technobabble made Wallace's eyes glaze over. He flipped to the pages ahead. He preferred reading articles on more mundane subjects like how to cut a piece of wood accurately or how to render modern gang graffiti on a 50-foot, single-door boxcar. At this point in life, the question of actually building a new layout was academic, anyway. Nobody in his right mind would try to shoehorn a model railroad into a motorhome, and the garage at the house in Escondido—even if Hannah were to take him back—was packed so full with *Acres of Money* membership boxes that the footprint for his old Western Pacific had long since disappeared. Hannah was now working full time in the business, and her garage didn't have room for a flea circus.

"Mr. Noe?"

Wallace looked up from his magazine.

There was something familiar about the old coot intent on interrupting him on such a peaceful morning.

At first Wallace mistook the man for the retired marine with the mustard-colored Bounder from the next street over. Their paths had crossed a time or two in the laundry room, and once at the park office while delivering their monthly rent checks, but then Wallace didn't know why a retired marine would be walking around the RV park wearing a white Stetson and snakeskin boots.

"Ernie Fernandez," said the old cowboy. "Used to be with the Escondido Police Department."

Just my luck, Wallace thought. One of the apes trying to put me away is a new neighbor, and he's come to recruit me for a game of freeze tag.

"Forgive me for not inviting you in," Wallace said. "I don't socialize with neighbors, new or otherwise."

"I'm no neighbor," Ernie said. "Living in a jar wouldn't suit me. My compliments. You disappear pretty good."

One of the few luxuries of living at HappyCamp on the Bay was that it was sufficiently isolated from the outside world. For Wallace, it always came as a shock when somebody was successful in tracking him down—Carson and Donald Duncan, eager to share their business plan, had done it last.

"Nice rig," Ernie said. "She yours?"

"Let me check with my attorney. I'll get back to you."

"That guy." Ernie chuckled. "He still after city golf cars?"

Wallace turned the page in his magazine. Here was good news: Walthers had a new line of streamline sleepers.

"Mr. Noe, I'd be much obliged if I could have a minute of your time—"

"Sorry, I'm busy."

"I'm envious. You have time to read. I retired last year and it's been nothing but hell ever since."

Wallace flashed his visitor a loathsome glare. "You want to talk to me about *hell?*"

Ernie lifted his Stetson and pushed a hand through his hair. His brow glistened with sweat. "I think you're gonna' wanna' hear what I have to say."

Wallace shifted his gaze back to his magazine. "What's your take on hidden staging with infrared detection of trains, Sergeant?"

Ernie raised a quizzical eyebrow. With a black cigarillo he indicated the wooden picnic bench near the concrete fire ring. "I been walking a lot of trailer parks. Mind if I sit?"

"Suit yourself," Wallace said.

The old sergeant wedged his thick frame onto the narrow bench, facing Wallace. He blinked up at the motorhome.

"Thirty-eight footer?" he asked.

"Thirty-six."

"What's her towing capacity, can I ask?"

"Come to talk motorhomes, Sergeant?"

"You a boxer, Mr. Noe? Ever train in a ring?"

"Nope."

"In that case I'm here to talk food chains. Know what it's like to watch a python eat a mouse?"

Wallace lowered his magazine.

"A trophic pyramid—that's a fancy term I learned in college," Ernie continued. "Every ecosystem has one. Our justice system, for instance. Sometimes you're the hammer and sometimes you're the nail. That's all it means."

Near the bathhouse a garbage truck was suddenly making an awful racket—lifting a metal dumpster overhead and shaking it with hydraulic arms. To the clatter of metal on metal, the dumpster's contents came spilling out. Wallace's tranquil morning had come to a grisly end.

Ernie squinted at the sun. "Gonna' be a hot one today."

"Weather doesn't concern me," Wallace said, going back to his magazine. "I can always go inside and take a nap."

"See, I can't sleep," Ernie said. "At first I blamed it on the homework. You'd expect a certain amount of stress, an old cuss like me trying to go back to school. Then one day I was in the arena, trotting my little granddaughter on a pony, and it dawned on me: things were haywire. A cop's supposed to help the good guys and put the bad guys in jail, not vice versa."

Wallace looked at the old sergeant.

"Fact is, Mr. Noe, I served in Vietnam," Ernie said, chomping the cigarillo. "I watched some good men die. They put it all on the line because they thought it was the right thing to do. I'd like to say I joined the police department for the same reason, but that'd be a lie. I was home from the war, I had a young wife, and I needed a paycheck. I didn't pick law enforcement, it picked me. I intended to go to college, get a degree, make something of myself. I wanted a career in business—a life like yours, you could say. My father was a grape picker in the San Joaquin Valley. That's neither here nor there, but when he took sick and died, my hopes of a college education passed with him. I soldiered on in police work, mainly because I needed the money—at that point I was supporting my mother, three sisters, and two ex-wives, and believe me, six women spread around this state don't come cheap. My point is, Mr. Noe, at the end of a purposeless life, when you're circling the drain, your only hope for redemption is that when push comes to shove you act honorably and do the right thing. Retired cops are a curious lot. For most of 'em, the stuff they can't get outta' their heads are the pictures of the dead bodies—ants in the eyeballs or brains in a motorcycle helmet." Ernie took the cigarillo out of his mouth and turned to Wallace. "For me it's the trivial case of a poor schmo who got caught up impersonating a police officer—"

Wallace tensed. "Trivial?"

"I found I couldn't look my granddaughter in the eye. It would mean my whole existence was a fraud. This thing about the brotherhood's a fact. It ain't much fun breaking off with family, especially when it's the main family you got."

Wallace stared intently at his visitor.

"I don't know who in their right mind would go into police work in these modern times," Ernie continued. "Gangbangers carry MAC-10s, drug lords fly around in private jets, scam artists wash checks and hijack identities with impunity—this whole world's gone to hell. Then you've got this new generation of law enforcement that trains like professional athletes and thinks like politicians. They're contemptuous of the common man and anything that approximates free will. All they want's a book deal and their own television show."

"You're talking about Detective Tetley," Wallace said.

"Turns out yours wasn't the only case," Ernie said. "I saw that thing with Kelly Starr on TV. When the chief said you pummeled that kid with your fists, I knew we had a problem. That was a common thread, that little phrase. A favorite embellishment."

"If you're here to tell me your junior detective's a liar, you should've saved yourself the trip," Wallace said.

"More than that, Mr. Noe. I interviewed the perpetrator—that Trout kid. I tracked down all the witnesses, I talked to them. At this point I'm prepared to say there were irregularities in the investigation."

"A little late, don't you think?"

"Mr. Noe, listen to me. My conclusion is there was no use of excessive force. Without that, the people's case falls apart. I'm offering to testify on your behalf. Detective Tetley is a bad cop. Exaggeration was his way of covering up for a chickenshit arrest."

"You're saying this can all just go away, like waving a magic wand?"

Ernie looked out over the bay. "It's been turned over to internal affairs. The chief's an honorable man. Tetley's days carrying a badge are numbered."

Wallace closed his magazine. "You didn't miss much, Sergeant, not having a career in business."

Ernie smiled wistfully. "Other than what might've been."

"Money's not all it's cracked up to be," Wallace said. "Do you know I once thought about becoming a cop?"

Ernie crossed his arms and grunted. "God help you."

"I wanted to be on horseback. I even looked into it. Turns out I was too heavy for consideration. My size worked against me."

Ernie shifted his gaze to the motorhome. "How's the sound system in this rig?"

"Why do you ask?"

"Ever heard of Don José, the singing Mexican cowboy?"

"Doesn't ring a bell."

"I'll get you a CD." Ernie took off his hat and set it on the picnic table. "I can't tell you why, but my aspiration is to write ballads. I'm taking courses in literature and philosophy at the community college. Imagine that—at my age, the muse has occupied my worthless old soul."

"This granddaughter of yours," Wallace said, "by any chance is her name Beatrice?"

Ernie seemed surprised.

"I believe you've got her confused with Beatrix, queen of the Netherlands," he said. "My granddaughter's name is Sally."

CHAPTER FORTY-FOUR

"Patience won't get off the phone," Morty said.

"Don't tell me," Wallace said. "Unmanned aerial vehicles is back?"

"The next generation of golf club," Morty said. "But the name needs work. They're calling it the Shank Stick—after the founder, Porter Shank."

Wallace rolled his eyes.

Entrepreneurs.

The only cardinal rule was no cocktail napkin presentations. No one got an all-partners' meeting in the conference room without a full business plan. Wallace was the founder and managing director of his own venture capital firm, Western Pacific Partners, and he was resolute that this time there would be no mergers, no boss to answer to, no capitulation to alien forces. If the ship were to sink, at least he would be at the helm.

Wallace started the investment fund using proceeds from the sale of his Merksamer Digital stock, but he wasn't alone in the endeavor. After settling the wrongful arrest lawsuit with the city—Wallace took one dollar plus attorney's fees, not feeling right about gaining personally off taxpayer money—Morty promptly shuttered his law practice and bought into Western Pacific as a partner. Patience signed on to the firm as well. She had passed the bar exam on her first try and joined the venture firm as its general counsel, but she was proving to be a tenacious deal junkie and had recently been named a full partner. Just that morning she had brought in an Internet security firm, an in vitro diagnostics company, and a start-up line of natural cosmetics. Wallace had quickly come to rely on her as an efficient filter. She was unapologetic about her workaholic habits. "You have to do your homework," she would say to Wallace. "You can't count on luck every time." She had little tolerance for an entrepreneur who didn't have an intimate knowledge of profit margins, cost structures, or the competition, and she made no bones about it when she thought someone wasn't leveling with her. For the obvious con men and flimflammers, she had a unique way of showing them the door. Wallace would hear an eruption of shouting from Patience's office—the tongue-lashing would invariably be in Vietnamese—and down the hallway, making a beeline for the lobby, would come the poor wretch clutching a computer bag, ducking his head, escaping within an inch of his life. Morty had a different way of dealing with charlatans: without saying a word, he'd get up and walk out. He often kept going, too—"I can't deal with the idiocy," he'd say to Margaret, the receptionist—and Wallace would see him an hour later, or more, walking up the block with a macadamia nut biscotti and a Starbucks.

On the docket this afternoon was a rare weekday social function for the three Western Pacific partners. It was May of 2000, more than a year since Wallace had funded Ruby Ridge Hobbies, and this was a celebration of sorts. The online company had posted extraordinary numbers. They had outgrown their first office space—the old Pullman-built baggage car—in a matter of months, and a second warehouse space after that. Today, with the help of mezzanine financing from a prominent Silicon Valley firm—not Jacaranda—they were moving into a new building on a high-tech industrial campus in Carlsbad. The ribbon-cutting ceremony was at four, with a catered authentic Santa Maria barbecue in the parking lot. The Ruby Ridge founders, Carson and Donald Duncan, would be trading in their engineer's caps for cowboy hats, and Wallace wasn't about to miss it.

"What's Santa Maria Barbecue?" Patience asked. They were riding in Wallace's black Chevrolet Suburban. The Cadillac had long since given up the ghost—the car blew an oil gasket one afternoon when Wallace was in line to pick up the girls from school, and on the spot he donated it to Pastor Maltby and the Four Gospels Theological Seminary. Wallace would still see the car around town, billowing black clouds of oily smoke, its leather seats stacked to the roof with bulk mail trays, a church volunteer behind the wheel.

"Tri-tip, beans, macaroni and cheese, and french bread," Wallace said, answering Patience's question about Santa Maria Barbecue. "It's a California tradition."

"Macaroni and cheese and tri-tip?" Patience made a face. She was a semi-vegan—had been since ingesting a bad piece of meat while she and Morty were on their honeymoon in South Lake Tahoe, Nevada.

"We should have packed lingcod and fish heads for my persnickety wife," Morty said.

The company parking lot was a sea of people—it looked more like a street fair. Rock music was blaring, children were bouncing in a castle-like inflatable playground, and already there was a long line for barbecue. Patience caught a whiff of the smoke and opted to stay inside the Suburban.

"You two go stuff your faces," she said. "I need to make some calls."

Since becoming a venture capitalist, Patience was rarely unyoked from her cell phone. On this day she was closely tracking three potential deals: a product sourcing company in Asia, a fingerprint biometrics company, and a Spanish-language ad agency. She was determined to capitalize on the country's changing demographics. She was already in late-stage negotiations with a local software company whose products helped immigration lawyers manage green card and H-1B work visa applications.

"My board of directors finally arrives," Carson said. He was waiting for Wallace and Morty in front of the Ruby Ridge. The old baggage car was the focal point of the new building. It sat on a grass pad and was now home to an elaborate model railroad—the Feather River Route, through the Sierras, from Oroville Yard to Portola, circa 1960s. During weekdays the company's editorial staff used the layout to evaluate new products: digital command control systems, accessories, rolling stock. On weekends the Ruby Ridge was open to the public as an operating exhibit. A model railroading club, led by Carson, met there on Thursday evenings. Wallace was an honorary member but had yet to make one of the meetings.

"You look good," Wallace said, shaking hands with Carson.

"They're making me eat salads," Carson complained. He had lost weight. He wore black sunglasses and expensive slacks.

"Are these all your employees?" Morty asked, looking around.

"Friends, families, advertisers, you name it," Carson said. "Everyone flocks for free food."

"Where's Donald?" Wallace asked. "I need to congratulate him on his numbers."

Carson gestured at the railcar. "Inside, running trains. Crowds make him nervous."

Morty wandered off to get his face painted.

Carson slapped Wallace on the back. "Come on, I'll give you the ten-cent tour."

Getting through the crowd was slow going. Carson stopped every few feet to greet employees and say hello to their families.

Inside the building they ran into Sanjay. He wore a cowboy hat and a red bandana with his board shorts and sandals.

"Hello, Wallace. Want to see something amazing?" In the palm of his hand he held what looked like a shirt button on a short string of wire. "It's called a cab cam. This is a camera and this is a transmitter. You situate it inside your engine."

"A modeler's dream come true," Carson said. "Experience your layout through the windshield of your own locomotive. We're getting video postings from all over the world. Just got one this morning from Azerbaijan."

"They're crashing our servers," Sanjay said.

Carson and Sanjay led Wallace through the building.

The modular office furniture was all on rollers—each workstation had a long tail that plugged into an overhead grid system. The cavernous facility reminded Wallace of a bumper car attraction at an amusement park. The rolling desks made for flexible work teams—SWAT teams, Carson called them—that could form quickly, tackle a project, disband, and move on to new assignments. There were no supervisors in the company, only coaches and team captains—Carson called them conductors. There were no private offices, either. Both Carson and Donald spent their days rolling around the company on workstations, like turtles. They participated on SWAT teams, too. It was only in corporate legal affairs that Carson was chairman and CEO, and Donald president.

"We're a confederacy of overgrown children," Carson liked to say, explaining his philosophy of eschewing traditional corporate structure. "We just get to play every day in a very cool sandbox, that's all."

For a moment Carson stood and stared across the room, as if he couldn't bring himself to believe what he was seeing. His eyes grew moist. He turned to Wallace and was about to say something when an attractive young assistant found him and spirited him away. The ribbon-cutting ceremony was about to begin.

Sanjay took Wallace on a detour to the server room. What Wallace saw surprised him. The machines would have fit easily inside his hall closet at home.

"That's it?" Wallace asked.

"Yes," Sanjay said. "Very simple."

Sanjay was Ruby Ridge employee number three, in charge of overseeing the company's technology. He had walked out on Carroll and Michael in a dispute over technical issues surrounding the Asbury Care implementation.

"I wonder if you'd mind kicking some tires for us," Wallace said. "Patience has a new software deal she's looking at."

"My pleasure. Anytime. She has my cell."

Sanjay was a resource Wallace had come to rely on. Whenever the two men got together, their conversation often turned to their former employer.

"Did you hear?" Sanjay said, his eyes full of mischief. "We just switched our health insurance to Cal Max. They gave us paper enrollment forms."

Wallace looked at him. He was both surprised and amused.

"Lenore says they pulled the business," Sanjay added.

"You talked to her?"

"The other day."

"And?" Wallace hadn't spoken to her in more than a year.

"She is very discouraged," Sanjay said. "She wants to come back to San Diego."

Wallace stopped.

"We could use her," Sanjay continued. "Carson agrees. But I was reluctant to make an offer—"

"Sanjay, don't be stupid," Wallace said. "Get her in here."

The men began walking again. Outside a mariachi band was playing. Carson's young assistant and another girl were stringing a red, white, and blue ribbon in front of the glass lobby doors. Carson and Donald stood nearby, sharing the finger loops of a giant pair of cardboard shears.

"How are Hannah and the girls?" Sanjay asked.

"Fine," Wallace said.

"Good to be home?"

"Like you can't imagine."

"You see? God's invisible hand."

"She did it for the children, Sanjay."

"Yes, yes. Very important," Sanjay agreed, looking over the colorful crowd. "Everything for the children."

The line for barbecue had grown even longer. The mariachi band's sharp trumpet notes carried in the wind. Children were jumping in the castle, oblivious to the ceremony that was about to take place.